DARK MONOLITH

HEROES OF RAVENFORD
BOOK 3

F.P. SPIRIT

Thanks to Tim for creating the world of Thac, and to Eric, Jeff, John, Mark and Matt for their roles in bringing the Heroes to life. Also, thanks to the rest of my friends and family who gave their time and support into the creation of this book.

BOOKS BY F.P. SPIRIT

The Heroes of Ravenford

Ruins on Stone Hill

Serpent Cult

Dark Monolith

Princess of Lanfor

The Baron's Heart

Rise of the Thrall Lord

City of Tears

Arinthar Collections

Tales From Thac

TABLE OF CONTENTS

Heals and Heels...1

Wins and Losses.. 10

The Fortune Teller.. 18

False Accusations 27

The Serpent's Head.. 40

Lloyd vs. Fafnar 53

Pearls 68

Lightning 80

Road to Vermoorden.. 90

House of Barmann 101

Theater of the Festive Spirits.................................. 109

Lake Monsters 120

Battle of the Bards 132

Dreams.. 143

Up the Creek 153

Black Gem 167

Temptress 179

Inazuma 194

Into the Darkwoods 203

Inside the Monolith 214

Chakras 220

Blades 234

Phantom Armor... 240

Runic Wheel of Fortune 252

Air 266

Above the Clouds 277

Water 288

A Walk in the Park 298

Earth 311

Fire 325

Stealle 336

Golden Sphere 347

The Woman in the Woods 354

Shadow of the Colossus 364

The Truth About Ruka 375

Above the Colossus 388

Hopes and Prayers 401

The Golem Master's Secret 411

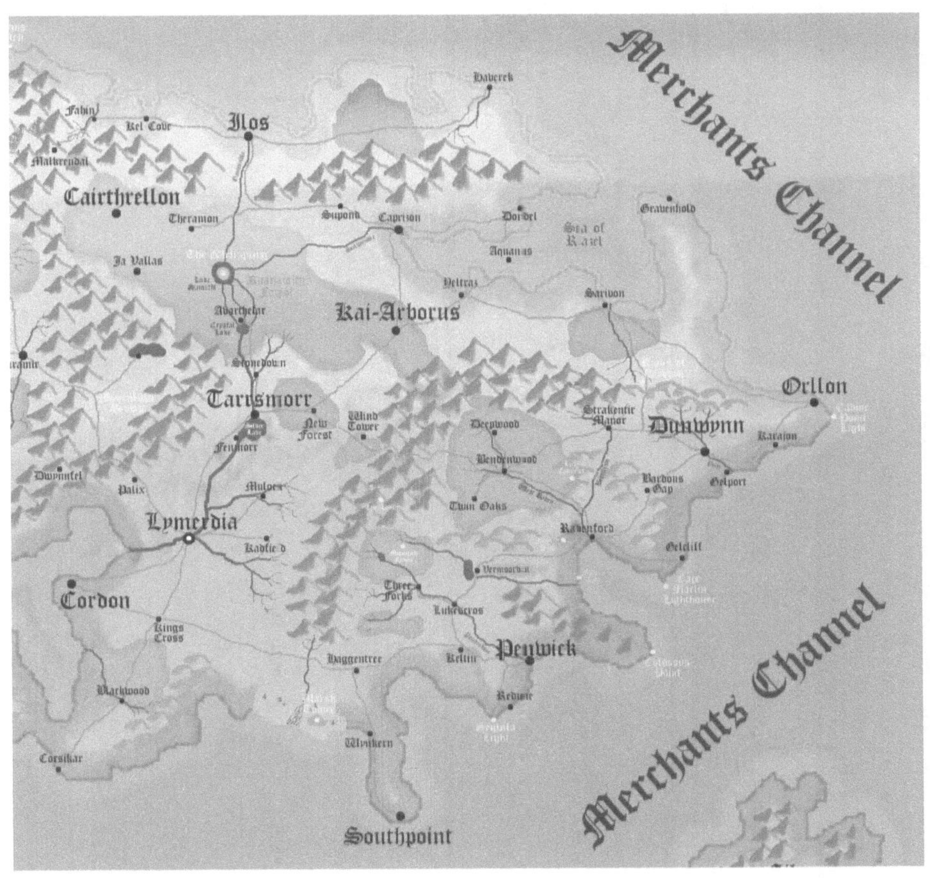

It has been nearly one hundred and fifty years since the end of the Thrall Wars, since the Thrall Lord and his minions reigned terror and destruction over the island continent of Thac. Chief among his lieutenants was the Golem Thrall Master, Larketh. The Dwarven master wielded a magic unparalleled even by today's standards. His golems were the strongest of constructs and utterly under his control. Unfortunately, Larketh's knowledge was lost with him at the end of that terrible war. To date, no trace of his works concerning golems has been found. Or if it has, it has been kept well hidden.

- Lady Lara Stealle, High Wizard of Penwick

1

HEALS AND HEELS

*If this were Dunwynn, those rogues
would have never made it past the gates*

Lloyd Stealle took a deep breath as he passed through the arched, double-door entrance to Ravenford Keep. It was something he immediately regretted. A sharp pain lanced up his side. It was definitely his ribs. One, or maybe even two, had been cracked during the battle with the Serpent Cult. The young warrior clamped his arm firmly to his side, giving no other outward sign of the pain he felt. It was a small price to pay for defeating the dark mages and their oversized serpents.

For reasons still unclear, the Serpent Cult had set its sights on the small seaport town. They had encircled Ravenford within a ring of monsters, assassins and demons. Caravans from the west were waylaid. Ships enroute down the coast were sunk. They even staged a home invasion of the town's master wizard, Maltar. Then, in one final brazen move, the Serpent Cult infiltrated Ravenford Keep. The dark mages had threatened the lives of everyone therein. That had been their last mistake.

Lloyd had come to care a great deal for the people of Ravenford over the last few weeks, and none more so than the Lady Andrella. Lloyd and his companions had taken the Serpent Cultists head-on in defense of the young lady and her family, the Baron and Baroness of Ravenford. It had been a deadly battle in the keep's courtyard, with casualties on both sides. In the end, Lloyd and his friends prevailed. Now, mere minutes after the battle had ended, he was being led into Ravenford Keep. His other arm was firmly linked to the spirited young woman whom he had come to care so much about.

The Lady Andrella Avernos was quite attractive, a fact that Lloyd had been keenly aware of from the moment he first laid eyes on her. Yet, there was more to the young lady than her tall, slender form, her long, perfectly coiffed strawberry blonde hair and her striking blue eyes. Andrella was rather intelligent, though she did her best to keep it hidden. She was also very strong-willed. Still, in quieter moments Lloyd had witnessed a gentleness about her, and a deep abiding concern for the people her family was charged with protecting. These were the qualities that he found most attractive.

"You were amazing!" Andrella gushed as she escorted him through the archway and across the black and white checkered floor of the keep's wide foyer. "The way you faced down those giant serpents then rocketed into the air to finish that horrible wizard." Her eyes glistened as she recounted his exploits.

"Oh, it was really nothing." Lloyd grinned sheepishly, embarrassed by her passionate description of what was merely his duty. After all, he had sworn to protect the Baron and his family.

Andrella abruptly halted and retracted her arm from his. She placed her hands on her hips and gazed up at him with a petulant expression. "Lloyd Stealle! You are far too modest." He felt himself flush even more as she stared at him, the frustration clearly written across her otherwise lovely face. After only a few moments, her eyes softened. Her expression changed and the corners of her mouth upturned slightly. "But I guess that is one of the things which makes you so endearing."

Lloyd was unsure how to respond. He found himself completely and utterly mystified by this charming young woman. It was amazing how fast her mood could swing from anger to delight.

"Anyway, let's get you healed up. She linked arms with him again.

Lloyd shook his head slowly but said nary a word. He had learned it was best to keep silent when faced with situations like this. The duo strode together into the keep proper and entered the main hall. Lloyd carefully scanned the large chamber—it had a vaulted, two-story ceiling, thick white columns interspersed at even intervals across the room, and four balconies on the second floor above them along either side of the lengthy room. The hall was decorated with plush red carpets, multicolored tapestries, and various portraits. There were a number of benches along the walls, some of which were already occupied.

Lloyd scanned those seats for Glolindir and Seth. After the battle, the duo was nowhere to be seen. Glo had disappeared, his absence made all the more ominous by the rantings of Voltark, the leader of the cult attack. He could still hear the evil mage's sinister voice in his mind. *You cannot defeat us! See how easily your wizard falls.* As for Seth, he had not been seen since before the Serpent Cult attacked.

As Andrella ushered Lloyd down the long hallway, he spied two familiar figures huddled close together on one of the benches. The first was clad in purple robes—the second wore an elegant bronze gown. A wave of relief suddenly washed over Lloyd. The purple-robed figure faced away from him, but there was no mistaking the long pale blonde hair and the tip of a pointed ear that peeked through those locks. *That's Glolindir!*

There was no mistaking his companion either. The long golden-blonde hair with faint greenish highlights, the vivid aqua blue-green eyes, and the shimmering bronze dress all clearly indicated that it was Ves. The young lady was the eldest of the mysterious three sisters they had first met on the beach at Cape Marlin.

Lloyd quickened his step, overjoyed at having found his missing friend. "Glo!"

The elven wizard spun around, a thin smile spreading across his normally serious face. "Lloyd! Glad to see you are alright."

A broad grin crossed Lloyd's face. "I could say the same. From what Voltark had said, I feared the worst."

Glo's face flushed with embarrassment. "Yes, well, I had a bit of a mishap."

Before he could say another word, Ves cut him off, her head slightly tilted as she gazed at him reprovingly. "Glolindir took the full brunt of a ball of fire, despite the fact that his protection spell had all but run out."

Andrella, still hanging on to Lloyd's arm, squealed with alarm. "I saw that! You were almost burnt to a crisp!"

Glo face scrunched up into a pained expression. "Yes, but I didn't really have much choice. After all, there was an entire crowd of guests behind me, including the both of you..." His eyes swept from Andrella to Ves.

Ves's expression softened, a slight smile spreading across her lips. "No, I guess you did not,"

Andrella gave the wizard a wry smile. "It was rather brave—even if it was stupid."

Glo glanced up at her and let out a short laugh. "Well, thankfully Ves was right there." He reached out and grasped Ves's hand. The young lady dropped her eyes down, her cheeks turning slightly pink. "Just glad I could be of service."

"Yes, Vestiralanna, thank you for taking such excellent care of our good friend," a stately voice rang out from behind them.

Lloyd spun around. The Lady Gracelynn approached them from the direction of the courtyard. Gracelynn Avernos was the Baroness of Ravenford and Andrella's mother. She was aptly named as the lady was the very picture of grace both in appearance and temperament. Perhaps an inch taller than Andrella, her lithe form seemed to glide across the hallway as she moved toward them. Her long chestnut hair flowed down from the small circlet across her brow and draped over the shoulders of her pale blue gown. Emblazoned on her chest was a golden circle with six rays spreading outward from it—the symbol of the god Arenor, the Hand of Light. Aside from being the Baroness of Ravenford, the Lady Gracelynn was also a very accomplished cleric.

Gracelynn led a procession of followers. Just behind her, Lloyd spied their friend Elladan, the elven bard still dressed in his white spangled outfit from the night's earlier performance. He was accompanied by the bardess, Shalla. The light-brown-haired songstress was dressed similarly to Elladan, except in white and green. Next to the two bards stood Aksel, their copper-haired gnomish friend and leader of the little band of companions, garbed in his white clerical robes. He was accompanied by the town head cleric, Abbot Qualtan. The erstwhile traveling companion of the Baron, Qualtan now appeared to be a rather sour-faced middle-aged man.

Behind them stood Sir Brennon and Sir Duncan, knights from Lloyd's own home city of Penwick. They were both dressed in the red doublet of the Penwick army, with shining rings of chainmail covering the rest of their bodies. Sir Duncan's doublet was ripped, his chainmail tarnished and broken in spots. Next to Sir Duncan, dressed in a white doublet and chainmail, was the fierce redheaded Knight of the Rose who had also joined them on the battlefield, the Dame Alana. The entire group was flanked by Francis and Relkin, the two town guards who had befriended Lloyd and his companions over these last few weeks.

Lady Gracelynn stopped in front of them. "And thank you, Glolindir, for your bravery. Were it not for your sacrifice, I'm afraid there would have been many more folks who would have perished this evening."

Glo merely bowed his head to the Baroness. The Lady Gracelynn smiled in return then turned around to address her entourage. "You were all quite brave, in fact, coming to our defense in our hour of need. Now let us repay you in some small measure. Please find an empty seat so we may tend to your wounds."

Ves leaned in closer to Glo. "That's my cue. We will talk later." She then let go of his hand, got up and joined Aksel, Qualtan, and the injured combatants. The entire group moved on down the hall.

Andrella prodded Lloyd, her tone quite firm. "That means you, too."

Lloyd sighed. He had been so distracted that he had almost forgotten about his own wounds. Now that she reminded him, he felt the pain again in his side. "Alright."

Gracelynn took the seat Ves had just vacated. "I'll be with you shortly. I just want to check on Glolindir first."

Lloyd nodded his understanding. "No problem, your Ladyship."

He knew first hand that Ves was an excellent healer. However, considering that Glo had almost died, it made sense that Lady Gracelynn would want to give him a quick once over.

Andrella tugged on Lloyd's arm and motioned with her head toward the next bench down. The others had left it vacant, probably assuming he would want to stay near his elven friend. Lloyd let Andrella lead him to the bench and they sat down. It was the first time he had sat since the battle with the Serpent Cult. It felt good. While they waited for Lady Gracelynn, Lloyd saw a slim figure zip by. The cap of short, sandy-blonde hair and the telltale pointed ears revealed that it was none other than Donatello. The wiry elf flashed him a quick twinkling smile then continued down the hallway. He did not stop until he caught up with the redheaded lady knight. Lloyd watched with keen interest as the slight elf smoothly gained the Dame Alana's attention.

Andrella let out a soft laugh. "Your new friend there appears to be quite the charmer."

Lloyd couldn't help grinning. "It would seem so."

Andrella slowly spun around, her eyes sparkling with laughter. The two of them stared at each other until Lloyd felt himself flush again. *She's so beautiful.* He could still remember the taste of her lips. At the end of the battle, she had rushed across the field, thrown her arms around him and kissed him ardently. Now he wanted nothing more than to taste those lips again. Lloyd slowly leaned toward her. Andrella responded in kind.

"I hope I didn't keep you waiting too long," a familiar voice spoke up behind him.

Lloyd froze in place, the blood rushing to his cheeks. He spun around and saw the Lady Gracelynn standing there. She watched them curiously, the trace of a smile on her lips. Still red in the face, Lloyd stammered his reply. "N-no, not really."

Andrella started to stand, but her mother waved her to stay where she was. "Sit, Andrella. The two of you just scoot over a bit, and I will have more than enough room."

Andrella smiled brightly at her mother, then she and Lloyd slid over as requested. Lady Gracelynn seated herself on the other side of him. "Please give me a moment."

She closed her eyes and folded her hands together, softly praying. It was a prayer to the god Arenor for divine power and guidance. Lloyd had heard that same prayer many times, his own sister being a priestess of the god of light. After a minute, her eyes snapped back open and she reached out, placing both her hands a few inches away from his side. White energy radiated from her palms, the light flowing over him and seeping into his body. The sharp pain in his side began to dissipate.

"The ribs are broken, so this may take a while," Lady Gracelynn explained to him, not taking her eyes off her work.

Lloyd nodded his understanding. He quieted his thoughts and focused on his breathing, doing his best to remain still. It was hard at first, but as the pain subsided, it became easier. He had just lulled himself into a semi-trance when the sharp click of boot heels echoed down the hall. Lloyd opened his eyes and saw Sir Fafnar marching down the hallway toward them. Lloyd let out a deep sigh. Fafnar was the last person he felt like dealing with right now.

Sir Fafnar Strakentir was a noble from the city of Dunwynn, far to the north. The knight had accompanied the Duke of Dunwynn to Ravenford, supposedly as the Duke's right hand man. The pompous knight had proceeded to throw his weight around town, interfering with the companions' efforts to protect the Baron and his family. Fafnar had even tried to get them banned from the keep. Luckily, that had not happened, or the consequences would have been disastrous.

Now the arrogant noble strode straight for them. He wore an insipid expression, his pencil-thin mustache and goatee making him look that much more absurd. Fafnar's shoulder length brown hair flapped as he walked, keeping time with the clicking of his boot heels on the stone floor. His fancy blue doublet was stained with grass, but otherwise the noble appeared unscarred by battle. In fact, Lloyd didn't remember seeing him on the field at all during the confrontation. That seemed rather surprising, considering how the man liked to brag about his fighting prowess. Lloyd had no time to contemplate the matter further as Fafnar stopped right in front of them. With a low bow, the foppish noble spoke in a fawning tone.

"Excuse me, ladies. I am glad to see that neither of you were hurt in that little fiasco." His eyes fell on Lloyd as he uttered that last word.

Lloyd refused to let this pompous fool get under his skin again, especially in front of Andrella and her mother. He kept his emotions in check, glaring silently back at the arrogant noble. The Lady Gracelynn also remained quiet, diligently concentrating on her work. Andrella, on the other hand, chose to reply, her response equally lofty.

"I thank you for your concern, Sir, but we were in good hands, I assure you."

"Really?" Fafnar arched an eyebrow, his voice taking on a snide tenor. "If this were Dunwynn, those rogues would have never made it past the gates."

Lloyd felt his anger rise. He nearly stood up, but then remembered he was being healed. With a great effort, he forced himself to remain still.

Andrella on the other hand, did not refrain from responding. "Is that so? Tell me, Sir Fafnar, where were you during all the fighting? I did not see you out on the battlefield."

Fafnar's cheeks reddened slightly. He pursed his lips, his face taking on an even more sour expression, if that was at all possible. "Ah, yes. It seems that some varlet thought it would be amusing to tie my bootlaces together. By the time I had them undone, the battle was over." The nobleman looked pointedly at Lloyd, and then over at the next bench where Glo still sat. Lloyd followed his gaze and noted that Elladan and Shalla now sat with the elven wizard.

A short laugh escaped Andrella's lips. Lloyd spun his head back around and saw the young lady had her hand to her mouth, her head turned to one side. Lloyd found it hard to contain himself. He gazed down at his boots in an effort to hide the grin on his face, however, his body spasmed with silent fits of laughter.

"Lloyd, you must remain still if I am to heal you properly," the Lady Gracelynn admonished.

"Sorry," he said, trying his best to keep his voice even.

Andrella recovered her composure, responding to Fafnar's plight in a placating tone. "I'm sure the prankster, whoever he was, meant no real harm."

Sir Fafnar's tone turned haughty once more. "That's quite alright, milady. I will prove my prowess at tomorrow's tourney, then you will see some real swordsmanship at work."

Lloyd glanced up. The arrogant noble stared directly at him. This was not some veiled accusation. That was a direct challenge.

Lloyd met Fafnar's gaze, his own voice cold as ice. "I look forward to it." The two glared at each other unflinchingly, the tension almost palpable between them.

"Yes, I'm sure you do," the fop finally responded, his tone dripping with conceit. He turned toward the Baroness and gave her a curt bow. "Lady Gracelynn."

The Dunwynn noble next turned toward Andrella and put out his hand. The young lady paused a moment then courteously extended her hand. As the noble bent to kiss it, she turned her head away. Lloyd watched the entire exchange with interest. When Fafnar stood back up, his disappointment was obvious. He quickly turned on his heel and strode away, his boots clicking sharply on the stone floor as he marched off. When he passed Elladan, Shalla, and Glo, he glared at them briefly, then continued down the hall.

Once he had passed, Elladan rose from his seat. The bard came over to join them, placing a hand on Lloyd's shoulder. "Lloyd, you better kick his butt tomorrow."

Lloyd nearly choked. His eyes moved from Andrella to Gracelynn, his face turning a light shade of red. Andrella's reaction surprised him.

"Please do!"

"Andrella!" Gracelynn chided her daughter.

Lloyd swung around to face the Baroness, yet she did not seem upset. In fact, there was the hint of a smile on her lips. Lloyd found their reactions heartwarming. Underneath all the titles and finery, the Avernos were just plain folks. They reminded him very much of his own family. For the first time in over a month, Lloyd felt like he was home again.

2
WINS AND LOSSES

These folks are ruthless and will stop at nothing

A short while later, Lloyd's ribs were healed. The Lady Grace-lynn took her leave, off to check on the rest of the wound-ed. Lloyd and Andrella turned to face each other, his mind quickly wandering back to where they had left off when last alone. He reached over and grasped her slender hand, holding it gently in his own. Andrella smiled softly as he began to lean in toward her. She tilted her head up slightly and closed her eyes as their faces drew nearer.

"Lloyd!"

He froze just inches away from Andrella's lips. "Come join us!"

That was Elladan's voice.

Lloyd reluctantly pulled back from the lovely young lady. He turned to see the bard standing in front of the bench where Glo and Shalla sat. He waved Lloyd over. Lloyd turned toward Andrella and sighed. "We probably should."

Andrella hesitated a moment, mixed emotions playing across her face. She sighed in turn. "Yes, I suppose you're right."

The duo stood up, still holding hands, and walked over to join the others. Elladan was in the midst of a vivid recounting of the battle with the Serpent Cultists. Glo and Shalla sat quietly, rapt in the bard's description of the clash.

"Lightning flared and thunder boomed. Yet another dark mage fell, his serpent mount sizzling. Lightning was met with fire. The crowd threatened, the elven wizard made the supreme sacrifice. Everyone held their breath, but in the end, the fierce ball of fire was stayed; but not without cost, for the wizard fell, charred and broken."

Elladan's voice grew soft at the end. Shalla reached over and patted Glo's hand. After a momentary pause, Elladan's voice rose once more.

"Yet the battle was not over. Swords danced, and serpents writhed. Fang and steel, coil and muscle, the fierce battle pressed on. And behind it all, two giant behemoths vied for supremacy over the field."

Lloyd found himself completely absorbed by this retelling of the clash. He had just lived it, and it had indeed been brutal and deadly. Elladan, however, made it sound like an encounter of near-epic proportions. The bard went on with his vibrant narration, until he reached the climax of the battle.

"The last dark mage, Voltark himself, hung suspended over the battlefield, threatening the host below with yet another magical barrage. A flash of lightning, a lance of light, and a rain of arrows, all bombarded the evil mage. The villain reeled, unaware of the red-clad warrior rising up from below, his swords alight with the fire of vengeance. There, high above the battlefield, he clove the dark mage in two with his fiery wrath and thus ended, once and for all, the threat of evil that hung over the keep."

When Elladan finished, silence fell over them. Lloyd was half honored and half embarrassed to be painted as a hero of such grand proportions. Andrella was the first to break the silence. She began to applaud.

"That was magnificent."

"Yes, it was indeed." Shalla stood up and kissed Elladan on the cheek.

"That does make quite a tale, doesn't it?" Elladan's lips parted to form a quasi-smile. "I'll have to make it into a song."

"You mean *we'll* have to make it into a song," Shalla corrected, elbowing him in the ribs.

Elladan grabbed his side but quickly recovered. He took Shalla by the hand, his smile widening. "*We* will write it into a song."

Shalla's feigned irritation quickly melted away. A wide smile spread across her lips as she eyed the bard fondly.

Lloyd suddenly remembered something that had been bothering him. He turned to Glo. "If you were that hurt, how did you manage to fire off that last bolt of lightning at Voltark?"

Glo peered at Lloyd, a perplexed look upon his face. "That wasn't me."

The response caught Lloyd by surprise. Not just anyone could cast a bolt of lightning. You had to be a fairly experienced magic user to do so.

"If you didn't shoot Voltark, then who did?" Elladan asked.

Glo's brow furrowed. "That is a good question."

Any further discussion was cut off when a voice rang out from down the hall.

"Gentlemen! Ladies!"

Lloyd spun around to see Donatello strolling up to them. Alongside the artist strode the redheaded lady knight, Dame Alana.

"Donnie!" Elladan stepped forward to greet his old friend. The slight elf walked up and grasped hands with the bard. "That was some fancy footwork out there."

"Indeed," the lady knight concurred. "His timely distraction saved Sir Craven and me from quite an unpleasant situation."

"From what I've heard, he makes a habit of saving fair ladies in distress." Shalla's full lips were upturned ever so slightly.

Alana turned toward Donnie, her expression darkening as she folded her arms across her chest. "Oh, *really?*"

Donnie raised his palms up in front of him, his face flushing with sudden discomfort. "Well, not so much a habit"—he swiftly changed the subject—"but where are my manners? Everyone, I would like to introduce you to the Dame Alana Benefilla. Alana is a Guardian in the order of the Knights of the Rose."

Elladan peered at Alana with clear admiration. "The legendary Knights of the Rose—tales of their valor date all the way back to the Thrall Wars and beyond."

Alana turned toward the bard, her expression brightening. "Why thank you, Elladan, is it?"

"Elladan Narmolanya, at your service," he replied with a low bow.

Alana turned to face Shalla. "And you are the Bardess Shalla, also from tonight's performance?"

"Shalla Vesperanna," the songstress responded with a curtsy equally as graceful as Elladan's bow.

"We must talk more," Alana said, moving closer and placing a hand on Shalla's shoulder.

Donnie cleared his throat and once again redirected the conversation, pointing toward Glo. "And this is Glolindir Eodin, acting town wizard."

"We were indeed lucky to have you and Sir Craven by our side this day," Glo said as he rose and bowed to the lady knight.

Alana nodded to him. "Thank you, good wizard. I could say the same of you."

Donnie continued introductions around the circle. "And this is the Lady Andrella, first daughter of Ravenford."

Andrella executed a graceful curtsy of her own. "As our good bard has already stated, the Knights of the Rose are well renowned. Your presence on the battlefield today was our good fortune."

A wide grin spread across Alana's face. "It is our pleasure to serve and protect your ladyship."

Donnie pointing toward Lloyd next. "And this is Lloyd Stealle, of the noble Penwick House of Stealle."

Lloyd stepped forward and extended his hand to the lady warrior. "You and Sir Craven were truly valiant out on the field today. It was an honor fighting beside The Knights of the Rose."

Dame Alana took Lloyd's hand and shook it vigorously. Her grip was rather impressive. "You are all too kind, Lloyd Stealle. You handle those swords as if you were born with them in your hands. It was our honor to fight alongside a warrior of such prowess."

Lloyd cheeks reddened at the praise. "I try my best, good Dame, but I am no knight."

Alana's entire face lit up at Lloyd's humble reply. She opened her mouth to respond, but their conversation was abruptly interrupted. Another familiar voice rang out across the large hall.

"Attention! Attention! The Baron of Ravenford would like to say a few words." Captain Gelpas, the head of the Ravenford guards, stood in the center of the hall. Behind him were Baron Gryswold, the Lady Gracelynn, and Abbot Qualtan.

Gryswold Avernos was dressed in his typical spartan military attire, a dark grey outfit with a longsword strapped to his side. The only decoration on his jacket was a small heraldic in the upper left corner. It was multicolored, with a background of red, white, and blue overlaid by a large black figure representing the dragon that he had slain to save the seaport town some ten years ago. Gryswold's powerfully-built shoulders appeared tense, his expression pensive—his dark brown hair, mustache, and beard making him look positively grim.

The Baron and Baroness stood amidst a crowd of party guests. Behind them were a mixture of Ravenford guards in their black and white uniforms, and Dunwynn men in the powder-blue outfits. Everyone in the hallway hushed as Gryswold began to speak, his deep baritone voice reaching across the area, thanks to the superb acoustics of the main hall.

"I want to thank *all* of you, Knights of Penwick, Knights of the Rose, and our very own Ravenford guards. Your swift rise to arms and prowess in battle has won the day for us." He paused a moment as cheers and clapping ran through the crowd, then continued, his voice rising over the throng. "But most of all I want to thank the Heroes of Ravenford. Had they not uncovered this foul plot and prepared us for it, the day might have turned out far differently."

More cheers broke out, accompanied by clapping this time as the crowd turned to face the companions. In lieu of Aksel, who had not yet rejoined them, Elladan stepped forward and spoke for the group. "It was our pleasure to serve."

The crowd clapped even louder and a few cheers of *Heroes* could be heard interspersed among those gathered. The Baron let it go on for a bit, then again raised his own voice above the assembly. "There is one sad note." The crowd quieted down, the mood turning rather somber once again. "Sir Calric, the valiant knight from Penwick, was killed by those accursed mages. He died with honor, protecting us with his very life. Gryswold swiveled to face the Abbot. Therefore, I would like to ask our good friend Qualtan if he could attempt to restore this brave knight back to life."

All eyes fell upon the middle-aged, white robed cleric. Qualtan eyes flickered around the waiting throng, his eyes shifting back and forth and his hands twitching slightly. After a moment or two, he turned toward the Baron. "Well then, I may be able to restore his spirit in the morning. That is, with proper prayer and donations..."

A few gasps went up through the crowd. Gryswold's jaw dropped, his mouth hanging open. He attempted to speak, but no words would come out. Finally finding his voice, he cried out in dismay. "Qualtan! Whatever has come over you?"

Qualtan averted his eyes as more murmurs sprang up amongst the gathering. Gryswold's face grew red, his eyes turning dark with anger, but before he could speak further, the Lady Gracelynn grabbed him by the arm and pulled him aside. Their exchange was rather quiet and could not be heard over the crowd, but Gryswold was fuming, his hands clenching into fists and unclenching. Somehow, Gracelynn managed to calm him down, and when he looked up again, he seemed in control once more. The crowd hushed as the Baron turned toward Qualtan.

"Very well. The town of Ravenford will pay for Sir Calric's resurrection. After all, he died defending us."

"Excellent," the Abbot simpered, "I'll head back to the temple at once to prepare for the morrow. Please have the good knight's body sent over so that we may preserve it until then." The white robed cleric quickly spun around and disappeared into the crowd.

"That was a less-than-divine attitude," Donnie observed.

Andrella's voice was rather subdued. "Abbot Qualtan is usually quite amenable. He has seemed rather distant, though, as of late— almost as if something were preying on his mind."

The Baron addressed the assemblage once more. "Very well then, we are done here. Once again, thank you all." Gryswold and Gracelynn adjourned themselves from the main hall, followed by the town guards and the Dunwynn contingent.

As the crowd dispersed, Sir Brennon came over to join the companions. "I wanted to personally thank you for your help today. It was an honor fighting beside you." The others responded in kind. A short discussion ensued about the day's events, at the end of which he said, "My apologies, but I must take my leave. Sir Duncan and I will be accompanying Sir Calric's body to the temple, where we will remain in vigil until they attempt to raise him on the morrow."

Alana nodded. "As I would do for one of my fellow knights."

Sir Brennon's gazed at her briefly, a look of understanding passing between the two. "Thank you." He then turned to Lloyd. "A moment if I may, young Master Stealle?"

Lloyd whispered to Andrella, "I'll be right back."

"I'll be waiting," she whispered in return.

Sir Brennon led Lloyd a short distance away from the others. "Lad, it is now up to you to represent Penwick at the rest of this gathering."

Lloyd suddenly felt as if a great weight had been placed on his shoulders. "I'll do my best."

The trace of a smile passed across Sir Brennon's otherwise grim countenance. "Of that I have no doubt. I must say that was quite some display of swordsmanship out there today. I've fought beside your father before, and you looked just like him on the battlefield."

Lloyd was honored. His father was the best swordsman he had ever seen. That was quite a compliment coming from the Penwick knight. "Thank you, Sir Brennon. That means a lot."

Brennon actually smiled this time, but his expression quickly turned serious again. His eyes briefly swept the area, then he stepped even closer to Lloyd, speaking in a very soft voice. "A piece of advice—the Lady Andrella seems to have taken a fancy to you. Just be warned that there are those who seek her hand for more than reasons of the heart. Watch your back, son. These folks are ruthless and will stop at nothing. If they see you as a threat, the next attack may not be on the battlefield."

Lloyd nodded. He had already experienced Fafnar's attempt to discredit them. He would not put it past the noble to try again. "Thank you for the advice, Sir Brennon. I will heed your words."

Sir Brennon placed a hand on Lloyd's shoulder. "Very good. Stay safe, young Lloyd Stealle."

3
THE FORTUNE TELLER

Sometimes I can even divine the future

Seth Korzair had watched the entire battle with the Serpent Cult from the roof of the keep. He had gone up there to keep an eye out for anything out of the ordinary. That is indeed what the dark-haired, black-clad little halfling found. Sitting quietly on the rooftop near the front of the keep was Ruka, one of Ves's younger sisters. The sandy-haired girl had hidden up here to avoid the pageantry below. She and Seth were of a like mind in that respect and in many others. Neither trusted anyone, both expected the worst from a situation, and they tended to hide their feelings behind a veil of sarcasm. Thus, when the serpents and their riders first exploded out of the ground, both of them played it cool.

"Think they need our help?" Ruka stood up and nonchalantly stretching her thin five-foot frame.

"I don't know." Seth's voice was measured as he gingerly moved his own three-foot frame to the edge of the roof. He carefully surveyed the battlefield below. *Three dark mages astride seven large serpents, versus Lloyd and Donatello—what could possibly go wrong?*

The two listened silently as Voltark made his pre-battle speech. They nodded appreciatively when Lloyd slew a large serpent and watched intently as Voltark's companions were felled by lightning bolts shortly thereafter. Seth finally spoke up after four chain-mailed warriors, the castle guards, and the Boulder joined the fray.

"No, I believe they're good." He sat back down at the roof's edge.

"Whatever you say." Ruka shrugged and seated herself next to him.

They watched the spectacle below until Glolindir was caught unprepared. Seth shot up, the blood draining from his face. He watched in horror as his friend was consumed by Voltark's fireball. He briefly relived that awful moment when his old master died. It had happened in much the same way. Seth held his breath as the fireball dissipated and Glo's burnt body fell over.

Ruka's voice was filled with uncharacteristic concern. "Don't worry. Look. Ves has him. She'll take care of him."

Seth saw a blonde figure, garbed in a bronze gown, catch Glo. Shortly thereafter, he saw the blue white light of Ves's healing power envelope his friend's body. Abruptly, Voltark's voice bellowed out from a spot over the battlefield. He gloated about his triumph over Glo and threatened the other combatants. Seth found himself quite irritated that the mage was not in knife-throwing range. "You know, he is starting to really piss me off. I just wish Glo could've gotten off one last lightning bolt..."

Ruka's reply was cryptic. "That can be arranged."

The girl drew out her short sword and pointed the weapon directly at the hovering mage. The blade began to glow, then a flash erupted from it, sending a bolt of lightning across the courtyard! It hit Voltark at the same time as a ray of searing white light and a pair of arrows.

Seth cried with glee. "Nice!"

"It was nothing." Ruka sounded rather pleased with herself, despite her nonchalant choice of words.

Seth then caught sight of Lloyd rising up from the ground, his blades alight with flame. He watched with keen pleasure as the warrior sliced the evil wizard in half. Both he and Ruka lost their composure, breaking into cheers and dancing with delight in a precarious circle at the edge of the rooftop. Just as quickly, the pair stopped, staring at each other self-consciously.

Seth was the first to speak, trying to mask his embarrassment. "You know, they don't make villains the way they used to. First sign of trouble and they just fall to pieces."

Ruka snickered. "Yeah. Guess he just couldn't hack it."

They both stood there, arms folded across their chests, their mouths twisted into lopsided grins. As things wound down in the courtyard below, Seth's thoughts went back to Ruka's sword. A weapon that could shoot lightning bolts was not exactly common. In fact, he could swear he had heard a legend about it at some point. He decided to say something to gauge her reaction. "By the way, nice sword you got there."

"Thanks." Ruka's tone was curt, her eyes remaining focused on the aftermath below.

Seth tried once more. "So where does one get one of those?"

"Family heirloom." She still refused to look his way.

Seth shrugged his shoulders. *Oh, well, nothing ventured.* "Anyway, now that that's over, I think I'll go back and check out the campsite. Someone needs to makes sure none of those creeps are still skulking about."

"Good luck." Ruka barely nodded.

"See you around." Seth made his way across the rooftop. The whole time, he could not get the image of that glowing sword out of his head.

Seth re-entered the performers' camp a short while later. It was situated halfway down the hill, between the keep and the town proper. Earlier in the day, he had spied a number of new wagons at the other end. Upon further investigation, he had found a large serpent hidden in one of those enclosed wagons. Seth now slowly crept between those same wagons, virtually silent and invisible thanks to his magic cloak. Without warning, an unfamiliar voice spoke behind him.

"Where are you going, little one?"

Seth started, quickly spinning around. A tall human female stood outside one of the wagons he had just passed. He could have sworn there was no one there a few moments ago. The strange woman was dressed in gypsy's garb, the most striking thing about her being her bright violet eyes. They were currently staring right at him, even though he was supposed to be invisible.

"Yes, I can see you," she said in a quiet voice, as if reading his mind.

Seth walked cautiously over to the woman, keeping an eye out for anything that might be a trap. He stopped a few feet from her.

"Who are you?" he whispered.

She pointed to herself in mock surprise. "Me? I am a mere fortune teller."

Seth eyed the woman suspiciously. This was no mere fortune-teller, especially if she could see him while he was invisible.

The woman wore an amused expression. "If you must, you can call me Elistra, but what you really want to know is how I can see you when you are invisible. Am I right?"

"You might be." Seth's tone was noncommittal. She was exactly right. Seth was no novice to magic—he knew that wizards and sorcerers could cast spells to see the invisible. They could even make items that would enable the wearer to see the invisible. Perhaps this woman was wearing such an item. She did have a number of rings on her fingers.

"No, it is nothing I am wearing," she answered his unasked question, still appearing quite amused. "Let's just say that I have certain gifts, and these gifts provide me with advantages that most people do not have."

Seth was not often taken by surprise, but he was not sure what to make of this Elistra. She was either really good at reading people or she could actually read minds. Seth had known quite a number of gypsy folk growing up, and he knew most of the cons. Thus, he was not that easy to read. She had caught him by surprise at first, but now he was on his guard. He decided to play along with her.

"So what are these advantages?"

Elistra placed a finger on her chin as if deciding how best to explain. "For one, I can see and hear things others cannot. For example, I can speak with spirits, and sometimes I can even divine the future."

Seth studied the woman carefully. "That must be pretty useful."

A full-fledged smile sprouted across her lips. "It can be at times."

So either she is psionicist, she is trying to con me, or she is just plain nuts. Psionicists had psychic powers—some could in fact read minds. Either way, Seth did not trust her.

Elistra continued in a casual tone. "But it is not all fun and games, I can assure you. It is a good thing that you are skeptical. There are dark forces at work here, and it is best that you are on your guard."

She folded her arms across her chest and regarded him silently, waiting for his response. Seth was not in the mood to play guessing games though. He stared back at her, refusing to speak. The gypsy woman finally gave up, letting out a deep sigh. Her tone was now serious, all traces of amusement gone. "Very well, I know that you and your friends are seeking them out. My instincts are telling me that I should help you uncover them."

"My friends?" Seth was unwilling to give her any bit of information.

"Yes, Seth, your friends. I know who you are and who your friends are as well. You Heroes have become somewhat of a force for good in this area in these last few weeks. That is something that will be sorely needed in the days ahead. If I can help you in some small way, then that will be beneficial for all involved."

Seth mulled her words over. It didn't surprise him that she knew who he or his friends were. There had been gossip about them all over Ravenford that could have easily spread to neighboring towns by now. Even Fafnar had alluded to knowing their name. Yet he was still not quite sure whether he believed her, so he decided to put her to the test. "That's all well and fine, but what I really need to know right now is if there are any more of these Serpent Cult folks around. Can your gifts tell me that?"

A smile crossed the gypsy woman's face. "Why, yes, they can actually."

Her head tilted back, and her eyes took on a faraway look. It reminded Seth of when Glo was in contact with his raven familiar. It only lasted a few moments, then her eyes cleared and her expression grew serious once more. "While I no longer detect serpents or dark magicians in the area, I do in fact feel something dark emanating from that carriage." She pointed to an enclosed wagon about a dozen yards to his left. It was not much different from the rest, other than the orange sides and green trim. Like all the others, the door was closed and the shades were pulled.

"Well then, let's go and check it out," Seth said, still wary of this strange woman.

Elistra laughed gaily at his measured response. "Oh, you are the doubter, aren't you? Very good. Do you want me to lead the way?"

Seth shook his head. "No. I've got this."

On their way over to the wagon, Seth wondered if this woman was playing some kind of elaborate game with him. There was always the possibility she was luring him into a trap. He was cautious, though, and trusted his own reflexes enough to get not caught. There was also the remote possibility she was telling the truth. Yet, Seth did not trust in the altruism of any mysterious benefactor. No, if she were helping them, he found it hard to believe that it was merely out of the goodness of her heart.

This Elistra was shrewd. She was playing some angle he hadn't quite yet figured out, but he would sooner or later, of that he had no doubt. When they reached the wagon, Seth climbed the short stairway to the door. Elistra stayed on the ground below. Checking the door, he found it was locked, but that was quickly remedied. Seth slowly opened it and peered through the doorway. There was a dull glow coming from somewhere inside. He turned to look down at the gypsy woman.

"Coming?" he mouthed the word.

She smiled and silently climbed the stairs behind him. As Seth entered the wagon, he heard a low moan.

"Help me," the disembodied voice lamented.

He scanned the inside of the wagon. There was a small room here in the front of the wagon, filled with chairs and a table with a number of grotesque-looking instruments on it, as well as magical paraphernalia. One of those items was a dimly-glowing lamp. A hall led down the center toward the back of the trailer. Abruptly, Seth's eyes fell upon a gruesome sight. There was a body, or the top half of a body, hanging on the wall. It appeared to be alive, or at least it was talking.

"Help me," it gasped. "Please. I am in pain like this. Please... kill me."

The figure seemed strangely familiar. He knew that face from somewhere. Then recognition dawned on him. He had seen this human back at Stone Hill. It was that dark wizard, Telvar!

"Is he alive?" he whispered to the gypsy behind him. "Half alive," she responded.

Despite himself, Seth snickered.

"No pun intended. It is an evil spell which keeps the spirit tied to the body, even though it is dead."

"Listen to me," the apparent corpse of Telvar continued. Its voice was strained as if it took a great effort just to speak. "They have my work, and they know... where I found it. Now they go... to seek the rest. They go to... the Monolith."

"What research do you mean?" Seth asked, all sorts of warning bells going off in his head. He still did not trust this whole situation, but he would continue to play along until he was sure one way or the other.

"The... golem master's... notes. Larketh's... notes," the animated corpse continued, its voice sounding as if it were in agony.

Seth raised an eyebrow. Many people knew about the golems, but no one knew about Larketh's notes—no one except for Maltar, the Baron, the Baroness, and Captain Gelpas. Somehow, he did not believe any of them would share that information. No, he was certain, now, that this was Telvar, or at least what was left of the dark mage. The half-alive wizard continued to speak.

"But the Master's book... Larketh's book... can be found... at the Darkwoods Monolith." He paused and gasped for air once more. "If the cult finds it... they will be able... to make their own golems... like in the old days. Golems that haven't been seen... since the Thrall Masters... walked the earth."

If what Telvar was saying was true, then this was extremely serious. The Thrall Master's magic was unparalleled in their respective areas of research. Even today, no one could make golems as powerful as Larketh had.

"Now please... end this spell," Telvar groaned with pain. "Set my spirit free."

Seth turned to Elistra. Can you do that?"

"Yes I can." The gypsy woman slowly stepped forward and raised her hands in concentration.

Seth watched the whole scene carefully. The evil mage peered at the woman standing before him, but there was no recognition in his eyes, nor any fear. She had been telling the truth and had sensed the presence in this trailer. She was not merely one of Telvar's torturers, using this as some kind of clever ruse to gain his trust. Seth still did not accept this woman at face value, but he could live with that for now.

What Telvar had just told them was far more important than any lingering distrust he had of this Elistra. If the Golem Thrall Master's work did fall into the hands of the Serpent Cult, they could supplement their army of serpents with an army of golems. He just imagined the town of Ravenford being invaded by dozens of serpents and Boulder-like creatures. Even with him and his friends by their side, Ravenford would not stand a chance. The Baron and his friends needed to be warned.

Abruptly, Seth felt a surge of power in the air. It was not quite magical, it was somehow different, but it was most definitely power. The light from the lamp on the table dimmed, and the half-corpse of Telvar sagged as the life went out of it. He and the gypsy woman now stood alone in the near darkness. Seth heard a ghostly *Thank you*, and then the lamp light brightened once again.

"He's gone," Elistra announced with a sigh.

"I need to report this to the others. Will you still be here in case they want to talk with you?"

"Wouldn't dream of being anywhere else," Elistra said as if she had been expecting the question.

Seth stared at her for a few moments, but the gypsy woman

merely gave him a calm smile. It was as if she was certain they would be calling upon her again soon. The halfling just shook his head, then vaulted out of the trailer and headed back toward the keep.

4
FALSE ACCUSATIONS

If you want to question the honor of my friends,
it shall be at the end of my swords

Back up at the keep, the rest of the companions had followed Gryswold and Gracelynn outside to the courtyard. There they began to assess what was left of the dinner that had been laid out for Lady Andrella's birthday. Unfortunately, there wasn't much left to be seen. The food was destroyed, the place settings melted, the great oaken tables charred, and the chairs smoldered kindling. Gryswold and Gracelynn stood, quietly surveying the aftermath. Andrella, however, was not so silent.

"My party is ruined!" The young lady turned and buried her head in Lloyd's broad chest, openly weeping. The young man did his best to console her, holding her close and talking to her softly.

Gryswold reached over and placed a large hand on his daughter's slim shoulder. "Now, now, Andrella. It will all be fine."

Andrella gazed up at her father, but then buried her head in Lloyd's chest again, her tears beginning anew. Gryswold dropped his arm, looking utterly defeated. The Lady Gracelynn pulled her husband aside, reached up, and placed her hands on his broad shoulders. Her eyes were filled with sympathy and understanding.

"Then we'll just have to start all over again."

Gryswold smiled at his kindhearted wife. He then straightened up, turned around, and shouted to the surrounding staff. "I want everything repaired here and ready within the hour."

Grabbing Gracelynn's hand, the two of them went to direct the recovery. Meanwhile, the companions surveyed the wreckage around them.

Aksel shook his head. "What a mess. I don't see how they're going to be able to fix all this in an hour."

Elladan wore a thoughtful expression. "If they commandeered the kitchens in all the inns they might get enough meals prepared. They could even borrow silverware if necessary."

Glo's eyes swept across the burnt tables. "They would still need seating for sixty. I guess they could cart up tables from the inns, too."

Aksel's face brightened. "It's a good idea. We should go tell the Baron."

Aksel and Elladan went to tell Gryswold, but something held Glo back. If the other casters had been prepared, they could have magically mended the tables and chairs. With just himself, though, it would take all night, and they would still be without food anyway. His eyes returned to Lloyd and Andrella, the young man still trying to console her.

Glo silently wished there was more he could do. He knew there was a spell that could in fact conjure up an entire feast. It would include tables, chairs, food, and drink. However, it was far beyond his current ability to cast. Glo scanned the crowd in the courtyard, not sure what he was looking for, then his eyes fell on Sir Fafnar. The Dunwynn noble glared at Lloyd and Andrella, his jealousy of the pair quite apparent. Glo watched curiously as the noble leaned over and whispered to the tall gentleman next to him. The man was none other than the Duke of Dunwynn.

Sir Kelvick was a tall, gaunt man with dark hair, a thin mustache, and a goatee. There were traces of grey here and there in each, but it made him look distinguished rather than old. He was dressed in a fancy blue outfit with the heraldic of Dunwynn woven into the fabric of the jacket. It was a golden crown floating above a crossed sword and scepter, all on a background of deep royal blue. The Duke stood there with a sour expression as Fafnar whispered to him. A slight smile crept across his face.

An eerie feeling came over Glo as he watched that smug smile. Kelvick snapped his fingers, and one of his menservants came running forward. After a brief exchange of words, the servant ran off. He returned a minute later with two scroll cases under his arm. Kelvick held out his hand, and the servant placed one of the scrolls into it. Glo stared intently at that scroll case. What could the Duke be up to?

No! It couldn't be. What were the odds that Kelvick would come to Andrella's party with scrolls of Feast? That would be incredibly presumptuous, even for the Duke of Dunwynn. Glo watched in disbelief as Lord Kelvick stepped forward. He cleared his throat, drawing everyone's attention to himself. "Ahem. Lady Andrella," he said in a voice loud enough for all to hear. "Please allow Dunwynn to assist you in your time of need."

Andrella paused her weeping and looked up from where she was nestled in Lloyd's arms. The Duke made a grand gesture of opening the scroll case, removing the scroll from it, and unrolling it.

"He missed his calling," a voice whispered behind him. "He is actually quite good with theatrics."

"What he is, is an unmitigated ass," another voice replied.

Glo nearly choked. He glanced over his shoulder and saw Shalla, Donnie, and the Dame Alana standing behind him.

Alana spoke up. "That is not a kind way to talk about such a high-ranking noble." The lady knight appeared quite serious at first, but then sighed, the corners of her mouth upturning. "Alas, from what I have seen, I cannot argue the point."

The trio smiled in unison at the lady knight. Meanwhile, Lord Kelvick was still engaged in his theatrics. He spoke in an officious tone. "Stand back, please."

Fafnar and the rest of the Dunwynn retinue moved forward. They unceremoniously cleared everyone out of the way.

"Kelvick, whatever are you doing?" a gruff voice spoke out. Gryswold and Gracelynn had rejoined them. They now stood next to their daughter and Lloyd.

"You shall see in a moment, Gryswold," Kelvick answered in a haughty tone. When enough room had been cleared, Kelvick read from the first scroll. It was a short incantation. When he finished, a glow of light appeared in the center of the area. The light grew brighter and then expanded until it was a few yards long, two yards wide and four feet high.

The bright light slowly coalesced until it formed into a long table, complete with seating for twelve. The table itself was magnificent— long and ornate, with twelve matching chairs, twelve fancy place settings, a frilly lace tablecloth, and six sets of candelabras down the center. Further, the selection of food on it was unbelievable. There was bisque, chowder, prime rib, lobster, chicken, fish, potatoes au gratin, sweet potatoes, corn on the cob, three different kinds of bread, butter, herb salad, apple pies, cherry pies, pudding, and a number of clear flasks filled with golden nectar. This was no mere meal; it was a banquet fit for a king. The spread made what the Baron had originally presented look quite meager in comparison.

Gryswold stood there stoically, not reacting to the Duke's conjuration. Gracelynn stared from her husband to her brother, a concerned look on her face. Andrella, on the other hand, seemed totally mesmerized. She had pulled away from Lloyd and stared in awe at the table before her. Kelvick did not stop there. He appeared quite pleased with himself as he received the second scroll from his servant and repeated his previous performance. When he was done, a second table appeared a couple of yards from the first, equally as marvelous.

The Baron finally decided to speak. "Well, Kelvick, although this is mighty gracious of you, there does not seem to be enough..."

He was interrupted, however, by his daughter. "Oh, Uncle!"

Andrella rushed toward the Duke and stopped in front of him, clasping her hands together like a schoolgirl. "It's lovely!" she gushed. She leaned forward and kissed Kelvick on the cheek.

Glo cocked his head to one side, and eyed the young lady uncertainly. *Can she really be that shallow?*

"You are quite welcome, Niece," the Duke said, beaming at her enthusiasm. He clearly had elicited the response he wanted from her.

"But, Andrella..." Gryswold began.

This time Kelvick cut him off. "Why don't you come and sit with us at the head table, Andrella?" he said, waving his hand toward the first table.

"I would be honored, Uncle Kelvick," she said, her cheeks aglow.

Fafnar cast a quick glance around, a smug look on his face as he put out his arm for Andrella to take. However, instead of grasping it, the young lady put up her hand in front of her. "Just a moment please." She spun around and ran back to stand in front of Lloyd. Breathlessly, she grabbed the young man by the arm. "Coming?" she said in a loud voice.

Glo nearly choked. *So this is what she was up to.*

Andrella had only pretended to be shallow, to beat her uncle at his own game. Now she was doing so, by inviting whom she wanted to the dinner table. Lloyd, however, seemed uncertain. He peered tentatively over at Gryswold, but the Baron was smiling. He nodded his approval.

"Go ahead, Lloyd. You've earned it."

Relief spread across Lloyd's face. He let the eager young lady lead him away. Fafnar appeared crestfallen. He stared unabashedly at the young couple as they headed toward their seats at the magnificent table. It appeared as if he was going to protest, but he was abruptly cut off.

Gryswold spoke again, raising his voice so all could hear. "In fact, I think that all those who fought today should get priority seating at these tables. After all, they did save our lives!" He turned toward the Duke, a broad smile on his face. "Don't you agree, Kelvick?"

The Duke of Dunwynn's face had gone ashen. He was obviously taken aback by both Andrella's choice of companion as well as the Baron's declaration. "Well... um... that's mighty generous of you, Gryswold... but..."

He never got the chance to finish. His sister, the Lady Gracelynn, interrupted him this time. "Well then, it's agreed!" She clasped her hands together, expertly mimicking her daughter's performance of a few moments ago. "Wizard Glolindir, Cleric Aksel, Bard Elladan, Master Donatello, Dame Alana please take a seat at the head table. And can someone please go fetch Sir Craven?"

The Duke's face reddened. "Gracelynn! You can't be serious! These people aren't the ones..."

Once again, Gracelynn interrupted him, speaking with mock chagrin. "Why, Kelvick! You are quite right. We shouldn't discount anyone just because of their station." She whirled around. "Captain Gelpas. Please inform guards Francis, Relkin, and Carlton that they may take their places with you at the head table."

The Captain of the Guard had a hard time suppressing a grin. "Yes, your ladyship." As he strode away, Elladan whispered briefly in the Baroness's ear. She nodded and then called after Gelpas. "And please have someone fetch the archer Martan from the top of the tower!"

The Duke's eyes went wide with horror. He was completely flustered now. His niece, brother in-law, and sister had expertly outmaneuvered him, turning his momentary victory into utter defeat. Andrella, taking up on her mother's cue, hammered in the last nail.

"Oh, Uncle Kelvick! I could not have asked for a better present than this wonderful meal, surrounded by the brave men and women who risked their lives to save us all." She turned to the rest of the party guests and asked, "What say you all? Is this not the most magnanimous gesture you have ever seen?"

The various nobles responded with cheers and salutations for the Duke of Dunwynn. Glo, with his keen hearing, caught the little bits of laughter intermingled with the applause. These nobles were not fools. It was obvious that the Duke was uncomfortable and had been diplomatically bested by the first family of Ravenford. Kelvick, however, was not one to openly admit defeat. He graciously accepted the applause, smiling and waving through it all. Fafnar, on the other hand, was obviously mortified by this turn of events. He stood by, morosely eyeing Andrella and Lloyd as they sat together at the first table. Glo tried hard to hold in his laughter. Donnie, Elladan, Shalla, and Aksel all had broad grins on their faces. Even the Dame Alana wore a bemused look.

Since there were only twenty-four place settings, a number of the guests decided to call it an evening and head back to their respective inns for a meal. When all was said and done, there were more than enough seats for those who were left at the second table. Baron Gryswold, Lady Gracelynn, Lord Kelvick, and Sir Fafnar all sat at that table along with the merchant Haltan. They were joined by Ves and her two younger sisters, Maya and Ruka, the latter of whom had finally decided to make an appearance.

Lord Kelvick took an immediate interest in Ves. He finagled the seating arrangement, managing to sit himself down beside the golden-haired young beauty. Three of the seats were held empty in honor of Sir Brennon, Sir Duncan, and Sir Calric. Servants ran two of the three meals over to the church for the knights who were holding vigil over their fallen comrade.

Martan, coming from the top of the tower, arrived last. The tall, lean, rugged-looking archer stood at the head table, stroking his short brown beard as he surveyed the occupied seats. With no room left at the first table, he had no choice but to sit at the second one. The humble archer was quite reluctant, especially with the high-ranking nobles who were seated there. Elladan, however, would not take no for an answer. He marched the man over directly toward Ves and tapped her on the shoulder.

"Ves, wouldn't you agree that our friend here deserves to eat with the rest of us?"

Ves had shown a sincere fondness for Martan on their adventures out at Cape Marlin. When she saw him now, she seemed delighted. "Martan!" She stood up, grasped his arm and kissed him on the cheek. Martan blushed a furious shade of red. "Well, of course! He can sit here with us." Ves turned to her sisters. "Ruka, Maya, please move down one seat." After the two girls moved over, Ves sat the reluctant archer down between herself and the Duke of Dunwynn.

When Elladan returned to their table, he wore a wide grin. "You should have seen the Duke's face when Ves sat Martan between them."

The entire table burst into laughter at the Duke's expense. Overall, Glo found the entire affair most satisfying. Thanks to Gryswold,

Gracelynn, and Andrella, an awkward situation had been turned into a tribute to those who deserved it most—and Elladan's little maneuver was the icing on the cake.

Cake! Glo's stomach growled. *Gods, I'm hungry.*

Three main courses later, Glo's appetite was sated. He had been ravenous after this last ordeal and even managed to keep up with Lloyd.

Now he felt refreshed and invigorated, as if he had gotten a full night's sleep. He knew it was in good part thanks to the Feast spell. The spell had magical properties beyond an ordinary meal. However, he also felt it was that he could relax for the first time in quite a while.

Glo's eyes flickered around the table, carefully observing his companions. They were talking and joking comfortably, as if they were seated at their regular booth in the Charging Minotaur. Elladan had borrowed one of the empty chairs from the other table and made room for Shalla. The lady bard now sat by his side, sharing his meal. Donnie was engaged in a lively conversation with the fiery lady knight Alana and her comrade, Sir Craven. Lloyd and Andrella sat close together, holding hands, feeding each other, and staring into each other's eyes. Even Aksel appeared complacent, sitting across from Captain Gelpas. From the bits and pieces he could pick up, the two were having a deep conversation about ethics.

Over at the other table, Ves doted on Martan, just as she had back at Cape Marlin. The archer, in turn, was far too entranced with the beautiful young woman to even notice Lord Kelvick's disdainful glare. All in all, his friends seemed quite content—all except for Seth. No one had seen the halfling since before the battle. Still, Glo was not worried. Seth could handle himself. He was certain the halfling was around here somewhere. His suspicions were soon confirmed. Kelvick's attention was so fixated on Ves and Martan that he completely missed the chicken leg that floated off his plate and disappeared into thin air. Glo stifled a laugh. Leave it to Seth to steal the Duke's food from right under his nose!

The meal was nearly at an end when a Dunwynn guard ran across the courtyard and up to Sir Fafnar. The guard bent down and whispered something into the noble's ear. Fafnar stood up and drew the man aside.

Elladan nodded his head toward the pair. "I wonder what all that's about?"

Fafnar spun around and glared at them, then rushed over to the Duke's side. He bent low and whispered into his ear. Kelvick, still preoccupied with Ves and Martan, sat suddenly up in his seat, wide-eyed.

Glo's apprehension grew. "I think we're about to find out."

The Duke turned toward the Baron and spoke in a voice loud enough for everyone to hear. "Gryswold, some alarming news has just come to my attention."

The Baron let out a heavy sigh. He had been relaxing quietly with his wife.

"What is it, Kelvick?" he replied in a less-than-enthusiastic voice.

"It seems that a Dunwynn guard was attacked by these ruffians that you call Heroes. He was robbed, beaten, and left lying on the banks of the river." The Duke threw down his napkin and stood up. "I will not stand for this, Gryswold! An attack on any of my men is an attack on all of Dunwynn. What do you intend to do about it?" He placing his hands on his hips and glared expectantly at the Baron.

Glo thought back to their encounter in town with the Dunwynn soldier. *Robbed? Beaten?* That is certainly not how they had left him. Was the Duke purposely exaggerating, or had that truly happened? No, he had been neither robbed nor beaten, but Lloyd's hands had been around the man's neck… Glo felt a momentary twinge of regret. Fafnar and his men had just finished insulting the entire town, and they had discovered the soldier following them, spying on them, on Sir Fafnar's orders. They had left him defenseless on the side of the road, but certainly not on the banks of the river. True, the Dunwynners were rude and obnoxious, but they did not deserve to be beaten and robbed.

Glo glanced at Elladan. The bard appeared equally surprised. The Baron stared back at the Duke, dumbfounded. Lady Gracelynn also appeared shocked. She was the first to respond to the accusation. "There must be some mistake, Kelvick."

Gryswold finally found his voice. "Just where did you come by this information?"

Kelvick's tone was indignant. "It is the word of my noble knight, Sir Fafnar here." He was obviously unaccustomed to having his word questioned.

Gryswold's expression was clearly skeptical. "Forgive me, but Sir Fafnar has made his disdain for our friends rather well known. Perhaps that has colored his judgment in this matter?"

Fafnar stepped forward, his face a mask of outrage. Kelvick put out an arm, restraining the knight. Fafnar stopped and took a step back. He visibly tried to calm himself.

Kelvick's entire body had gone rigid. "Baron Gryswold, do you question the honor of one of my knights?"

"I do!" came an angry voice from Glo's table. He spun around to see Lloyd standing, his face flushed, his hands gripping his sword hilts.

"Ever since this so-called knight of yours met us, he has cast nothing but insults our way. He has questioned our honor and even our right to defend this town. Yet we put all that aside because there were far more important matters at hand—but no more!" Lloyd kicked his chair back from behind him. "If you want to question the honor of my friends, it shall be at the end of my swords."

"Lloyd!" Andrella rose from her seat, grabbing the young warrior's arm.

Elladan, on the other side of Lloyd, also stood, placing a hand on his friend's shoulder. Sir Fafnar stepped forward again, his own hands straying to his weapon hilts. The Dunwynn guards behind him followed suit. Captain Gelpas and the Ravenford guards, Francis, Relkin, and Carlton, also rose to their feet. Seeing the Dunwynn guards' reactions, they grasped their weapon hilts as well. Lord Kelvick raised a hand to stay his men. He turned to glare at Lloyd and replied in an imperious tone, "And what gives you the right to question the honor of one of my knights?"

Gryswold stood up. "Kelvick! The House of Stealle is one of the noblest houses in all of Penwick."

Lloyd glared at the arrogant Sir Fafnar. "I may not be a knight, but as the Baron said, I have the right. Therefore, *Sir* Fafnar, I challenge you, noble to noble. Let our blades decide who is honorable in this and who is in the wrong."

"And where better than at the tournament tomorrow?" Elladan quickly interjected.

"Stay out of this, elf," Kelvick sneered.

Gryswold slammed his fist down on the table. "That is enough! You come into my house and insult my guests, all based on hearsay. I will not stand for it!"

Everyone turned toward the Baron. His face was practically scarlet, his nostrils flaring. Mixed emotions played across Kelvick's face. It was obvious that the Duke had never been spoken to in such a manner. He appeared to have no idea how to react. Gracelynn quickly stood up next to her husband and took his arm. She spoke in a calm voice. "Gentlemen, this has gone quite far enough. While I do not approve of my brother's attitude, he does have a right to air his grievances."

"Gracelynn!" Gryswold spun toward her, a shocked look on his face.

Kelvick visibly calmed at her statement, a smug expression crossing his face. It quickly disappeared, though, as Gracelynn turned on him. "However, *you*, dear brother, are forgetting that you accuse the very people who saved our lives a little more than an hour ago. Are you certain that you want to make these accusations? Perhaps Sir Fafnar was mistaken? It has been a fatiguing day, after all."

Kelvick's expression grew uncertain as he considered her words.

Fafnar stood with his arms folded across his chest. "I stand by what I said. These ruffians assaulted one of my men."

Elladan eyed the Lieutenant carefully. "This wouldn't be the same guard that you sent to keep an eye on us earlier today?"

Fafnar glared at the bard. "Yes, those were his orders. I did not trust you and believed you needed to be watched."

Lady Gracelynn chided the Dunwynn noble. "That was quite presumptuous of you, Sir Fafnar. This is not your town, and thus it is not your right to do so here."

Fafnar turned toward the Baroness, quite obviously taken aback by her comment. After a moment's pause, he answered her. "I am sorry, your ladyship. I was just concerned for the Duke's well-being, is all."

Gryswold finally got a hold of himself. "Yes, well then, you should have brought your concerns to us instead of taking these matters into your own hands."

There was another long pause as Fafnar regarded the Baron. Finally, he nodded. "Yes, your lordship. It will not happen again."

"Sir Fafnar?" a voice spoke up from their table. It was Aksel. "May I inquire as to the health of your guard? When we left him, he was merely asleep, thanks to a lullaby from our bard. We certainly did not want to see him hurt in any way."

Glo could not help but smile. Aksel's regard for others was unshakable. Fafnar, however, regarded the little cleric with disdain.

"He will be fine, no thanks to you and your friends. However, despite your pretty speech, I still hold the lot of you to blame for his condition."

"Which he would not be in if you were not overstepping yourself," Gryswold reminded the Dunwynn knight.

"Gentlemen, this is getting us nowhere," Kelvick spoke up again. He turned toward his Lieutenant. "Sir Fafnar, you were indeed over-zealous." Fafnar's face fell at the Duke's chastisement. "However, an attack on a Dunwynn personage cannot go unanswered." He paused for a moment, as all eyes turned upon him. "Were this Dunwynn, I would demand immediate retribution. However, as this is Ravenford and a noble from Penwick was involved, I ask that you, Sir Fafnar, see to the righteousness of our cause at the tournament tomorrow."

"Yes, your lordship." Sir Fafnar bowed respectfully to the Duke.

Kelvick pushed back his chair. "Now, if you will excuse me, I have had enough for one day." He bowed to the Baron and Baroness. "Gryswold. Gracelynn." He nodded to his niece. "Andrella." He then strode away, waving his entourage to follow him.

Fafnar glared one last time at Lloyd, then hurried after the Duke. As the Dunwynn contingent marched away, the air where Kelvick had been sitting shimmered and Seth appeared. The halfling grabbed an uneaten chicken leg and took a large bite out of it, and swallowed the huge morsel. "I thought they would never leave."

Seth's irreverent attitude broke the tension. Even Gryswold chuckled at the halfling's timely entrance.

"Welcome, Master Seth, it is so good of you to join us."

Unfortunately, the brief respite was cut short. Seth turned to Gryswold, his expression quite serious. "Thank you, your lordship. Unfortunately, I am the bearer of bad news. There is a real problem that we need to discuss.

Gryswold's face turned solemn. "What does the matter involve, Master Seth?"

"The Serpent Cult, your lordship. Regretfully, they are not going away all that easily. In fact, they may become even more of a danger if we don't put a stop to their new plans."

That doesn't sound good. Glo wondered where Seth had come across this new information.

Gryswold appeared to agreed. "That sounds extremely serious. Perhaps we should take this matter inside."

"Your lordship?" It was the Dame Alana. "If there are matters that concern the foul Serpent Cult, the Knights of the Rose are more than ready to stand with you."

Gryswold smiled at the lady knight. "That is most appreciated, Dame Alana. Very well then, let us adjourn to the side chambers off the throne room to discuss this new threat."

Gryswold stood, a slim smile stretched across his lips. "Thank you all for attending my daughter's party today. My apologies if the entertainment was a bit melodramatic."

He then took Gracelynn's arm, and the two of them strode away toward the keep.

5

THE SERPENT'S HEAD

It is more than just the Thrall Master's legacy
that is driving the Serpent Cult

A short while later, the companions reconvened with Gryswold, Gracelynn, Gelpas, and Andrella in the meeting chambers off the throne room. This time, they were joined by the Dame Alana and Donnie. Once everyone was seated, Seth began the narrative of his encounter with the gypsy woman, Elistra, and the subsequent discovery of Telvar. He finished his story with the information the half-dead mage had provided concerning the Serpent Cult's interest in the Golem Master's work and the monolith in the Darkwoods.

The conversation then turned to the implications of the Serpent Cult getting their hands on Larketh's works and making themselves an army of golems. They had all seen firsthand what just one golem could do. Earlier that day, the Boulder had literally ripped the largest serpent on the battlefield in half.

The Dame Alana rose up at the other end of the table. "I think our course is clear. We must find this monolith and stop these foul creatures before they can make away with these golem plans."

"Indeed, you speak the truth." Gryswold paused a moment to collect his thoughts. "We must set up a strike force to go to the monolith and put a stop to these cultists. And I cannot think of a better group than the one assembled in this room at the moment."

Lloyd stood up next to Dame Alana. "It would be our honor, Baron Gryswold. Once I clear our name tomorrow, we will be ready for such a journey."

"And I can send Sir Craven ahead to gather our squads from the Wind Tower," Alana added. "They are five light cavalry each. It would give us a fighting force to be reckoned with."

Gryswold's expression brightened considerably. "That would be most appreciated."

"They should probably meet us in Vermoorden," Elladan said, his eyes turning upward as he envisioned the route they should take. "The town is on Lake Strikken. There is a river that runs west out of the lake and up into the Darkwoods. If we hire a ship, it will save days of travel."

"Excellent!" Gryswold slammed his hand on the table with force. He had appeared anxious when they first heard the Serpent Cult was still plotting and scheming. Now, with a clear course of action before them, the Baron was enthused once more.

They still needed to determine the exact location of the monolith, but Glo might be able to use the scrying orb they had taken from Voltark to find its location. Then again, perhaps they had another option. "Baron Gryswold, perhaps we should question this fortune-teller further. She seems to know quite a bit about the Serpent Cult. She may know more about the monolith."

"You may be right, Glolindir." Gryswold turned to Gelpas. "Send someone to bring the fortune teller here."

"Right away, your lordship." Gelpas went to the door and passed instructions to the guards stationed there.

Smaller conversations broke out around the table, but Glo remained silent as he mulled things over. They had already found one of the Golem Master's works at the ruins atop Stone Hill, specifically a manual of stone golem creation. If the monolith held a copy of that book, or manuals to create more powerful golems, then the cult could indeed make an army of constructs to supplement their serpents.

Still, it would take time and skill to create those golems. However, the companions had also found the Boulder at Stone Hill. If the monolith held more constructs like that, then the cult could have a ready-made stone army. Then there was that scroll they had procured for Maltar, the one with the Armageddon spell—a giant fireball that could destroy an entire city. Larketh hadn't written that spell, it was far more ancient than he, dating all the way back to the time of the mad Emperor Naradon. Still, if he had anything like that sealed away in the monolith...

Glo forced himself to stop and take a deep breath. There were too many unknowns to start panicking just yet. The Serpent Cult might be after Larketh's works, but what was their end goal? Why focus on Ravenford? They had certainly gone to a lot of trouble, recruiting orcs, goblins and worse. Was Andrella really their target, or was it instead the Duke? Perhaps both? All pomposity aside, Dunwynn was in fact one of the most powerful forces in the area. It would make an excellent launching point for an invasion of eastern Thac. Was that the cult's plan, or was their goal the entire continent?

Glo's head began to hurt. There were still too many questions, and not nearly enough answers. Somehow they needed to gain insight into who, or what, was behind the cult. They needed to cut the head off the serpent, so to speak, to put an end to their plans. Only then could they be sure that Ravenford was safe.

About twenty minutes later, there was a knock on the door. Captain Gelpas went to open it and stepped slowly aside, a rapt expression on his face. Into the room strode a woman, perhaps in her mid-twenties, dressed in gypsy garb. She wore a red and black top that exposed her midriff, a red skirt that almost reached her knees, and lacy black stockings that disappeared into a pair of black leather boots. Atop her head, she wore a black cap adorned with yellow stars and a red hood draped over it. Her honey blonde hair was braided in places, framing her heart-shaped face, slim nose and strong cheekbones.

Yet what stood out the most was her eyes—they were bright

violet. Glo had never met anyone with eyes that color before. He found them quite intriguing. The gypsy's eyes flickered around the room, pausing as they fell on him. She wore an amused expression, almost as if she could read his thoughts. Glo found himself smiling back.

Gryswold addressed the newcomer. "And you are, Mistress... ?"

"Elistra, your Lordship," she responded, executing a perfect curtsy. It was so well done, in fact, that it appeared as if she was a lady at court.

Gryswold repeated the name. "Elistra. Thank you for coming." A brief smile crossed his lips for the first time since they had entered the room. "Master Seth told us how you helped him a short while ago."

A serene smile spread across Elistra's lips. "I was just glad I could be of service."

Gryswold motioned toward the table. "Please, sit down and join us."

Glo got up and pulled a chair over for her. Elistra's eyes fell on him as she sat down, wearing that same amused expression. "You're such a dear."

Glo found himself mystified as he sat back down. *What is it she finds so amusing?*

Gryswold began introductions all around. He first presented his wife and daughter and then asked the others to introduce themselves. Before Glo could speak up, Elistra turned to face him.

"Ah, the mage. You must be Glolindir."

Glo hesitated before replying. "I did not realize I had a reputation."

There was a mysterious twinkle in her eye. "Maybe not just yet—but you will. You definitely will."

Glo found himself even more mystified than before. He opened his mouth to respond, but Elistra had already turned toward the little gnome cleric seated across from them. A shrewd smile crossed her lips. "And the healer. You must be Aksel."

"I am," Aksel replied, his expression remaining neutral.

"Well met, young cleric. The power of your faith is only matched by the kindness in your heart."

Aksel eyed the woman quizzically. "Thank you."

Elistra continued down the table, next turning to the elven bard. "And the entertainer. You must be Elladan."

"Well, I guess I do have a bit of a reputation," Elladan said with a partial smile.

"That you do." Elistra nodded, her expression still amused. "And the warrior. Lloyd," she went on, turning toward the tall young man. Lloyd sat at the other end of the table between the Lady Andrella and the Dame Alana.

Lloyd appeared perplexed. "Do I know you?"

"No, but I know of you," she replied in a lofty tone. She paused a moment, glancing at Andrella. "The lovers," she whispered in a voice so soft that Glo wouldn't have heard it if he hadn't been right next to her. Elistra gave him a brief glance and winked before turning back to Lloyd. "Your heart is in the right place, young Master Stealle. Trust your feelings. They will not lead you astray."

Lloyd appeared even more puzzled by those words, his brow furrowing, but then Andrella grabbed his arm. The young man turned to look at her and all traces of bewilderment vanished from his face.

"And the knight," Elistra continued, addressing the Dame Alana.

"Well met, Mistress Elistra," Alana said quite courteously. "Pardon if I ask, but is this some sort of witchcraft?"

An amused smile graced Elistra's lips. "Not at all, my dear. It is merely the tarot." Her eyes passed over at all those present. "The cards are what led me to this town in the first place."

Seth snorted over on the other side of the table. Glo's eyes narrowed as he watched the gypsy woman, but she appeared quite sincere. Glo was familiar with the tarot—his mother, Aerandir, had introduced it to him. She was a very skilled psionicist and had taught him a bit about the subject.

Psionics is the manipulation of spiritual energy, the force of an individual's life essence or soul. It is different from arcane or divine magic which is fueled by mana, the energy that flows in and around all things. In that respect, psionics is more akin to a martial discipline, like that of the Spiritblade. Yet, like an arcane caster, a psionicist focuses their abilities via the mind, or perhaps more accurately, their will. Tools like tarot cards were merely to amply the focus of psionic power. They could be used in the same way a wizard used spell components.

In the meantime, Elistra moved on to Donatello, referring to him as the "Swordsman."

"Milady," Donnie stood and bowed with a flourish.

For the first time since she entered the room, Elistra sounded uncertain. "There are many mysteries that surround you, young elf, but stay the course and you may very well find what you seek."

Donnie squinted at her suspiciously but said nothing more, instead merely sitting down. However, his eyes remained firmly fixed on the gypsy for quite some time after that.

There was a long pause in the conversation until Gryswold finally broke the silence. "So, Elistra, can you please tell us what you know about the Serpent Cult and this Darkwoods Monolith?"

Elistra's eyes flickered around the table before speaking. "I did meditate on the subject of this monolith while waiting for your summons, and I did see a vision." She closed her eyes, her head tilting back slightly. "A tall structure made of very dark stone, almost black in fact, standing high above the trees in the middle of a large clearing. It is surrounded by a dense forest, although I did get the sense of water not too far away." She paused a moment before continuing, her brow furrowing as if she were trying to see clearer. "And there were mountains, definitely mountain peaks in the background, both to the north and the west."

"That's the northern end of the Darkwoods," Elladan spoke up. "The Korlokesel range turns east for a bit at that point before stretching north once again." His eyes took on a faraway look as if he were trying to picture the area in his mind. "And if there is water nearby... it would have to be... the West Stromen. That is the river that runs northwest from Lake Strikken into the Darkwoods." He finished with a nod toward the gypsy woman.

Elistra nodded back at the bard. "I'm glad my vision was useful. However, there is more I would impart to you." Her face took on a serious cast for the first time since she had entered the room.

Gryswold sat forward in his chair, his own expression turning grim. "Go ahead, Mistress Elistra."

She gave the Baron a brief nod. "I am sure Master Seth has detailed the gravity of the situation. However, things may be even more serious than you realize."

Glo raised an eyebrow. "More serious than an army of serpents and golems?"

Elistra turned to face him. This time there was no amused expression on her lips. "Yes, for it is more than just the Thrall Master's legacy that is driving the Serpent Cult. It may very well be an actual Thrall Master."

Elistra's pronouncement caused a commotion around the table. There was a gasp or two, and then everyone started to speak at once. Glo remained silent, lost in his own thoughts. *An actual Thrall Master? How could that be?* They were all destroyed nearly a hundred and fifty years ago, or at least that is what we were all told...

Elladan, Donnie, Lloyd, Alana, and Gryswold were all trying to speak over each other. Seth sat quietly watching the pandemonium while Andrella and Gracelynn tried to get Lloyd and Gryswold, respectively, to sit back down in their seats. Elistra, in the meantime, sat back, calmly gazing around the table.

A loud voice blurted out, "Quiet!"

Glo spun around and saw Aksel standing up on his chair. The little cleric eyed everyone with a look of consternation. The others went silent, shocked at the normally soft-spoken gnome. Aksel stepped down off his chair, took a deep breath, then turned to face the Baron. "Sorry, your lordship, but this is getting us nowhere."

The corners of Gryswold's mouth upturned slightly. "No, no, you are quite right, Cleric Aksel. Please, the floor is yours."

Aksel's eyes briefly swept around the table. They all sat down in turn, chagrinned looks on most of their faces. He then turned to face Elistra. "Would you care to elucidate on that statement?"

The gypsy sat forward in her seat. "Certainly. Let me be clear. I am not saying that the head of the cult is one of the great Thrall Masters, perhaps a lesser one, but my intuition tells me that a true Thrall Master is behind the resurgence of the cult, and my insights are seldom wrong."

Aksel sat back in his chair, his hand going to his chin. Around the table, eyebrows were raised and glances exchanged, but no one else said a word this time. Glo was intrigued by the words Elistra had just used. Intuition and insight were key psionic phrases, especially if one was a clairvoyant. The more he watched the gypsy, the more he was convinced she was the genuine article. *Well, I had been wondering who, or what, was behind the Serpent Cult. A Thrall Master was not the answer I had expected, though.*

Aksel sat quietly, mulling over Elistra's declaration. "Are you saying the Thrall Masters did not die?"

Elistra looked sharply at the little cleric. When she answered, her tone was very measured. "It is not so much whether one or all of them died. This master may or may not be the same individual they were a hundred years ago, but mark my words, there is a Thrall Master on the rise again. He, or she, is out there today, scheming and planning to recover their lost power."

Aksel eyed Glo curiously. Glo gave a subtle nod in response, acknowledging his belief in this strange woman's words. Aksel let out a heavy sigh then turned his attention back to Elistra. "If what you are saying is true, then this is indeed far worse than anything we had previously imagined."

It was Elladan's turn to speak. "Now hold on a minute. No offense, Elistra, but I've read just about every history book on the subject. I've even read Dreamweaver's original works, the same bard who chronicled the end of the Thrall Wars. They were all pretty clear that the Thrall Masters were destroyed."

All eyes turned to Elistra, but the enigmatic young woman appeared unphased by Elladan's assertions. When she spoke, her tone was calm and even. "I've read most of those same books, good bard, including Dreamweaver's works. Unfortunately, you cannot always believe what you read. Historians tend to write the past the way they wish things had been, not necessarily the way they actually were." She paused as if to emphasize her point. "Think of it this way, would you really want to tell a populace that had almost been decimated that the monsters that did so had escaped? And furthermore, that they might come back to plague them again one day?"

Glo silently nodded. Elistra's explanation made a lot of sense.

He, too, had read those same histories. He had to admit, he always found it strange how neatly everything was tied up at the end of the Thrall Wars. Life had a tendency to be far messier than that. Before anyone else could respond, Glo added his two cents. "It makes sense if you think about it."

From his expression, Elladan still did not seem convinced, but Aksel pursed his lips and nodded. "Go on."

Glo's eyes swept across table as he ticked off on his fingers. "First of all, how else would the Serpent Cult know to look for Larketh's notes at Stone Hill? Second, it would take someone rather powerful to summon that Barghest demon we ran into at the cape. Third, only someone really confident in their own power would send assassins after Maltar. Fourth, members of the actual Wizards' Council have disappeared, and they make Maltar look like a novice!"

Glo paused to glance around the gathered group. Donnie, Alana, Lloyd, and Andrella all nodded in agreement. Aksel had his hand on his chin, deep in thought. Gryswold, Gracelyn, and Gelpas stared at him, but did not appear to disagree. Even Elladan seemed to be coming around, his brow furrowing as he considered the merit of Glo's words. Only Seth sat there impassive, fingering his knife nonchalantly as if waiting for the others to make up their minds. "The recruitment of the orc bandits, the goblin army, the use of assassins, and the collection of powerful artifacts all point to the same thing—a potent, well-trained mind organizing and controlling all these pieces. Up till now, I was not sure to what end, but if it were a Thrall Master striving to regain power, then it would all fit."

Finished with his argument, Glo sat back down. Elistra leaned over, placing a hand on his arm.

"Nicely done," she whispered to him. He could smell her perfume—a cross between lavender and honeysuckle. He found it strangely soothing.

"So you have no idea which Thrall Master is it?" That was Elladan. He sat forward in his chair staring intently at Elistra. "The Golem Master, Larketh? The Undead Thrall Master? The Thrall Lord himself?"

Elistra locked eyes with the bard, her gaze as intense as his. "It would be too easy to assume it is Larketh, but that would be mere conjecture."

"It doesn't really matter which Thrall Master it is. Either way, we still need to stop them," the Dame Alana declared.

"Dame Alana is right," Aksel said. "Our immediate goal is to stop the Serpent Cult from gaining Larketh's works."

Gryswold spoke up from the head of the table. "Agreed. The plan remains the same. We send a strike force to the Darkwoods Monolith, and I am counting on you to lead that force."

"That's all well and fine," Seth spoke up for the first time in a while. Everyone turned toward the halfling. "But if we are going to do this, then let's keep it as quiet as possible. We don't want Dunwynn sticking their noses in any of this. They'll just get in our way."

There were a few chuckles around the table but mostly nods of agreement.

"I hate to say it, but I have to agree with Master Seth," Gryswold said.

All eyes fell on the Dame Alana. The lady knight sighed audibly. "Very well. We will keep this information just amongst us for now. There will come a time, however, when we might need Dunwynn's strength."

Elladan gave the lady knight a half-smile. "Maybe, but until that time, let's play it close to the vest."

Elistra spoke up again. "Just one more thing—would you mind if I go along with you on this journey?"

"I think it would be a good idea," Aksel answered before anyone else could respond.

"She has my vote," Lloyd expressed his approval. "And mine," Alana agreed.

"She's been useful so far," Seth said with a nonchalant nod.

"Fine with me," Elladan agreed with a semi-smile.

"And what about you, Wizard Glolindir?" Elistra asked turning to face him again. "Do you want me to come along?"

Glo eyed her curiously. She stared at him with a straight face, but he could see the mirth in her eyes.

"Oh, most definitely," he replied. "After all, we cerebral types need to stick together."

She gazed at him for a moment then burst out laughing. It was a light, airy sound, almost musical in nature, and Glo found it quite charming.

Gryswold rose from his chair. "Now that that is settled, I think it's time we call it a night. After all, tomorrow is a big day."

As they rose to leave, Elistra turned to Glo and whispered, "Thank you for believing me." She reached out and touched his arm again.

"You're welcome," he replied. "I could tell your insights were genuine."

Her eyes were filled with curiosity. "Really? And just how do you know that?"

It was his turn to smile. "My mother is a rather accomplished psionicist. She taught me enough of the basics that I can recognize it in others. I would guess that you are a seer... and... a bit of a telepath."

Elistra gazed at him with clear respect. "You really do know your psionics, then."

Glo found himself intrigued by this woman. She had a keen mind and was rather attractive. Further, she seemed quite approachable.

"You know," Elistra continued, her eyes dropping shyly away from his, "it's not a subject I get to talk about very often." She paused a moment, then looked back up at him. "Would you care to continue this discussion? Perhaps over a drink?"

She was obviously a strong woman, but at that moment she seemed quite fragile, almost lonely in fact. Glo found himself suddenly wanting to spend more time with her.

"I would love to," he said with all sincerity. He extended his arm, and she gleefully looped hers through it. As the two of them walked toward the door arm in arm, Glo heard Gryswold clear his throat.

"Oh, and just one last thing."

Everyone turned around to look at the Baron. "Lloyd, about tomorrow—kick his butt, son."

Lloyd and Andrella exited the throne room together, the young lady giggling uncontrollably. Lloyd pulled her aside. "What's so funny?"

Andrella, between fits of silent laughter, managed to get out the words, "I... can't... believe... he said... that..."

"Oh, yeah," Lloyd responded, feeling somewhat embarrassed. "That did kind of catch me by surprise."

Andrella held her chest, trying to regain her composure. Lloyd smiled down at the delightful young lady, but his mind was wandering elsewhere. He knew quite well of Larketh, the Golem Thrall Master. The dwarf was single-handedly responsible for the overrunning of Penwick some hundred years ago. Still, something bothered him. Andrella finally calmed down and gazed up into his eyes.

"What's wrong?"

"Nothing really. It's just... what's a thrall?"

A delicate smile crossed her lips. "You mean, you don't know?" she said, her tone mocking.

"Do you?" he shot back, feeling foolish for having asked the question in the first place.

Her hands went to her hips. "Of course I do. It's... it's..."

"It's someone who's been enslaved," a familiar voice said from behind them. Lloyd whirled around to see Elladan standing in the middle of the hall, a partial smile on his lips.

"I was just going to say that!" Andrella declared.

"Sure you were," Lloyd teased the obstinate young lady.

Elladan's half-smile spread into a full grin as he strode their way. "The Thrall Masters were dangerous because they had absolute control over hundreds of creatures—powerful creatures that couldn't normally be controlled..."

"Like golems!" Andrella interjected.

"Like golems." Elladan nodded.

"See," she said elbowing Lloyd in the ribs, "I do know what I am talking about."

Lloyd grabbed his side. "I... never... doubted you for a minute." He turned to Elladan. "So how did they control those creatures?"

Elladan's expression grew puzzled. "No one really knows. I've read everything I could get my hands on about the Thrall Masters, but nowhere does it say how they controlled their slaves."

"Maybe you should ask Elistra," Andrella said in an innocent voice.

Elladan gave a short laugh. "She does seem to know quite a lot, doesn't she?" His expression turned thoughtful for a moment, then his semi-smile returned. His eyes moved from Andrella to Lloyd. "It is a true mystery, but one for another day. It's getting kind of late, and Shalla is waiting for me. I'll let you two be." He gave Lloyd a quick wink, then spun around and strode away.

"Thanks, Elladan!" Lloyd called after the bard.

"Well then," Andrella said, her voice dropping very low and throaty, "are you ready to call it a night yet?"

Lloyd turned to see the heated look in the young lady's eyes, and it made him flush.

His voice dropped to a whisper. "No, not really." He leaned forward and kissed her passionately on the lips.

6
LLOYD VS. FAFNAR

The two of them collided in the center of the arena,
blade to blade, fire and ice

The late morning sky was a deep, tranquil blue, completely cloudless in all directions. The golden rays of the sun nicely warmed the courtyard of Ravenford Keep below. It should have been blissful after the events of these last few days, but unfortunately for Lloyd Stealle, he could not enjoy the gorgeous weather. His future, and the future of all his companions, rested squarely on his shoulders this day.

The young warrior stood in the entryway of a white tarpaulin tent, one of a pair that had been set up for the tournament's combatants. In front of him, a sixty-by-sixty-foot area had been cordoned off into a makeshift arena. On either side, stands had been erected. Those stands were currently packed, filled with townsfolk, visitors, and even performers from last night's show. It had spread around like wildfire that Lloyd was to fight the arrogant Sir Fafnar, and it appeared that the entire town had turned out for the battle.

Directly across from him stood a royal box with Gryswold and Gracelynn seated in the center. Immediately to their right sat the three knights from Penwick: Sir Brennon, Sir Duncan, and the recently revived Sir Calric. One chair over from Lady Gracelynn sat Lord Kelvick. The seat to either side of him lay empty. The chair to his left had been reserved for Sir Fafnar, but the haughty noble currently waited in the tent next to Lloyd's. Lloyd, however, was far more interested in the empty chair between Gracelynn and the Duke. That seat was reserved for Lady Andrella. After last night, Lloyd was sure she would be there to cheer him on. Yet he still had not seen her this morning.

"She'll be here," Elladan's voice sounded from behind him.

Lloyd spun around to face the bard. Elladan and Glo stood there watching him. The rest of the companions had been there earlier, but had left to grab seats in the quickly filling stands. The two elves had opted to stay with him until it was time for his match. They both stood there watching him with shrewd smiles. Lloyd grinned sheepishly back at the duo. They knew him far too well.

"I agree with Elladan," Glo said. "Andrella wouldn't miss this."

Lloyd was about to reply when he heard the sounds of steel on steel. The match prior to his had begun. One of the castle guards, Carlton, was facing off against a large warrior named Brum. The warrior wielded a huge two-handed sword, and Carlton was having a hard time getting near him. Lloyd did not think the battle would last very long. The large warrior, being rather good-natured, was not trying very hard. Once he did, it would be over quickly. Abruptly he heard the tent flaps rustle behind him.

"Am I too late?" an all-too-familiar voice said.

Lloyd spun around just in time to see Andrella come flying through the entrance. She was breathing rather heavily, her face nearly as red as the dress she was wearing. It was a brightly-colored red gown, the identical shade of his home city's colors.

"No, the other match is still going on," Elladan answered. "I think it will be over soon, though."

"Well, I got here as fast as I could. That darned dressmaker took forever finishing this gown!" Andrella rushed across the tent, finally stopping directly in front of him.

Lloyd stood there openmouthed, unable to take his eyes off her. "You... look... breathtaking."

"Thank you, noble sir." Her face lit up with a bright smile and she executed an elegant curtsy.

"Ahem..." Elladan cleared his throat. "We'll just be going now."

"Good luck," Glo added, a hint of amusement in his voice.

"Thanks, guys," Lloyd said, not taking his eyes off the beautiful young lady in front of him. He heard the tent flaps rustle once more, and then he was alone with her.

As soon as the tent flap fell, she reached up, threw her arms around his neck, and drew him down toward her. She kissed him ardently, dispelling any residual doubts he had been feeling. His head swam as he tasted her lips on his, smelled the fragrant odor of her hair, and felt the warmth of her soft body pressed against his. Time seemed to stop as they stood locked in each other's arms. After what seemed like forever, Lloyd reluctantly pulled himself away. Andrella arched back, her face flushed as she looked up into his. She paused a moment to catch her breath, then her expression changed to one of concern.

"Is something wrong?"

"No, not really. It's just—I need to focus if I am to win today."

"Oh, and I distract you too much. Is that what you're saying?" She pushed against him, pretending to be angry.

A wide grin spread across Lloyd's face. "A distraction I would love any other time."

Andrella blushed, giggling like a schoolgirl. "My dear, Lloyd Stealle... flattery will get you everywhere."

It was his turn to blush.

All of a sudden, she pulled away from him. "Oh, I almost forgot." She reached around her neck and removed the bright red scarf that had been wrapped around it. "Here." She moved to his side and tied the scarf around his upper left arm.

Lloyd examined the scarf—the letters AA were embroidered on the fabric. It had to stand for Andrella Avernos, the young lady's initials!

Andrella stood back with her hands on her hips, looking over her handiwork with an expression of satisfaction. "There, you are now my chosen protector. Go out there and make me proud."

Lloyd could tell she was trying to make light of the situation. What she had done was truly touching. First, she was wearing his colors, and now she had tied her scarf on him. He bowed low and replied in a voice that was intended to mimic Fafnar's, "Thank you, milady. I will do my best to earn your faith in me."

Andrella laughed. "You are far too modest, my Lord Stealle," she said in a mock formal tone. She laughed once more and threw her arms around his neck, her voice growing soft. "It is one of your most endearing qualities."

She pulled him down and kissed him again, this time more ardently than before. Lloyd's head swam once more, the heat rising throughout his entire body. When Andrella finally pulled back, she was out of breath. Her face was flushed as she gazed at him longingly, but then she gently pushed away from him. Her breath was still heavy as she tore her eyes from his. Andrella gazed downward, straightening out her dress. When she looked up again, she half smiled at him, her face still slightly red. "Good luck out there today," she said, reluctantly turning and heading toward the exit. As she reached the tent flaps, she turned and gazed at him one last time. "You better win!" With that, the Lady Andrella pushed open the tent flaps and skirted through them.

Lloyd stood there alone with a silly grin on his face. Andrella was most certainly a handful. He briefly wondered what he had gotten himself into, but the truth was, he couldn't imagine his life without her now. Sudden cheers rang out from the direction of the arena. Lloyd spun around and opened the tent flap. The fight was over. He was up next! Closing his eyes, Lloyd called upon his spiritblade training. His breathing slowed and his mind emptied. When his eyes snapped open a minute later, he was ready.

Let the battle begin!

Lloyd entered the arena at the same time as Sir Fafnar. The Dunwynn knight's demeanor had not changed since the prior evening.

He still had that same sour expression on his face. The only major change to the knight was his battle attire. Bright silver links of chain-mail were now clearly visible under his pale blue tabard. His short coat still bore the heraldic of his city across the chest, and lieutenant bars on the shoulders. Strapped to his waist was the same sword and axe that the noble had worn the first time they encountered him.

The crowd cheered as the two combatants appeared. Fafnar, however, refrained from looking around, starting across the field to-ward the box where the Baron waited. Lloyd fell in beside the knight, marching briskly across the arena. He and Fafnar were nearly the same height, the Dunwynn knight perhaps only an inch shorter, but the noble's lithe form was in stark contrast to Lloyd's muscular physique.

As they crossed the field, a soft chant of *Heroes* sprang up amongst the crowd. Lloyd peered into the stands, quickly spying Aksel, Seth, Donnie, Elladan, and Glo. All were seated in the first row. Aksel, his face impassive, nodded to Lloyd. Seth, being Aksel's polar opposite, stood up and yelled out across the field.

"Lloyd! Give him the old one-three!"

The old one-three? What happened to two?

Glo sat next to Seth and Aksel, his expression nearly as stoic as the little cleric's. Elladan stood on the other side of the wizard, lute in hand, leading the crowd's chant. He nodded, his eyes resting on Lloyd. The flamboyant Donnie was also on his feet, waving his hands as if conducting the audience. He briefly turned Lloyd's way and winked.

The duo was so inspiring that Lloyd broke out into a grin. He scanned up the stands and immediately recognized three of the spectators in the second row behind his companions: Ves, Ruka, and Maya! The Greymantle sisters had all come to cheer him on. Ves gave a short wave while Maya, the youngest, stood on the bench and waved both her arms back and forth at him vigorously. Even Ruka, the reserved young teen, nodded to him, the corner of her mouth lifted upward. Next to the sisters sat the mysterious gypsy, Elistra. She smiled at him serenely as if she had already divined the out-come of the match. On Elistra's left stood Shalla. She had her lute out, playing along with Elladan and the crowd. Beside Shalla sat the Dame Alana. The lady knight stood up as he glanced her way, drew her sword and saluted. Lloyd nodded in response.

Cheers and chants came from the other stand as well. Lloyd immediately spied Kailay, the blonde barmaid from the Charging Minotaur, on that side. Next to her sat her sister, Gristla. He also saw the merchant Pheldan and his granddaughter, Xelda. There was even Captain Rochino from the *Endurance*. All chanted *Heroes*, waved, or gave him the thumbs up. Lloyd was stunned by the turnout. Everyone they had helped at one time or another was there to cheer them on.

The two combatants finally reached the other end of the arena. They stopped in unison directly in front of the Baron and Baroness. Gryswold stood up and raised both his arms. The crowd went silent. Over to the Baron's left, Andrella settled into her seat. She glanced at Lloyd and winked. Lloyd smiled briefly in return, but his attention snapped back to Gryswold as he began to recite the rules of combat. It was more or less a formality, as everyone present already knew them. The two combatants would fight until one yielded or was unable to continue. This was not a battle to the death, but accidents were known to happen.

During the Baron's speech, Fafnar quietly whispered to Lloyd, "Is that the Lady Andrella's scarf you are wearing?"

Lloyd gave the noble a sidelong glance—he wore an infuriated look. Lloyd, not wanting to be rude, declined to respond.

"The likes of you does not deserve her attention," the irritant noble continued. "I will put an end to that soon enough," he added, his voice rising above a whisper.

"What was that, Sir Fafnar?" Gryswold interrupted them.

Lloyd suppressed a smile, keeping his eyes firmly fixed forward. The Baron wore a grim expression as he glared down at the haughty Dunwynn noble. Fafnar, caught in the act, did not immediately respond. When he did, his tone was placating at best. "I was merely wishing my opponent... luck."

"Hmm, yes, I'm sure you were," Gryswold said. From his expression, it was obvious he did not believe a word the noble had said.

"Anyway, please take your positions. On Captain Gelpas' mark you may begin the match."

Lloyd spun around and strode toward the center of the arena, side-by-side once more with Sir Fafnar. The crowd began to cheer again, the noise becoming quite loud. When they reached the center of the arena, the two combatants spread out, taking positions about a half-dozen yards from each other. They both drew their weapons, took fighting stances, and eyed each other intently. Fafnar held a longsword in his right hand and brandished a single-bladed hand axe in his left.

Up until now, Lloyd had not taken the foppish noble seriously— he had thought his weapons merely for show because the sword and axe was a difficult combination to pull off. The axe, being both short- er and lighter than the sword, made it faster to swing, but also gave it less range, and the difference in weight between the two weapons would throw an unseasoned fighter off balance. Now Lloyd noted the well-guarded stance and the comfort with which the Dunwynn knight held his weapons. If he was as well-practiced with them as he appeared, the relative lightness of axe would allow for exceedingly quick attacks. Lloyd shifted his own stance slightly. Fafnar might be more of a challenge than he originally thought.

Captain Gelpas had followed them out to the center of the arena. He now stood directly between the two men. Holding his sword out in front of him, the Captain gazed at each of them in turn. "Good luck," he cried over the din of the crowd. He then stepped back, lifted his sword and yelled, "Begin!"

The crowd quieted as the two men slowly circled each other. They cautiously closed the distance between them until they were just a blade's reach away. Each made a few feints, testing the other, but these were easily parried or avoided. Suddenly, before Lloyd could react, Fafnar closed the gap between them. The knight deftly slipped under his guard and landed two blows into his midriff as he passed! Luckily, his armor took the brunt of the attacks, but he still felt them. Lloyd whirled around with his blades, attempting to catch the knight before he was out of range, but somehow Fafnar avoided the first blow and neatly parried the second one with his axe. *Gods, he's fast, and nimble to boot! The man rivaled Donnie.*

The crowd had gone silent—it appeared that no one expected the haughty Sir Fafnar to land the first blow. Lloyd was going to have to be a lot more careful. He readjusted his stance again, shortening his grip on his weapons in preparation for closer combat. As he did, Fafnar spun around and immediately launched himself back toward him. Lloyd was not expecting such a reckless maneuver from the prim and proper noble. Before he knew it, the knight was under his guard again and landed two more blows, one of them nearly penetrating his armor! Lloyd swiftly swung around and set himself for a single swipe at the retreating noble. He brought his right hand around and connected with the knight, the tip of his black blade slicing neatly through the man's armor and biting into his side. The crowd let out a collective cheer.

Fafnar, recoiling from the blow, took a few steps back, putting some distance between himself and Lloyd. His face reddened as he examined his side. He was bleeding through his armor. It was not a deep or debilitating wound, but it must have stung nonetheless. The Dunwynn knight's eyes fell on him. "How dare you!" His expression hardened and he fixed Lloyd with an icy cold stare. "Now you shall feel my true wrath."

Lloyd stood ready for the next attack, but instead the Dunwynn noble just stood there. A look of fierce concentration filled the man's face, and Lloyd could feel the power building around him from where he stood.

Could it be? Was Fafnar some kind of... spiritblade?

In answer to his silent question, Sir Fafnar's blade and axe frosted over, seemingly turning to ice in front of him! Lloyd was stunned by this new development. He had never heard of a technique that could turn weapons icy. It was as if they had studied the same arts, only substituting ice for fire. There were murmurs from the crowd around them. They appeared as surprised as Lloyd. Fafnar charged forward again. He moved in quite swiftly, but this time Lloyd was prepared. He parried the knight's sword with his own, but Fafnar ducked under Lloyd's left arm. He caught him in the side with his icy hand axe. Lloyd felt the cold right through his armor as Fafnar continued by. A few shocked cries went up around them, one in particular from the royal box.

"Lloyd!" That was Andrella.

Fafnar did not immediately turn and attack again this time. Instead, he kept going until he was well out of the range of Lloyd's blades. Keeping one eye on his opponent, Lloyd took the opportunity to check his side. Sure enough, there was a slit in his armor and a red slice in his skin beneath it. The wound was covered over neatly with a cold patch of ice!

"Blood for blood!" Fafnar sneered at him from a safe distance.

That was enough! Lloyd felt his anger mount. Almost without thought, his blades lit on fire. Murmurs arose from the crowd and a few voices cried out.

"Go for it, Lloyd!" That was Elladan.

"Now that's more like it!" That was Donnie.

Lloyd smiled grimly at Fafnar. "Two can play at that game."

"We shall see, knave!"

Lloyd purposely goaded the arrogant noble, knowing he could not resist responding. While the knight fired back his reply, Lloyd took advantage of the moment and executed a quick spiritblade move. Time slowed as he made the appropriate motion and envisioned the results in his mind. Lloyd reached deep within himself, finding that spark of spirit. It felt as if a floodgate had opened, the energy rushing outward, coursing through his body. The entire process took only a second. While Fafnar's mouth still hung open, Lloyd leapt ten feet into the air and dove down toward the surprised knight. Gasps went up around them as the young warrior plummeted down toward his intended target.

Yet Fafnar did not try to dodge out of the way. Instead, the knight closed his own eyes and stood perfectly still. Just as Lloyd was about to pounce, Fafnar suddenly shot up into the air! Lloyd was taken completely by surprise. He passed through the space where Fafnar had just been. Luckily, his reflexes kicked in—he neatly curled into a ball as he hit the ground, tumbled forward, and came up in a fighting stance. Lloyd quickly spun around, searching for his opponent.

Fafnar now floated high above him, nearly twenty feet in the air. Lloyd watched in amazement as the knight pointed his sword down at him. A ball of ice formed at the tip and an icy projectile launched itself from the blade, careening downwards at a frightening speed. Lloyd reacted immediately, bringing his two flaming blades up and crossing them in front of him. He felt the impact as the ball of ice hit his blades and broke apart. Ice chunks went flying in all directions, causing Lloyd to duck his head.

Screams of fright sounded all around him. When he opened his eyes a few seconds later, he was unharmed, but now he had a new problem. A thick bank of steam rose high in front of him, hiding the Dunwynn knight from his view. Lloyd knew an attack was imminent. Calming his mind, he tried to anticipate the direction of the next assault. He felt it before he saw the dark form appear in the mist.

Lloyd brought up his black blade to block the impending attack, but as it turned out, the blow was not aimed directly at him. Instead, it struck his blade. Without warning, the weapon was jerked from his hand! The blade went flying across the field and fell to the ground a good dozen feet away. Screams and jeers arose from the crowd as Lloyd realized what had happened. Fafnar had used his axe to disarm him, hooking his blade with the L-shaped weapon. The knight had miscalculated, though, having put too much force into the blow to disarm him.

Fafnar currently stood before him, off-balance, the knight's exposed back facing him. Lloyd swiftly seized the opportunity. He brought his other blade around in a high arc toward Fafnar's unprotected flank. Having no other choice, the Dunwynn knight quickly spun around, bringing his own sword up to block Lloyd's. He had no time to set himself, and could not counter the warrior's greater strength.

The force of Lloyd's blow drove the knight down on one knee. Thus, he was off-balance when Lloyd unleashed a devastating right fist directly into his opponent's jaw. The young warrior connected with a resounding crack that could be heard across the arena. Fafnar's body actually lifted off the ground, flipped into the air, and was sent flying backwards. The Dunwynn knight landed in a heap nearly two yards away.

The crowd roared, coming to its feet. Cries of "Take that, you creep!" and "Way to go, Lloyd!" were mixed in with the shouts, but

Lloyd was only focused on one thing. As soon as Fafnar went down, he spun around and sprinted for his black blade. Lloyd closed in on the weapon and had nearly reached it when he heard a scream from behind.

"Aaahhh! How dare you!" the voice roared.

Lloyd did not stop. He launched himself the last few feet and landed atop his black blade, grasping the hilt with his right hand as he rolled into a ball. He continued tumbling forward, coming up onto his feet in a fighting stance, both blades again in hand. Lloyd whirled around to face his opponent.

Fafnar lifted himself off the ground, his face twisted into a mask of rage. He launched himself forward with a cry. "You'll pay for that, varlet!"

"Enough of this!" Lloyd spat as he also started toward the knight.

The two of them collided in the center of the arena, blade to blade, fire and ice. Steam rose around them as their weapons clashed over and over. Lloyd knew the knight's tricks now, and would no longer allow him to slip under his guard. Yet he could not land a blow on Fafnar, the wiry knight being too quick. The two of them separated, glaring at each other. Suddenly, the Dunwynn knight's face went blank once more.

Lloyd silently swore at himself for giving his opponent this opportunity. He quickly launched himself forward, determined to catch Fafnar before he could begin his next assault, but as he swung at the man, the knight's axe rushed up to block it. The same thing happened with his other blade. No matter where Lloyd tried to strike, a sword or axe was instantaneously there to block his attack. *Blade wall.*

The name of the technique reverberated through Lloyd's mind. It was as if Fafnar was surrounded by a wall of impenetrable weapons. There really was no way around it. It could not be kept up indefinitely, but if he kept on hacking away at it, Lloyd would wear himself out.

An idea dawned on him. Stepping back, Lloyd summoned up his spirit energy again. Advancing forward, he went to strike Fafnar once more. This time, blade and axe clattered against each other with the same astonishing speed. The same thing happened with their other hands. Both men's weapons were now moving almost faster than the eye could see. It was as if there was a wall of flashing steel between them as they circled around each other. The crowd grew hushed as they watched the incredible display of swordsmanship. Neither warrior nor knight could get through the other's defense. It was the perfect offense. Lloyd could now keep up with Fafnar without tiring himself out. This went on for nearly a minute until Fafnar finally drew back. He was fuming at how his clever defense had been nullified.

"Block this, then!" Fafnar lifted his blade and pointed it at Lloyd.

Lloyd felt the surge of power but did not react, confident his blade wall could handle whatever was coming. He was taken by surprise though, as a blast of icy wind blew from the tip. It expanded outward into a cone of snow and ice that completely engulfed him. *My blades are no good against this! It's like trying to fend off the very air.*

Before he knew it, Lloyd froze over. The flames on his blades went out, and he was covered with a thick layer of ice. The crowd booed and jeered while Fafnar stood there gloating. The knight slowly approached Lloyd, crying out in a voice loud enough for those in the stands to hear.

"So then, knave... do you give up?"

"Don't do it, Lloyd!" a voice shouted from the crowd. "You can't let him win!" came another cry.

Fafnar angrily spun around to face the stands. "He has no say in the matter! He has lost!"

Lloyd barely heard him. He still might have a chance. There was a spiritblade technique he hadn't quite mastered yet—it invoked a state of body that did not require movement like most other skills. It was indeed a long shot, but if he could get it to work, he might still have a fighting chance. Lloyd stilled his mind. Some corner of it noted that Fafnar had turned back to face him. The knight was still gloating.

"What's the matter? No retorts? Nothing to say, man of Penwick?"

Time slowed at those last few words. Lloyd felt that spark of spirit again and knew he had connected with his innermost being. Drawing on that power, he pulled it forth and pushed it outward from his body in all directions. It was a huge strain, and he felt himself sweating from the effort.

Fafnar's voice rang out. "Whatever are you doing? You're stuck. You can't..."

The ice surrounding his body began to crack.

Fafnar's voice rose in pitch. "That's... impossible!"

Straining with every fiber of his being, Lloyd pushed outward one last time. The icy prison that held him broke apart. Lloyd's eyes snapped open. Chunks of ice and snow flew in all directions. Fafnar jumped back out of the way as a huge piece of ice went flying past him. Lloyd seized the opportunity—he began to concentrate, the world slowing around him once more. He swiftly reached the point where body, mind, and spirit were all one, then the world flashed past him, and he was suddenly behind Sir Fafnar.

The knight was taken completely off-guard. Lloyd reached out and grappled him with one arm. Fafnar tried to break free, but then froze in place as the tip of Lloyd's sword pressed up against his back. Around him, the audience began to cheer wildly. There were cries of "Way to go, lad!" "That'll show him!" and "Who's stuck now?"

Lloyd kept his eyes firmly fixed on his opponent, holding him firmly in place. "Do you give up?"

Fafnar stiffened. Even from behind, he could tell the knight was livid. Lloyd remained wary, carefully watching for signs of spiritblade moves. None came. The Dunwynn noble remained firmly in his grip, still seething at having the tables so effectively turned on him.

"I do not!" Fafnar spat from between clenched teeth.

The audience died down, but there was still underlying chatter in the stands. Fafnar tried to thrash around, but Lloyd tightened his grip. He held him fast, the tip of his blade digging into the knight's back. Fafnar finally ceased his struggling.

"Do you give up?" Lloyd repeated, his tone as calm as ice.

Fafnar would not answer. He remained firmly stuck in Lloyd's grip, refusing to yield. The two of them stood locked in that position for perhaps another half minute when a voice rang out across the arena.

"The match is over!"

Lloyd peered in the direction of the voice and saw the Baron standing in the royal box. He waved his hands out in front of him, signifying the end of any further actions.

"And the winner is... Lloyd Stealle!" Gryswold declared emphatically.

A huge roar went up around them, the entire audience standing up and cheering as one. Mixed chants his own name and "Heroes!" erupted from both sides of the arena. Lloyd slowly released Sir Fafnar and stepped away from him.

Fafnar turned around to face him, his expression boiling with anger. "You were lucky, knave. That move would not work a second time."

Lloyd glared at the arrogant noble. "It doesn't matter. I'd beat you again, even without it."

Fafnar glowered at him, his face a mask of rage. He began to retort, but was interrupted as another loud voice rang out across the arena.

"Sir Fafnar! We are done here!"

Lloyd glanced in the direction of that voice. It was the Duke of Dunwynn. He too now stood, his eyes fixed on his recalcitrant knight. Fafnar spun toward his liege, his anger quickly dissipating. Crestfallen, he bowed to the Duke. "At once, Lord Kelvick."

Fafnar spun around again and hissed under his breath, "A fortnight from now, here in Ravenford."

Lloyd nodded. "Agreed."

Fafnar stormed off back toward the tents, the crowd cheering his exit. Lloyd watched as the noble retreated, then sheathed his swords and crossed the field toward the royal box. The Duke had disappeared, but Gryswold, Gracelynn, Andrella, and the knights from Penwick all stood and clapped for him. His eyes were focused, though, on the young lady whose scarf he wore. Andrella then surprised him. Despite her fine gown, the young lady vaulted down onto the field. She met him in front of the royal box, pulled him down, and kissed him firmly on the lips. Another round of cheers went up through the crowd as the two young nobles locked lips. When Andrella finally let go, Lloyd found himself breathless.

"That was some battle!" she cried.

"Indeed it was!" Gryswold agreed over the din of the crowd.

"Well done." Sir Brennon commended him.

The Baron raised his hands and hushed the audience into silence. His voice boomed across the arena. "As this was not only a match but a matter of honor, I now declare all charges against these fine gentlemen dropped!"

Cheers exploded around the arena, but this time Gryswold did not stop them.

7
PEARLS

S tay still," Aksel admonished. The little cleric stood over Lloyd, pouring healing light into the young man's wounds. Lloyd assured Aksel that he was fine, embarrassed at being scolded for fidgeting again. He sat on the edge of a large four-poster bed in one of the castle's guestrooms, a spacious, well-furnished chamber on the fourth floor of the keep.

Light streamed in through a pair of tall windows inset into the outer wall, brightening up the area with the midday sun. Andrella had insisted on bringing Lloyd up here to heal his wounds and rest after the intense battle. It was probably just as well, for the spot where Fafnar had sliced through his armor went far deeper than he originally thought. It was, in fact, lucky that it had been iced over since it actually slowed the bleeding. Once he had peeled his armor off, it began to bleed profusely. Lloyd also had a mild case of frostbite, most likely from being encased in ice, and a few bruises here and there. Fafnar must have hit him far harder than he thought. Even so, Lloyd still felt they were making a much bigger deal out of it than was necessary.

Andrella hovered over his other side as Aksel continued to work. "Stop arguing with the healer. You're being a baby. Now sit still like he asked you to."

Lloyd turned his head and stared at the young lady, his face reddening even further. "Really? Not you, too?"

"Let me guess, I sound like your mother," Andrella teased.

"No, more like my sister. If it was my mother, she wouldn't say a word. She'd just cast a spell of holding on me."

The sound of snickering came from the other side of the room. Lloyd turned his head and saw Seth, perched on a comfortable chair, a wicked grin on his face. "Sounds like my kind of wizard!"

"Oh, so suddenly you like the 'shoot now, ask questions later' type?" Glo interjected. The elven wizard sat on a small couch across from Seth.

"Never said I didn't," Seth shot back. "Your work at the lighthouse was dazzling..."

If looks could kill, Glo would have bored two holes through Seth's skull. Before he could retort, Andrella interrupted them. "Lighthouse? You mean the Cape Marlin Lighthouse? I heard reports that it burnt down."

There was a huge thump back by the sitting area. Seth had fallen off his chair and was rolling on the floor, laughing hysterically.

"What's with him?" Elladan nodded at the chortling halfling. He and Donnie had been wandering around the room, admiring the plush décor.

Glo, appearing quite chagrinned, turned to face Andrella. "With everything that's gone on since we got back, there was never a good time to tell anyone..."

The elven wizard paused a moment, then launched into the story of their encounter at the lighthouse. He went into great detail about the lost ships, the apparently vacant lighthouse, and the fake "light" up the coast that had led those ships astray. He then described the goblin party and the demon they had faced, and how that confrontation led to the destruction of the lighthouse. He finished with the recovery of the ship's cargo and the attack of the goblin army on the shore. Lloyd noted that Glo left out any mention of Ves, Ruka or Maya. The others interjected from time to time, especially Donnie and Elladan, who had not traveled with them to the cape. The Lady Andrella stood there quietly throughout the entire tale, listening patiently until Glo was done. Silence pervaded the room afterwards until Andrella finally spoke.

"It seems to me that you were just defending yourselves, and there was no loss of life, so I would say you have nothing to be ashamed of."

Glo let out a huge sigh, his shoulders visibly relaxing until Andrella continued. "However, the lighthouse will need to be rebuilt, and that will require funding..."

"Say no more," Aksel swiftly interjected. He had just finished with Lloyd. "We will be more than happy to make a substantial donation into that fund."

"Thank you, Cleric Aksel," Andrella said with a gracious nod. "I will explain the entire matter to my parents. Consider it closed."

Lloyd looked at Andrella with renewed respect. She had handled that quite well. She would make a fine ruler one day. The young lady sat down on the bed next to him, leaned over and whispered in his ear. "How was that?"

"Perfect," he whispered back. "Just like you."

Andrella's eyes misted over. She threw her arms around him and kissed him.

"Get a room, you two!" Donnie quipped.

Lloyd and Andrella both stopped and turned to stare at the slight elf.

"Oh... wait..."

Donnie spun around, his eyes sweeping their surroundings, a mischievous grin on his face. The couple burst out laughing at his comical antics. The door to the guestroom suddenly opened, and the Baron and Baroness stood in the entryway. Gryswold was in good spirits, practically grinning from ear to ear as he strode into the room. "How's our boy doing?"

"All healed up," Aksel reported.

"That's excellent news! I was hoping to see him win the rest of the tournament."

Lloyd reached back and grabbed his armor, currently strewn across the bed, then vaulted to the floor below, eager to get ready for his next match.

Aksel cleared his throat. "Ahem, about that..."

Lloyd stopped in his tracks. All eyes turned toward the little cleric.

"I hate to do this to you, Lloyd, but as your healer I would be remiss if I did not."

Lloyd sighed heavily. He had lived with a healer in the house most of his life. He knew what was coming. "Let me guess. You don't want me to finish the tournament."

Aksel's expression was one of keen sympathy. "I am truly sorry, but between the injuries you sustained from the battle with those serpents, and now your bout with Fafnar, your body really needs to rest—especially if we are headed out on a mission first thing in the morning."

Lloyd sighed once more. He knew Aksel was right, but he couldn't help feeling disappointed. Abruptly, he felt a light touch on his shoulder. He turned to see Andrella standing next to him, an empathetic look on her face. "You've already won in my eyes."

Lloyd reached down and took her slim hand in his own, the two of them standing there gazing at each other. The room grew awkwardly silent until Glo changed the subject. "Excuse me, your lordship. I was just wondering, what will become of Sir Fafnar?"

All present turned to face the wizard. Gracelynn was the first to reply. "You don't have to worry about my brother or any of his people. They have withdrawn to their rooms and are leaving for home later this afternoon."

"All things considered, I doubt we will be seeing much of them, if at all, between now and then," Gryswold added.

"Thank you, your lord and ladyship," Glo said. "I am sorry for all the trouble this has caused."

Gracelynn's expression filled with compassion as she gazed upon the wizard. "Do not be sorry. My brother can be—difficult at best."

Gryswold, however, turned red in the face at the mention of

the Dunwynn noble. "Personally, if I had my way, Fafnar would get more than a slap on the wrist. Refusing to yield like that was very unknightly."

"Do not worry," Gracelynn said to Gryswold. "If I know my brother, Sir Fafnar will be properly chastised for his behavior. The Duke does not take inappropriate behavior lightly."

"Couldn't happen to a nicer guy," Donnie commented.

"I must confess, I will not be shedding any tears over his misfortune," Elladan said with a quasi-smile.

Gryswold let out a huge sigh. "Very well then—it is best you make your repairs and any preparations for tomorrow's journey. We will be occupied with the tournament for the rest of the day, but I am opening the armory up to you."

"Thank you, your lordship." There was a note of surprise in Aksel's voice.

Gryswold continued. "Furthermore, I will provide you with a note for the town merchants. You may stock up on whatever supplies you require at our expense."

Elladan responded this time. "That's very generous of you, your lordship. I can promise you that anything we purchase will be at a fair price."

A faint smile spread across Gryswold's lips. "Of that I have no doubt. Let's just say this will expedite things with certain merchants."

A half-smile crossed Elladan's lips. "Ah, yes. Like our good friend Haltan."

Donnie eyed the bard curiously. "Sounds like I missed an interesting time."

"Why don't you join us when we go back to visit him?" Elladan winked.

"Wouldn't miss it." Donnie grinned.

"Very good then," Gryswold said. "I will send Lieutenant Relkin shortly to assist you. We will meet back here at the keep first thing in the morning."

The companions and the first family of Ravenford parted ways, the Lady Andrella rather reluctantly joining her parents as they headed back to the tournament. Aksel, Glo, Lloyd, Seth, Elladan, and

Donnie went downstairs to meet Lieutenant Relkin for their trip to the armory.

A short while later, the Lieutenant let the companions into the Ravenford armory. The armory was actually broken into two rooms, one for weaponry and the second for armor and shields. They spent a good hour exploring those rooms. Seth managed to restock his throwing knives, and Donnie found a particularly nice rapier and short sword to replace the ones he had nicked up on the tough skin of those serpents in yesterday's battle. Yet they were truly surprised to find three *mithral* chain shirts.

The silvery metal was extremely lightweight, yet sturdy. Forged into chain mail, a mithral shirt was just as strong as regular chain, but half the weight. It would make the perfect armor for someone like Lloyd or Donnie, who tended to move around a lot in battle. The two of them ended up taking a mithral shirt each, although Lloyd did have one complaint.

Lloyd dubiously eyed one of the silvery shirts. "It's not red."

"Seriously?" Seth stared at the young man as if he were crazy.

"You can just wear your Penwick tabard over it for now," Glo said. His expression was quite serious, but his eyes were alight with amusement.

"If you really want, I can paint it red for you," Donnie offered.

Lloyd's face suddenly lit up. "Could you really do that?"

"I don't see why not." Donnie took the chain shirt from Lloyd and examined the links. "I will need to come up with a fairly resistant stain, though," he mused under his breath.

The last shirt went to Elladan, since neither Seth, Aksel, nor Glo wore armor. When they were finished with the armory, the companions split up, promising to meet again for dinner that evening. Elladan and Donnie took the note the Baron had promised them, and headed off to shop for supplies. Lloyd reluctantly went back to the inn to rest. Aksel proceeded to the temple since they were leaving early the next morning. Glo had a pre-arranged meeting with Ves, and Seth went to watch the rest of the tourney.

Glo found Ves waiting for him in the Druid's glade on the outskirts of town. She sat all alone on a large flat gray rock in the center of the quiet glade, surrounded by thick grass. The clearing was dotted here and there with vibrant green bushes and brightly colored pink and yellow flowers. Ves gave him a reserved smile as he strode up to join her.

"Where is Almax?" Glo asked. Almax was the old Druid who had accompanied the three sisters to Andrella's party. Glo had expected to see him here since the glade was his charge.

"He is out in the woods, gathering herbs and attending to the plants and animals in the area." Ves acted quite strangely, having a hard time looking him in the eye.

"And your sisters?" He swept the glade with his eyes, but saw no sign of the two younger girls.

Ves did not turn to look at him, but instead stared out at the grove of trees that surrounded the glade. Her shoulders were taut, and she appeared rather pensive. "Maya went with Almax. She loves running around in the woods. As for Ruka, she is competing in the tournament."

"Ruka?" Glo was surprised that the girl would have entered the tournament. "Are you sure that's a good idea?"

"Trust me, she can handle herself," Ves replied, her tone defensive. It was the first sign of emotion she had shown since he had entered the glade.

Glo responded in a soft voice. "Of that I have little doubt. I just thought you would be more concerned that her powers might get away from her..."

Her shoulders tensed up even more, if that were possible, her blue-green eyes practically boring into him.

Glo through up his hands defensively. "I mean you are trying to keep your true natures a secret... after all."

"Ohhhh!" Ves exclaimed. Her shoulders relaxed, her expression softening. "That is what you meant. You were worried about us trying to keep a low profile."

An embarrassed smile crossed Glo's lips. "Yes. That's what I meant. I guess I don't always express myself as well as I should."

A warm smile lit Ves's face. She reached over and patted the rock next to her. "Please sit down."

Glo graciously accepted her invitation, sitting down on the flat grey rock. It was warmer than he expected, most likely from the rays of the afternoon sun. Once seated, he turned to face Ves. She stared back at him, appearing as if she wanted to speak, but hesitating as if searching for the right words. "That attack by those serpents yesterday was... troubling. You and your companions were very valiant in the way you fought them off."

"We only did what we thought was right. The Baron and his family have been very good to us, and we wanted to protect them from this Cult."

A look of surprise registered on her face. "So, the Baron's family was the target of the attack?"

"We believe so."

Ves silently considered his words. She seemed rather preoccupied, as if she were struggling with some internal conflict. "I am not... overly fond of dark magic. I could sense the evil flowing from those creatures. It was warped and... quite unsettling."

A shudder passed over Glo as he relived nearly being consumed by Voltark's fireball. "I must admit the entire experience was harrowing."

Abruptly he felt a hand on his. Ves was staring at him, her eyes filled with keen sympathy. "That was rather insensitive of me, after all you went through."

A wan smile spread across Glo's lips. "Thanks."

There was a warmth in Ves's eyes as they sat there silently together in the glade. Something intangible passed between them at that moment. It was as if they bonded in some ethereal way, then the moment was gone. Ves pulled her hand away and spoke. "Were you able to find out anything more about these dark mages? Do you know where they came from? Were they indeed part of this Serpent Cult that you told us about?"

Glo paused before answering. He felt on some deep level that he could trust Ves. However, the sisters had abandoned them a couple of days ago, never showing up like they promised in front of Maltar's home. Still, yesterday Ves had saved his life. Without her timely intervention, he would have died from the wounds he had received. Glo finally decided to listen to his gut. "Look, Ves, I trust you, but trust is a two-way street. If I am going to answer your questions, I need to know that you trust me as well. Are you willing to go down that road at this time?"

The young woman's face fell, and she averted her eyes. She seemed torn as she considered his words. When she finally spoke, her voice filled with trepidation. "This is... difficult. You already know that I have made a promise, and I cannot break it. However, you and your companions have been nothing but kind to us. You don't even really know us, but you have accepted us at face value, even when it is obvious that we are more than we seem."

She raised her eyes and peered at him once more. "And if that were not enough, yesterday on the battlefield, you proved the kind of people you are, yet again."

There was a hint of moisture in her eyes, but she quickly reached up and brushed it away. When her eyes rested on him again, her expression was determined, as if she had reached a decision. "So although I cannot break my earlier promise, I can make you another promise. My sisters and I can be powerful allies. We have much magic at our disposal. My promise to you, then, is that wherever you are, if you need help, we will be by your side. To that end, please take this."

Ves reached into a small pocket that he had not even noticed before, and pulled out a small amulet. It had a round, lustrous, moon-colored gemstone, the size of a large pebble, inset in the center, surrounded by a bronze border. It was attached to a simple bronze-colored, sturdy chain. She held out her hands, proffering the amulet to him. Her voice was low as she gazed up from her hands to his face. "This is a Pearl of Friendship. With it you can contact us anytime, anywhere."

Glo felt a sudden warmth rise up in his gut. He had not known such items existed, but he recognized it immediately as being quite valuable and rare. It was therefore not something that one offered lightly, and signified that the young woman was indeed placing a great deal of trust in him. When he replied, his words came out thick with emotion. "This is a priceless gift. I am honored that you would entrust me with it."

She reached out, grasped his hand, and placed the amulet into his palm, then laid her hand on top of his. "I have seen the goodness in your heart... in all of your hearts, and want you to know that I do, in fact, trust you."

He could see the sincerity of those words mirrored in her eyes. Any reluctance he may have felt before melted away. "And I you."

The two of them sat there, hand in hand, staring at each other, and Glo felt that strange bond once more. They he noticed something he had missed before. There was a sadness in Ves's eyes—a deep abiding loneliness, as if she had spent her entire life walled off from everyone around her. He suddenly felt a deep desire to reach out to this young woman, to show her that she was not alone. Yet something held him back. He pulled his hands away and cleared his throat. "Ahem. Yes, now, I was going to tell you what we found out about those creatures..."

A look of surprise momentarily crossed Ves's face, but it quickly disappeared. The corners of her mouth upturned slightly, and a small laugh escaped her closed lips. Glo paused, somewhat mystified by her reaction. "Did I do something wrong?"

A genuine smile spread across her lips. "Oh, no, quite the contrary."

"Then what is so amusing?"

Ves began to blush. "Let's just say... business would the farthest thing from most men's minds... were they here alone with me."

It was Glo's turn to blush. "Yes... well... there are... pressing matters at hand."

"Oh, I absolutely agree," she said with a serious nod. "I just meant that your dedication is... refreshing."

Glo was now more confused than ever. He gave her a puzzled smile as he wrestled with his tangled emotions. "Very good, now where was I?"

He told her everything that they had found. He affirmed that the serpents and the black mages were indeed part of the Serpent Cult, that their apparent target was the Lady Andrella and/or the Duke, about the discovery of Telvar and the monolith in the Darkwoods, and finally, the suspected return of a Thrall Master. He went on to explain how they believed the disappearances of the wizards from the council, as well as her father, and now Maltar, were somehow all related to this. When he was done, Ves appeared even more troubled than she had when he first saw her here in the glade.

"It is just as I feared. Father has gotten himself into more than he may be able to handle on his own."

Glo nodded, his own expression grave. "That may well be. I just wish we had some clue as to where he is. We really do we want to help you find him."

Ves attempted a smile.

"For now, though, we must gather ourselves and our allies and set out for this Dark Monolith. We must stop the Serpent Cult from getting its hands on the Golem Master's work.

"Indeed, that is probably the most important thing at the moment."

Ves agreed. "But I do appreciate your desire to help us with our father." She slowly rose from her seat on the rock. In the meantime, I will find Almax and tell him all this. The Druids should know what is coming as well."

Glo also stood. "That is an excellent idea."

Ves smiled briefly at him. Without warning, she stepped forward, stood up on her toes, put her arms around his neck, and kissed him on the cheek. It only lasted for a moment or two, then she quickly pulled away.

Glo felt the blood rush to his face.

Ves gazed at him rather fondly. "Once again, thank you for your concern—and all that you have entrusted me with."

"I could say the same," he managed through an embarrassed smile. "Well, it is getting late, and I still have much to do before we leave tomorrow..."

She nodded, her countenance turning solemn. "I understand. Good luck on your journey."

They smiled at each other one last time, then both turned and went their separate ways. As Glo strode away, a strange sense of sadness washed over him. He glanced over his shoulder one last time, but Ves had already disappeared into the woods and was now out of sight.

8
LIGHTNING

My apologies for thinking you were just an ordinary girl

Seth sat high up in the stands of the packed arena, waiting for the start of the tournament finals. Everyone was disappointed when they heard that Lloyd had resigned from the competition. Rumors flew around the arena, anything from "He had been badly hurt in his dual with Sir Fafnar," to "He had run away with the Lady Andrella," that is, until the young lady showed up again in the royal box with her parents. The rumor that eventually surfaced to the top was far closer to the truth—that the Heroes had an important mission to carry out for the Baron, and that it took precedence over the tournament.

So the competition continued without the favored Penwick warrior. It turned out to be quite interesting, nonetheless, with two very different combatants eventually rising above the others. Those two finalists now stood across from each other in the center of the arena, waiting for the signal to begin the final match. On the one side was the redheaded Knight of the Rose, Alana. She stood at the ready in her gleaming silver full-plate armor, her longsword in one hand and her shield held firmly in the other. The lady knight had reached the finals by soundly defeating her competition, her prowess enabling her to best much larger, stronger opponents, even the huge barbarian Brum.

The second finalist had taken the crowd completely by surprise, all except for Seth, that is. He had a fairly good idea what Alana's opponent was capable of. Standing casually across from the lady knight was none other than Ruka, the middle sister of the Greymantles. The sandy blonde-haired girl was wearing her standard leather tunic and held that short sword of hers loosely in one hand. Seth had seen firsthand what that sword could do. He had watched with keen interest as she felled opponents nearly twice her size on her way to the finals. Despite the fact that no lightning bolts were thrown around, he had no doubt that they all felt the "shock" of her small blade. The phenomenon of Ruka had the crowd going wild. She quickly became the town favorite in place of Lloyd.

Seth's mouth twisted to one side. *This is going to be a very interesting final.*

Dame Alana Benefilla had been a Knight of the Rose for almost five years now. She was fourth generation in a line of knights dating back over a hundred years. Her father and older brother, also part of that order, were both rather high-ranking knights themselves.

Her current mission to pay the order's respects to the Lady Andrella, the heir to the Duchy of Dunwynn, took a surprising turn last night when the Serpent Cult attacked during dinner. The foul creatures had been repelled, largely due to the efforts of the Heroes of Ravenford. An unorthodox order, they nonetheless fought bravely and with exceptional skill against the minions of darkness. What's more, their uncovering of the Cult's further schemes and the possible rise of a new Thrall Master was indeed fortuitous. It was the sworn duty of the Knights of the Rose to stand against evil, and she would proudly support any such effort.

Right now, however, she was proving her mettle in the Ravenford tournament. She had to admit, she was quite disappointed at not being able to face Lloyd Stealle. She was extremely impressed with the young warrior's prowess. Still, her opponent in today's final was quite far from ordinary, and would prove to be an interesting challenge.

As the crowd quieted down, Alana carefully assessed her opponent. A slender blonde girl, not more than fifteen years old, stood across from her wearing only a simple leather tunic, a rather crude-bladed bronze short sword with a strangely elaborate hilt grasped loosely in her one hand. Alana had observed this "girl" during her previous matches, and had seen what she had done to opponents nearly twice her size. Well, Alana was not going to be fooled like the others. Despite the girl's casual stance, she noted the intensity of her gaze and the tight smile across her lips as she prepared for combat.

The crowd hushed as Captain Gelpas gave them the order to begin, lifting his sword and stepping away from the center. The first lightning bolt solidly caught Alana before she could take a step toward her opponent. It was not a killing bolt by any means, but it was more than enough to rattle her teeth. Stunned cries arose from the crowd. No one had seen the girl cast spells in her prior matches.

After the initial shock, Alana quickly sidestepped, moving in with a feint. She kept her guard up all the while, seeking any further sign of casting. There was none, other than a small frown and a quick change of the girl's eye color from green to amber. Alana managed to dodge the worst of the second bolt, which sprung from the teen's sword, but the charge was numbing nonetheless. Cries of alarm broke out amongst the crowd once more, followed by a low chanting of the girl's name.

Ruka! Ruka!

Alana paid them little heed. Instead, she bore down and quickly closed the gap between herself and the little caster. She leapt forward the last few feet and struck immediately with two solid blows. The crowd hushed, and she had a brief surge of guilt, worrying that she may have mortally injured the young warrior. Her worries, however, were short-lived. If anything, Ruka was invigorated by the attacks, replying with a series of skilled strikes, almost too fast to follow. The last blow landed with more strength than any of the opponents she had just fought, and carried an extra charge of electricity to boot!

The two of them stood there in the center of the arena, trading blows as the crowd roared with delight. Her strikes landed easily on the unarmored girl, but appeared to have little effect. Meanwhile, Ruka's blows pierced Alana's heavy armor more often than expected, with deft skill and shocking strength.

Alana kept careful watch on Ruka's eyes, turning her enchanted sword to avoid any further lightning strikes. It seemed like an effective strategy until, without warning, the girl simply reached out with her other hand, touching Alana's armor almost casually. The electric charge caught Alana full on, and she was knocked back off her feet onto the ground. The crowd hushed as she laid there, rattled far beyond mere physical blows. Alana quickly recovered her wits. *What a clever move!* She had not seen that one coming at all. As the lady knight rose to her feet, she realized that she would not be able to win this match without deadly force, some- thing she would never resort to against a good, honest soul. Thus, instead of renewing her attack, the Dame Alana Benefilla, Knight of the Rose, stood up straight and gave a knightly salute to her erstwhile opponent, conceding defeat to the blonde teenage girl.

The murmurs in the crowd hushed once again as Ruka watched her opponent cautiously. As Alana sheathed her sword, the audience went wild! Cheers sprang up all around for the girl who had just won the Ravenford tourney. Chants of *Ruka, Ruka* could be heard amongst the roar.

A grinning Ruka met Alana in the middle of the arena and sincerely thanked her for a good go of it, more like a little girl after an enjoyable game of hearthstones than a bloodied combatant. Alana raised an eyebrow, but merely congratulated the young warrior on her victory. The two of them then walked side by side to bow before the Baron and Baroness, and Ruka was crowned the tournament winner and presented with the five-thousand gold-piece prize for the win.

Early in the morning, the party gathered up on the hill just outside the castle gate. It was another clear day, only a few puffy white clouds dotting the otherwise empty blue sky. The sun still hung over the eastern horizon, sending a yellow-orange streak across the bay toward the shore.

Glo sat astride a tall chestnut mare they had rented from the town livery, his familiar, Raven, perched comfortably on his shoulder. The rest of the companions were present and accounted for, with the additions of the archer Martan, the gypsy Elistra, and the Dame Alana. Baron Gryswold, the Lady Gracelynn, and the Lady Andrella had all come out to bid them farewell. Captain Gelpas and the Bardess Shalla were also present.

All of the travelers had their mounts packed for travel. Alana's horse in particular was rather impressive—a roan warhorse with a broad back and a powerful build; his head was covered with a white hood that had a single scarlet red rose across the forehead. Thick white cloth was draped over his shoulders and ran under his saddle, all the way back to his hindquarters. This cloth was also decorated with a scarlet rose on either side. Glo had heard Alana and Lloyd discussing it earlier. The covering was referred to as a "caparison." Alana explained that it bore the standard symbol of the Knights of the Rose.

Alana now sat comfortably astride her large warhorse, looking as if she were born in the saddle. Glo had previously thought Lloyd's white and brown paint was large, but Alana's roan was definitely the more massive of the two. The lady knight herself was decked out in shining silver full plate. Her sword was strapped to her side, and her silver shield with the heraldic of a golden griffin hung off her left arm. She held her helmet under her right arm as she waited for the journey to begin.

Donnie rode up next to the lady knight, sporting the new pair of boots he had purchased at Haltan's shop the day before, *Boots of the Spider*. The enchantment on them would enable the wearer to scale walls and stick to the slipperiest of surfaces. From their retelling of the encounter, Haltan had been most unhappy when Elladan showed him the purchase note from the Baron. The merchant was obviously uncomfortable with the prospect of overcharging the Barony of Ravenford, especially with Elladan's knowledge of fair pricing.

The companions had also made one other large purchase the night before. At Elladan's prompting, they had decided to buy the Charging Minotaur. They had amassed a small fortune from their adventures, and the bard convinced them the inn was a solid investment. It would also provide them with a place to park the Boulder. The creature was too slow-moving to take on this trip, and further, he would be too heavy to take on a small ship upriver. They left him standing outside the inn, aptly renaming it the Golden Golem. Elladan had further convinced them to hire Shalla on as the manager of their newly-acquired investment. That way she could keep an eye on the Boulder, the inn, and even provide entertainment for the townsfolk. After a lively bit of haggling, which included a cut of any profits, Shalla agreed to take on the position.

Now the songstress stood off some ways from the group with Elladan, the two entertainers saying their goodbyes. The handsome bard swept Shalla off her feet and kissed her soundly on the lips.

Andrella had pulled Lloyd aside as well, the young couple holding each other tenderly, whispering back and forth and trading brief, passionate kisses of their own. Elladan and Shalla were the first couple to part, the songstress holding onto his arm and laughing gaily as she accompanied the bard back to his mount. Lloyd and Andrella soon followed, holding hands as they slowly walked toward the horses.

Elistra sat on the mount next to Glo's. She leaned over and whispered to him, "They are adorable."

Glo turned in his saddle to face her. "Which couple?" he responded, smiling impishly.

"Lloyd and Andrella, of course, silly," the gypsy woman admonished, fixing him with a droll stare.

"Luckily for them, the Baron and Baroness agree with you." Glo nodded toward the royal couple.

Gryswold and Gracelynn stood arm in arm in front of the castle gate, observing their daughter and the young noble from Penwick. They were whispering softly amongst themselves, each seeming rather content with their daughter's choice of suitor.

Andrella reluctantly let Lloyd go. "Good luck!" She stepped back as he mounted his steed. Shalla, still standing there, reached a slender arm around the young lady's shoulder. Andrella gazed up and smiled at the tall woman.

Aksel swiveled around in his saddle. "Are we ready now?" His eyes specifically fell on Elladan and Lloyd.

"Ready," Lloyd said, his eyes still straying to Andrella.

"Yes," Elladan agreed, a partial smile on his lips as his eyes fell one last time on Shalla.

"Then let's head out!" The little cleric turned forward once more and spurred on his canine mount.

As they moved out, Glo noted that Gryswold and Gracelynn walked down to stand with Andrella and Shalla. Gelpas was not far behind. The five of them stood together at the top of the hill as the little band trotted down the road and toward the town below.

"Good luck!" Gryswold cried as they were almost out of earshot. "Come back safe," Andrella added to her father's cry.

Glo turned his head just in time to see the young lady throw herself into her mother's arms and bury her head in her bosom.

When the companions reached the south edge of town, they spied a familiar figure laying across a large boulder on the side of the road. It was Ruka! The girl rose up from her comfort- able position and stretched her arms wide. "Well, it took you long enough."

Aksel stopped his mount and held up his hand, signaling the others to do so as well. Glo was rather surprised to find the middle Greymantle sister waiting for them along the road. "What are you doing here?"

She jumped down from the boulder she had been resting on. "I've come to join your little quest. Ves filled me in on what you were going to do. I thought I would come along and make sure you stayed out of trouble."

"Not to mention there might be loot where we're going," Seth added with a half-twisted smile.

Ruka grinned back at the halfling. "You know me too well."

"Wait a second," Donnie's voice rang out from the ranks. "You can't be seriously thinking of letting this girl join us?" He urged his mount forward, reigning his horse in at the front of the line. "She's just a child!"

A hush fell over the group as Glo, Aksel, Seth, and Lloyd exchanged glances. They had seen firsthand just what the Greymantle sisters could do. Ruka turned to face Donnie, her hands on her hips and her head tilted slightly. She peered at the elf as if sizing him up. Donnie's expression grew more and more uncertain under the weight of that stare. It probably did not help that everyone else had fallen silent, no one daring to support his assertion. Finally, Ruka shifted her gaze to Glo.

"Who's the new elf?" she asked, nodding toward Donnie.

"Donatello, young dame," Donnie replied, smoothly dismounting his horse and lightly landing on the ground. "At your service," he added, doffing his riding cap and bowing low in front of the young teen. "And you are Ruka..."

"Rukastanna ta Yatharia Greymantle," she announced with obvious pride. The expression on her face was a mixture of amusement and curiosity. That was quickly replaced with her customary smirk. "...and I can handle myself, *thank you.*"

Donnie opened his mouth to reply, but was interrupted by a familiar voice from the rear of the company. "Trust me... she can." They all turned to see the lady knight, Alana, spur her warhorse forward. She drew up next to Donnie. "This young woman beat me fair and square in the Ravenford tourney yesterday."

No one other than Donnie seemed surprised by her statement. The slight elf's eyes swept from Alana to Ruka, his jaw hanging open. "This young girl beat *you?*"

Ruka's body tensed and there was a dangerous edge to her voice. "Yes, as a matter of fact, I did." There was a quick flash of amber across the girl's normally green pupils, and a sudden palpable tension in the air, made even more ominous by the rumble of thunder off in the distance. Glo scanned the heavens, but there was not a dark cloud to be seen in the sky. The tension just as quickly faded, Ruka's eyes returning to normal.

"But you were very good." Ruka nodded to Alana. The lady knight bowed her head and smiled in response to the girl's praise. Ruka then turned her gaze back to Donnie. "And if you don't believe her," she added fiercely, "I can show you right now how I did it!" Thunder rumbled once more off in the distance as if to punctuate her assertion.

Donnie threw up his hands in front of him. "No, no, that won't be necessary. If the Dame Alana says that you are that good, *then you are that good*. My apologies for thinking you were just an ordinary girl." He punctuated his speech by flashing her a charming smile.

Ruka seemed momentarily taken aback, her cheeks flushing slightly. She quickly recovered, her mouth curving to one side. "Apology accepted. Now can we get going, or are we going to stay here all day?"

"My thoughts exactly," Seth agreed.

Ruka flashed the halfling a wicked grin.

"Well, let's go then," Aksel said. He addressed Ruka. "Do you want to ride with one of us?"

Her nose wrinkled as she considered his proposal, but she quickly shook her head. "No, I'll just fly." Ruka turned toward Glo. "Can you let your raven loose? It would be nice to have some *intelligent* company to talk to up there." She ended with a quick glance in Donnie's direction.

Glo chuckled to himself. "Surely." He spoke a single word to his winged companion. *"Revia."*

Raven spread her black wings and propelled her tiny body off his shoulder, winging her way upward. Back on the ground, Ruka's expression was one of deep concentration. Her entire body began to glow, growing brighter and brighter until all that was visible was a brilliant white light. It was so intense that Glo had to shield his eyes. The glow appeared to transform, shrinking and shifting into the form of a bird. The brilliant radiance faded, and when it was finally gone, there now stood a magnificent white-tailed hawk. The hawk spread her large wings and lifted off the ground. It quickly rose skyward, joining Glo's raven far above. The two birds circled around each other, then took off along the road to the south.

"Nice going there, Donnie," Seth commented.

Donnie, once again in his saddle, stared beseechingly at the rest of the riders. "How was I supposed to know?"

His mournful plea elicited chuckles from the rest of the group. Dame Alana reached over and placed an armored hand on his shoulder.

"Your intentions were well-meant at the least," she said sympathetically.

"*Thank you.*" Donnie smiled at the lady knight. "At least *someone* understands me." He cast a reproachful glance at the others.

That produced yet another round of laughter from the group.

9
ROAD TO VERMOORDEN

I don't think talking to your dinner is wise

The road between Ravenford and Vermoorden had once been referred to as the Knight's Road. These days it was called either the Old Knight's Road or just the South Road. The road itself had been built in the old days, when Thac was still young. Ancient spells had been set in place to keep the cobblestones clear and smooth. Not even the grass grew near the edge, at which point brambles, thickets, and wild hedges grew in abandon.

The companions were quite familiar with this road. It was the same one that led through the Dead Forest and past Stone Hill. A couple of hours into their journey, they came within sight of the barren peak standing by itself off to the west of the road. Elladan proceeded to sing a tune he had written about their adventures in the ruined keep atop that hill. The bard had not been with them during their first visit, but the story was entertaining, if somewhat embellished. It wasn't too long before they exited the dreariness of the Dead Forest. There were few, if any, inhabited farmsteads in the wild south of Stone Hill. The road soon turned west, away from the coast, in the direction of Vermoorden. Glo knew little about the town, but Lloyd appeared quite well versed in its history.

"Vermoorden was originally a refugee camp," he told the riders. "The founders were folks from Dunwynn."

"Not Dunwynn again," Seth said with clear annoyance.

Lloyd spun around in his saddle to face the halfling. "No, you misunderstand. These were refugees from Dunwynn. They were kicked out for disagreeing with the city's rigid principles of unrelenting law and xenophobia."

"Oh, then that's okay. Why didn't you just say so in the first place?"

Lloyd gave the halfling a quick grin. "The refugees struck out southward and finally came to stop in Penwick..."

"...which is how you know all about this in the first place," Seth interrupted.

Lloyd spun around to look at him again. "Would you like to tell this story?"

"No, no, go ahead. You're doing just fine." Seth waved him to continue.

Lloyd shook his head slowly then went on with his story. "Anyway, as I was saying, this all happened about seventy years ago. The Baron of Penwick back then didn't want Dunwynn refugees in his town. So he granted them the rights to the lands east of Lake Strikken..."

"...which is not exactly prime real estate, for reasons you'll see when we get there," Donnie finished for him with a wry smile.

"You know of the town?" Lloyd turned in his saddle to face the slight elf.

"I may have passed through it on an occasion or two," Donnie admitted.

"Well, don't keep us in suspense. Tell us what you know." Elladan urged his friend.

"Well..." Donnie began, "I don't know that much really. Lloyd is obviously the expert."

"Lloyd?" Elladan turned back toward the young man.

A pained expression crossed Lloyd's face. "What Donnie says is true… it is not the choicest of locations." Lloyd's voice fell almost to a whisper. "Not all Penwick rulers have had the best interests of the townspeople in mind." He hesitated as if there was something more he was going to say on the subject, but then continued with his story. "Anyway, the refugees turned around and headed back north until they reached the shores of the lake. There they formed the settlement which became Vermoorden."

"So this Vermoorden is actually a fiefdom of Penwick?" Aksel asked with interest.

"Oh, no, no, not in the slightest," Donnie answered.

Lloyd nodded. "Vermoorden is an independent town. It is run by a Lord Mayor, who is actually elected into office."

Glo arched an eyebrow. "Elected into office? What a novel concept."

"Indeed," Aksel agreed. "It does sound like a fair way to choose a ruler."

"Well, it would be if the elections were fair," Donnie noted with clear sarcasm.

Elladan turned to his friend, his eyes narrowing. "Okay, out with it. You obviously know more than you're telling."

Donnie's eyes flickered around the rest of the riders. "Well, let's just say that Vermoorden has a dark side to it."

"Just how dark?" Seth asked, his tone measured.

Donnie turned to face him. "Well, for one, Vermoorden has no agreements with other towns. Because of that, it is known as a great place for those with shady backgrounds to reside."

Elladan nodded. "So it's a haven for questionable folks."

"Unfortunately, that's not the worst of it," Donnie said with a meaningful glance around the group. "Vermoorden also might have the reputation of being a place to go if you need services that operate outside the law."

"What kind of services?" Alana asked.

Donnie turned toward the lady knight. "Rumor has it that the town is home to a guild of assassins."

Alana's eyes flew wide open. "An assassins' guild?"

Glo's own eyes narrowed as he stared at the slight elf. "And just how do you know all this?"

"Oh, I get around," Donnie replied with a nonchalant wave of his hand. "As I said, I've been through Vermoorden once or twice."

"Through the bars, no doubt," Elladan added, his lips curving into a half smile.

Donnie spun toward his old-time friend and grinned. "Naturally."

Elladan let out a short laugh. "Which explains how you heard all the town gossip."

"Is there a better way?" Donnie shrugged his shoulders.

A snort sounded from the front of the riders. That was Seth. "Sounds like a real nice place we've chosen to pass through."

Aksel, next to Seth, cleared his throat. "I'm sure as long as we do just that, merely pass through, we'll be fine."

"I hope you're right," Seth retorted, still not sounding convinced.

The travelers continued their journey until the sun started to disappear behind the Korlokesel Mountains far to the west. They had made good time, covering half the distance between Ravenford and their destination, but traveling in the open at night was not wise. There were things skulking about in the wild, and not all of them were friendly.

Further, before leaving Ravenford, they had heard rumors of a large green dragon seen to the north. Unlike their copper cousins, green dragons are not friendly—in fact, black, red, green, blue, and white dragons are inherently evil. In addition, dragons can fly quickly over long distances, so even this far west, an encounter with the dragon was not out of the question. Therefore, the companions decided to make camp and start out again at first light.

Martan found a small clearing a short distance from the road, surrounded by a dense stand of pine. It was the perfect place to spend the night—out of sight of any watchful eyes. A hawk and raven circled the grove in the darkening sky overhead, keeping watch as the others busily pitched tents and unsaddled horses.

Once the camp was setup, Elladan began preparing dinner. The bard's prowess with cooking was nearly as good as his ability to entertain. Aksel sat in front of his tent, chanting his evening devotions. Glo perused his traveling spell book by a small light conjured on the end of his staff, trying to decide what spells he would memorize come tomorrow. Elistra sat across from him, cross-legged, deep in meditation. Lloyd had headed out to the road to stand the first watch. Donnie went with Martan and Alana to brush down the horses. The slight elf continued his quest to woo the lady knight. Alana, on the other hand, showed little signs of succumbing to his charms.

The only two missing were Seth and Ruka. The former had set out a short while ago into the surrounding woods to "scout the area." Glo smiled to himself, thinking it more likely that Seth was trying to sneak up on Ruka. The two had developed a kind of rapport since the night of the Serpent Cult attack. When no one else was quite sure where Seth was, the shape-shifting girl had a knack for pinpointing his location. Thus, Seth had found an excellent partner with whom to train, and Ruka appeared to enjoy the exercises as much as the halfling, if not more.

Ruka reappeared among the horses at the edge of camp just as the contents of the stew pot sent tendrils of steam across the clearing. Not a whinny or shuffle from the animals betrayed her arrival. Even Aksel's and Seth's riding dogs just wagged their tails. Ruka greeted each of the animals in turn before joining the others at the campfire. She had a half dozen large trout on a string at her side.

"Did you see Seth out there?" Glo asked.

"Nope," Ruka said, settling on a large stone by the fire. "Heard him, smelled him, and crossed his trail twice, but never saw him."

Glo smiled. Those two were cut from the same cloth. His gaze fell on Elistra. The seeress had just finished her meditation, and nodded toward Ruka with a knowing smile. Ruka spread out a cloth and began cleaning the fish while the others started on the stew. Elladan filled up a steaming bowl and held it out to her. Ruka hesitated, sniffing the contents of the proffered dish.

"What's in it?"

"Secret seasonings known only to the ancient Elvish Lords," Elladan said with a quasi-smile.

"No, I mean the meat." From the expression on her face and the way her mouth watered, it was obvious Ruka was tempted to take the bowl. Yet for some reason, she held back.

Elladan sighed and cast a quick glance over at Martan. "It's venison, though the recipe calls for pork."

"Not my fault," Martan protested between mouthfuls. "The pig farmer wouldn't sell me any. He made up some crazy story about a little dragon stealing his whole pen."

Ruka's face flushed ever so slightly as she held up a hand in front of her. "Oh, then I think I'd rather not. I just spoke with several deer. I don't think I could eat one of their relatives in good conscience."

"Mom always told me never to name any of the animals that we were going to eat. I don't think talking to your dinner is wise, either," Alana interjected. Everyone turned to look at the lady knight, but she merely shrugged and took another bite of stew.

Ruka appeared as if she were about to reply, then abruptly cocked her head to one side as if she had heard something. A twisted smile spread across her lips as she took the bowl from Elladan and held it aloft in her hand.

"That doesn't count. My stomach growled," came the disembodied voice of Seth. The bowl appeared to float in the air for a second before the halfling appeared. He sat down with it in hand and hungrily consumed the stew.

Ruka's smirk spread into a bonafide grin. "Yeah, that was a close one—thank the gods for Elladan's stew."

Looking at her grinning like a kid across the campfire, it was hard to imagine Ruka as anything other than the young teenager she appeared to be. Glo had to remind himself that she was far more than just a shape shifter, and he strongly suspected that her current form was not her true shape.

"Then why eat fish?" Elistra asked as Elladan handed Ruka a plate of trout.

"The bounty of sea and stream are the just due to the masters of wind and wave," Ruka replied with a faraway look in her eye, as if quoting something she had heard many times before. "We honor their life and respect their death as they feed our children."

The group went silent as they considered what she had said.

"Oh, and fish are stupid and not worth talking to," Ruka added with a twist of her lips. A few short laughs trickled around the campfire in response to her remark.

"Respect all beliefs, but hold true to your own." Alana recited the familiar passage as she rose. "Still, I'll stick with the bounty of the lands that the gods provide and that are cooked by the hand of our fair elf friend." She turned to Elladan. "It was deliciously rendered and most appreciated."

Elladan glanced up from his cooking pots and gave the lady knight that now-familiar half-smile. Alana briefly smiled in return, then addressed the rest of the company. "Excuse me, all. I shall go relieve Lloyd in his guard duties so he may also enjoy this meal."

"Wait, fair lady, I shall accompany you!" Donnie rose in one smooth motion, spinning an empty stew bowl on a finger, then tossing it to Elladan. The bard gave him a nudge with his elbow and a wink as he passed.

"There is no need, really." Alana's voice could be heard as the two headed up the path toward the road.

"Ah, perhaps not, but to miss the moonrise on a face as lovely as yours would be a sin to all artists!" came Donnie's reply.

"But you've forgotten your paints..." Alana could be faintly heard.

"Ah, but there are so many forms of art..." Donnie's voice faded into the darkening woods.

Glo exchanged an amused look with Elistra. Suddenly he heard a roll of thunder off in the distance. On a hunch, he cast a quick glance at Ruka. Her bright green eyes appeared to have amber flecks in the firelight, her pupils briefly contracting vertically like some great cat.

"Sounds like a storm's coming," Martan noted, briefly pausing in his effort to gather the empty bowls and plates from around the campfire. His comment seemed to rouse Ruka from her thoughts.

The young teen blinked, her eyes returning to normal. Abruptly she shot up from her seat next to the fire. "Well, you people can sit here snuggling, playing house with your tents, and eating poor forest animals!" she spat out angrily. "But there are real monsters out there..." She took a deep breath, appearing as surprised at her outburst as the rest of the companions. "...somewhere," she added rather awkwardly, then stormed out of camp.

Moments later, Lloyd came rushing in. "Did I hear someone say something about monsters?" He seemed quite anxious, his hands gripping the hilts of his blades.

"Nothing to worry about." The corner of Seth's mouth rose as he got up from his seat. "The biggest little monster in the area has already left," he added as he walked to the edge of camp. Reaching the trees, Seth waved once, then vanished into thin air.

Lloyd stood there with a bemused expression until Martan offered him a bowl of stew.

The birds chirped their early morning greetings as Martan walked from the campsite down to where a bend formed a pool in a nearby creek. He had a water skin over his arm and held a pile of dishes that still needed washing from the previous night's meal.

When he reached the stream, Martan froze in his tracks—Elistra was already there, seated on a large flat rock that tilted into the water. The seeress was barely dressed, wearing only thin black silk undergarments that strategically covered her most private areas. Her bright red travel clothes were laid out on the other end of the stone, drying in the morning sun. Martan felt the blood rush to his cheeks as he watched her slowly comb her long honey hair, currently damp from being washed in the stream.

"Good morning," she greeted him with a friendly smile. She did not seem concerned in the slightest about his presence there.

"Morning," Martan muttered, averting his eyes. He swiftly turned away, deciding to head further downstream. It wasn't so much Elistra's current state of dress that unnerved him, but rather the odd stare of her violet eyes.

Three strides were all he took before observing the second set of clothes, a pile of dark leather fabric, folded exceedingly neatly on the bank near the deeper part of the stream. A sword and dagger lay next to them. Martan froze yet again, uncertain what to do. He recognized the outfit as belonging to the girl, Ruka, and immediately decided there was something that urgently needed his attention back at camp. It was too late for the poor archer, though. His eyes went wide as a familiar head rose out of the stream, his feet firmly rooted in place out of fright.

Ruka held a pair of fish in each hand—she was also completely naked. The teen strode calmly past Martan and laid her catch out on a stone. She then turned toward him, raising a hand in front of her with sparks jumping across her fingertips.

"What're you staring at?" she asked menacingly.

It was surprising how scary this teenaged girl could be. Martan felt the short hairs on his arm stand on end as he desperately tried to keep his expression neutral. "N... n... nothing."

A soft laugh suddenly filled the air. Both Martan and Ruka turned toward Elistra. The seeress was staring at the teen with an amused expression.

Ruka's eyes narrowed as she peered at the gypsy. "What's so funny?"

Elistra let out another short laugh. "Your hair—it's ridiculous."

Somehow this morning, Ruka's hair had become a startling, garish pink color. Martan felt relieved to have the attention diverted off of him. He debated running while he still could.

"I didn't get it right?" Ruka's tone was flat and strangely emotionless.

Elistra chuckled and shook her head. "No, horribly, horribly wrong—unless you were going for the carnival jester look."

Martan involuntarily flinched in anticipation of the explosion. Ruka, however, just sighed, her hand going to her hair. "I was going for red. I couldn't tell from the stream's reflection. That bad, huh?"

Elistra nodded, her expression changing to one of sympathy. "I'm afraid so, although he may go for the other enhancement you are working at."

Ruka's face reddened at the remark. "What do you mean?" she asked, sounding suddenly more like an embarrassed school girl. Yet before Elistra could answer, Ruka sighed again. "Never mind, it was a pain holding this change anyway."

Elistra nodded once more as if she understood, and said something that sounded like "morphic resonance."

"Huh?" Ruka stared at Elistra with an uncertain expression.

Martan had never heard the term either. Then again, he had never really studied much of anything other than the bow.

"It's just a term scholars use to describe a common effect of shape change magic. Shape changing requires altering your spirit image and invoking the magic to match your physical form to that image. The maintenance of an altered form is primarily handled by the subconscious mind, and the more the altered aura is in sync with your psyche, the easier it is to maintain. Forms that are fundamentally in sync with yourself are easier to assume, become familiar, and gain morphic inertia."

Ruka stared silently at the seeress for a few moments, then muttered irritably. "That was as clear as mud."

Martan couldn't have agreed more. The entire explanation had gone right over his head.

"It just means be yourself and let the magic determine the form for each creature type," Elistra explained.

Ruka laughed, though it sounded more ironic than cheerful. "Myself? That is the one thing I can't be in front of..." She paused and shook her head. "He sees me as just a plain little girl."

Elistra's voice grew soft. "You are hardly plain, but you are just a girl, regardless of your form."

"I'm older than you!" Ruka snapped. The crackle of electrical power was once again in the air, making Martan take a step backward, into the stream.

"You might be surprised," Elistra responded calmly, "but regardless, I was speaking of mental and spiritual maturity. The magic knows what it is doing. After all, it comes from within you. It manifests one of your true forms for that type. It would be a feat, but with practice, you could overcome morphic resonance. You are a natural shape shifter, and could make yourself appear as anyone. Still, what would it gain you? The greatest risk of shape shifting is the risk of losing yourself. Would it be worth it to get him to like you when you are just pretending, and not being true to yourself?"

Martan was sure lightning was going to strike this time, but instead Ruka let out a long breath. "I guess you're right..."

Her form blurred for a second, then her hair returned to sandy blond. Martan also noted one other obvious change. He felt suddenly embarrassed standing so close to the naked teen. He involuntarily took another step backward and lost his balance as his rear foot landed on nothing but water. He pitched over and fell into the deep part of the stream with a splash. The pans he had held in his hand went clattering onto the creek stones all around him. As he righted himself in the water, he heard the high-pitched laughter of the gypsy woman and the teenaged girl. Suddenly, the sound of rustling came from the trail to camp.

"Donatello, is that you?" Elistra called out in a loud voice.

With barely a flash of pale posterior, Ruka snatched her clothes and dove into the bushes.

"I heard a crash. Is everyone alright?" Alana asked as she stepped onto the little embankment.

"Just Martan being a klutz," Elistra said with a grin. "Apparently, no one told him this is the girls' bath time."

"Well, I think that is just stupid," Alana said as she pulled her tunic over her head. "Aren't we all comrades on the campaign trail?"

Martan was busy moving downstream and tried not to look back. Out of the corner of his eye, he caught sight of Ruka coming out of the bushes, and he doubled his pace.

"Good morning, Ruka," Alana said, her tone quite cheerful.

Ruka stared at Alana's half-naked form for a moment, then blushed and ran off. Alana turned toward Elistra with a bemused expression. "What was that about?"

"I think you won this battle, lady knight," Elistra chuckled.

10

HOUSE OF BARMANN

Vermoorden isn't all that sophisticated a place

The Old Knight's Road continued westward, paralleling a set of foothills to the north. Those low rolling hills, thickly lined with trees, bordered the south end of the Bendenwoods. South of the road, lush green grass stretched as far as the eye could see. Elladan said that the East Stroman also paralleled the road some twenty leagues south of here. The river sprang out of Lake Strikken and ran nearly straight east to where it emptied into Merchant's Bay at a place called Fisheye Cove.

Somewhere in the midafternoon, the road began to curve southwest. According to Lloyd, the road would soon turn south altogether and run along the east coast of Lake Strikken, down to Vermoorden. If one continued along the road, in another day they would reach the city of Lukescros, and Lloyd's home city of Penwick in two days more. The first hint that they were approaching their destination was a strong musky smell wafting through the afternoon air. Apparently, there was a swamp at the north end of the lake, a fact which their nostrils verified.

"I hope the whole town doesn't smell like this," Seth commented, holding his nose.

"There are sections..." Donnie responded dryly.

"Great. Just great." Seth tried to wave the smell away with his free hand. "No wonder the Baron of Penwick gave these lands up."

A short while later, they got their first glimpse of Lake Strikken. The shimmering waters were visible off through the trees to the right of the road. The woods soon thinned out, and the companions were treated to a clear view of the lake. It was a wide expanse of water, the late day sun causing the smooth surface to shimmer and sparkle.

Alana appeared mesmerized by the view. "It's quite beautiful."

"Indeed it is," Donnie said. "When all this is done, I need to come back here with my easel. You wouldn't care to join me, would you?"

"Perhaps," came her noncommittal reply.

The opposite shore was a couple of miles away. It was lined mostly with woods, though a solitary peak stuck out at the northern end. North of that, one could see the wide mouth of a river.

"That's the West Stromen, and where we need to head next," Elladan told them.

"Shall we hire a boat first, or do you intend to start swimming from here?" Seth's mouth bent to one side.

"Swimming would not be an option for me," Alana responded, showcasing her full plated armor with one hand. "I would sink straight to the bottom of the lake, I'm afraid."

"Fear not, for I would dive in to save you, milady!" Donnie declared, finishing with one hand pointed upward for dramatic effect.

Seth gave a short, closed-mouth laugh. "Then you'd both drown."

A large hill rose between the lake and the road, eventually blocking their view of the waters. Southward, the top of another hill appeared through the trees. A walled structure stood atop that peak, obviously quite large, to be seen from this distance.

"That's Vermoorden Keep," Lloyd told the others.

"Home to the most honorable Lord Mayor of Vermoorden," Donnie added with a sarcastic edge to his voice.

For some reason, the sight of the keep gave Glo an eerie feeling. He stared intently at the structure but saw nothing to justify the strange sensation. He glanced upward and noted Raven flying peacefully overhead, spiraling around the treetops along with Ruka, still in the form of a white-tailed hawk. Well, the weird feeling certainly wasn't coming from his familiar. Abruptly, he felt as if he was being watched. Glo spun around in his saddle and saw Elistra staring at him intently.

"Yes?" he asked the gypsy woman.

"Oh, nothing," she answered with that mysterious smile that said she knew more than she was telling.

Glo sighed and turned back to the keep once more. It was just an ordinary keep on closer inspection. *Must be my imagination acting up after a long, tiring day on the road.*

The first building cropped up on their right, signifying they had finally reached the town of Vermoorden. It was a small building with a wide porch, and numerous barrels and sacks stacked outside. A sign across the front read *General Store*. They cantered past the building and soon reached an intersection. The road to their right ran down toward the lake. A rather large wooden structure stood along that path, seated on a stone foundation. A fancy sign stretched across the front, covered with scripted, multicolored lettering. The sign read *The Theater of the Festive Spirits*.

Elladan raised an eyebrow. "Now that's an interesting name for a theater."

Donnie made a square in front of him with his thumbs and index fingers and gazed critically through it. "The sign's rather well done, too, though I'm not sure I would have chosen those exact colors."

There were a few more buildings farther down the south road. A baker's shop stood to their left, and a store with a sign that said *Tackle, Harness, & Leather Goods* on their right. Just beyond the bakery was a fenced-in area that enclosed a large wooden building, and some smaller ones that stood behind it. There was a sign out front that read *House of Barmann: Food, Lodging, and Ale*. The party came to a halt in front of the sign.

"This is where I stayed on my trip up from Penwick," Lloyd told them. "It's actually pretty nice inside."

Aksel scanned the western sky. The sun was well past its zenith, slowly arcing its way down toward the Korlokesel Mountains off in the distance. "Well, it is late in the day, and it will be nightfall in a couple of hours. We should probably get some rooms for the night. Once we settle in, we can look for a boat to take us upriver tomorrow."

"Consider it done," Elladan said. The bard spurred his horse forward and led the companions into the courtyard. There they all dismounted, Elladan asking Martan to take his reigns. He then headed toward the main building. A man walked out of the front door to meet him. The man appeared middle-aged, his hairline receding and greying along the temples. He wore a loose-fitting shirt with a dingy pair of overalls. In his hands, he held a towel with which he gingerly wiped off his hands.

"This is a fairly large party," the man called out to them, his tone rather gruff.

Elladan gave him a semi-smile. "Good day to you, friend. I'm Elladan. And you are..."

"...I'm the owner of this establishment," the man replied, pointing to the large sign above the inn. "Barmann, if you can read."

Glo spiked an eyebrow. This man certainly did not seem very friendly for the owner of an inn.

"Vermoorden isn't all that sophisticated a place," Donnie whispered to those around him.

Elladan ignored the man's abrasive behavior, extending his hand to the unkempt owner of the inn. "Pleasure to meet you, Barmann. We are in need of a few rooms. How about we sit down inside and discuss it over a glass of ale."

Barmann slowly extended his own hand and shook with Elladan, sizing up the party as he did so. "Very well. Follow me. He spun around and walked back toward the main building, not looking to see if Elladan was following. He did, however, call out toward the stables, "James, help these folks unsaddle their horses!"

A young boy, no more than thirteen, came running out of the stables. He held a shovel in one hand and was covered in hay. "Right away, Barmann!" he cried, dropping the shovel and running over toward the companions.

Elladan halted and smiled. In one swift motion, he reached into his purse and flipped the boy a silver coin. The young James stopped in his tracks and caught the coin, staring at it as if he had never seen one before. He looked up from his hands to Elladan, his mouth hanging wide open. "Th... thanks, mister."

Elladan let out a short laugh. "Keep the change, kid."

Barmann had watched the entire exchange. When Elladan turned back to face him, his gruff expression had softened measurably. "I'm sure we can work out something reasonable for you and your friends."

"After you, my friend." That familiar half-smile returned to Elladan's lips as he ushered Barmann into his own inn.

After his kind gesture and a round of drinks, Elladan got them the best and largest rooms at the inn, up on the second floor. The only condition was that they had to pair up. It was no surprise when Aksel and Seth immediately chose to bunk together, as did Lloyd and Glo. Donnie glanced wistfully at Alana, but the lady knight had already elected to room with Elistra. Crestfallen, the artist/swordsman picked Elladan as his roommate. That just left Martan and Ruka. Martan appeared terrified, but Ruka quickly put his fears to rest.

"Trust me, I'm not sleeping inside any stuffy old room. I'm used to sleeping outside, under the stars."

"But what am I going to do with a whole big room to myself, then?" Martan asked with wonder.

"Enjoy it?" Donnie immediately answered with a wink.

In the end, Elladan got Martan downgraded to single room on the first floor. Martan seemed far happier with the choice, stating that it was much more what he was used to.

While the others unpacked, Aksel, Donnie, and Lloyd went to find a ship for the next leg of their journey. As it turned out, Donnie had some knowledge of sailing. He and Lloyd had a lengthy discussion about it on the way down to the docks. The trio followed the south road past the keep and turned at the next intersection. This road led westward toward the lake, passing through the heart of town. Vermoorden was not large by any stretch of the imagination, but this road was lined with cottages on both sides. All, however, were in various states of disrepair.

"It's a nice place to visit," Donnie quipped.

"Vermoorden is not a wealthy town," Lloyd agreed. "In truth, after all the invasions, there are sections of Penwick that look worse."

Donnie raised an eyebrow but made no further comments.

At the next intersection, Aksel observed a temple up the road. It was not a very large building, but appeared to be well kept. He also noted a separate smaller building on the grounds, most likely the rectory. Aksel made a mental note to visit the temple when they were done with the business of renting a ship. The trio finally reached the southwest side of town. After passing a few boathouses, they saw the lake spread out before them. A number of piers jutted out into the waters, but only a few vessels occupied berths there—and of those, even fewer appeared seaworthy.

Donnie peered skeptically at the few ships moored there. His mouth contorted into a half grin. "We might just need to get out and paddle."

Aksel brow furrowed—Donnie's glib assessment was not wrong. "Let's hope not. It's still a long ride upriver to the monolith."

After much searching, Lloyd finally pointed out a vessel. "Let's try that one."

Donnie held a hand to his chin. "Hmm. That one does look reasonably seaworthy."

The trio walked along the pier, stopping at the gangplank of the vessel in question. A solitary figure stood up on deck—a man with long black hair, a thick black beard, garbed in a long blue coat, his head adorned with a tricorne hat. The lone man stood at the railing, a spyglass in hand, looking out at the lake.

"Ahoy," Lloyd called up to him.

"Ahoy, yourself," the man replied, his tone gruff as he continued to gaze through his eyepiece.

"Sounds friendly," Donnie whispered to the others.

Lloyd raised an eyebrow but did not comment, instead calling up to the man once more. "We're looking to hire passage on a ship."

"I'm not taking any passengers right now," the man yelled back, his eye still glued to the spyglass in his hands. "In fact, no one is on these docks."

It was Donnie's turn to raise an eyebrow. His eyes moved from Aksel to Lloyd, a bewildered expression on his face, then he turned back toward the gruff man on the ship deck above them. "Why's that?"

The man on deck finally put his spyglass down. He shook his head briefly and muttered something as he turned to stare down at them. His expression was grim at first, but as he looked them over it slowly changed to one of surprise. The man swiftly crossed the deck and climbed down the gangplank. As he drew closer, Aksel got a clearer look at him. He was rather tall and lean, with craggy facial features. Aksel stifled a laugh. *All he is missing is the eye patch and a parrot on his shoulder.*

When he reached the bottom of the gangplank, the man stopped and regarded them carefully. "You're not from around here, are you?"

Lloyd responded in a good natured tone. "We just arrived from Ravenford. We're looking for passage upriver."

A grim smile crossed the man's lips. "Well, that's a problem then. See, there's monsters in the lake, and the little beasties seem to take great pleasure in attacking any ship that sails these god-forsaken waters."

"Well, that has to be bad for business," Donnie commented, clearly sympathetic for the sailor's plight.

The man let out a deep sigh. "Aye. It's been impossible to move anything on the lake or the rivers in the last few weeks."

Lloyd eyed him incredulously. "So you've been stuck in port this whole time?"

An angry scowl crossed the man's face. "Yeah. A few folks tried to make it past them."

"And?" Lloyd asked.

The man leaned in and spoke deliberately. "They're all sitting at the bottom of the lake, lad."

Lloyd was about to comment when Donnie chimed in. "Why, that's a crime! How's an honest sailor supposed make a living if the waters aren't safe?"

The man gazed at Donnie, his expression softening. "Aye, that's the truth of it." He squinted at the slight elf. "What'd you say your name was?"

Donnie performed a low bow and then proffered a hand toward his companions. "Donatello, at your service. And these are my friends, Lloyd and Aksel."

The man nodded curtly and pointed a thumb at the ship moored behind him. "Nice to meet you. I'm Captain Morled, and this is me ship, the *Rusty Nail*."

Donnie rubbed his hands together. "Well then, Captain, I think we may be able to help you with your lake monster problem."

Captain Morled expression turned skeptical. "And how you gonna do that, laddie?"

Donnie's lips parted into a mischievous grin. "Well, we have a few more friends who are rather good at casting spells—the kind of spells which water creatures don't exactly like, if you know what I mean."

"Plus, there are a few of us who are pretty good with these," Lloyd chimed in, his hands resting firmly on his sword hilts. "Just in case any of these beasts decide to come up on deck."

Captain Morled eyed them up and down once more as if re-evaluating his initial opinion of them. After a moment's pause, a wicked grin broke out across his face. "Well now, maybe we do indeed have something to discuss. Why don't you folks come aboard?" He spun around and started back up the plank, waving for them to follow. "We'll pop open a bottle of rum and you can tell me more about these friends of yours."

"Lead the way, good Captain!" Donnie answered jovially, falling in behind Morled.

Aksel peered at Lloyd—the young man appeared impressed with Donnie's handling of the situation. Aksel had to admit that the slight elf did seem to have things well in hand. He decided to let him continue bartering with the Captain for now and see how it played out. Aksel swiftly fell in behind Donnie, motioning for Lloyd to follow.

11

THEATER OF THE FESTIVE SPIRITS

The sword began to glow as the bolt swirled around and was slowly drawn into it

Giant octopi? And how are we supposed to fight something like that?" Glo stood in the middle of his room gazing incredulously at his companions.

"Can't you just do your lightning bolt thingy?" Donnie responded, a charming smile gracing his lips as he pointed his finger and waved it around in the air.

Glo glared at his fellow elf, doing little to hide his exasperation. The Serpent Cult already had at least a day's head start on them, if not more, and now they would have to waste precious time dealing with lake monsters. Still, none of this was Donnie's fault. Glo bit back the sarcastic reply that was on his tongue and forced himself to smile. "That 'lightning bolt thingy,' as you refer to it, is a fairly high-powered spell—one that I can only cast a few times a day." He glanced at Aksel. "Do we even know how many of these creatures there are? And what if it takes more than one bolt to kill these things?"

"Stop worrying so much."

The familiar voice drifted through the open window. Glo turned his head to see Ruka, sitting cross-legged on the roof outside his dormer, her lips twisted and her eyes dancing with amusement. "If you need to fight sea creatures, I can lend you a hand."

Glo arched an eyebrow. There was no questioning Ruka's abilities—she was an incredibly fast swimmer, could breathe underwater, and even communicate with marine life. She also had access to powerful magic, electrical if he had to guess. Glo recalled the assassin she had chased over the side of the *Endurance*. He had been practically fried when she hauled him back aboard. Glo had to admit, with Ruka's help they might just pull this off.

Of course, Donnie knew nothing of her aquatic abilities having not been with them at Cape Marlin. The slight elf walked over to the window, leaned on the sill and said, "I know you can handle yourself, young lady, but what can you do against sea monsters?"

Instead of immediately responding, Ruka slowly got up and sauntered over to the window. She sat down and swung her legs over the sill, forcing Donnie to move out of the way. Once again on her feet, Ruka reached over and patted the elf on his cheek. "Awww, worried about me?"

The normally talkative elf seemed at a loss for words for the first time since Glo met him. Ruka's smirk widened as she walked past the bemused elf and strode across the room. She stopped directly across from Glo, drew her short sword and addressed the curious wizard. "Go ahead, shoot me with a lightning bolt."

Ruka's words broke Donnie from whatever spell he was under. The slight elf vaulted from the window to the center of the room, placing himself directly between Glo and the girl. He gazed wide-eyed from one to the other and cried, "What? Are you nuts?"

Ruka's smile turned into an outright grin at the elf's panicked state. Glo, not sure what to say, was spared the need when a familiar voice interrupted them.

"I wouldn't stand there if I were you."

Seth sat comfortably on one of the beds, taking in the whole show. From the half-twisted smile on his face, he obviously knew something he wasn't telling them. Alana, who had also remained silent up till now, casually strolled to the center of the room.

"Donnie..." she said in a deceptively dulcet tone. As the elf turned to face her, she gently reached forward and placed a hand on his chest. Donnie froze on the spot, his brow furrowed with curiosity. "Trust me on this—she knows what she is doing."

Before Donnie could utter a reply, Alana pushed him backwards onto the empty bed. Snickers and snorts erupted from the onlookers. Glo joined in, but his curiosity was piqued more than his funny bone. Alana also knew something more about Ruka than the rest of them.

Meanwhile, Donnie had landed gracefully, immediately righting himself. He peered at Alana with a hurt expression, then shook his head, and folded his arms across his chest. "You're all crazy!"

Alana ignored him, instead turning to Ruka and Glo. She flashed them both a sweet smile and said, "You're all clear." Alana then also moved out of the way, sitting down on the bed next to Donnie. The slight elf's expression immediately changed from pouty to amorous.

Ruka nodded to Alana, then spoke once again to Glo. "Go ahead, shoot me."

Glo narrowed his eyes, looking from Ruka to Seth and Alana. "You're sure about this?"

Seth and Alana both nodded. Ruka merely stood there, confidently holding up the small sword in front of her. Abruptly an image flashed through Glo's mind. It was of Ruka's younger sister, Maya, dancing out into the center of Cape Marlin Light as a large stone careened down at her from above. Glo had cringed as it struck the girl, but amazingly the stone had broken into bits, leaving the young girl totally unharmed. *These Greymantles are made of sterner stuff than they look.*

Glo shrugged. "Very well. However, the rest of you might want to move back a bit..."

While Glo prepared his spell, everyone shifted as far away from the center of the room as possible. Donnie now sat at the head of the bed with his hands covering his eyes. "Tell me when it's over."

Alana, still next to him, reached over and pulled his hands away, holding them with her own. "She'll be fine. Trust me."

Glo caught this through the corner of his eye, his concentration mostly on his spell. As he finished weaving his arms through the air, he called out one last warning. "Okay, here it comes."

Ruka merely stood her ground, the corner of her mouth rising slightly.

"*Pessulum Electrica.*"

Glo let loose a bolt of lightning. In the blink of an eye it arced across the room. Just before it reached the blade, the energy suddenly bent around it! The sword began to glow as the bolt swirled around and was slowly drawn into it. The blade grew brighter and brighter until it shone white hot, sparks flying as small arcs of electricity danced all around it. Within seconds, any trace of the bolt was gone, the blade's light quickly fading until it turned completely dark once again. There had been the briefest of thunderclaps before the bolt hit the sword, but now the room was dead silent.

Everyone stared at the darkened blade—everyone except Donnie, that is. The slight elf must have shut his eyes despite Alana's assurances. "Can I look now?"

Before anyone could answer him, Seth let out a cry with uncharacteristic enthusiasm. "That... was... cool!"

Everyone seemed to agree. The words *amazing, awesome* and *incredible* were bantered around the room. Glo smiled, but was too caught up in his musings to speak. A sword that could absorb lightning bolts was rare indeed. He had heard legends of such a sword—there was even a name that went along with it, but whatever it was it escaped him at the moment. Glo couldn't help wondering if this was that same sword, and further, how Ruka had come into its possession.

Meanwhile, Ruka turned to face Donnie. She fanned her arms across her body and said, "See, I'm fine. And what's even better—" she strode toward the window, "—is this." Ruka raised the short sword and pointed it out the open window. The blade started to glow once again, and shortly thereafter a bolt of lightning leapt out from it, skirting over the nearby treetops. A clap of thunder capped the demonstration.

"Now that's impressive," Elladan exclaimed.

"Just how many charges can your sword hold?" Aksel asked.

"It can actually hold quite a few," Ruka responded before turning back to Glo. "If you can cast that spell again, we can store some more bolts in the blade."

A genuine smile spread across Glo's lips. This lake monster hunt was looking more and more feasible. "I can cast it a couple more times, but I suggest we take this outside, just to be safe."

"Probably a good idea," Aksel agreed. The little cleric addressed the group at large. "Once we rid the lake of these monsters, Captain Morled agreed to take us up river to the Darkwoods. The lake is rather large, though, and no one is sure exactly how many monsters there are, so we are to meet the Captain down at the docks at first light."

Glo turned back to Ruka. "Well then, let's charge up that sword of yours as soon as possible."

Ruka nodded. "Meet you at the north end of town." Without another word, she shifted into a hawk and took off out the window.

While Glo went to gather his gear, Donnie and Alana left the room. The others, however, straggled behind. Aksel in particular seemed as intrigued as Glo by Ruka's blade. "A short sword that can absorb and shoot lightning bolts. Very interesting."

"It's a family heirloom," Seth informed them with a wry twist of his lips.

"Family heirloom," Glo repeated. "Maybe the girls' father had come across it at some point?"

Aksel stroked his chin. "Could be. Rodric Greymantle was one of the greatest wizards that ever lived. If the sword was his, then that certainly makes sense."

"Well that's one interesting family," Elladan noted wryly.

Lloyd let out a short laugh.

Seth glanced up at the tall warrior. "What's so amusing?"

A grin broke out across the young man's face. "I think I finally found a family that is 'stranger' than my own."

Night had fallen when the companions met for dinner in the common room—everyone except for Ruka, that is. After charging up her weapon, she had told Glo she was going to find her own meal. Glo had returned to the inn, only to find Elistra waiting for him. The two of them did some scrying using the crystal ball they had confiscated from Voltark nearly a week ago. Their efforts confirmed Glo's worst fears, which he now shared with the others. "The Serpent Cult has already reached the monolith."

The table fell silent, all eyes turning on him. Aksel was the first to speak, his voice stone cold. "What exactly did you see?"

"A number of men in dark robes and some giant snakes. They stood in front of a dark structure in the middle of a wide clearing. It was very dark and very tall, reaching high above the surrounding trees.

"It was the same one I saw in my vision," Elistra concurred.

Murmurs went around the table, but Aksel held up his hand, signaling for silence. "Did they go inside?"

Glo nodded slowly. "There was no visible entrance at first. Then one of the dark-robed figures recited a verse, and a door appeared in the side of the structure. The entire group then went inside."

It was Elladan's turn to speak. "That's not good. Judging from our present location, and the distance we need to travel upriver, we are probably still two days away from the monolith."

"And how long by horseback?" Lloyd chimed in.

Elladan's nose wrinkled as he thought it over. "Three, maybe four days depending on whether we can find a trail through the woods."

Aksel shook his head. "It can't be helped, then. We can only hope they don't find what they are looking for before we get there."

Glo knew Aksel was right, but he could not shake his growing discomfort. The discussion turned toward the hunt for the lake monsters, but Glo only half listened to the conversation—visions of dark mages, serpents and an army of golems playing through his mind.

Once the companions finished dinner, Aksel excused himself and headed over to the temple to offer up his evening prayers. Donnie persuaded Alana into going for an evening walk, with Elistra dragging Glo along to clear his mind. Martan adjourned to his room, saying something about checking the fletchings on his arrows. Seth went off in search of Ruka who still had not returned from the forest. With nothing else to do, Elladan decided to check out the Theater of the Festive Spirits. He saw no use in sitting around and worrying about things that were out of their control. It didn't take much prodding to convince Lloyd to join him.

The theater was not the newest building, nor was it necessarily that large. There was a good-sized stage, though, and more than ample seating to fit the entire town, from what Elladan reckoned. He had played in better places, but he had played in worse as well. A thin, light-haired man stood in the middle of the stage, holding a lute in one hand.

He was dressed rather fine, wearing a puffy white silk shirt with a fancy vest over it, light brown pants, and knee-high brown leather boots. The man busily directed a couple of stage hands, a small, mousey-looking man with spectacles, wearing grey robes, and a tall, thin, hawk-nosed woman with long brownish hair, garbed in a robe of iridescent blue. Elladan and Lloyd sat down in the farthest row to watch the rehearsal.

"No, no, no," the man said. "The timing's all off. Let's try it again." The man lifted his lute and played a jaunty tune. At the same time, the woman made some gestures with her hands. A cloud of fog appeared at the bard's feet, quickly spreading across the stage. She quickly made a second set of gestures and four globes of light appeared around the stage.

The bard nodded to the man in grey. "Now you, Rhith."

Rhith nodded back in response then began to conjure. Suddenly, there were two bards up on stage, both the spitting image of each other. The second bard mimicked everything the first bard did.

"Shadow image spell," Lloyd leaned over and whispered.

Elladan raised an eyebrow. He already knew that, but was surprised that Lloyd did. Elladan made a mental note to ask Lloyd later where he had learned about spells.

"And again," the bards said in unison up on stage.

Rhith cast the spell once more, and another copy of the bard appeared next to the other two. Now three bards played in the fog. Abruptly, the lights started to dance around the trio. The bards played a tune in earnest, all three of them synchronized in both movements and sound. All in all, it was a very good performance.

When it was over, Elladan and Lloyd both stood up and clapped. The bard jumped down off the stage, shading his eyes with his hand, searching the back rows. Finally, his gaze settled on them.

"Thank you," he called up to them. "I didn't realize we had an audience."

Elladan strode down toward the front of the theater, motioning for Lloyd to follow him. "That was well done," Elladan complimented the bard. "The special effects blended nicely, not overshadowing the song. It's important that the music stands out first and foremost."

A knowing smile spread across the bard's face. "Thank you, my friend. That was spoken like one who is used to performing."

Elladan gave the man a bent smile. "Guilty as charged." He bowed before the other bard and introduced himself. "Elladan Narmolanya, at your service. And this is my friend and colleague, Lloyd," he added with a wave of his hand toward the tall young man.

The other bard bowed in return. "Pleased to meet you both. I am Balmaroh." He motioned up toward the stage. "And these two folks are Rhith, my illusionist, and Newin, my wizard."

Newin gave him a curt nod. "Hello."

"Hi," Rhith waved giving them a self-conscious smile.

"Pleased to meet you," Elladan and Lloyd said almost simultaneously. Elladan turned back to Balmaroh. "You are quite good with that lute. What would you say to a duet?"

Balmaroh tilted his head and smiled. "I'd say, why not?"

With a wave of his hand, Elladan's lute appeared out of thin air. The bard held it up and then began to strum a quick beat. Balmaroh soon joined in, the two bards taking turns with various combinations of chords and runs.

Elladan nodded to Balmaroh. "Not bad." Balmaroh grinned back. "Not bad yourself."

Finally, Elladan broke out into song. Balmaroh joined him, nicely picking up the harmony.

I went to a land.
Wasn't it grand.
Not too much sand.

I want to go back.
To slash and hack,
My way through Thac

I left the Great Forest
to go on a trip to the west
My sword and my senses were sharp
on the boat from Essex

I sat in a dive
On the docks of Orllon
Looking for fun

A trader bound for Ilos
She would need guards
And a couple of bards

She told me we'd leave in the morning
and started to laugh
She bought me some drinks
and she stole my sword and my pack

And when I awoke I was alone
On a boat bound for home

I'll get my revenge
When I slash and hack
My way through Thac

The two bards finished, hanging on the last word and adding in a flashy combination of chords. When they were done, they sat there grinning at each other. Lloyd, Rhith, and Newin all clapped in appreciation.

"That was fun!" Balmaroh exclaimed. Elladan grinned. "Yes, it was."

"We should have a competition!" Balmaroh said suddenly. "Things have been slow around here lately, I must confess. And with someone of your caliber to compete against, it would be sure to drum up business."

"Sounds like fun—but we need a catchy name for it." Elladan's hand went to his chin. Balmaroh did the same. Names flashed through Elladan's mind like *Duel in Vermoorden* and *Bard vs. Bard*, but nothing that quite caught his fancy.

Out of the blue, Lloyd suggested, "How about *The Battle of the Bards*?"

Elladan stopped and stared at his friend. That wasn't half bad, actually. "I like it!"

"As do I!" Balmaroh agreed.

Lloyd obviously had an ear for this sort of thing. Elladan clasped him on the shoulder. "You've been holding out on me. If I had known you were this creative, I would have had you do more than just stand and beat the drums at Andrella's party."

Lloyd's face reddened at the praise. "It's no big deal, really. It's just that I have a friend back home who's into this sort of stuff."

Elladan gave Lloyd a quasi-smile. "Well, whoever your friend is, he's quite good."

"She," Lloyd corrected him.

Elladan arched an eyebrow. "She, then." Lloyd was just full of surprises today. Elladan wanted to know more about this mystery 'friend" of Lloyd's but Balmaroh interrupted him.

"Is tomorrow too soon?"

"It might be," Lloyd answered. "We have to go out on the lake."

Newin interrupted them, her tone rather high pitched. "Out on the lake? You do know there are monsters out there?"

Elladan's eyes turned toward the wizard and he winked. "That's okay, there won't be any by late tomorrow."

In truth, Elladan wasn't all that worried. He had grown up around magic, and Glo, for all his self-berating, was one of the most promising young casters he had ever seen. As for Ruka, that sword of hers would be devastating to sea creatures. Between the two, Elladan bet those lake monsters wouldn't stand a chance.

Newin, not knowing any of this, peered at him rather skeptically. "I hope you two know what you're doing."

"I concur, friends Elladan and Lloyd," Balmaroh added, his concern quite evident from his expression. He held their gaze for a moment or two, then a smile spread across his lips. "After all, we wouldn't want anything to get in the way of our performance."

Elladan gave their new friend another semi-smile. "Set it up for tomorrow evening. We'll have made short work of those monsters by then."

Lloyd, as if on cue, nodded, folding his arms in front of him confidently.

"Maybe we'll even bring you back dinner." Elladan winked.

12
LAKE MONSTER

Four enormous tentacles reached over the railing amidships

T hese waters seem awfully calm," Donatello said. The slight elf stood on the sterncastle of the *Rusty Nail*, next to the ship's wheel. Donnie had been on small ships like this before. This was a schooner, the long main deck having two masts, the foremast being shorter than the main mast. By the way the sails were rigged, he could tell this boat was set for speed, rather than hauling large amounts of cargo.

It was a typical configuration used by smugglers or privateers, once again, something he was not unfamiliar with. Donnie suspected Captain Morled was a bit of both, but he kept that to himself. The others had more than enough to worry about with these lake monsters. Morled currently manned the ship's wheel. Donnie stood next to him making casual conversation, but in reality he was keeping an eye on the sea dog. If he tried anything, Donnie would be there to deal with him swiftly.

"It usually is this time of year," Captain Morled was saying.

"Do these monsters roam the lake, or are they typically in one spot?" Donnie asked.

"They've been seen all over, but more often than not they are at the mouth of the East Stromen, the river leading out to sea. We should be getting close to that area in the next 15 minutes or so."

"Keep an eye out," Donnie shouted to the others. "We'll probably see them in the next quarter hour."

Alana and Lloyd stood in the center of the main deck, near the hatch to the cargo hold. Both warriors were decked out in full fighting gear—Lloyd in his new red-stained chain-mail, something Donnie had stayed up all night working on, and Alana wearing the gleaming full-plate armor of a knight.

Donnie was impressed by Lloyd's prowess with the sword. It was phenomenal the way he could light his blades on fire, flash behind an enemy, and cleave even huge serpents in two. It made him a force to be reckoned with. More than that, Donnie found the concept of the *spiritblade* intriguing. He appreciated anything having to do with the sword, being quite good with a blade himself. In fact, he had learned from some of the best, but that seemed a lifetime ago.

Donnie's thoughts suddenly shifted to Alana. As much as he admired her beauty, the lady knight was nonetheless an impressive warrior in her own right. She had held her own admirably against those giant serpents back in the courtyard of Ravenford Keep. He had argued with her, prior to coming on board, about the wisdom of wearing full plate on a sailing ship. The lady knight, however, had insisted she would be fine. He finally gave up trying to convince her otherwise, but promised himself he would keep a close eye on her. If anything were to happen to the red-haired beauty, he would never forgive himself.

Donnie gazed out toward the bow of the ship. The wizard Glolindir stood there with the seeress Elistra by his side. The elven wizard had his raven familiar out in front of the ship, scanning the waters ahead. The gypsy seeress was also using her abilities to anticipate any impending danger.

Donnie had noticed the duo spending more and more time

together these last few days. Always an advocate of love, he hoped things would work out between the two. Glo seemed unusually shy and awkward, though, around women. Luckily, the seeress did not appear shy at all. Donnie suspected that if a first move was made, she would be the one to do so.

Lifting his eyes toward the top of the foremast, Donnie spied the crow's nest up there. It was currently occupied by the halfling, Seth, and the young teen, Ruka. That pair had sharp eyes. From their vantage point, they should be able to see anything in the waters around them. Donnie imagined the duo would be having a contest to see who could spot the first monster. Seth and Ruka seemed to thrive on competition, especially with each other. He did not detect anything romantic between them, but Donnie had seen stranger relationships in his time. Heck, he had been in stranger relationships.

A glance over his shoulder confirmed that the archer, Martan, stood at the aft of the vessel. Martan kept a sharp eye out behind them, in case any creature attacked from that direction. The archer was a quiet one, mostly keeping to himself. He seemed rather morose most of the time. From what Donnie had heard from Lloyd, Martan had a thing for Ves, Ruka's older sister. Her absence might explain the archer's glum attitude.

In front of the sterncastle, just below him on the main deck, sat Donnie's old friend, Elladan, and Aksel, the little gnome cleric. Both waited for a sign that a monster had been spotted and that their talents would be needed. Elladan had not changed at all since the last time Donnie had seen him. Flamboyant and charismatic, the bard drew the eye of everyone when he entered the room. He had also left behind one of the most beautiful women that Donnie had ever seen, Shalla, in Ravenford. The bard certainly had not lost his touch.

Aksel was another quiet one, until it mattered, that is. An unlikely leader, the little gnome had managed to garner the respect of everyone in the group. Donnie had originally been surprised that Aksel was the leader of the Heroes. He had expected it to be Lloyd, or even Elladan, but Aksel showed an aptitude for strategy and leadership that Donnie had not seen in many. He would have made a fine captain of a ship, or baron of a town, for that matter.

Their voyage across the lake went on uneventfully, the waters remaining calm and quiet, no one spotting anything out of the ordinary. Donnie had just begun to wonder if there really were monsters in the lake when he heard a cry from the bow of the ship.

"There's something large in the water close by!"

It was the seeress, Elistra. Donnie scanned the waters around them, but saw nothing. He was about to yell back, when he heard a cry from above.

"I see it!" Ruka called out.

"Where?" Donnie shouted up to her.

"Off the starboard bow!" Seth yelled back this time.

Everyone turned to starboard just in time to see a familiar figure in black leather execute a perfectly arced dive from the crow's nest into the waters below. It was Ruka. Donnie's fear for the teen's safety once again reared itself. He ran to railing with a shout. "Is she crazy?"

When Donnie reached the rail, he scanned the waters with his keen eyes, immediately spotting a dark shape under the water maybe ten yards away. Whatever it was, it was huge. Donnie yelled back over his shoulder, "Ten yards off to starboard!"

"Got it!" he heard Morled cry back.

The small vessel eased into a wide arc in that direction, all aboard now intently searching the waters below for some sign of their small comrade. Abruptly, the silence was shattered by a loud noise like cannon fire. A tall plume of water rose into the air over the spot where Donnie had seen the dark shape. A large wake swiftly expanded out from the center of the explosion, rushing toward the ship.

"Hang on tight!" Donnie shouted in warning.

When the upturned waters reached the Rusty Nail, the ship was lifted upwards, rocking the deck wildly. Donnie held on tight to the railing, quickly glancing around to make sure everyone was okay. Luckily, his warning had given the others time to find something to hold onto. Donnie peered back down into the churning waters, looking for any signs of Ruka or the monster. The lake waters had just begun to settle when a second plume erupted in the same spot.

"One more time!" Donnie yelled.

Once again they all held on as the vessel was rocked from the wake of the explosion. When it finally settled, they heard a cry from above.

"She got it!"

Donnie searched the waters once more—sure enough, a giant shape broke the surface. The creature was huge, easily forty feet long if he had to guess. Donnie had heard rumors of such creatures during his time at sea, but had never seen an octopus that large before. As they drew closer, he noted two large blackened circles along its torso. They looked like burn marks. Donnie shook his head in amazement. Ruka had dispatched the huge creature just as she claimed she would. It suddenly dawned on him that she was still out there. Donnie scanned the waters frantically, but she was nowhere to be seen!

"Can anyone see Ruka?" he cried.

"I'm right here!" came Ruka's voice from down on the main deck.

Donnie spun around and saw her just climbing on board near the bow of the ship. He stood there, staring at her dumbfounded.

"Well, that's one," she said, nonchalantly shaking the water out of her hair.

Donnie dashed over to the railing above the main deck and cried down to her, "That was amazing! I am sorry I ever doubted you."

Ruka peered back up at him, her mouth bending to one side. "Told you I could handle myself." Her eyes lingered on him a moment or two longer, then she spun back toward the foremast. "No time for pleasantries just yet, though."

"There are more of them out there," Elistra concurred. "I can feel it."

Ruka nodded to the seeress then scurried up the foremast back to the crow's nest, taking up her original position.

Donnie shook his head and muttered under his breath, "That is one strange girl. Impressive, but strange."

Captain Morled brought the *Rusty Nail* about and put them back on course toward the mouth of the East Stromen. Another quarter hour went by when abruptly Seth's voice rang out from above.

"I see another one! Off the port bow! Headed this way!"

Donnie shifted his gaze toward the port side of the ship and spied a large shape moving toward the ship. It was about twenty yards out and was still underwater, but as it got closer the creature finally surfaced. Large tentacles reached out ahead of it, easily twenty feet long and a good two to three feet thick. Up at the bow, Glo began the motions of a spell, but before he could unleash it, a bolt of lightning flashed down from the top of the foremast. It arced its way to the creature below, striking with a loud clap of thunder. The sea monster halted its advance, sparks playing across its body. Wisps of dark smoke rose from the spot where the bolt had connected with the monster.

The attack must have given the creature second thoughts—it abruptly turned away from the vessel, slowly submerging back underwater. Glo, apparently caught by surprise, had stopped mid-spell. He swiftly began the motions again, but before he could unleash it, a second bolt of lightning shot out from the foremast. It caught the giant octopus from behind, this time halting its retreat. Arcs of electricity played across the monster's frame for a few moments, then the creature's huge bulk went limp. It rose back to the surface and floated there, unmoving.

Cheers erupted from around the vessel, but faded as loud laughter drifted down from the crow's nest above. The sound was punctuated by a familiar sardonic voice.

"Ruka two, Glo zero."

Another hour went by, cruising around the south side of the lake, but there were no more sightings of the lake monsters. At that point, Donnie turned to Captain Morled. "Do you think we got them all?"

"There are more," Elistra voice rang out from the deck below. "I am sensing something up by the north side of the lake."

Morled's eyebrows raised, his mouth opening slightly. He motioned for Donnie to take the wheel, then stepped over to the railing, his eyes falling on the seeress. "The north side? Are ya sure, miss? The beasties have never been spotted up there before."

Elistra gazed up at the Captain with that all-knowing smile that

Donnie found so infuriating. She had caught him by surprise, back in Ravenford, with her proclamation that he should *"stay the course and you may very well find what you seek."* He had never told anyone, not even Elladan, that he was in search of something. Donnie had known too many charlatans to believe that Elistra was the real deal. Yet somehow she had known.

His musings were interrupted by Glo's response to the Captain. "Well, there don't seem to be any more monsters down here. Would it hurt to take a look up north?"

Morled let out a heavy sigh and shrugged. "I guess not." He strode back to the wheel, taking it from Donnie and proclaimed, "Oh, well, here goes nothing."

Captain Morled slowly spun the ship around in a wide arc and set course for the north side of the lake. Another hour passed before they reached the northern end of Lake Strikken. Donnie could tell they were getting close when a foul, musky smell assaulted his nostrils. The odor had to be from the swamp they passed on their way to Vermoorden. It was close to midday, and the sun was directly overhead, its reflection making it difficult to see anything underwater. They were traveling along smoothly when a shriek rang out from the seeress.

"Look out!"

The boat suddenly rocked as if it had been struck. Elistra's warning had saved them from falling overboard, giving everyone barely enough time to grab onto something.

"I think we found another one!" Elladan shouted. "More like it found us!" Donnie yelled back.

The *Rusty Nail* swayed back and forth as the small vessel tried to right itself, but the deck was still rocking when Elistra called out again.

"Get ready!"

Everyone steadied themselves as the ship pitched starboard. Donnie caught a brief glimpse of a white-tailed hawk flying from the foremast before four enormous tentacles reached over the railing amidships. Lloyd and Alana rushed forward, blades swinging as they engaged the flailing limbs. The warrior's twin blades were alight with flame, and the lady knight's sword gleamed as if filled with the light of the heavens. The old timbers of the small craft gave out a moan of protest as the boat pitched over even further.

"I'm not sure how much more of this she can take!" came Captain Morled's cry.

"Never fear, me hearties!" a voice called out from below in a perfect imitation of the Captain's voice. The hum of strained rigging lines was suddenly drowned out by the twang of an inspiring tune, its stirring beat immediately calming the nerves and energizing the body.

Donnie caught sight of Glo skidding crazily across the heaving decks—the wizard was trying to get a clear shot at the creature, but its flailing tentacles were in the way. Multiple arrows suddenly whizzed past Donnie, embedding themselves into the monster's head. A quick glance over his shoulder showed Martan lashed to the starboard railing, bow in hand, while deftly drawing another arrow from his quiver.

Back on the mid-deck, Lloyd spun wildly, fighting off two tentacles at once. His flaming blades made each cut sizzle, the giant limbs flinching away from him with every swipe. Alana expertly fended off another huge tentacle, but Donnie spied a second one snaking toward her from behind. He immediately sprang into action, drawing his sword and vaulting over the railing. He hit the deck below and rolled forward, shooting up directly behind Alana. Donnie spun around just in time to fend off the limb that had been reaching for the lady knight.

"Got your back!" he cried over his shoulder.

"Much appreciated!" Alana yelled back before launching a fearsome assault on the tentacle in front of her. The lady knight's glowing blade sliced deep into the slimy flesh of the huge lake monster, inky-colored blood spurting out from the wound.

Abruptly the deck reared up around them, throwing nearly everyone off their feet. Donnie rolled with the fall and came up in a half-crouch, blade ready. The tentacles had pulled back, exposing the monster's maw, those limbs writhing as if the creature were in agony. Through the flailing tentacles, Donnie caught a glimpse of the creature's arrow-riddled head. Planted directly in a huge eye was a small black dagger, the comparatively tiny weapon buried up to the hilt in the creature's iris. A foul-looking liquid oozed from the wound. Donnie nearly let out a cheer when he caught a gleam of silver out of the corner of his eye. He turned his head to a chilling sight—Alana charged forward, blade first, at the monster's maw. The weight of her armor must have kept her on her feet, and now she was rushing in for a killing blow. Donnie watched in awe as the lady knight thrust out with her gleaming blade, burying it deep into the exposed underside of the giant octopus. The creature recoiled once again, this time completely letting go of the vessel.

The *Rusty Nail* responded by rocking away from the creature. Unfortunately, Alana's blade was still buried deep into it, and the lady knight would not let go. Without thinking, Donnie sprinted forward and leapt for the rigging. He grabbed hold of one of the mast lines, slashing it free with his sword in one quick motion.

The slight elf swung clear across the deck, reaching Alana just as she was about to fly over the rail. Donnie instinctively let go of the line and grasped for her waist, hoping his momentum would be enough to save the armor-laden knight from a deadly fall into the waters below. By the grace of the gods, his plan worked. The lady knight was bowled over, her sword coming free with her. It clattered to the deck as she and Donnie tumbled over each other.

The duo continued to roll, finally coming to a stop near the foremast. Alana lay on top of Donnie, her breath coming in ragged gasps as her armor-clad form weighed on top him. Yet despite his aches and pains, Donnie gazed fondly into her emerald green eyes and managed a sparkling smile. "Shouldn't you have bought me dinner first?"

A broad grin spread across the lady knight's lips. "And here I thought you were a cheap date."

The sound of an explosion brought them back to the battle. Donnie and Alana picked themselves up in time to see the monster go limp in the water. The ship rocked slightly from the resulting wake, then finally righted itself. The *Rusty Nail* had managed to hold together after all.

Donnie let out a deep sigh and turned to gaze fondly at Alana. "Now where were we..."

His statement was caught off by a shout from above.

"Look out! To the stern!"

Donnie spun around in time to see another giant octopus rear out of the water behind the ship. Its tentacles reached forward, attempting to grasp the stern of the vessel. Donnie and Alana rushed forward once again, the lady knight retrieving her sword on the way to the sterncastle. Martan, still lashed to the railing above, was launching volley after volley into the approaching creature, but he was nearly out of arrows, and his assault had not slowed the monster's progress.

Abruptly, a bolt of lightning flashed over their heads, catching the giant octopus square in the maw. Donnie glanced over his shoulder and spied Lloyd hovering in midair above the main deck, holding onto Glo with one arm. The wizard pointed ahead. "Let's get closer!"

Lloyd nodded and launched forward, toward the stern of the vessel, as Glo began the motion of a spell. Donnie rushed up the steps of the sterncastle, with Alana right behind him. The giant octopus had stopped in its tracks after the first bolt struck, but now moved forward again, its giant arms flailing as it grasped for the back of the vessel. The creature had nearly caught hold when a second bolt flashed overhead. This one went right over the tentacles and caught the creature in the head. The lake monster halted, arcs of electricity playing across its body and smoke rising from its sizzling torso. With one giant heave, the creature collapsed into the water and lay unmoving.

Donnie breathed a sigh of relief. He peered at Alana and received a quick smile in return before the two of them headed over to where Lloyd and Glo were landing. Elladan strode up to the duo as and clasped both on the shoulders. "That was some quick thinking, you two!"

Aksel was right behind him. "Yes, nice teamwork," the little cleric agreed.

"Yeah, not bad," came Ruka's voice. They all turned to see the young teen standing by the rail, dripping wet. "But by my count, I still have you beat two to one."

A wide grin broke out across the wizard's face. "I wouldn't have it any other way."

Donnie found himself strangely elated to see Ruka safe and sound. On impulse he strode over to the girl, scooped her up, and spun her around.

"You... were... magnificent!"

Ruka was caught off-guard, going stiff in his arms at first, but then proceeded to laugh and hug him back. After another spin or two, Donnie put her down. He stood there, still grinning at her, absolutely impressed with the girl's bravery. Ruka uncharacteristically grinned back, her cheeks flushed. Abruptly, she spun around and gazed out over the waters, her voice cracking strangely. "Is that the last of them?"

"I do not sense any others," came Elistra's immediate reply. "I believe the lake is clear."

Morled chuckled gleefully, slapping Donnie on the back. "Well then, we did it. I didn't think we were going to make it there for a while, but we did it!"

"I never had any doubt," Elladan declared, fixing the Captain with his infamous half-smile.

The *Rusty Nail* pulled back into port around mid-afternoon. Captain Morled had them tie one of the giant octopi's bodies to the ship and haul it back for everyone to see. When they approached the docks with the beast in tow, a crowd swiftly gathered. Excited murmurs traveled through the throng, the onlookers staring at the huge creature with wonder. Shouts were intermixed with the loud buzz of the gathering.

"You gotta see this!"

"Look at the size of that thing!"

"I can't believe they caught one!"

Captain Morled grinned from ear to ear as they drew up alongside the docks. He shouted over the noisy din, "Not just one! We killed them all!"

His statement elicited more cries.

"No way!"

"I don't believe it!"

"Is it true?"

The companions stood at the ship's rail curiously watching the chaos unfold. Elladan gave Aksel a quick glance, the little cleric nodding back. The bard's voice boomed out across the docks, magically soaring over the loud buzz. "People of Vermoorden, the lake has been cleared out of all monsters like the one behind us—courtesy of our good Captain Morled and the Heroes of Ravenford..."

Donnie, standing beside Elladan, nudged the bard and nodded toward Alana. "...and the Knights of the Rose," Elladan swiftly added.

The mob's reaction was mixed. There were a few cheers here and there, but the crowd grew noisier as folks talked excitedly among themselves.

"Heroes?"

"Morled's a hero?"

"What's Ravenford got to do with this?"

"What are the Knights doing here?"

Abruptly the throng parted, an older gentleman pushing his way through. Garbed in dark blue robes, he had a pocked-marked face, greying hair, and a long beard that hung down to his chest. The crowd quieted as he halted and peered up at the Captain. "Is all this true?"

"'Tis indeed. I saw it with my own eyes." Morled nodded toward the stern of the ship. "Four lake monsters, as dead as this one."

At that point, cheers broke out in earnest. Chants of *Heroes of Ravenford* and *Knights of the Rose* were repeated over and over.

"What they really should be chanting is *Ruka, Ruka*," Seth noted in a voice loud enough for all aboard to hear.

Ruka gazed almost fondly at the halfling, but her expression swiftly turned into an ironic smile. "That's alright. I know what I did. I don't need cheers from some stupid crowd."

13
BATTLE OF THE BARDS

Our humble little town is honored by your presence

It was only mid-afternoon when the companions arrived back in Vermoorden. Many of them wanted to quickly pack up and set out again for the monolith, but it did not look like that would be possible. First and foremost, the Rusty Nail had taken damage in their fight with the lake monsters. Second, they needed to wait for Sir Craven.

The knight was due to arrive the next morning with the two squads of cavalry he had retrieved from the Wind Tower. Third, the man in blue robes, who turned out to be the town magistrate, insisted they throw a victory celebration. At Elladan's prompting, the festivities were scheduled to coincide with "The Battle of the Bards" later that evening.

Shortly after dinner, the Heroes and their friends walked over to The Theater of the Festive Spirits. The entire town seemed to be gathered there, many folks still milling around outside the large hall.

Upon entering the theater, the companions were greeted by the town magistrate, Fraith. He led them through what was a nearly-packed theater, down to the front row. A stately-looking woman with long, jet black hair and a pale complexion sat alone in the center of the otherwise empty aisle. When she saw them, she stood up. Fraith introduced them.

"This is the Lord Mayor DeWyness."

"And these must be the Heroes of Ravenford," Mayor DeWyness replied, simultaneously giving them the once over. She had a positively snobbish air about her that made Glo cringe. It reminded him far too much of the snooty elves from the Great Houses of his home city—not to mention Sir Fafnar and the Duke of Dunwynn. He did not wish to prejudge her, but from his experience, people like that had a tendency to look down on others. Glo found that kind of attitude insufferable. People were people, and should be treated with respect, no matter their station in life. With a nod to Aksel, Elladan stepped forward and introduced each of the companions in turn. Much as Glo expected, the Mayor remained rather aloof until he got to Lloyd.

"Hmm, a young Lord from the noble Penwick House of Stealle? Our humble little town is honored by your presence," DeWyness practically purred.

Lloyd's reply was typically humble. "Thank you, Lord Mayor. It is our privilege to help in any way we can."

DeWyness gave the young man a feeble smile. When Elistra was introduced, the Mayor's face took on a puzzled expression. "Have we met somewhere before? You look exceedingly familiar."

That mysterious smile crossed the seeress's lips. "I get that all the time. It's the eyes."

Uncharacteristically, Ruka had decided to join them this evening. The companions had previously agreed it best not to disclose her real name, her father being a legend and all. Elladan introduced the young teen as Ruka Grey.

DeWyness arched an eyebrow as she regarded the girl. "Isn't she a bit young to be traveling with a group such as this?"

"She is my apprentice," Glo answered before anyone else could respond. The more time they spent with this woman, the more uneasy he felt around her. Perhaps Elladan and Seth were rubbing off on him.

DeWyness shifted her gaze to Glo. "Well then, aren't you rather young to have an apprentice?"

A thin smile spread across Glo's lips. This woman was obviously not very familiar with the elven race. "Lord Mayor, I may appear young, but in actuality I am one hundred and twenty years old—easily old enough to take on an apprentice."

The Mayor opened her mouth to reply, but Ruka cut her off.

"He's an adequate teacher. I'll keep him for now."

DeWyness turned to regard Ruka. She stared at the young teen for a few moments, then began to laugh. It was a cold, hollow sound. "Oh, I like this one," she declared to herself. A smug smile abruptly crossed her lips. "If you ever tire of the elf, come to me. I'll show you what a real wizard can teach you."

"You're a wizard, Lord Mayor?" The revelation had caught Glo by surprise.

"Indeed, young elf," DeWyness responded, her tone rather haughty. "And I'd dare say a better one than you."

Glo spiked an eyebrow but declined to comment. This DeWyness had a rather high opinion of herself. He wondered how good of a wizard she actually was. DeWyness stared at Glo a moment longer, then addressed the entire group. "Anyway, we are grateful for the service you have provided for our fair town this day. I trust you have received your reward?"

"There was a reward?" Seth spoke up for the first time.

DeWyness nodded. "Yes. Five thousand gold pieces for clearing the lake of those troublesome pests." She turned toward her magistrate. "Fraith, make sure that these folks receive that money."

Fraith gave a slight bow. "Yes, your Mayorship."

"Now, since you have provided our town with a much-needed service, please join me as honored guests." DeWyness waved at the empty seats beside her.

The companions slowly filed into their seats, all except for Elladan. Balmaroh was already up on stage, and Elladan headed up to join him. He had only taken a few steps before DeWyness called out after him.

"Oh, and good bard..."

"Elladan, your Mayorship," he spun around and corrected her.

"Hmm, yes. Elladan," she purred the name, "if you would be so kind as to tell the story of your little lake battle first, I am sure my constituents would appreciate it." She finished with a wave of her hands to the now completely packed theater.

Elladan responded with a partial smile. "Yes, your Mayorship."

Glo felt a sudden wave of apprehension flood over him. He did not want the truth about Ruka getting out, especially in front of DeWyness. Abruptly, a wry smile spread across his face. Elladan and Seth were definitely rubbing off on him. Elladan climbed up on stage and the two bards had a brief exchange. Balmaroh then stepped forward and addressed the audience.

"People of Vermoorden!"

The theater quieted down.

"We have gathered here this evening for The Battle of the Bards!" Some cheers went up through the crowd.

"But first, my good friend Elladan here will tell the tale of the battle earlier today with the lake monsters."

The audience began to cheer in earnest. Elladan stepped forward and motioned with his hands for the crowd to settle down.

"Thank you. Thank you very much. Now then..."

Elladan began the tale of their battle on the lake. As Glo had heard him do so often, Elladan made the trip sound like a quest of epic proportion. He embellished in spots, but when it came to Ruka's accomplishments, the bard rather adeptly attributed them to Glo. Lloyd, Alana, Seth and Donatello were credited with killing off the one monster that had clamped onto the ship.

When Elladan finished his tale, the crowd erupted, coming to its feet. When the applause finally died down, DeWyness turned toward Glo, a sickly sweet smile on her otherwise cold features. "Perhaps I was too hasty in my estimation of you, good elf. You seem much more capable than I originally thought."

"Thank you, your Mayorship," Glo replied, not feeling any more comfortable with the woman.

"I might be able to use someone of your abilities in my staff," DeWyness purred. "If you are ever interested, feel free to come by my keep."

Glo forced himself to smile. "Thank you, your Mayorship. I will give that some consideration."

As Glo sat back in his seat, he felt an elbow jab him in the side. He turned to see Ruka, with a lopsided grin on her face. "You seem much more capable than I originally thought," she whispered, mimicking DeWyness almost perfectly.

Seth, seated on the other side of Ruka, let out a wicked laugh. Glo fixed the duo with an acid stare. Before he could respond, however, he felt a hand on his arm. He spun around as Elistra leaned in close and whispered, "Do not trust that woman."

They were so close that their noses almost touched, the seeress's eyes like two violet orbs blocking out all else from sight. He could feel the warmth of her skin and smell the scent of her perfume—a heavenly lavender. His senses flooded, Glo momentarily lost focus. Abruptly, he broke out of his trance, mentally chastising himself for his brief lapse. "Oh, I don't," he whispered back. Elistra merely nodded, but there was a trace of that knowing smile on her lips as she pulled away from him.

With the storytelling done, The Battle of the Bards began in earnest. Balmaroh insisted that Elladan, as his guest, should go first. Elladan politely accepted. He had already arranged with Glo and Lloyd to put on the same performance he had given at Andrella's party. When they were ready, Lloyd set the beat with his drums and Glo created a fog bank on stage.

Once again, Elladan's dark silhouette appeared in the cloud, dancing lights alit behind him. When he stepped out of the fog, Glo set off a pyrotechnic effect. The one thing that was different was Elladan himself. For some reason, the elven bard made no fighting poses, nor did he dance around, instead, standing still as he sang. The result was a nice performance, but without the same energy as his previous show. When he was done, the crowd applauded, but not with the same wild abandon as in Ravenford.

Elladan strode off stage and took his seat between the Mayor and

Elistra. Glo leaned over next to the seeress and whispered past her to the bard, "What happened up there?"

Elladan peered back at Glo, and whispered to him with a wink, "Never beat a bard on his home turf. It's bad form."

Now it was Balmaroh's turn. The crowd grew quiet as the hometown bard gave his performance. Rhith and Newin set up the same effects they had used in rehearsal the night before. The result was stunning, making it sound as if three voices were singing at once.

She flies
On wings on high
Carried by winds,
Oh, why can't I?

The zephyr's love
Lifts her above
I serve a mighty Lord
With faith and sword
But my heart
Is weak as a dove

The song went on for a few more verses, and when Balmaroh was done the audience gave him a standing ovation. The Mayor climbed up onto the stage and officially declared Balmaroh the winner of the battle. Surprisingly, she also invited the companions up on stage, presenting them with the key to the city. In reality, it was just an oversized, plain brass key, but no one complained. The audience cheered once again.

"Guess we're all winners tonight," Balmaroh cried over the applause as they all took turns bowing.

"I wouldn't have it any other way," Elladan shouted back, giving Glo a quick wink.

Early the next morning, Sir Craven arrived in Vermoorden, accompanied by two cavalry units of the Knights of the Rose. Twelve armored riders, both men and women, followed the knight into the courtyard of the House of Barmann. Two younger riders, not as heavily geared, trailed after them, carrying pennants, one with a golden griffin, the other a crescent moon.

Alana hailed her fellow knight. "Well met, Sir Craven."

Sir Craven reined in his mount, signaling the rest of the riders to a halt. "Well met, Dame Alana."

The riders dismounted and formed up into ranks. Alana performed a brief inspection, Sir Craven by her side. When she was done, she introduced the companions, then nodded to Aksel and took a step back. Aksel stepped forward, but paused a moment before speaking. He was not used to giving speeches—that was more Elladan's forte. Aksel swept his eyes over the gathered troops. These were stalwart men and women, standing in perfect formation, immaculate in their white tabards with rose insignias and shining silver chain mail. It was an inspiring sight. Suddenly Aksel knew what he wanted to say.

"Thank you for coming on such short notice. This is a critical mission we are undertaking, with the fate of all Thac possibly laying in the balance. Things may get very dangerous when we reach our destination, but I can't think of better allies to have at our side than the Knights of the Rose."

The men and women responded by drawing their swords and saluting him in perfect unison. Aksel had never been saluted before—it made him feel all warm inside. A genuine smile broke out across his face and he waved back to the troops before turning to Alana. "Let's go inside and grab some tables. Your people could probably use breakfast, and we have much to discuss."

Alana nodded and stepped forward once more, her voice ringing out across the yard. "Stable your horses, then regroup inside for breakfast. This will be the last town we will see for a while. Make sure you have all the supplies you need and that all your gear is in good condition. Now dismissed!"

"Yes sir!" came the unified response. The dozen or so riders broke ranks, leading their mounts to the stable. The stable boy, James, stood in the doorway gawking at all the horses to be tended.

Donnie, standing next to Lloyd, nudged the tall man. "Let's go give him a hand."

Lloyd's eyes moved from Donnie to Aksel. Aksel gave Lloyd a brief nod. Lloyd grinned, then took off with Donnie toward the stable. Aksel watched them for a few moments, truly touched by the kind gesture. He already knew Lloyd was good hearted, but Donnie was proving to be as well underneath that roguish exterior. As Aksel turned his attention back to the courtyard, he noted the two youngest riders had remained behind. The one with the banner of the moon had gone to take Sir Craven's mount as well as his own, while the second one approached Alana. He stopped a few paces from her, and gave a crisp salute. Alana saluted back.

"This is my squire, Syndir," she told the others.

Syndir gazed around the group, his eyes filled with curiousity, then quickly returned his attention to Alana. "Your mount is in the stable, my lady?"

Alana gave him a brief smile. "Yes, he is."

Syndir responded with a curt nod. "Very good. I shall make sure he gets a good brushing down." The young squire gave a crisp salute, then spun on his heel and led his horse to the stables after the others.

Alana watched after him for a few moments, a proud expression on her face, then turned to the others, ushering them toward the inn. "Gentlemen, shall we?"

Aksel and the others filed inside. Barmann must have seen the large group outside his establishment and roused his staff. They already had a number of tables lined up together at the back of the common room for their numerous guests. The companions picked a large table and sat down with Alana and Sir Craven. The conversation remained light while they waited for Lloyd and Donnie to rejoin them. It wasn't too long before the duo reappeared, along with the rest of the Knights of the Rose.

The common room was soon packed, Barmann himself helping to wait the tables. The aroma of breakfast soon wafted in from the kitchen, and before long everyone was treated to a hearty meal. Eggs, hotcakes, bacon, sausage, biscuits, potatoes, juice, and ale were all served in plentiful heaps. Appetites were finally sated, and the men and women of the cavalry slowly filtered out of the inn to prepare for the trip ahead.

Once breakfast was cleared away, Elladan pulled out a large parchment and unrolled it across the table. It was a detailed map of the area surrounding Lake Strikken, including Vermoorden, the town of Three Forks, the city of Lukescros, and the Darkwoods. Glo and Elistra joined the bard in pinpointing the exact location of the monolith. Between the wizard, the seeress, and Elladan's knowledge of geography, they swiftly identified its position, just south of the source of the West Stromen, the river that fed into the north end of Lake Strikken. Now that they had located the monolith, the next question was the best way to get there. Elladan leaned over the map, placed a finger on Vermoorden, and slowly traced a line north and then west.

"According to the map, there are no roads through the Darkwoods. Your best bet is to head north from here and make your way around the swamp until you reach the West Stromen. From there, you could follow the river into the Darkwoods till you reach its tributaries. At that point, you would need to cross over and head south to reach where we believe the monolith to be."

Alana and Sir Craven had been leaning over the map, intently following the bard's directions. Now the duo sat back and conferred. They seemed mostly concerned about the type of terrain they would run into and the difficulties of leading armored riders through a dense forest. After a few minutes, Aksel spoke up. "Alana, Sir Craven, pardon me, but how long do you think the journey will take you?"

The two knights paused in their conversation and turned to Aksel. Sir Craven's hand went to his chin, stroking the short dark beard that decorated his chin. Alana's brow furrowed with deep concentration. Sir Craven was the first to break the silence. "Well, considering the distance to be traveled, the type of terrain, and the fact that we have light cavalry units... I would guess about three days."

Alana nodded her head slowly. "I agree with Sir Craven's assessment. Light cavalry moves faster than heavily armored knights, but once they hit the woods the going will be slow."

Aksel let out a sigh—that was way too long. The Serpent Cult had already been at the monolith a full day. The longer they had to search the place unhindered, the more likely they were to find Larketh's works. He glanced at Glo and saw his own concern mirrored in the wizard's eyes. Maybe it was best that they go ahead of the knights after all. Aksel turned to Elladan. "How long did you say it would take to reach the monolith by river?"

Elladan eyes swept over the map. "I'm not the expert on sailing here, but based on the distance, I thought it wouldn't take more than a day."

Both Donnie and Lloyd stood up, leaned over and examined the route upriver. "That's neglecting the fact that we would be headed against the current," Donnie pointed out.

"Also, not to mention that we may run into rough water," Lloyd added.

Aksel's eyes moved from the slight elf to the tall man. "So how long would you two estimate?"

Donnie and Lloyd exchanged glances.

"Two days," Lloyd answered.

"Three actually," Donnie corrected him.

"*Three?*" The word nearly exploded out of Glo's mouth.

Donnie threw up his hands and shrugged. "Well, the *Rusty Nail* was pretty roughed up by that giant octopus. Morled said it won't be ready for the trip up river until tomorrow."

Aksel sat back and took a deep breath. It seemed as if they had little choice. "So either way, it will take us three days to reach the monolith. And you're certain there's no other ship that could take us?"

Donnie shook his head. "Trust me, we were hard pressed finding the *Rusty Nail.* All the other ships were either too small or in bad shape."

Lloyd nodded. "I have to agree. I wouldn't trust sailing on any of them up the river into the Darkwoods."

Aksel's eyes flickered around the table. It was filled with grim faces, all except for Elladan. The bard, wearing his typical half-smile, tried to cheer the others up. "Well, since there's no hope for it, we might as well make the best of our time. I vote we stay here and use the extra day to prepare ourselves."

Aksel nodded slowly—Elladan had a point. He peered around the table once more. "What do the rest of you think?"

Lloyd shrugged his broad shoulders. "I guess I could use the time to train a bit more."

"If you do, then I will stay and train with you," Alana added, her eyes alight with the thought of working with the young warrior.

"I wouldn't mind joining you either," Donnie chimed in. "You never did show me how you do that thing where your blades catch on fire." The swordsman made a whooshing sound which he emphasized with some hand motions.

A grin swept across Lloyd's previously glum face. "I can try, but it took me years to get it down."

Donnie flashed him a sparkling smile. "I'm a fast learner."

"I guess I could research some new spells," Glo mused aloud.

"And I could see if I can divine anything more about the Serpent Cult's progress," Elistra said.

Seth, Ruka and Martan all agreed they could make use of the extra day. Aksel imagined Seth would spend the time honing his sneaking skills with Ruka like he had done on their way to Vermoorden. With everyone agreed, Aksel made the final decision. "Okay then, I guess that settles it. We'll stay in Vermoorden for the day."

Sir Craven nodded his approval. "Very well. Once we've finished resupplying ourselves we'll head out. We'll follow the path you laid out for us and meet you at the monolith three days from now."

Aksel gave the man a brief smile. "Thank you, Sir Craven. Thank you, Alana. Let's just pray we are in time to stop the Cult..."

14
DREAMS

Shortly before noon, the companions bade farewell to Sir Craven and company. They watched the armored riders disappear
up the road to the north, then went their separate ways. Glo left
to study, Elistra to meditate, Aksel to pray, Lloyd, Alana, and Donnie
to train, Seth and Ruka to play their strange game of hide-and-seek,
and Elladan and Martan to stock up on any supplies they may need
on the next leg of their journey.

The rest of the day went agonizingly slow for Glo. He sat alone
on his bed in the room he and Lloyd shared, the spellbooks of Telvar
and Voltark spread out before him. Try as he might, he could not
concentrate on his research. After a few hours, his eyes grew tired of
staring at the pages opened in front of him. Frustrated and tired, the
young elven wizard sat back on the bed and closed his eyes.

The forest was dark, the tall trees looming far overhead, blocking out any sight of the sky above. A worn path cut through the woods before him, the barest glimmer of daylight in the far distance. He searched all around, but his friends were nowhere to be seen. He considered calling out their names, but the forest was eerily silent, making him wary of calling attention to himself.

Glo slowly picked his way along the overgrown path, stepping over dead branches and tangled underbrush that barred his way. He kept a cautious eye on the dark woods that surrounded him, a growing sense of foreboding hovering at the edge of his senses. When he finally reached the end of the pathway, the woods opened up into a wide clearing. In the very center, a tall black structure rose far above the trees, nearly touching the grey skies above. It was the Darkwoods Monolith! There was no mistaking it. It looked exactly like the structure he had seen in his crystal ball.

Glo felt a strange sense of urgency as he rushed across the clearing. Where were the others? Was the Cult still inside? Had he made it in time?

As he approached the monolith, he observed an arched doorway at the base. It lay open, a dim reddish glow just visible beyond. Glo was running now, only stopping when he finally reached the door. He took a deep breath, then gingerly stepped inside. A huge chamber lay before him, glowing urns burning with fire lining the edges of the vast room. In the very center stood a giant stone statue. Glo eyed the figure carefully, quickly determing it was in the shape of a dwarf. The dwarf wore long, flowing robes, and held a large tome in one hand.

That must be Larketh.

Abruptly, the air before him began to shimmer. A transparent visage began to form, swiftly coalescing into the small but familiar figure of a halfling. Glo's eyes went wide in horror.

"Seth?"

"Yes..." the visage responded in a strangely hollow tone.

Glo's voice broke as he stared at the ghostly figure. "What... happened to you?"

"What do you think?" Seth shot back, his voice wavering strangely as he talked.

"You're... dead." Glo forced himself to say that last word, not wanting to believe it, despite the irrefutable proof in front of him.

"Duh," came the immediate reply. There was no mistaking it. This was Seth, or more accurately, Seth's ghost.

Moisture welled up in Glo's eyes. It was his fault. He had fallen behind somehow, letting his friends down. "I'm... I'm so sorry, Seth."

"Don't be sorry," Seth's visage continued in that wavering tone. "There is still time..."

"Time for what?" Glo cried out, still distraught over the death of his friend. "And why on earth are you talking like that?"

Seth's ghost smirked at him, his voice suddenly normal. "I'm talking this way because I'm dead, and I thought it would be amusing." Glo almost screamed at the halfling in frustration, but Seth held up a hand. "There is still time to save the others, you nitwit." The visage then spun around and floated quickly toward the center of the room. "Follow me..."

Glo took off at a dead run after Seth's ghost. He led him to a stairwell in floor of the chamber. Winding steps disappeared below. Glo raced down the staircase after the floating visage, doing his best to keep the ghost in sight. The stairs seemed to go on forever, farther and farther down into the earth below. After what seemed like an eternity, he spotted a doorway.

Glo raced through the archway and into a wide chamber. Piles of gold and silver were stacked against the walls with large chests scattered here and there. Some were half open, gems, jewels and more treasures visible inside. An open path led across the center of the chamber to a wide platform. On that platform, a familiar figure in red spun around, a sword in each hand, driving back the four large serpents that surrounded him.

"Lloyd!" Glo shouted with relief.

Lloyd spun around, his eyes falling on Glo, the momentary lapse his undoing. At that moment, the largest serpent lunged for the young warrior.

"Look out!" Glo cried in horror.

He watched in terror as the large serpent caught the warrior from behind, lifted his body up with its giant maw, shook him around fiercely, then flung him aside like a rag doll. Lloyd's body landed in a pile of gold next to the center platform. Glo stared at his friend's unmoving figure, mortified at what he had just witnessed. Abruptly he realized there were more bodies lying next to Lloyd's. All of his friends were there: Seth, Aksel, Elladan, Donnie, Elistra, Alana, Martan, and even the girl, Ruka. He felt momentarily numb, but that feeling was quickly replaced as unabiding anger welled up from somewhere deep inside him.

"You... you murderers!" Glo screamed at the top of his lungs.

He swiftly pulled a pinch of sulfur from his pouch and began the motions of a spell. As he did so, the largest serpent changed, shifting into a black-robed figure.

"That won't save you!" Glo yelled with fury. He finished the motions, speaking the word that would invoke the spell. "Augue!"

A red hot ball sped from his hands, homing in on the mage and the large serpents. Man and beast stood as if frozen, watching the ball race toward them, not even attempting to move out of the way. The fiery sphere swiftly reached them, exploding into a huge dome of raging flames. The figures were engulfed, quickly disappearing from sight. A few seconds later, the flames subsided. The serpents were all gone, turned to ash, but the lone figure of a black mage stood there, completely unharmed. A shrill laugh emanated from behind the dark hood, followed by a strangely familiar voice.

"Is that the best you've got?"

Glo's eyes went wide, the blood draining from his face as he recognized that voice. The dark figure reached up and pulled back its hood. It was Glo's father, Amrod!

"I told you to stay home, little elf..."

Glo woke with a start. He sat up on the bed, his body drenched in sweat. Glo nearly started again when he saw the tall figure standing over him, but it turned out to be only Lloyd.

"You were crying out in your sleep," Lloyd told him, the young man's face lined with concern.

"Elves don't sleep..." Glo murmured, the answer more out of reflex than anything else.

"Well, your eyes were closed..."

Glo suddenly felt a wave of emotion overtake him. *Lloyd is alive!* Without another thought, Glo jumped up off the bed and threw his arms around the young man. "I have never been so glad to see anyone in my life!"

Lloyd appeared taken aback by the sudden display of affection. He stood there awkwardly hugging Glo back. "Umm, thanks... I guess. Anyway, sleeping or not, it sounded like you were having a nightmare."

Abruptly, Glo came to his senses. He swiftly pulled away from his tall friend. "Um, yes, as a matter of fact, I was."

A look of puzzlement crossed Lloyd's face. He cocked his head to one side, his brow furrowing. "So let me get this straight—you don't sleep, but you dream?"

"Yes and no," Glo replied, a smile etched across his lips for the first time since "waking". He paused a moment, trying to find the words to explain elven rest to his friend. "As a spiritblade, you know how to meditate, right?"

"Yeah, though I'm not very good at it."

Glo's smile widened at his friend's admission. "Well, elves basically meditate instead of sleeping. It helps us rest, and it replenishes our bodies."

Lloyd nodded slowly, understanding dawning on his face. "Okay, but then, how do you dream?"

Glo let out a short laugh. It was a fair question. "Well, it doesn't happen all the time, but if an elf enters into a deep enough trance, he, or she, can indeed dream."

Lloyd nodded once more, the lines in his face finally disappearing. "I guess that makes sense. Still, that must have been one heck of a dream."

"You don't know the half of it." Glo body involuntarily shuddered, the vision of his father's face atop those black robes firmly etched in his mind.

The next morning, the companions stood on the deck of the Rusty Nail, headed up the West Stromen toward the Darkwoods. The journey had been fairly quiet thus far. The weather was clear, and Lake Strikken was calm once again. They had reached the mouth of the river in just under an hour, and had began the slow voyage upstream. The land was clear on either side of the river. Beyond the southern bank, lush green plains spread out as far as the eye could see. The land on the northern bank was similarly filled with green grasses and sparse vegetation until it rose up to meet a chain of rolling, tree-lined hills in the distance.

This was the same chain the travelers had seen on their way to Vermoorden, the one which bordered the south end of the Bendenwoods. According to Captain Morled, they would not reach the edge of the Darkwoods until much later in the day. Still they were making good time. Even so, many of the companions had grown anxious, not knowing if the Serpent Cultists had already found the Golem Master's works.

Glo sat on a wooden crate on the deck of the Rusty Nail, silently wondering what waited for them inside the Darkwoods Monolith. He was still unnerved by the nightmare he had the day before. Glo had tried scrying on the monolith again, but to no avail. He had seen no further sign of the dark mages, nor of their serpents. Elistra sat on the crate next to him, her eyes closed and legs crossed as she meditated. The seeress had been unperturbed by his failure to scry on the cultists further.

"Larketh's secrets are not so easily unearthed," she had told him with that mysterious smile of hers.

Glo decided to divulge his dream to the seeress, thinking that maybe she could make some sense of it. He reached over and lightly tapped her on the shoulder.

"Elistra?" he said softly.

"Yes," she responded, not opening her eyes.

"Do you have a moment?" he asked tentatively, already having second thoughts about discussing his strange dream. Elistra's eyelids slowly opened, and two deep pools of violet stared back at him.

"Certainly." Her eyes sparkled at him with curiosity. She spun around to face him, remaining cross-legged all the while. "What is it?"

Glo hesitated briefly, then told her about the dream. Elistra listened intently, not interrupting as he described the details to her. When he was done, she remained silent, her eyes taking on a faraway look. Glo waited quietly until she came out of her trance-like state. Abruptly, the seeress moved closer, a sympathetic smile on her face. She grabbed his hands and held onto them lightly. Her words were measured as she spoke.

"That was indeed an interesting dream. While some dreams are prophetic, I am not getting that sense from what you have told me."

Glo let out a deep sigh, the anxiety he had been feeling for the last twenty-four hours suddenly washed away.

"Still, there are elements of your dream I do find very interesting." Glo raised an eyebrow, his nerves kicking up again. "Such as?"

"Well, for one, the fact that the Serpent Cult had already found Larketh's treasures."

"And for two?" He was certain she would mention the appearance of his father.

An impish smile crossed her lips. "For two, is the fact that all your friends were dead or died in the dream."

That was not what he had expected to hear. "Is there a third point?"

Elistra's smile spread into an outright grin. "Yes, in fact. You are getting the hang of this. The third point is that your greatest nemesis turned out to be your father."

There it is. Glo shook his head, his face flushing. He kept talking to hide his embarrassment. "And all these points are..."

"...your greatest fears," she finished for him, squeezing his hands tightly.

Glo let out a sigh, finally understanding what she was getting at. "Oh... I see. My mother used to call them fear dreams. She used to say it was your subconscious mind's way of making you face your fears."

"Your mother is quite knowledgeable."

He shook his head, a wry smile crossing his lips. "She definitely knows her way around the mind." Glo had found that out at a young age. He was never able to lie to her. Somehow his mother could always tell when he was hiding something and coax the truth out of him. Elistra gave him a warm smile, then turned to face toward the deck once more. She still held onto his one hand though. The two of them sat there side-by-side, holding hands and watching the antics on deck.

Over by the railing, Donnie and Alana were taking in the sights. The two had grown closer over the last couple of days, the lady knight warming to the swordsman after his daring part in keeping her from falling overboard. Encased in full plate armor as she was, a tumble into the lake would have been a death sentence. The duo were not content long, though, their peace interrupted as a white-tailed hawk strafed over them.

Donnie jumped back from the rail and threw his hands up over his head. "Ruka! Cut that out! I don't know what's gotten into you!"

The rest of the companions, scattered across the deck, stopped what they were doing to watch the show. Glo glanced at Elistra—a knowing smile graced her lips. Across the deck, Donnie continued to be pushed away from the railing, dodging the swooping hawk at each pass. Alana, still at the rail, wore a bemused expression as she watched the swordsman bob to and fro.

"How long do you think before he figures it out?" Elistra asked quietly.

Glo chuckled softly. He was no expert in matters of the heart, but even the densest person could see Ruka's interest in the slight elf. "I'm not sure. I don't think his mind quite works that way. He seems to think of her as a mere child."

"There is nothing mere about her," Elistra said with a tone of absolute certainty.

Elladan sat on a crate on the opposite side of the deck. He had been playing a soothing melody until Ruka began her assault on the hapless elf. Now he played a jaunty tune, throwing in jibes here and there. "Watch your head there, Donnie! Those claws are sharp!"

Aksel and Seth leaned side-by-side against the opposite rail, watching the antics unfold across from them. They had always been an unlikely duo, but seemed to have developed a friendship despite the fact that they were polar opposites. Seth lips bent further each time the hawk dove past the swordsman. Aksel's expression remained serious the entire time. Martan was up in the crow's nest on the foremast. The archer had mostly kept to himself since Ves had left them. A quiet man anyway, he now seemed heartbroken since they had gone their separate ways. Glo felt a brief pang of sympathy, understanding only too well how the archer felt.

Glo suddenly felt something soft on his shoulder. A sidelong glance confirmed that Elistra had laid her head on him. Not looking up, the seeress whispered, "Penny for your thoughts."

"Oh... nothing in particular. Just enjoying the show. I guess I'm also relieved to have gotten that dream off my chest."

A contented sigh escaped her lips. "Good. It's about time you relaxed."

Glo laughed softly. "Me? Relax? Not likely. Not when we have no idea what's really waiting for us at the monolith."

"Well, there's a simple answer to that!" Elistra lifted her head, then suddenly stretched out and laid it on his lap. Glo was momentarily startled, but grew calm as he stared down into those violet eyes.

"And what might that be?" he replied taking the bait.

"Why, it's destiny of course."

She stared up at him, her expression gravely serious. Glo stared back at her with uncertainty. Abruptly, Elistra burst out laughing. She rolled off his lap and onto the deck, giggling the whole while. "Oh, stop being so serious!"

Glo was completely taken off-guard. "I'll give you serious!" He leapt forward, grabbed her, and started tickling her mercilessly. It turned out that she was very ticklish. Elistra squirmed this way and that, giggling uncontrollably as she tried to get away from him. Glo, however, was unrelenting.

"Stop!" she cried in-between fits of laughter. "Sto... oo... op!" she cried louder.

Glo stilled his fingers. "Do you give up?"

Instead of answering, she tried to wiggle away once more.

"Oh, no, you don't!" Glo resumed moving his fingers. Again, Elistra squirmed and giggled, thrashing around underneath him. Once more, Glo stopped. "Do you give up?"

"I... I give... I give!" she cried this time, almost out of breath from laughing so hard.

Glo began to laugh as well. Without warning, Elistra threw her arms around his neck, dragged him to the deck, and rolled on top of him. The two of them lay there in each other's arms, laughing like two little kids. Glo suddenly realized that it had gone quiet around them. He gazed up and saw that everyone was now staring at them. Even Ruka had stopped strafing Donnie. The hawk had landed on a beam and peered down at them, twisting its head from side to side almost quizzically.

"Get a room!" Donnie shouted.

"Maybe we should!" Elistra shot back, not missing a beat.

She gazed down at Glo and gave him an exaggerated wink. Glo

felt the blood rise to his ears. This enigmatic woman had a way of keeping him completely off-balance. Elistra began to laugh once more. She slowly got up and went to sit back down, gleefully chortling all the while. In the meantime, Elladan played a jaunty tune about a sailor and a tavern wench who was his eventual undoing. As Glo retook his seat, he saw that Donnie had taken Alana by the hand and was dancing around the deck with the lovely lady knight—that is, until Ruka dove off her perch and began buzzing him once again.

"Ruka! Enough already!" Donnie yelped, letting go of Alana and dodging those swooping claws.

"Ahhhhh, young love," Elladan crooned, wearing that all-too-familiar half-smile.

The door to the cabins opened behind them. Lloyd stepped out on deck, stretched his arms wide and yawned. "What'd I miss?"

Elistra wore a mysterious expression as she answered his query. "Not much. Just a touch of spring fever."

15
UP THE CREEK

It was late in the day when they entered the Darkwoods. The vegetation grew gradually thicker on either side of the river. Tall dark trees shot up on the banks, their long branches extending out over the West Stromen. Before long, the sky all but disappeared, except for a thin blue strip down the very center of the river. The rest of the sky was blotted out by a dark canopy of branches and leaves. Elladan stood at the railing with Donnie and Glo.

"Do you feel it?" Glo asked, the wizard's voice low.

"It is somewhat oppressive," Donnie answered, his voice equally soft, his quick eyes keenly scanning the passing shoreline.

"It reminds me of a somber tune," Elladan commented. He took out his lute to play, but then stopped himself. He felt uncomfortable out here in the open, not being able to see beyond the trees on either bank. "Maybe this is not the best time," he murmured, putting his lute back away.

"It almost reminds me of the Dead Forest," Glo said, his voice still hushed.

Elladan nodded. "I remember that place." They had passed through the forest on the way to the ruins atop Stone Hill. Those woods had felt stifling, almost as if they were trying to suck the life out of you. He felt a brief shiver pass up his spine as he recalled the memory.

Donnie shifted his gaze away from the shore to his companions. "Didn't we pass through those woods on our way to Vermoorden?"

Glo nodded. "Yes. It's not the kind of place that is easily forgotten."

Donnie shrugged. "It didn't seem quite that bad. I have seen worse places, like this one time..."

Without warning, the ship pitched forward. The three elves grabbed onto the railing just in time to avoid being thrown overboard. The Rusty Nail came to a stop, its sudden halt accompanied by a loud grinding noise. As the ship righted itself, Martan yelled down from the crow's nest.

"There's a giant chain across the river!"

Elladan leaned out over the railing. Sure enough, a length of thick chain stretched across the front of the ship, holding it firmly in place. Elladan followed the chain with his eyes—it ran all the way to the shore and disappeared in the trees beyond both banks. Glo sounded as incredulous as Elladan.

"How in the world did we miss seeing something like that?"

Donnie, on the other hand, did not seem surprised at all. "It's an old river pirate trick," the slight elf explained. "You lay the chain just under the surface and when a boat hits it, it gets pulled taut."

Any further discussion was cut off by Seth's cry from above. "Incoming!"

They all ducked just in time. A hail of arrows flew overhead, embedding themselves into the deck behind them. The Rusty Nail suddenly looked like a pincushion. From the angle of the shafts, the volleys had come from both sides of the river.

"We're surrounded!" Elladan warned the others. A sudden screech from above caused them all to glance upwards. A familiar white-tailed hawk launched itself from the crow's nest and flew swiftly toward the southern bank.

"There goes Ruka!" Alana yelled.

"She won't go alone!" Donnie shouted in response. He leapt up and ran for the bow, nimbly dodging the next volley of arrows. When they were done, Donnie vaulted up onto the railing and launched himself off the boat, landing deftly on the length of chain that held them fast. He balanced precariously on the thick chain for a moment or two, then took off at a dead run toward the south bank.

"Glo, Lloyd, quick! Take the other bank!" Aksel's voice range out across the deck.

"Already on it!" Lloyd replied as he rose up into the air.

"Same here!" Glo added, also rising off the deck.

"Wait for a song!" Elladan cried. He swiftly invoked the magic that made his lute appear and played a tune to inspire them. The pair hovered there for a few moments, then shot upward as the next hail of arrows whizzed overhead. Elladan had to duck down to avoid being skewered—when he looked up again, Lloyd and Glo hung unharmed in the air just above the mast. With a brief wave, the duo flew off toward the north shore, quickly gaining the cover of the trees.

"I should be helping them."

Elladan turned and saw Alana and Elistra at the rail behind him. The lady knight stared intently at the south bank, her body tense with frustration. Elladan felt a sudden pang for her. Though a full-fledged knight, she was obviously still young and her growing feelings for Donnie were clouding her judgement. Elladan reached over and laid a hand on her shoulder.

"Trust me, Donnie can handle himself."

Elistra placed a hand on Alana's other shoulder. "And he has Ruka with him." As if to accentuate the statement, the south woods suddenly lit up with a blinding flash. A crash of thunder followed shortly thereafter. Elistra nodded her head toward the shore. "Looks like she's already at work."

A slim smile spread across Alana's lips, though her knuckles were still white where she gripped the rail. Abruptly, the sky behind them lit up. They all turned as a second crash of thunder reached their ears.

"Glo as well," Elladan said with a smile.

Aksel's voice suddenly rang out across the deck. "The arrows have stopped."

He was right—there were no more arrows coming from either shore. It was a good sign. Elladan chuckled softly. "Looks like they've got their hands too full to be taking pot shots at us."

Any further comments were interrupted by a voice from above.

"Is Seth down there with you?" Martan called down to them.

Elladan glanced up and saw the archer hanging over the edge of the crow's nest, looking down at them. The companions scoured the deck, but Seth was nowhere to be seen.

"There he is," Elistra called out.

She was pointing toward the north shore. Elladan followed her gaze, but still saw no sign of Seth. His eyes narrowed as he struggled to see the halfling, but to no avail. "Where?"

Elistra shifted her gaze toward him, her expression swiftly changing to one of surprise. "Oh, I'm sorry. He must be invisible. He's walking across the chain. He's almost at the shore."

Aksel strode up next to them, leaned over the railing and gazed intently at the north shore. "Why doesn't that surprise me?" His tone was filled with exasperation. "Oh, well. One of these days maybe he'll learn to tell me before he goes running off on his own."

Elladan placed a sympathetic hand on the young gnome's shoulder and shook his head. "I wouldn't hold my breath."

When Donnie reached the south shore, he leapt off the chain and vaulted into the woods. As he rushed through the thick underbrush, the sky in front of him lit up and the forest reverberated with the crash of thunder.

That has to be Ruka. She's in trouble!

The agile swordsman pushed himself even harder, afraid of what he might find ahead. Seconds later, the underbrush parted and Donnie screeched to a halt. Ruka, her back to him, stood not twenty yards away, surrounded by a number of small figures. They didn't look much larger than Aksel or Seth, but were definitely not halflings or gnomes. These creatures had orange-hued skin, beady yellow eyes, and sharp, pointy teeth. Their ovoid-shaped heads appeared far too large for their small bodies.

Goblins. I hate goblins.

Goblins were foul, man-eating creatures. They were cunning and ruthless, and not to be taken lightly, despite their diminutive size. Five goblins stood in a circle around Ruka, armed with wicked little curved swords. A sixth lay dead at her feet, its small body burnt and still smoldering. Ruka stood calmly in the center, brandishing her sword, her voice rather nonchalant.

"Ok, who's next?"

The goblins hesitated, having seen what that blade could do. Donnie used those moments to his advantage, noiselessly drawing his own weapons and slowly moving forward across the clearing.

If I can just take a couple by surprise...

Any further thoughts were interrupted by a deep growl emanating from the bushes on the opposite side of the clearing. Donnie froze in his tracks, straining his eyes to see what was hidden there. Moments later, a large figure erupted from the brush and slowly shambled into the clearing. It had a brutish face, a short wide neck, broad shoulders, and mottled green skin. The figure carried a huge wooden club in its right hand, easily the size of one of the goblins.

Troll!

Donnie felt a slight fluttering in his stomach. He had run across his share in the past and it had always been deadly. Not only were trolls as strong as they looked, they were also fast. Even worse, if you cut one, the wound would immediately start to heal. Donnie pushed down his nerves—he needed to keep his wits about him if they were going to survive this encounter.

The troll stopped at the edge of the clearing, its beady red eyes surveying the area. Its gaze swiftly settled on Ruka, an evil grin forming across its cruel inhuman face. Those crimson eyes then dropped to the smoldering form lying on the ground. The grin on the creature's face quickly disappeared. It threw its huge head back and lifted its arms up into the air, a savage roar bursting from the beast's mouth.

Well, this just keeps getting better and better.

A regular troll was bad enough, but an enraged troll was even stronger. Donnie's mind raced as he adjusted his strategy. His swords would do no good against the thick skin of the troll. Plus, it was on the other side of the circle and he would have to get through the goblins to get to it. The goblins had to working with the troll or they would have already bolted and run. So his best bet would be to distract the nasty little creatures. If he could keep them off Ruka's back, she might be able to keep the troll at bay with that short sword of hers, at least until help arrived. Admittedly, it wasn't the greatest plan, but it was the best he could do on such short notice, and they had just run out of time.

The troll stopped roaring, dropped its arms, and glared at Ruka. Strangely, the young teen didn't even flinch. The goblins, not the bravest of creatures, had been startled by the troll, even though it was on their side. Now, having regained their courage, they jeered at Ruka.

It's now or never!

Donnie threw caution to the wind and launched himself toward the nearest two goblins. The creatures heard him coming too late. He slipped between them before they could bring their weapons to bear, his swords neatly skewering each creature through the neck. Both goblins dropped to the ground clutching their throats.

"Nice move, Donnie!" Ruka yelled over her shoulder.

"Thanks, milady!" Donnie grinned, though he wasn't quite sure how she knew it was him. The thought quickly left his mind as the three remaining goblins turned to face him.

Donnie fell back into a defensive stance and slowly backpedaled, hoping to draw the creatures away from Ruka. It worked like a charm—he had garnered the undisputed attention of the single-minded little pests. Donnie managed to pull the goblins a good ten feet away before the troll charged. He watched in horror as the huge creature rushed the girl. The troll was on top of Ruka before Donnie could move a muscle. Every nerve in his body screamed as it swung its club at her.

"Ruka!" Donnie cried in anguish, expecting to see her crushed under the weight of that club.

Time appeared to slow as the weapon closed upon the girl's skull, yet Ruka did not attempt to move out of the way. Instead, she dropped her sword and threw both of her hands up in front of her. What happened next was impossible—Ruka stopped the troll's club in mid-swing. The clearing went silent. Everyone froze, staring in disbelief. Donnie, not believing his eyes, blinked and looked again. Ruka still stood there, the troll's club held firmly in her outstretched hands.

She caught the club! Ruka caught the troll's club!

Donnie was so elated he nearly missed the faint golden glow that surrounded Ruka's body. It was just barely visible, but it was there. There was no time to think about it now though. The troll had been thrown off-balance by the abrupt halt of its attack. It grunted angrily as it righted itself, then tried to yank its club back. Try as it might, though, it could not budge the weapon.

Donnie watched on in awe as Ruka's hair rose on its own accord, the crackling glow of electric arcs dancing across her body. The arcs swiftly grew in intensity, abruptly flying up the handle of the club. They reached the troll in moments, racing up its arm and engulfing its entire body. The troll screamed with rage as the electricity danced across its torso, burning it and singeing it in numerous places at once. Yet, try as it might, it could not let go of the club.

Donnie shook himself, realizing there were still three goblins standing in front of him. The little creatures were rooted in place, mesmerized by the spectacle taking place before them. Donnie silently dispatched one of them, the other two not even noticing.

Meanwhile, Ruka had finished her onslaught. The arcs of electricity died down around her and then disappeared completely. The troll, finally able to let go of its club, staggered backward, blackened scars still smoldering on its green mottled skin. The large creature stared down at the girl, growling and snarling with rage.

The two remaining goblins finally moved. They dropped their swords and backed away from the girl and the troll. One of them backed up almost directly into Donnie. He took the opportunity to slit its throat.

This is almost too easy.

Meanwhile, the troll glared at Ruka. It appeared as if it was gaining the courage to attack again when the creature's eyes suddenly went wide. Its shoulders drooped, and just like the goblins, it also began to back away from the girl. The troll only took a few steps when it spun around and started to run. Donnie didn't have time to question the strange spectacle. The last goblin, spurred on by the troll, decided to run as well. Yet as it turned to flee, Donnie caught it and quickly dispatched the foul little creature. He looked up just as Ruka cried out after the retreating troll.

"Oh, no, you don't!"

Ruka dropped the huge club, and instead of retrieving her sword, pointed a finger at the fleeing monster. A bolt of electricity erupted from her hand and flashed across the clearing, slamming hard into the back of the creature. Thunder boomed around them as the troll dropped to its knees.

Ruka glanced briefly at Donnie, her features unreadable, then swiftly snatched up her sword. She pointed it at the kneeling creature, the blade already beginning to glow.

At the very last moment, Ruka shifted her aim and let loose a bolt at a nearby tree. It struck the trunk square on, a loud splitting sound accompanying the roll of thunder. A second later, the tree began to fall. Too late, the troll realized the danger it was in. It could not move out of the way fast enough, and was slammed to the ground by the thick trunk of the falling tree.

Once more, Ruka aimed her sword. The glowing blade let loose another bolt, this one striking the trunk of the tree. Thunder rolled across the clearing once more as the fallen tree burst into flames. The troll, pinned underneath the trunk, groaned one last time and then went limp and silent.

Donnie was dumbfounded. His eyes flickered from the burning troll to Ruka and then back again. Abruptly Ruka laughed. Her teen-age chortle was a sharp contrast to the raw power he had just seen her display. Ruka sheathed her sword, spun around, and walked up to the dazed swordsman. She stopped less than a foot in front of him and gazed up into his eyes. Her voice was soft and throaty.

"Thanks for the assist."

Donnie found himself speechless for the first time in a very long while. He had just watched this girl dispatch a full grown troll without so much as breaking a sweat. Further, in doing so she had demonstrated strength far greater than Lloyd, and a command of lightning that easily outclassed Glolindir. Donnie had no idea what to make of this girl. Ruka continued to gaze quietly up at him—it was a look he had seen before, and he knew exactly what it meant. He stared into those emerald green eyes, and was mesmerized for a moment. Abruptly he shook his head.

Get a grip on yourself, man!

Donnie took a quickly back step and executed a deep bow. "Ahem. It was nothing, milady." He stood up and flashed her one of his best smiles. "It was really you who did all the work."

Ruka took another step, ending up once again less than a foot from him. "Maybe, but you did risk your life coming to my rescue."

There is that look again.

Donnie needed to divert her attention away from him, fast. "I think we should make sure that troll doesn't break loose." He stepped gingerly around her, walking hastily across the clearing toward what was left of the creature. Donnie cast a nervous glance behind him and saw that Ruka followed only a few short paces behind.

Donatello, what have you gotten yourself into this time?

At the same time Donnie entered the clearing, Lloyd and Glo reached the north shore. Glo came to a sudden halt, signaling for Lloyd to stop as well. Feral grunts sounded from the woods ahead, followed by another volley of arrows. The projectiles sailed just below the duo, soaring over the river and toward the Rusty Nail.

Lloyd started forward, but was held back by a sudden hand on his arm. He glanced over his shoulder at Glo. The wizard shook his head once, then made some swift hand motions indicating the two of them should separate and circle the woods ahead. Lloyd nodded his understanding. With a brief smile, Glo spun in mid-air and flew off to the east. Lloyd did the same but in the opposite direction. He flew in a low arc, keeping just above the trees.

When the next volley erupted from the dark forest, Lloyd was directly west of it. The young warrior clenched his teeth. *That will be the last attack on my friends.*

Lloyd drew his blades and launched himself straight at the source of those arrows. Seconds later, the trees parted into a wide clearing. A number of orange-skinned figures stood there, all with bows in hand. *Goblins? What are they doing here? No matter.*

Lloyd set his jaw and dove down into the clearing, his blades bursting into flames as he closed in on the nearest goblin. The creatures were too busy nocking their arrows to notice him. He was on top of the first goblin before it ever saw him.

Lloyd took a mighty swing with his black blade, cleanly lopping the creature's head off. The dead goblin crumpled to the ground as he continued past. Five more goblins were lined up in front of him, and Lloyd was determined to cut each one down.

He was on the second one in moments, swinging with his other blade. It bit deep into the goblin's side, causing the creature to yelp in pain. The goblin tried to back away, but before it could, Lloyd brought his black sword around and cleaved its head off. The goblin's cry had alerted the others, though.

The four remaining goblins looked up in surprise. Lloyd did not hesitate, barreling forward as the foul little archers raised their bows. He slammed into the next goblin before it could take a shot, knocking it backwards toward the other two.

As it flew through the air toward its comrades, three arrows embedded themselves in the goblin's back. It was dead before it hit the ground. The next goblin dropped its bow, turned and ran, the others doing likewise. Lloyd's eyes narrowed. *Oh no, you are not getting away that easy!*

Lloyd took off after them, closing fast on the nearest goblin. He almost caught up to it when something large came crashing out of the brush. A dark figure leapt into the clearing, crouching there on all fours, its cruel yellow eyes scanning the area. A vicious snarl escaped its snout, its jaws opening to reveal a row of razor sharp teeth.

"Barghest!"

Lloyd hissed the word as he recognized the creature—a demon in the form of a wolf, but twice the size and with a goblin's head. He had seen one before, back at Cape Marlin, but this was no time to be reminiscing. Lloyd spun his body around and planted his feet in the dirt, skidding to a quick halt. The young warrior fell into a fighting stance and prepared for the fight of his life.

The goblins he had been chasing ran headlong into the Barghest. The demon reached out with one huge claw and swatted the lead goblin, sending it flying across the clearing and into the trunk of a nearby tree. It was dead on impact, its lifeless body falling to the ground in a heap. The other goblins skidded to a halt and attempted to turn and flee, but the Barghest was on top of them in a single bound. It rent them to shreds in a matter of seconds. When it was done, it lifted its huge head, blood dripping from its fangs, and fixed its baleful eyes on Lloyd.

As Lloyd prepared himself for the inevitable charge, the sky suddenly lit up around them. A bolt of lightning flashed across the clearing, striking the demon square in the back. Thunder rolled as the Barghest screamed, a horrifying wail that chilled the air. Its flesh sizzled and a thin trail of smoke rose from the demon's hide. Lloyd traced the bolt back to the edge of the clearing, a good fifty yards away. A figure in a purple robe stood between the trees, its hand still extended from the spell it had just cast.

A grim smile spread across Lloyd's lips. *Nice shot, Glo.*

His smile quickly faded as the demon whirled around. Without a sound, it launched itself forward, racing straight for the elven wizard. Lloyd immediately sprang after it, trying his best to catch up, but the four-legged demon was way too fast. It left Lloyd far behind, covering half the distance to Glo in mere seconds.

"Lloyd, duck!" came a cry across the clearing.

Lloyd threw himself to the ground as the clearing lit up once more. A flash of light flew over his head, causing the hairs on the back of his neck to stand up. When Lloyd lifted his head, he saw the Barghest had halted. It stood halfway between him and Glo, shuddering as electrical arcs danced across its dark grey fur. Lloyd leapt up and launched himself forward, running as fast as he could. He had only closed half the gap when the beast snarled. Lloyd tried to draw its attention with a battle cry, but the creature ignored him, leaping forward and hurtling toward Glo once more.

Lloyd knew he would never catch it on foot. He had only one chance. Clearing his mind, Lloyd reached inside, searching for that spark of inner spirit. Time appeared to slow as he made contact. The energy surged up from deep inside him, spreading through his body and into his limbs. Still running at full speed, Lloyd pushed off the earth with a great heave. His body rocketed forward, faster than he had ever flown before.

Despite its great speed, he was now closing in on the Barghest. Somehow, the demon must have sensed his approach. It skidded to a halt and whirled to face him, its jaws salivating and snapping as he flew directly toward them. Lloyd held his blades ready, preparing for the worst when a sudden glint caught his eye. A flash of silver came out of nowhere and landed right in the demon's eye! The beast yelped in pain and pawed at the knife hilt that stuck out from its bleeding socket.

Seeing his chance to end this, Lloyd dropped the other blade and grasped his star metal sword with both hands. Ten feet... five feet... he lifted the blade to strike when the demon lashed out with its other paw. Lloyd felt searing pain slice rake his side. He nearly flinched, but willed himself to ignore the pain, swinging downward with all his might.

The young warrior unleashed a devastating blow that caught the demon in mid-torso. The black blade sliced through flesh and bone alike, passing unobstructed through the creature's body. Then he was past the beast, hurtling through the empty air. A blood curdling scream erupted behind him, reverberating all around the clearing.

Lloyd slowed down and curled into a tight ball. He hit the ground and rolled over three times before finally coming to a stop. He immediately leapt to his feet and spun around, his black blade held ready in front of him, but there was no need. The Barghest lay cloven in two, thick black blood seeping from either half of its huge, dark torso.

Lloyd stood up and breathed a sigh of relief. *It's over. I killed it! I killed the Barghest—a demon nonetheless. First a giant serpent and now a demon.* Lloyd could just imagine the look on his father's face when he told him. His dad would be proud. Even his brother, Pallas, would not be able to make light of this. No more calling him "little Lloyd," or telling him to "get the lead out, iron pants."

Lloyd was startled out of his reverie when Seth abruptly appeared out of thin air. He stood over the demon's cloven torso, the corner of his mouth upturned. Lloyd grinned at the halfling. "You couldn't have timed that better."

Seth's smirk grew even wider. "What can I say? I'm that good."

"Just don't let it go to your head," came a voice from behind them. Lloyd spun around to see Glo walking toward them. "That goes for both of you. You're both good, but we got lucky this time. In a head to head battle, we would not have fared so well."

Glo's words brought Lloyd back to reality. He was right—they had gotten lucky. Seth, however, was not so willing to concede the point. The halfling folded his arms across his chest and fixed the wizard with an acid stare.

"Speak for yourself. I know I'm that good."

Glo shook his head, the trace of a smile gracing his lips. "I guess there's no point in telling you to be more careful in the future?"

"None whatsoever."

Seth's expression did not change. Glo cast a quick glance at Lloyd, but the young man knew by now there was no arguing with Seth. Lloyd merely shrugged in response. Glo let out a deep sigh and turned his attention to the dead demon. "The real question is, is this the same Barghest that we saw at Cape Marlin? And if so, what is it doing here in the Darkwoods?"

A sudden chill ran up Lloyd's spine. "I'd hate to think there are more than one of those out there."

"Well, either way, it was waiting for someone," Seth interjected. "That was a very deliberate ambush this thing had set up, from both sides of the river at the same time."

That's right! In the heat of battle, Lloyd had forgotten all about the other bank. Now he suddenly remembered Ruka and Donnie had both headed over there.

Glo mirrored his thoughts. "We should probably check on the others."

"You two go ahead," Seth told them. "I'm going to search the bodies and see if I can find any clues as to what these things were doing here."

"Good idea," Glo agreed.

Lloyd nodded to the halfling. "We'll see you back on the ship."

Glo and Lloyd took a few steps back. As Lloyd grabbed onto his cloak, the elven wizard cast his flying spell.

"*Fugere*," they both said simultaneously.

As the duo lifted into the air, Lloyd peered down at Seth. The halfling was already busily rummaging through the demon's corpse.

16
BLACK GEM

I guess my minion must have failed. No Matter.
Now you shall be mine

When Lloyd and Glo reached the other bank, they found Donnie and Ruka surrounded by the bodies of more goblins and one large mountain troll. The two of them were physically fine, but for some reason Donnie seemed rather nervous. Ruka, on the other hand, was uncharacteristically pleasant. Lloyd was not sure exactly what was going on with them, but he had to admit he was impressed with how they had handled themselves. "Nice job you two. We had a run-in with a troll back in the Bendenwoods. They're not all that easy to kill."

Donnie motioned toward the young teen. "It was all Ruka. If she hadn't been here, I'd still be running that thing around."

Ruka punched the elf in the arm then smiled sweetly up at him. "Donnie, you say the nicest things."

Donnie grabbed his arm. "Thanks," he managed, half-smiling, half-grimacing.

Lloyd wasn't all that surprised. The Greymantle sisters were definitely more than they seemed. He had witnessed shape-shifting, feats of strength, and near invulnerability. Add to that Ruka's sword and the defeat of a mountain troll was not all that farfetched. Lloyd grinned at the pair. "Either way, it's still impressive."

"So what about the other side?" Donnie asked.

Lloyd told them about their run in with the goblins and the Barghest, but didn't go into detail about how they killed the demon. When he was done, Glo chimed in.

"Lloyd's being modest. He cleaved that Barghest right in two."

Ruka turned to Lloyd and eyed him up and down, her expression one of clear respect. "Now that's impressive."

Lloyd felt the heat rise in his face. "It was more luck than anything else."

"Perhaps," Donnie interjected, "but I know a thing or two about swordsmanship, and it takes more than just strength to cleave an opponent like that."

Now Lloyd's cheeks were downright burning. Thankfully, Glo picked that moment to change the subject.

"Well, if we are done here, we should probably take down that chain across the river. If we're lucky, it might not have damaged the boat."

The foursome headed down to the riverbank. It wasn't long before they found the end of the thick chain wound around a large tree. Between Lloyd and Ruka, they were able to detach it and clear the way for the *Rusty Nail*. Ruka swam out to check the hull of the vessel while Lloyd and Glo flew Donnie back to the ship. When they landed on the deck, Seth was already there, wrapped in a towel and drying off.

"A little warning next time before you cut the chain," the halfling admonished.

"Don't tell me you're afraid of a little water?" Donnie teased.

Seth glared at the slight elf. "Better than being afraid of a little girl."

As if on cue, Ruka called out from over the side, "The hull's fine!"

Donnie nearly jumped out of his skin. Lloyd and the others

chuckled as they strode over to the railing. Ruka tread water just off the starboard side of the vessel.

"You coming back on board?" Donnie yelled down to her.

"Nah, I'm going to take a look upstream and make sure there are no more surprises waiting for us."

"I'll send Raven with you," Glo called to her.

"Thanks!"

Ruka gave them a quick grin then shifted shape, her form replaced by a white-tailed hawk hovering just above the water line. She was quickly joined by Glo's black bird, and the two took off, spiraling up into the sky. The others watched as they rose upward then shot out toward the west, following the river upstream. Once Ruka was out of sight, Donnie filled the others in on the details of their battle with the troll. He seemed especially concerned with her amazing feat of strength. When Donnie was done, he stared at the others expectantly. Lloyd merely shrugged, being no stranger to the girl's abilities.

Seth's response was equally nonchalant. "And..."

A short laugh escaped Elladan's lips. Aksel's expression was impassive. Alana gazed at him with keen sympathy. Glo and Elistra exchanged a meaningful glance.

"You knew!" Donnie pointed an accusing finger around the group. "You all knew about this!"

"Duh," Seth responded, clearly enjoying Donnie's chagrin.

Glo was a bit more sympathetic. "Well, it's not that we really know anything..."

Donnie spun toward the wizard, his eyes narrowing. "But you suspected... so what else aren't you telling me?"

After a moment silence, Elistra stepped forward and placed a gentle hand on Donnie's cheek. An enigmatic smile crossed her lips. "Oh, Donatello. I'm afraid you still have much to learn."

She patted him lightly, then turned and walked away. Donnie's eyes followed her, his hand rising to the spot where she had just touched his cheek. Alana stepped forward next and took him by the arm. "I think you and I need to have a little talk."

As Alana led Donnie away, their conversation trailed off.

"You need to let this go," Alana was saying.

"But... it isn't... natural..."

"Why? Because she's a girl?"

"No... no... that's not what I meant at all..."

Seth snickered.

"That's a battle he ain't gonna win," Elladan said, gazing around at the others with a knowing grin.

Lloyd did not envy Donnie, having had his share of being "talked to" in the past. It was usually from his sister, Thea, his mom too busy with town business, experiments, and magic school. Although his brother Pallas seemed to relish pointing out his shortcomings as well. Lloyd had always tried to accept their "advice" graciously, but the words still stung. It had left him with a burning desire to prove himself. In fact, it was one of the driving forces behind him setting out on his own.

"Coming, Glo?"

Elistra's voice stirred Lloyd from his thoughts. The seeress stood by the doorway to the cabins, looking expectantly at the wizard.

Glo arched an eyebrow. "Where am I going?"

Elistra's eyes danced with amusement. "Why to rest, silly. After all, you did just use some powerful spells."

Glo's brow furrowed. "Yes, I guess I did."

"Well, come on then." Elistra motioned for him to join her.

Glo glanced around at the others, shrugged, then strode across the deck toward the seeress. As the door to the below decks closed behind them, Seth snickered and Elladan let out a short laugh.

"That's two," the bard commented.

Lloyd started to laugh, but stopped as a sharp pain lanced through his side. It was the spot where the Barghest had caught him. Aksel was immediately by his side.

"Looks like you caught a nasty wound there. Let's get that healed up." Aksel motioned for Lloyd to follow him as he too strode toward the doorway to the cabins.

"Alright."

Lloyd let out a deep sigh as he fell in behind Aksel. He couldn't believe the demon's claws had cut clean through his new chainmail. In truth, Lloyd had been lucky. He would have been gutted if he had been wearing his old leathers. Pallas and Thea had always said he was reckless. Perhaps they were right.

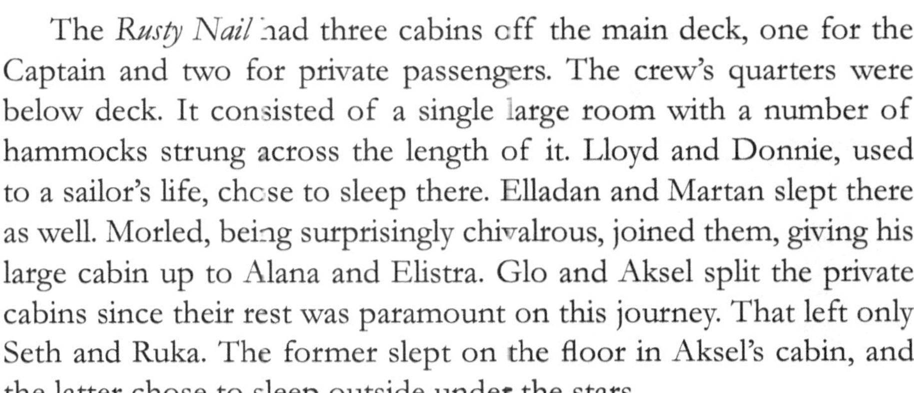

The *Rusty Nail* had three cabins off the main deck, one for the Captain and two for private passengers. The crew's quarters were below deck. It consisted of a single large room with a number of hammocks strung across the length of it. Lloyd and Donnie, used to a sailor's life, chose to sleep there. Elladan and Martan slept there as well. Morled, being surprisingly chivalrous, joined them, giving his large cabin up to Alana and Elistra. Glo and Aksel split the private cabins since their rest was paramount on this journey. That left only Seth and Ruka. The former slept on the floor in Aksel's cabin, and the latter chose to sleep outside under the stars.

When Glo reached his cabin, he found he was not very tired. It was too soon after battle, and he could still feel the adrenaline pumping through his veins, but Elista insisted that he rest. She sat down on the bed in front of him, legs crossed, and forced him to do the same thing. He sat there, facing the seeress, his legs bent in front of him in what he found to be the most uncomfortable position possible. Elistra, her eyes closed, chanted to him.

"Now breathe in... and out... in... and out."

Glo tried to follow along, but could not see how she relaxed with her legs all bent up like this. He was about to say something when they heard a knock at the door.

"Who's there?" Glo called.

The door opened and Seth strode into the room. When he saw the two of them, his mouth curved into a lopsided smile. "Hope I'm not interrupting anything."

Glo glared at him. "Really? Like this?" He pointed to the awkward way they were sitting.

Seth's smirk widened. "You never know—some people have strange habits."

Elistra spun her head around to look at the halfling. "Was there a reason for your visit?" she asked pointedly. "After all, I am trying to get him to rest."

Seth appeared completely unaffected by her sarcastic tone. "Yeah, actually, there is something I need to show you—both of you."

Glo's patience was wearing thin. "Well, what is it?"

"Not here. Meet me over in my cabin in a few minutes." Before Glo could say another word, Seth spun around and strode out of the room, closing the door behind him.

Glo turned to Elistra. "Now what do you think that was about?"

"We'll find out soon enough," she responded in an insufferably patient tone. "Now we still have a few minutes. Try to relax. Breathe in... and out... in... and out..."

When they arrived at Seth's cabin, Aksel and Lloyd were already there. The little cleric had just finished healing Lloyd's wound. The young warrior picked up his chain-mail shirt off the bed and held it out in front of him. There was a foot-long gash in the links just under the left armpit. Glo gulped. That had been from a grazing blow. He couldn't imagine what the damage would have been if the demon had really connected.

"Don't worry, Lloyd, we'll have that mended in no time," Aksel was saying.

"So what'd I miss?" Elladan's voice came from behind them. Elistra and Glo moved out of the doorway, making room for him.

"Not much," Glo said. "We just got here ourselves."

"Where's Donnie?" Seth asked.

Elladan let out a short laugh. "Alana's still giving him a piece of her mind. I didn't have the heart to disturb them."

Seth shrugged. "No matter, we can fill him in later."

Glo's eyes narrowed. "So what's with all the secrecy?"

Seth's voice grew quiet. "I found an interesting item on our demon friend. I thought it might be best to check it out away from prying eyes."

"He means Morled," Elladan translated for them.

Seth gave the bard a short nod then reached into a pouch on his belt. When he drew his hand back, there was a black gem in his palm. It was rather large, easily the size of the halfling's fist. There was also something strange about the stone. Despite its dark color, a light emanated from it—a light that pulsed like a heartbeat. A sudden gasp caused Glo to spin around. Elistra stood there, her hand over her mouth. She flushed when she saw them all staring at her.

"Sorry. It's just... I wasn't expecting such a dark aura."

Aksel was the first to answer. "No, that's quite understandable. There is something not quite right about this gem. I wonder..." After a moment's hesitation, the little cleric cast a quick spell. A dark glow began to emanate outward from the gem. It grew until it radiated a good two feet in all directions.

Seth snorted. "Humph, definitely evil."

Elladan turned to Glo. "Can you identify it?"

Glo reached for the gem, but was stopped by a light hand on his arm. He turned to see Elistra holding on to him, her brow furrowed.

"Be careful with that."

Glo raised a single eyebrow.

"I sense more than just a simple gem," she explained further.

A slight smile spread across Glo's lips. It was not the first "evil" gem they had come across. He was about to tell her the story of the gem they found underneath the Ruins on Stone Hill when Aksel interrupted him.

"Hold on a minute."

Glo watched as the little cleric spun his arms in an unfamiliar pattern. As the spell released, a white circle formed around the entire cabin. It lingered there for a few moments, then faded from view. Aksel gave Glo a brief nod. "There, that should help to protect against evil influences."

Glo was impressed. Aksel must have just added that spell to his repertoire during their brief stay in Vermoorden. Seth stepped forward and held out the gem. Despite Aksel's assurances, Glo still felt uneasy taking the stone from the halfling's grasp. The gem was surprisingly cool to the touch, its surface perfectly smooth. Glo reached into his pouch, pulled out a small vial, and drank the contents. Holding his empty hand over the gem, Glo spoke a single word, "*Eandem.*"

A faint yellow glow intermixed with the black one surrounding the crystal, then quickly faded. The elven wizard fixed his eyes on the gem, staring deep into its crystal facets. Nothing happened at first, but abruptly the facets appeared to waver and an image appeared inside the gem. It was fuzzy at first, but it slowly cleared and Glo found himself looking into a woman's face. She had pale, porcelain skin, framed by long, raven black hair with deep brown eyes, almost bordering on black. She had a thin nose, extremely high cheekbones and blood red lips. This woman had a very strong demeanor—she radiated power—a lot of power. She had not been looking his way initially, but Glo froze as she turned toward him. He heard a cold voice in his mind.

Did you find them?

Who? Glo thought before he could stop himself.

The dark woman's eyes narrowed, her gaze growing even more intense. *Oh, you are one of them. I guess my minion must have failed. No matter. Now you shall be mine.*

Glo felt a sudden pressure on his forehead, accompanied by soft words in a language he did not know. There was a dark edge to those words, repeated over and over in his mind. The pressure built swiftly, clouding his vision, and making him dizzy. Glo tried to fight it at first, but the pressure was so intense, and the words so cruel, that his concentration wavered. Just when he thought his head was going to explode, a hand grabbed his chin and turned him away.

That will be enough! A second voice resonated through his mind. It sounded like Elistra, but this voice was also filled with power.

Everything went silent, but Glo could still feel the pressure. Yet there was something else now—he had the sense of a great struggle, as if two powerful combatants were waging a mental war over his mind. Abruptly the struggle stopped, and the silence was shattered by a piercing scream. Glo tried to cover his ears, but it was to no avail. Thankfully, the scream died swiftly. What followed was a wail in that first cold voice. *This is... not... over...*

Those last words faded as if said from a great distance. The pressure had disappeared, and his vision was clearing. Glo found himself staring into a familiar pair of violet eyes. Elistra held his head gently between her hands, his own hands still clutching his ears.

"Are you alright?"

Glo turned to see Aksel staring at him, his eyes wide with fear. Lloyd and Elladan wore similar expressions. Even Seth showed signs of concern.

Elistra answered for him. "He will be. Just give him a minute."

Glo grabbed her hands, gently removed them from his face, then walked over to Aksel's bed and sat down. Elistra came with him, still holding onto his hands.

The others gathered around as Glo explained what had happened. He described the dark woman, the voice in his mind, and the pressure on his skull. He left out the part about Elistra's voice and the power struggle he had sensed, letting the others think that Aksel's spell had broken the connection. Yet, as powerful as the dark woman was, Elistra had proved a match for her. Even counting the spell's assistance, she was still far more powerful than she let on. Glo did not want to question her in front of the others, but he would definitely confront her the next time they were alone.

When Glo was finished, Seth was the first to speak. "Well, that answers that."

Lloyd eyed the halfling curiously. "Answers what?"

A familiar twist spread across Seth's lips as he peered up at the tall man. "Whether the river trap was set specifically for us."

Seth's statement sent cold shivers up Glo's spine. The mental attack had distracted him, but now that Seth pointed it out, there was no mistaking the dark woman's intent. She had specifically sent the Barghest, the troll, and even the goblins looking for them. It was a sobering thought that she could muster such powerful enemies to her side. Strangely, Elladan's response was the exact opposite of Glo's. The bard let out a short laugh.

"Looks like our little victory in Ravenford put a real crimp in their plans."

"And made us a target," Seth agreed.

Lloyd's eyes moved from Seth to Glo, his brow furrowed. "Do we have any idea who this woman is?"

Glo shook his head. There had been no indication of who she was, not even a name.

"Well, whoever she is, she did send a Barghest after us..." Aksel began.

"...and how much you want to bet it was the same one from Cape Marlin," Seth continued.

"...which would make her part of the Serpent Cult," Lloyd finished the thought. Despite that realization, the young man still wore a puzzled expression. He shifted his gaze to Glo. "Back at Maltar's, you said controlling demons wasn't easy."

Glo's lips tightened as he recalled the large summoning circle in Maltar's home—it was made specifically to imprison demons. Summoning one and holding it was hard enough, but controlling one while it was roaming free in the world was something else entirely. "It isn't. This woman must be very powerful to control a demon such as a Barghest."

"Almost like a Thrall Master," Elladan said speculatively.

Glo's eyes darted to the bard, another chill racing up his spine. *Did I just have an encounter with a Thrall Master?*

Seth folded his arms across his chest and let out a derisive snort. "Thrall Master, or not, she knows we beat her demon. It doesn't take a genius to figure out she'll be sending something just as bad our way—or worse."

Glo spiked an eyebrow. He did not relish the thought of facing another demon. Aksel, as usual, was pragmatic about the situation. "Well then, it would be best to be on our guard from here on out. In the meantime, we can't just leave this gem just lying around."

"I could crush it," Lloyd offered.

Elistra fixed her eyes on the young man and pursed her lips, her tone tentative at best. "You might find that more difficult than you think."

"Do you know something more about this gem?" Seth asked. He stared intently at the seeress, his eyes filled with suspicion.

Elistra faced the halfling, seemingly unfazed by his glare. "No, not this particular gem, but I've seen ones like it. They are used to locate, communicate with, and control beings over great distances."

Glo's eyes suddenly went wide. *That's it! That's how she controlled the Barghest—through the gem.* Perhaps this dark woman was not quite as powerful as he originally thought.

"Locating and communicating don't necessarily sound evil," Elladan said.

"You're right," Elistra agreed. "The gems themselves aren't exactly evil, but they do resonate the power of their current owner. As you've already surmised, this one is owned by a decidedly evil being. Unfortunately, destroying it could create a psionic backlash on anyone nearby."

Lloyd's mouth hung partially open. "Whoa. Is that as bad as it sounds?"

Glo, stirred from his thoughts, answered the young man. "Let's just say it could hurt your mind as much as your body."

"Yes." Elistra gave the wizard a short nod. "And if the owner of this gem is as powerful as I believe, the psionic backlash would be deadly."

The blood drained from Lloyd's face. "Oh. That would be bad."

Seth chortled at the young man's reaction. "Thank you, Captain Obvious."

As Lloyd gave the halfling a dark look, Elladan weighed back in to the conversation. "So then we don't destroy it, but will it work across dimensions?"

Elistra's eyes widened, her nose wrinkling as she pondered the bard's question. After a few moments of silence, she finally answered. "It might not, but I am not completely certain."

"Sounds like it would be worth a try," Elladan responded while at the same time removing what appeared to be a common cloth sack from his belt. He opened up the sack and held it out toward Glo. "Put it in here."

Though the sack appeared plain, Glo immediately recognized what it was. Elladan held in his hands a *Portal Bag*, a magical item that acted like a small portal to another plane. The bag was actually larger inside than out, so it could hold items far bigger than it would otherwise appear.

Aksel seemed impressed with the bard's plan. "Very nice, Elladan. You pick that up at Haltan's?"

Elladan tilted his head toward the little cleric and gave him a quasi-smile. "Sure did. Got it off him for next to nothing."

"I'm sure he was less than happy about that," Seth noted in a dry tone.

Elladan responded with a curt laugh. "He was positively miserable about it."

"Good," Seth said, a satisfied smile spreading across the halfling's face.

Glo slowly reached out, held the gem over the bag, and after a moment's pause, dropped it. The gem fell through the opening and then disappeared from sight. Glo suddenly realized he had been holding his breath the entire time. Despite the fact that the connection with the dark woman had been broken, just holding onto the gem had made him nervous. Now he let out a huge sigh. Elistra, still next to him, placed a comforting hand on his shoulder.

Meanwhile, Elladan closed the drawstrings tight and put the bag away. "Well, that's that."

"We shall see soon enough," Elistra said under her breath.

17
TEMPTRESS

The nymph hung on his shoulder, her body
practically wrapped around him

Ruka returned late in the afternoon. She had scoured the river a few miles ahead, but found no more signs of goblins, demons, or trolls. When night fell, Lloyd and Donnie helped Morled pull in the sails and drop anchor. They kept the ship in the center of the river, as far as possible from either bank.

Martan, Ruka, and Seth took turns at watch in the crow's nest, yet the night passed uneventfully. The Darkwoods remained quiet, the only sounds being those of crickets and the occasional nocturnal forest creature. The only source of light they saw was the silvery moon as it passed overhead on its journey across the nighttime sky.

The next day, everyone was up early, with the exception of Ruka. She had taken the last watch, and it was now her turn to sleep. Not one to sleep indoors, Ruka curled up silently in the crow's nest next to a nervous Martan. With no room in the crow's nest, Seth sat in the rigging just below, carefully scouring the river and banks ahead. The sun had barely risen when they weighed anchor and got underway.

Since their encounter the previous day, and the incident with the dark lady in the gem, the companions chose to be more cautious. Not traveling at night would cost them an extra day, but it was better than not arriving at the monolith at all.

Down on main deck, Lloyd sparred with Alana. Warrior and knight danced back and forth, Alana matching Lloyd's strength and agility with experience and skill. Aksel knelt on a crate just outside the door to the cabins, his eyes closed as he offered up his morning devotion. Elistra and Glo sat opposite the little cleric, on the same two crates they had occupied the day before. Elistra, eyes also closed, sat cross-legged, deep in meditation.

Glo, having just finished the morning review of his spell-book, did not wish to disturb either of his friends, so he quietly got up and went to join Elladan and Donnie. The duo stood by the rail, Elladan taking pleasure in needling his elven friend. "So have you decided?"

"Decided what?" Donnie responded, his shoulders taut and his tone more than a little defensive.

One corner of Elladan's mouth raised slightly as he placed a hand on Donnie's shoulder. "Why, which girlfriend you are going to pick."

Donnie's jaw tightened. "She is not my girlfriend!" he blurted out just a bit too emphatically. Donnie immediately covered his mouth and cast a quick glance over either shoulder.

Glo found it difficult to keep a straight face as he strode up to join the two. "I'm sure Alana will be sorry to hear that."

Donnie spun to face the wizard, his head cocked, a sarcastic smile across his lips. "I didn't mean Alana."

"Ah, I'm glad you clarified that." Glo nodded, the corners of his mouth upturning despite his best efforts.

"But the little one wants to be," Elladan prodded.

Donnie's eyes swept from Glo to Elladan, the slight elf shaking his head. "She is way too young for me. Don't you two have any morals?"

"At least as much as you," Elladan responded, a quasi-smile finally breaking out across his lips.

Donnie glared at the bard, causing Elladan to burst out into fits of laughter. The sound was a nice change of pace after all that had occurred yesterday, and Glo found himself joining in. Donnie glowered at the two of them, but after a few moments, he too began to laugh.

"Cut out that racket!" Elistra's voice rang out from across the deck. "Some of us are trying to be productive!"

The trio quelled their laughter, although snickers and giggles continued to escape their lips. Glo cast a quick glance toward Elistra, but the seeress still sat cross-legged on her crate, her eyes firmly shut. Abruptly he felt a hand on his shoulder. Glo spun his head to see Elladan leaning in close. "Looks like you've got a live one there, my friend."

Glo turned his gaze back toward the spirited seeress, the warmth rising in his cheeks. "You could say that."

Donnie strode up beside him. "It reminds me of this one time..."

Whatever he was going to say was drowned out by a cry from above.

"Holy dragon dung!"

The deck grew quiet as all eyes turned upward. Martan stood in the crow's nest, his gaze fixed on the southern shore. The archer's face was so red that you could see it from the deck below. Seth, standing next to Martan, pointed toward a spot on the south bank as he called to the folks below. "Umm, guys, you're going to want to see this."

Glo, his curiousity piqued, followed Seth's finger toward the tall trees along the shoreline. He spied nothing at first, until his eyes honed in on the largest of the trees a short distance up the bank. A thick branch jutted well out over the waters—and upon that branch stood a fair-skinned woman with long, flowing auburn hair. Strange as it was to see her there, what really threw him off was the fact that she was completely naked. Glo's cheeks felt on fire as he stared at the nude woman.

"Oh, my," the words slipped from Donnie's mouth.

"You can say that again," Elladan agreed.

Glo was stirred from his reverie by a loud noise that sounded like a slap. He spun around and saw Lloyd holding the back of his head.

Alana, next to him, folded her arms across her chest. "What would that nice Andrella say if she saw you gawking like that?"

"Sorry," Lloyd managed, his face turning a bright shade of scarlet.

"You're lucky it wasn't you sparring with her," Elladan murmured to Donnie.

Alana's gaze shifted their way. "What was that, Elladan?"

Elladan seemed totally unphased by the lady knight's ire. "Oh, nothing. I was just commenting that she is probably a woodland nymph."

Alana's eyes narrowed. "Yes, I'm sure you were."

Aksel and Elistra strode up to the railing. The little cleric's expression was impassive. "She may very well be, but we should probably make sure."

"I'll go and check," Elladan offered, a bent smile spreading across his lips.

Elistra regarded the bard for a moment, then her eyes shifted to Glo. He could feel the intensity of her gaze—it was as if she were trying to bore into his mind. The experience was rather sobering, and it shocked Glo back to his senses. He turned to Elladan. "Just be careful. With all that's happened so far, she may not be what she seems."

Elladan nodded. "Trust me, I'll be careful. And anyway, Lloyd can come with me for protection." He waved a hand toward the young man.

"Sure," Lloyd responded. A smile crossed his lips, but then his eyes fell on Alana and it abruptly faded.

Alana, her lips pressed tight, stared from Elladan, to Lloyd, her eyes finally settling on Donnie. "What? Don't you want to go along, too?"

Her tone was mild, but there was an intensity in her eyes that spoke all too clearly how she felt about the matter. Donnie immediately picked up her intent. He raised up his hands in front of him and responded perhaps just a bit too dramatically. "What? Me? No. I'm just fine right here."

Alana continued to stare at him, her eyes narrowed and a frown across her brow. Elistra had watched the entire exchange with a thinly veiled smile. Alana turned to the seeress, shook her head, and said a single word. "Men."

Elistra gave her female compatriot a knowing smile, then her eyes shifted back to Glo. Her gaze seemed merely curious this time, but the young elf felt himself flush once again. Alana and Elistra were not wrong; they were all acting like a bunch of schoolboys. You would think none of them had ever seen a naked female before. Glo let out a heavy sigh, then turned to Elladan. "Whenever you're ready."

"Lloyd?" Elladan asked the young man.

Lloyd briefly adjusted his sword hilts, then nodded.

"Ready," Elladan said.

As Lloyd invoked his flying cloak, Glo cast the same spell on the bard. The duo then launched themselves into the air. Over in the trees, the woodland nymph suddenly climbed up off the branch and disappeared into the forest. The bard and warrior flew across the river and into the forest after the nymph.

"Be careful!" Elistra called after the duo. She turned to the others, a deep frown across her brow. "I don't like this."

An empty feeling grew in the pit of Glo's stomach. "Perhaps we should wake Ruka and send her after them?"

Donnie shook his head. "She only got to sleep a short while ago."

"Let's give it a few minutes then," Aksel decided.

Donnie helped Morled bring the Rusty Nail to a stop. By the time they had reined in the sails, Martan called down from above, "I see them! They're coming back!" There was a short pause, then he added, "They're bringing company!"

Glo leaned out over the railing and peered downstream. Their two companions were indeed flying back toward them, except that Lloyd carried the nymph in his arm.

"I don't like this at all," Elistra repeated, the tension in her voice almost palpable.

"Agreed," Aksel said, his expression stony.

The pit in Glo's stomach grew as his companions approached. After what seemed like an eternity, Elladan and Lloyd finally landed in the center of the deck. As the young warrior put the nymph down, Elladan strode quickly over to them.

"What's going on?" Aksel asked in a soft voice.

Elladan leaned in close and whispered, "When we approached the nymph, she cast a charm spell on us. Thankfully, I was unaffected, but Lloyd fell under it. I tried a counter-spell, but it didn't work. So I suggested we fly back and introduce her to all our friends, hoping one of you could break the spell. Luckily she agreed."

Glo glanced over to where Lloyd stood with the nymph. The young warrior remained perfectly still, a blank expression on his face. The nymph hung on his shoulder, her body practically wrapped around him.

"Maybe I should go over there and slap some sense into him again," Alana said, her ire rising once more.

Glo shook his head. "It won't help if he's charmed."

Elistra stared intently at the creature, her eyes narrowed and her brow deeply furrowed. "There's something off about that creature. I'm certain she is not what she appears to be."

"Well, there's a way to find out and snap Lloyd out of his spell at the same time," Aksel said quietly. "If one of you can keep her distracted, I can dispel any magical influences in the area before she realizes what is happening."

"I'll keep her occupied!" Donnie offered, perhaps a bit too eagerly.

Alana cast a dark look at the elf, then turned her back and stormed away. Donnie's face fell. He started to follow her, but Elladan reached out and placed a restraining hand on his friend's shoulder. "First things first."

Donnie let out a short sigh, then spun around and followed the bard to greet the naked nymph.

"Aren't you going, too?" Elistra asked Glo, with just a trace of amusement in her tone.

Glo had to admit, the nymph was very alluring—it would be easy to succumb to her physical charms. However, that is not what attracted him to the opposite sex, or at least not solely, he corrected himself. "No. I'm fine where I am."

"Good," she said softly, stepping closer and putting her arm through his.

While Elladan and Donnie approached the nymph, Aksel headed in the opposite direction. He stopped next to Alana, with his back to them, and covertly prepared the spell which would free Lloyd.

"Good morning, my lady," Donnie addressed the woodland creature. "Welcome aboard the Rusty Nail."

The nymph slowly unwrapped herself from Lloyd and sauntered up to the slight elf, her every move practically dripping with sensuality. Long auburn hair flowed downward over the pale skin of her shoulders, just barely covering the roundness of her breasts. A pair of smoldering blue eyes fixed themselves on Donnie, as the she reached out a finger and placed it on Donnie's chest. Those pouty pink lips parted, a breathy voice passing between them. "Is this your ship?"

Glo could hear Donnie gulp all the way from the other side of the deck. "Um, no, my lady, it is not. Tell me, what's a beautiful girl like you doing in a place like this?"

From someone else, that might have sounded cliché, but it was obvious from Donnie's tone that he was trying to be amusing. His ploy worked—the nymph giggled, then responded in the same breathy voice. "I was wandering around the forest all by myself. I was rather lonely, and wanted some company." She emphasized that last word. "Then I saw your boat. I was so happy when these handsome men flew over to get me." All during her speech, she continued to run her finger around Donnie's chest.

Glo heard a decided "Humph" from the deck behind him. Alana was obviously not buying any of the nymph's story. Donnie, however, was getting more than he bargained for. The nymph's forwardness was causing even the worldly elf to blush. Donnie reached down and gently grabbed her hand, carefully moving it away from his chest. "I'm just glad we could be of assistance, my lady."

"Who's your new friend, Donnie?" a familiar voice interrupted them.

Glo glanced up and saw Ruka perched on the lowest yardarm of the mainmast. Her expression was a mask of calm, but Glo suspected she was seething underneath.

Donnie spun around to face the teen, his eyes wide. "Oh... Ruka! I... didn't see you up there."

"That's because your eyes were focused elsewhere," Alana called from across the deck.

Donnie's gaze shifted to the lady knight, little beads of sweat forming on his brow. "I was just greeting our visitor."

"I'm sure that's what you were doing," Alana replied, her voice practically dripping with acid.

The tension in the air was almost palpable. Unfortunately, the exchange between the two women and Donnie was drawing too much attention to Alana, who stood dangerously close to Aksel. Glo nearly said something, but thankfully Elladan had the presence of mind to step in.

"Well, it is a pleasure to have you here, my lady," he addressed the nymph. "I am so glad you took up my suggestion to come and visit us." He executed a graceful bow, finishing with a partial smile.

The nymph turned toward the bard. "You are indeed the charmer," she responded in her breathy voice. She sauntered forward and placed a finger on his chest. "And here I thought you didn't like me."

She stared up at him, a seductive smile on her lips, and walked her fingers up his chest. Somehow, Elladan managed to maintain his cool—he grabbed her hand and took it gently into his own. "Now, whatever gave you that idea?"

The nymph never got to answer. As her lips parted, a brilliant circle of violet light engulfed the entire deck around them. It swiftly faded, but so did Lloyd's blank stare—the young man blinking his eyes rapidly as if awakening from a deep sleep. At the same time, the creature in front of Elladan began to change. Her hair and complexion remained the same, but her eyes darkened and her lips turned blood red. The most striking change, however, was the two tiny horns that now stuck out from her forehead, and the bat-like wings that protruding from her back.

"Succubus!" Elistra practically hissed the word.

Glo's eyes went wide, his heart suddenly beating fast in his chest. A succubus was another demon—not as strong as a Barghest, but deadly in their own right. A succubus charmed its victim with its seductive powers, luring them into acts of passion. Once there, it drained them of their very life force. This was not a creature to be trifled with. Unfortunately, with Elladan and Donnie in the way, Glo did not have a clear shot at it. Elladan, now seeing what he was dealing with, dropped the demon's hand and took a long step back.

"What's the matter?" the succubus said, her voice huskier, yet still breathy. "Don't you find me attractive anymore?"

Elladan attempted to recover—he stopped backing up, once again flashing her his half-smile. "Oh, but I do."

The succubus stepped forward and poked the bard in the chest, her dark lips pouty as she did so. "I... don't... believe you." Before Elladan could respond, the demoness whirled around toward Donnie, her voice taking on a seductive tone. "You do, don't you?"

Donnie's face went abruptly blank. When he responded, his voice was wooden. "I do, milady."

"Then protect me," she said, stepping away from Elladan. Donnie drew his rapier and pointed it menacingly at his old friend.

Elladan threw up his hands and backed away even further. "Whoa now, Donnie. Watch where you point that pig sticker."

A sudden blur flew across the deck, a small figure slamming into the slight elf and knocking him over. The sword flew out of his hand and went clattering away across the wooden surface. Ruka then sat up and straddled Donnie, pinning him down by the arms.

"Got him!" she cried out, not taking her eyes off her captive. Under other circumstances, the sight would have been comical, but at this critical moment, it was anything but.

The demoness raised a blood-red, long nailed finger to her lips and tapped them slowly, her voice filled with feigned concern. "Oh, my, I seem to have lost my toy." She shrugged her bare shoulders, glancing around the deck with a smoldering stare. "No matter. It looks like there's plenty more here to play with."

Behind the creature, Lloyd had come to his senses, drawing his swords and taking a defensive stance. At the same moment, a voice rang out from the deck behind them.

"I'll give you something to play with, foul creature!"

Alana rushed past, directly for the succubus, brandishing her gleaming sword. The demoness's eyes went wide at the sight, immediately launching herself up and backwards, her bat-like wings fluttering wildly. For a moment Glo couldn't understand her reaction, then it dawned on him—Alana, a holy knight, carried a holy sword. While a normal blade wouldn't scratch a demon's thick hide, a holy sword would be deadly to it.

The succubus rose quickly off the deck, Alana just barely missing her. As she hovered out of reach, the succubus recovered her former composure. She addressed Alana, her tone dripping with disdain.

"Oh, and what do we have here? Ah, I see. It is a little girl playing knight. Be careful with that sword, little girl. I might just feed it back to you."

"You're welcome to come down and try!" Alana cried back, not phased in the least by the demon's hollow threat.

While the succubus had saved herself from Alana's wrath, she had made one fatal mistake—by hovering in the air, she had put herself directly in Glo's line of sight. Seth and Martan must have had similar thoughts, for in the seconds it took the wizard to weave his spell, a knife blade and two arrow shafts descended from above. Unfortunately, both the arrows and the blade bounced neatly off the creature's tough torso, leaving her completely unharmed. The demoness threw her head back and let out a wicked laugh.

Let's see her laugh at this, Glo thought. *"Pessulum Electrica."*

Glo let loose a bolt of lightning. In the blink of an eye, it arced upward the short distance to where the demoness hovered, striking her directly in her midsection. Arcs of electricity played across her body for a few moments, then abruptly winked out.

The demoness still hovered there, her wings beating slowly, without so much as a scratch on her body. Glo's eyes went wide when he realized what he had just done. Every novice knew that demons were immune to electricity. They had been ever since the Third Demon War some 6,000 years ago. Glo shook his head. Something was definitely wrong here—his mind felt as if it were in a fog.

The demoness eyed him with an amused expression. When she spoke, her voice was smug. "Trouble thinking? I seem to have that effect on people."

Glo grimaced, not knowing what to do. Without a clear head, he was useless. At that moment, a familiar form stepped forward and placed itself between him and the succubus. It was Elistra. The seeress stood with her hands on her hips, gazing up at the demoness defiantly. "Not all of us."

The succubus fixed her gaze on the seeress. The two locked eyes, glaring at each other with an inhuman intensity. Glo could almost feel the silent battle between the two, his skin nearly crawling from the psychic energy in the air. Demoness and seeress remained still in their soundless clash for what seemed like an eternity, until the succubus abruptly gasped and twisted her head away.

Elistra let out a soft laugh. "Don't feel too bad—your mistress didn't fare much better."

The demoness spun back to face Elistra, a hateful glare in her dark eyes. Glo, his head clearing, was completely impressed. Whatever Elistra had done, had broken the succubus's spell on him. It was the second time her gifts had saved him in the last 24 hours. The seeress gave Glo a brief smile, then continued to needle the demoness.

"So, let me guess, since the direct approach didn't work, your mistress sent you to seduce the males." Elistra brought a finger to her chin and examined the succubus critically. "Guess she couldn't find anything better on such short notice."

The demoness's eyes went blood red. "Take that back."

Elistra merely laughed in response. Alana stepped back and took a stance next to the seeress, brandishing her gleaming sword. "Why don't you come down here and make her?"

The succubus eyed that sword uncertainly. Once again, Glo was impressed. Together, these two women were able to do something the men couldn't—stand up to the demoness on both a mental and physical level. The question was how long this stalemate would go on. If the succubus was able to reassert her control over just one of them, the others would end up fighting their friend. Another spell, one that could actually hurt a demon, might tip the advantage their way.

Glo began to lift his arm when, without warning, an ethereal, glowing axe appeared in the air in front of the demoness. It caught her by surprise, swiping across her body and actually drawing blood!

Glo cast a glance behind him and saw Aksel wearing a fierce look of concentration, then a piercing scream drew his attention back to the succubus.

"Who dares!"

The creature touched the cut across her torso, then lifted her fingers to look at the blood on them. Her face took on a dreadful cast, then she opened her mouth, bared her fangs and hissed, all traces of her former beauty gone. A faint smile crossed Glo's lips. *Guess she's not untouchable after all. Well, let's add to that.* He raised his arm, pointed at the demoness, and spoke two words, *"Radius Ardens."*

A red-hot beam leapt from his fingertips and lanced upward toward the succubus, hitting her square in the chest. She let out another horrific scream as the skin blackened and sizzled between her semi-exposed breasts. The demoness stared down at her torso, the fire gone out of her eyes, her voice sounding hollow. "You burnt me. You actually burnt me." She peered down at the elven wizard, tears welling in her eyes. "Look what you did to my perfect skin."

For a moment, Glo felt sorry for the creature, but then he felt a soft hand on his shoulder and heard Elistra's voice whisper in his mind. *Don't fall for it.*

Glo glanced at the seeress and gave her a curt smile. Elistra winked back at him. The demoness, foiled yet again, fumed in the air above them. "I'll get you for this! I'll get all of you!"

Her large bat-like wings snapped apart and, with a strong flap, she launched herself at Glo, Elistra and Alana. The trio braced themselves, but at the last moment she swerved and headed straight for Lloyd. It was an incredible aerial maneuver, happening so fast that no one had time to react. The creature flew up to Lloyd and kissed him on the cheek before anyone could stop her. Lloyd's expression immediately went blank.

"Oh, no, not again," Elladan groaned.

"Oh, yes, again," the demoness swore in triumph. She flitted behind the tall man and said in a dulcet voice, "Fight for me."

"Yes, mistress," came the wooden reply. The young warrior marched forward, his face taking on a deadly cast.

Alana stepped in front of the others, her shield up and sword ready. "Stay behind me," she called over her shoulder.

Glo felt his own muscles tense as Lloyd advanced on Alana. This was no sparring session; Lloyd's expression was deadly serious.

Elladan mirrored his thoughts. "This isn't going to be pretty." A lute suddenly appeared in the bard's hand and he began playing madly. Glo felt an immediate lift in his spirits—even Alana seemed to stand taller, if that was at all possible.

"Just hold him off a minute," Aksel's voice rang out behind them.

A brief nod was all Alana had time for before Lloyd was on her. He was not holding back, his blades flashing almost faster than the eye could see. Alana did her best to keep up with him, deftly parrying his savage blows with her own sword and shield.

"Cut her, slash her," the succubus urged, her voice filled with malice.

Alana, refusing to attack, was pushed backward until, inevitably, a blow broke through the lady knight's guard. It was Lloyd's black blade. The star metal sword cut neatly through the thick steel gauntlet of her right arm, the deep wound seeping red liquid over Alana's silver armor. The succubus chortled with glee.

"Blood for blood," she cried exultantly.

Alana drew back, her shield in front of her, the gleaming sword barely clutched in her injured hand. Lloyd, not hesitating, renewed his assault, raining swift blows down on the lady knight. Alana struggled to fend off his attacks with her shield alone, but it was a losing battle. The others watched on, frozen in horror, until a sharp cry rang out across the deck.

"Lloyd, stop!"

Lloyd halted his attack, the young man's head spinning toward the source of that scream. All eyes turned to see Donnie prone on the deck, Ruka still on top of him, pinning him down. The slight elf's eyes were wide, his expression frantic. "Ruka, get off me—I have to help her!"

Yet before Ruka could move, his plea for help was answered with a white circle that fanned out across the deck. The brilliant light engulfed everyone, including Lloyd. The young man blinked, his expression changing as awareness returned to his previously vacant eyes.

The succubus let out a deep sigh. "Now why did you have to go and spoil all my fun?"

Lloyd's arms dropped to his side. "What just happened?" he asked groggily.

"She charmed you again," Elladan explained.

Lloyd grimaced, but then his face turned ashen as his gaze fell on Alana. Blood was now dripping freely from the lady knight's wound onto the deck.

"Did I do that?" he asked in a hushed tone.

"You did indeed," the demoness chortled behind him.

Moisture welled up in the young man's eyes, his voice cracking as he apologized. "I'm so—sorry."

A weak smile spread across Alana's lips, her face filling with compassion. "It's alright, Lloyd. You weren't yourself."

A wicked laugh rang out as the succubus launched herself back into the air. "That's quite magnanimous of you, lady knight. But now that you've spoiled all my fun, who's going to play with me?"

Anger welled up inside Glo. This had gone on long enough. "Oh, I'll play with you," he declared, lifting an arm toward the creature once more.

"So will I!" Lloyd said heatedly, the young man's face red with anger. Before anyone could stop him, Lloyd grabbed his cape and launched himself upward.

"Stay in the circle!" Aksel cried after him.

Lloyd nodded his understanding as he closed on the demoness. Unfortunately, Glo had to stay his hand as the young man flew up between him and the dark creature.

The succubus appeared amused, the trace of a smile gracing her lips as Lloyd drew even with her. She spoke to him in that same innocent voice she had used when they first met her. "Oh, so you're going to play with me now?"

Lloyd was far from in the mood to play, gritting his teeth as he responded to the foul creature. "You made me hurt my friend. Now I'm going to hurt you."

The demoness let out a wicked laughed. "You? Hurt me?"

Lloyd was done talking. In the wink of an eye, he lashed out with his black sword. The blade caught the demoness across the torso, crossing the cut that Aksel had previously made. The new wound began to bleed as well. The demoness wailed in response.

"You cut me! I can't believe you cut me!"

Her expression abruptly changed once more, and this time, long claws sprouted from her fingertips as she bared her fangs. The demoness then flung herself at Lloyd, but the young warrior had grown adept at airborne combat. As she swiped at him, he caught her clawed hand with his left blade, then spun his body around and sliced her again with his black blade. The sword crossed her skin, leaving yet another wound, this time along her side. The succubus rapidly withdrew, flitting back outside of the protective circle Aksel had conjured. Her face was now a mask of rage.

"You... will... all... die!" she declared vehemently.

As she hovered there fuming, she was besieged from four different directions: a knife from Seth, arrows from Martan, a beam of white light from Aksel, and another red hot ray from Glo. The arrows and knife both bounced off her tough skin, but the white light and red ray scorched her flesh.

The demoness arched her back up to the heavens and let out an ear-splitting scream. The companions winced from the shrill sound, covering their ears. The nearby trees were emptied of birds, the avian creatures scared away by the harsh cry of the wounded demoness. As the sound trailed off, the forest about them grew silent.

The succubus still hovered in the air above the ship, huffing with anger, her expression one of sheer hatred. Abruptly, she let out a second scream, this one as high-pitched as the first. Before they could recover, the demoness launched herself straight up at an incredible speed. She flew high up above the trees, circled once, and then disappeared into the forest to the south.

18
INAZUMA

Lloyd hovered high over the Rusty Nail, scanning the treetops for the demoness. Meanwhile down below, a familiar voice caught everyone's attention.

"Can I please get up now?"

Aksel's eyes swept back down toward the deck, where he saw Ruka still perched on top of Donnie. The slight elf wore a plaintive expression. The young girl's face reddened somewhat as her eyes fell on the elf upon whom she sat. "Oh, right," she responded, quickly getting up.

Donnie rose as well, dusting himself off. "So, last I remember, Elladan and I were talking to that succubus. Next thing I know, I'm lying on the deck with Ruka on top of me, and Lloyd's battling Alana. Anyone care to tell me what happened?"

Elladan fixed his elven friend with a bent smile. "Oh, nothing much—that succubus just took over your mind is all."

Donnie grinned sheepishly, a hand going to the back of his neck as his eyes turned toward Alana. "Ah, that explains it. I didn't hurt anyone, did I?"

The lady knight shook her head. "No, this wound isn't from you. Ruka stopped you before you could do any harm."

Elladan let out a soft chuckle. "Yeah, she tackled you like a charging boar. I'm surprised you're not aching all over."

"Actually, I am," Donnie responded, rubbing his shoulder gingerly.

Ruka stood behind him, her head hung low, her voice filled with regret. "Sorry."

Alana walked over to the girl and put her good arm around her shoulders. "Well, I think she was just marvelous."

She smiled down at the young teen. Ruka peered up at her, the trace of a smile crossing her lips. "How about we women warriors go spend some time away from these men," Alana told her, casting an accusatory glance around the deck.

Ruka gave a swift nod. "Yes, let's."

The duo then turned away and strode off together to the other side of the ship. Donnie threw up his hands and shrugged, glancing around at the others plaintively. "What'd I do?"

"Oh, Donnie..." Elistra said with a sigh, then walked off to join Alana and Ruka.

Aksel watched after her with concern. The succubus had not really caused any physical harm other than Alana's arm, something he could heal fairly easily. Her presence, however, seemed to have created a rift in their group. Up until now, they had all worked together effectively, having each other's backs when it counted. If this falling-out was allowed to continue, though, it could disrupt their ability to work as a team and jeopardize their entire mission.

Although he himself had not caused the rift, Aksel felt deeply responsible for it nevertheless. The others looked to him for leadership, and that made it his responsibility. In truth, Aksel had never led a group like this before. Oh, he had been in charge of a number of projects back home, both in school and at the temple.

The elders, old Bockworth in particular, had thrust him into a position of authority a number of times, despite his desire to be just like everyone else. Those assignments, however, had been either group lessons or community action projects, not life and death situations. Thus, nothing had prepared him for the great weight that now rested so squarely on his shoulders. Aksel's thoughts were interrupted as Lloyd descended from above.

"There's no sign of the Succubus anywhere. It's as if the Darkwoods just swallowed her up."

Lloyd seemed quite frustrated by his inability to catch the demoness. Elladan placed a comforting hand on the young man's shoulder. "It's okay, you did the best you could."

"Thanks," Lloyd said, though his expression remained grim.

A strained smile crossed Aksel's lips. At least some of the group was still getting along. The real problem seemed to be gender-related, exacerbated by the appearance of the succubus. Still, if he could just get them all to concentrate on the mission again, things might fall back into place. Unfortunately, here out on the river, they were sitting ducks. The succubus could return at any time and make more trouble for them. He decided to broach the subject with the others. "Maybe it's time we left this river."

Glo brought his hands up into a steeple in front of his mouth, his brow creasing as he mulled over Aksel's words. After a few moments pause, he spoke. "Second attack in two days. They obviously know where to find us."

Aksel turned to Elladan. "Do you have that map handy?"

Elladan pointed his thumb toward the cabins. "It's in my knapsack down below."

"Can you go get it? Maybe you and Captain Morled can figure out our current position. Then we can decide what to do next."

"Sure thing." Elladan spun on his heel and headed for the door to the cabin area.

"While he does that, I'm going to go and see if Alana needs any healing," Aksel told the others. The truth was Alana, being a holy knight, could probably heal that type of wound herself, but Aksel felt it his duty to ask.

"I'll come with you," Donnie offered, a pensive expression on his face as his eyes swept across the deck. Aksel followed his gaze to where Alana, Ruka, and Elistra stood apart from the others. Alana cast a quick glance in their direction, then immediately turned away. Aksel let out a short sigh—it appeared this was not going to be easy. He turned back to Donnie and spoke to him as delicately as he could manage. "That might not be the best idea right now."

Donnie hung his head, his tone resigned. "If you say so."

Aksel felt sorry for him. Donnie obviously liked the lady knight, but the allure of a succubus was difficult for even the strongest-willed of men to resist. Still, if Donnie truly cared about Alana, he should have shown just a bit more restraint around the temptress. Aksel attempted to cheer him up. "Don't worry. I'll try to convince them to rejoin us once I am done."

"Thanks," Donnie responded with another wistful glance in the direction of the lady knight.

Aksel left the others behind and strode over toward the three female members of their team. He could not hear their conversation, but from their tone of voice, both Alana and Ruka still seemed somewhat agitated. When they became aware of Aksel's approach, the three fell silent. Aksel halted in front of Alana and noted a blood-stained kerchief tied around her arm. He peered up at her solemnly, wondering why she had not healed it herself, but then noted her flushed cheeks. She was obviously still angry, not a state of mind in which it was easy to connect with your god.

"May I heal your arm?" he asked her as politely as possible.

Alana seemed somewhat taken aback at first, but after a moment or two broke into an embarrassed smile. "Oh, yes, why of course."

She held out her arm and allowed him to gently unwrap the bloody kerchief. The armor had been neatly sliced open, exposing the skin beneath. Across the length ran an ugly, open scar, with blood still welling inside. It was not the deep wound he had expected to find, but the blood he had seen leaking onto the deck before, and the stains on her skin and armor could not have been caused by such a wound. Aksel eyes fell on Alana. "You healed this yourself?"

Her expression was woeful. "I tried, but I was a bit too distracted to do an effective job."

Aksel gave her a brief smile. "I understand. Healing is not easy, even in the best of circumstances."

Alana attempted a wan smile, but her face flushed even more, this time from embarrassment. Aksel returned his attention to the wound. He scanned deep into her arm, making sure that no tendons were cut, then held his hand over the wound and called forth the white light bestowed upon him by his goddess. The healing energy flowed from his hand and bathed the wound, causing flesh and skin to mend together and close completely.

He stood in silence among the three women during the few minutes it took to heal the wound. When he was done, Alana withdrew her arm and twisted it around, an expression of marvel upon her face. She glanced down at Aksel and gave him a genuine smile. "Thank you so much. I dare say our own holy clerics of Cormar could not have done a better job."

Aksel grinned in response. "That is high praise, indeed."

Alana took a deep breath before speaking once more. "Aksel?"

"Yes?" he responded uncertainly.

"Thank you for being such a gentleman. It would be nice if certain folks behaved more like you." She finished with a quick glance across the deck.

Aksel raised an eyebrow, uncertain how to respond. In the end, he merely said, "Thank you."

"So what happened to that witch?" Ruka interjected.

Aksel chuckled softly, certain that the young teen was purposely curbing her tongue. "Lloyd checked in all directions, but there was no sign of her. It seems to have disappeared for the moment..."

"...but could return at any time," Elistra finished for him.

Aksel nodded to the seeress. "Yes. We were thinking it might be best to leave the river."

Elistra pursed her lips. "It makes sense. This was the second attack in two days. There's little doubt they know where to find us."

Aksel couldn't help smiling—Glo had said almost the same exact thing. It was uncanny how alike these two were. His smile quickly faded—there was still a lot to do and night was fast approaching. Aksel turned to Alana. "Elladan and Morled are trying to figure out our current position. Perhaps you can join them and help figure out where Sir Craven and your company might be. Maybe we can even set up some kind of rendezvous point?"

Ruka snorted. "Humph. Sounds better than waiting out here for that overgrown harpy."

The young teen's comment made them all laugh, breaking any remaining tension. Alana, still chuckling, placed an arm around Ruka's shoulder. "Very well, let's do this."

Aksel led them back across the deck. Donnie stood alone at the tiller, the others nowhere in sight. The slight elf smiled self-consciously at Alana. The lady knight shook her head and let out a deep sigh, smiling despite herself at the irrepressible elf. Donnie told them that Seth had returned to the crow's nest, while Elladan, Morled, and Glo had adjourned to the Captain's cabin below.

Aksel, Alana, and Elistra left Donnie at the wheel, and headed down to the cabin, while Ruka returned to the crow's nest above. Inside the Captain's cabin, Morled and the two elves pored over a large map spread across the single table in the room. The three of them had already figured out their current position. Further, they estimated that if they kept sailing until dark, it would put them within a couple of hours' ride of where they believed the monolith to be.

Alana joined in and they were soon able to place the position of her company on the map. If they were right, Sir Craven and the armored riders would reach a good rendezvous point not too far from where they intended to dock sometime late the next morning. Aksel told them he could use a spell he had just learned to communicate with Sir Craven first thing in the morning. In the end, everyone agreed to the plan.

The Rusty Nail continued its passage upstream until just before the sun set. Everyone was on edge, keeping a keen look-out on both the northern and southern shores. Luckily, the rest of the day passed by uneventfully. At sundown, Morled set course for the northern bank. They pulled up to the shore, drew the sails, and dropped anchor. A watch was set and everyone else went inside to their cabins for a much-needed rest.

It was the middle of the night and Seth could not sleep. He was still wound up from the day's events, and decided to get up and check out things on deck. Martan stood in the crow's nest, busily scanning the shorelines. Seth thought it best not to disturb him, instead moving silently around the ship, checking for any sign of intruders.

As he passed the sterncastle, Seth heard a soft voice drifting down from above. As far as he knew, no one else was awake. Seth grabbed his cloak and made himself invisible, then slowly climbed the stairs that led to the upper deck. When he reached the top, the voice abruptly stopped. Seth froze in place, his eyes searching the dark deck for any sign of intruders, but there were none.

After a few moments, the voice started up again. It was coming from behind a large storage chest at the very rear of the vessel. Seth paused a moment to consider his next move. If he went directly for the chest, he would end up on top of whoever was hiding behind it. However, if he slid far enough along the railing, he should be able get a glimpse behind that chest. His mind made up, Seth stole over to the railing and slowly made his way toward the stern.

As he drew closer, Seth was able to pick out individual words. They were not in the Common tongue, but it was a language he knew nonetheless. It was Draconic, the native tongue of dragons. Furthermore, he now recognized the voice—it belonged to Ruka. Seth nearly revealed himself at that point, but froze once again when he heard a second voice answer Ruka in the same tongue. It was the voice of an old man. The dialect was a bit strange, but Seth could just make it out.

"Why do you waste your time with these elves and the others?" the old man was saying.

"They're interesting," Ruka replied evasively.

"You mean the one elf is interesting," the old man corrected her.

Seth, now thoroughly intrigued, inched his way closer until he could see behind the storage chest. Ruka sat cross-legged on the deck, with her back up against the chest. She held her short sword out in front of her, the blade glowing, but not as bright as it were going to discharge a bolt. Seth peered closer and realized the strange glow had a shape to it. It was the image of an old man.

"Grandfather!" Ruka replied, her voice rising from embarrassment.

"Admit it, child. It is this elf that intrigues you."

Ruka paused a moment before answering. When she spoke, her tone had returned to normal. "It's not like that. At first I just wanted treasure—but then this group seemed fun."

"And that drew you to them."

"Yes! Ves is always so stuffy. We always have to do the right thing when she is around, but she is not Mother and she doesn't get to tell me what to do!"

There was more than a trace of bitterness in her tone. For the first time, Seth felt sympathy for the young teen. He knew only too well what it was like to have family members who wanted to run your life.

"And what of Maya?" the old man asked softly.

"She's just a child. She adores Ves and follows her blindly."

"So you took this opportunity to go off and have fun. Is that it?"

"Yes." Ruka nodded.

"And then you fell in love with this elf."

"I'm not in love with him!" she said, perhaps a bit too loudly.

Her head shot up and her eyes furtively scanned the deck, looking to see if she had been overheard. Seth held his breath. She had caught him once too often that way, and he had learned from his mistakes. Ruka tilted her head upward toward the crow's nest. Seth followed her gaze, but saw no reaction from Martan. The archer continued to scan the shoreline, oblivious to the argument going on down here at the stern of the ship. In fairness, her rebuttal had not really been that loud, and Martan did not have the hearing of a halfling or an elf.

After a few moments, Ruka sat back and resumed the conversation with her "grandfather." The timbre of her voice had changed, though—it was almost too pleasant. "Inazuma, Donnie is different. He may act roguish, but there is far more than that to him. He has one of the purest hearts I have ever seen."

There was a slight pause before her grandfather answered. "Ahhhh, now we come to it. His heart has resonated with yours. Yes, that explains much. Very well, child. I will not interfere. But if he ends up disappointing you in the end, do not say I did not warn you."

"Very well, Grandfather," Ruka replied, sounding quite pleased.

The image before her wavered and vanished, and she went to sheathe the sword. Seth decided to get out of there while he still could. He carefully backpedaled along the rail, holding his breath until he reached the stairs. There was no sign of Ruka, but he remained invisible, breathing softly and sparingly. When he finally made it back to his room, Seth dismissed the invisibility spell and strode over to his bedroll.

"Out for an evening stroll?" Aksel's voice came from under the bedcovers.

"Yep," Seth responded without flinching. He was not about to let the cleric know that he had surprised him.

"I trust it was uneventful?"

"Well..." Seth paused a moment, then told Aksel all about the strange conversation between Ruka and her sword. When he finished, Aksel sat back, his hand slowly stroking his chin. Seth lay down on his bedroll and waited patiently for his friend to comment. Finally, the little gnome sat back up again. "That is one interesting sword. I seem to remember that name, Inazuma, from somewhere, but I cannot place it right now. Still, how many named lightning short swords were ever made?"

Seth, finally feeling tired, snuggled further into his covers before answering. "Not many, I'm guessing, but the whole thing with Ruka talking to the image..." Seth paused and yawned. "And calling it Grandfather..." Seth yawned once more. "That was... just... freaky..."

"Go to sleep, Seth," Aksel told him. But Seth was already fast asleep.

19

INTO THE DARKWOODS

*It was as if the absence of light encouraged the shadows
to warp and twist the trees here*

First thing in the morning, Aksel contacted Sir Craven. It was a brief conversation due to the limitations of the spell, but still they were able to set up a rendezvous point. The knight had been lucky enough to discover an old beaten path that paralleled the river. He told the companions to find the trail and wait for him there. Everyone gathered their belongings and congregated on the main deck about an hour after dawn.

After bidding Captain Morled farewell, the companions disembarked the Rusty Nail onto the northern shore of the West Stromen. Aksel sent Seth and Martan to scout ahead. Ruka volunteered to help as well, turning into a hawk and taking to the skies. Glo sent Raven along with her, and the airborne duo swiftly disappeared above the trees to the north. Meanwhile, the others stayed near the river, watching the Rusty Nail as it slowly turned and headed back downstream. Before too long, it was out of sight and they were alone in the forest.

Seth, Martan, and Ruka all returned a short while later. The halfling and tracker had scouted a mile ahead, with no sign of anything other than normal forest wildlife. Ruka had gone a bit further and found the trail they were looking for about two miles north of the river. With that in mind, the companions set out northward. Even though there had been no further succubus sightings, Aksel still wanted to be cautious. He put Martan and Seth out in front, with Ruka and Raven airborne once again. Alana and Lloyd followed them, then Glo and Elistra. Aksel paired himself with Elladan, then had Donnie bring up the rear.

The marching order put them in a good position to respond if anything happened, and also kept Donnie and Alana as far apart as possible. Donnie had been trying all morning to get back on Alana's good side. The lady knight was cordial to him, but still remained somewhat aloof. Yet her behavior did not seem to dissuade him, making the slight elf only try harder.

The Darkwoods continued to live up to its name, the trees so tall and thick that the sun barely shone through to the forest floor below. While not as eerie as the Dead Forest, there was a palpable heaviness to the woods. It was as if the absence of light encouraged the shadows to warp and twist the trees here, the trunks and branches growing at odd angles, creating shapes that fueled the fearful imagination. The underbrush was thick, and the forest floor was rather mossy, being so close to the river. It gave off a dank smell, the musky scent rather pungent.

"I hope the whole forest doesn't smell like this," Donnie complained as the companions slowly made their way through the thick vegetation.

"It's only near the river," Seth responded. "It gets better farther inland."

Sure enough, only a few hundred yards inland, the dank odor began to dissipate. The forest floor grew less slick and even the trees opened up a bit. The companions' morale visibly brightened and they were now able to move forward at a quicker pace. An hour later, they came across the trail Ruka had found, cutting across their path from east to west.

The trail was indeed old and beaten, appearing as if it hadn't been used in years. Nevertheless, the overgrown dirt pathway was still quite visible under the fallen branches and vegetation that covered it in so many spots. Elladan cautioned against staying too long out in the open, so Martan found a grove of dark, twisted trees a short ways north of the trail where they could easily keep it in sight. Ruka and Raven continued to scout in the air while the companions waited for Sir Craven and company to show.

The wait turned out to be worthwhile. Donnie managed to finally break the ice with Alana. Aksel had watched with some concern as the slight elf continued to try to win her over, but Donnie had a way about him. Before long, the lady knight was conversing, and even smiling, with the slight elf. Aksel breathed a sigh of relief. That was one less thing he had to worry about.

A short while later, Ruka came flying in from the east. "I spotted riders on the trail five miles east of here. They were decked out in chainmail, and the horses had white caparisons decorated with red roses, just like Alana's."

Alana nodded. "Indeed, that is Sir Craven. How long do you estimate before they get here?"

"The trail is pretty overgrown as far as I could see, so I would guess maybe an hour."

Sure enough, just over an hour later, Sir Craven and company appeared up the trail. Greetings were traded, and the companions made ready to travel with the riders. Thankfully they had planned ahead, thus Sir Craven had Alana's war horse, Lloyd's paint, Seth's and Aksel's riding dogs, and three more spare horses with him. Elladan and Donnie shared one of the extra horses while Glo and Elistra mounted another. Martan was given the last and was sent to scout out ahead. Ruka went airborne once more, flying off with Raven westward along the trail. The path, overgrown as it was, was still wide enough for two horses. Aksel and Seth rode in the front of the company, followed by Sir Craven and Alana.

"We've still got about a day's march ahead of us," Sir Craven told them. "Assuming this path continues as we suspect, by this time tomorrow we should be in eyesight of the monolith."

"And then the real fun begins," Seth added dryly.

The companions and troop of knights continued the rest of their long, slow march westward along the overrun path through the Darkwoods.

"I've got good news and bad news," Ruka announced. It was early the next morning, and the shape-shifting teen had just returned from a scouting mission of the forest ahead. The others were just packing up camp and preparing to move out.

"What's the good news?" Donnie asked as he stuffed his bedroll into a saddlebag on the rear of his horse.

"I found the monolith."

Glo felt a surge of excitement through his body. He dropped his own bedroll and rushed over to the young teen. "Where?"

Ruka's mouth bent into a lopsided smile. "That's the bad news. We're on the wrong side of the river."

Elladan looked up from a saddle bag on the other side of the horse he and Donnie shared. "The wrong side?"

Ruka nodded. "Uh huh. The monolith is in a wide clearing about three miles southwest of here—across the river."

Seth, still feeding his riding dog, wore a twisted smile himself. "And you're sure it's the monolith?" he asked, without looking up.

Ruka fixed the halfling with an acid stare. "Well, if it isn't, then someone else dropped a tall, stone building smack in the middle of the forest."

Glo chose to ignore the banter and get back to business. "What exactly did this building look like?"

Ruka spun toward him, her eyes turned upward as if envisioning what she had seen. "It's a tall stone structure, probably three times as high as the surrounding trees. It's got a fairly thick base but is not nearly as wide at the top." She paused a second, then added, "Oh, and it's completely black."

Glo felt a hand on his arm—Elistra now stood next to him. He exchanged a glance with her and she nodded to him.

"That's it, then," the seeress said.

Elladan, done with his packing, walked over to join them. "Well that's all well and fine, but how are we supposed to cross the West Stromen then with horses and these heavily-armored folks?"

He spread his arms, pointing out the company they were in. Ruka let out a short laugh. "Actually, it's not as bad as you think."

"How's that?" Aksel strode up to them with Sir Craven and Alana by his side.

Ruka's mouth twisted once again. "There really isn't much of a river anymore this far west. It's more like a couple of streams."

Elladan shook his head, a half smile crossing his lips. "Well, why didn't you just say so in the first place?"

Ruka shrugged. "You didn't ask me."

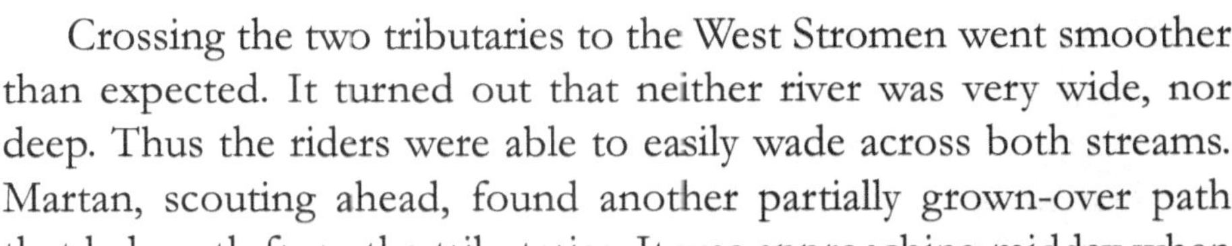

Crossing the two tributaries to the West Stromen went smoother than expected. It turned out that neither river was very wide, nor deep. Thus the riders were able to easily wade across both streams. Martan, scouting ahead, found another partially grown-over path that led south from the tributaries. It was approaching midday when the companions caught their first sight of the monolith.

The tip of a dark spire appeared through a rare gap in the thick trees of the Darkwoods. The pinnacle rose well above the forest, the overhead rays of the late morning sun gleaming off the dark stone obelisk, giving it an almost glossy appearance. Alana called the riders to a halt. Ruka and Raven winged skyward once more, while Martan and Seth went ahead on foot. They all returned a short while later. Alana, Craven, and the others gathered around to hear their report.

"The place is deserted," Ruka informed them.

"We did an entire perimeter sweep. There was no sign of any-one," Seth confirmed.

"Although, we did find tracks leading up to the monolith," Mar-tan added. "Mostly of the two-legged variety, but there were some that definitely weren't human."

"None coming out?" Lloyd asked.

"None," Martan affirmed.

Aksel, still sitting on his riding dog, stroked his chin slowly. "Then they must still be inside."

Lloyd turned to him, a crease across his brow. "After three full days?"

It was a fair question, one that Glo had puzzled over himself. He had finally consulted Elistra, and based on her knowledge of Larketh, they pieced together what they believed to be the answer. "If this is indeed one of Larketh's old strongholds, it could be filled with all manner of traps for the unwary."

Elistra, still seated on their shared mount, explained further. "Indeed, the Golem Master was not known to be a trusting soul. It is not unthinkable that he would have all sorts of defenses inside his lair."

"Hmmm," Elladan murmured. "So they went in and they haven't come out yet. Odds are, they are either dead or still haven't found what they came for. That leaves us with one question—what's our next move?"

"Well, I say we go in after them!" Lloyd said, slamming his fist into his other hand.

Alana placed a gauntleted hand on the young man's shoulder. "Spoken like a true warrior."

Glo's eyes swept across the group—everyone appeared anxious to move ahead except for Aksel. The little cleric's expression was pensive. Glo walked up to him. "What's troubling you?"

Aksel gazed up at him, his brow still furrowed. "It's as you said, if the cultists are still in there, then there has to be a good reason. What you and Elistra said about traps and defenses makes the most sense, but if that is the case, then we are likely to run into those as well."

"If there are traps, you can leave those to me," Seth said confidently.

Aksel shot the halfling a glance, then gave him a short nod. "True, but I'm not quite certain it's a good idea to drag everyone in there with us."

Alana pulled Sir Craven aside and the duo had a brief conversation. When they were done, she turned to the others. "Sir Craven will stay out here with our men and set up camp. They will guard the entrance and make sure no one else follows us in."

Aksel nodded, his brow finally unfurrowing. "Thank you, Alana. That is an excellent idea."

With that settled, the company remounted and resumed follow-ing the path south through the forest. The foliage thickened, cutting off their view of the monolith once again. A bit farther on, the path curved, veering west through the woods. A few hundred yards ahead, sunlight gleamed through an opening in the trees. All at once, the forest opened up and in front of them stood an enormous structure. The surrounding trees were ancient oaks and maples, easily reaching over a hundred feet. The monolith was easily three times that. The entire structure was made of that same dark stone they had glimpsed earlier, the rays of the midday sun granting it a glossy black sheen.

When Glo reached the edge of the clearing, a shiver ran up his spine. It was just like the nightmare he'd had a few days ago. The tall black structure stood in the center of the wide clearing, reach-ing high above the trees. The only difference was that the sky was a clear blue, and he was not alone. The riders behind them fanned out across the clearing, the treeless area spanning a perfect circle as wide as the courtyard back at Ravenford Keep. There was not a shrub or a single tree anywhere in the circle.

Martan nodded to the ground in front of them. "The tracks lead this way."

He spurred his mount forward, the others following him to the east side of the tower. As they circled the monolith, Glo paced out the length and width of the base. It turned out to be a perfect square, nearly one hundred feet long on all sides. The riders halted about ten yards from the base and scanned the structure. After a few moments of silence, Lloyd spoke up.

"I don't see any doors."

"Well, there has to be, unless the cultists know how to walk through walls," Seth noted dryly.

Glo had to suppress a laugh. He had been in a dark mood since entering the clearing, and Seth's humor seemed to help ease it. "Oh, there's definitely a doorway. I've seen it."

Glo tried to recall the vision he had seen in the scrying crystal just a few days ago, but instead, his nightmare reasserted itself. He saw an arched open doorway with a dim reddish glow just beyond. Elistra, still seated behind him, suddenly tightened her grip around his waist and lay her head against his back. *It was only a dream,* her voice said in his mind. Glo turned his head and gave her a brief smile, then took a deep breath and tried once again to picture what he saw. This time he was successful. Three dark-robed cultists stood in front of the monolith. There was no visible entrance in front of them. One of them stepped forward and recited a verse. Abruptly, a doorway slid open in the side of the structure. Glo related his vision to the others.

"Let's take a closer look then," Seth offered.

Glo dismounted and followed Seth and Martan to where the tracks disappeared into the monolith. Elistra and Elladan trailed close behind. Even at this distance, there was no visible sign of the doorway that Glo knew to be there. The dark stone appeared seamless, completely flat without a single break. Glo reached out and placed a hand on the wall. It felt as smooth as it looked, and it was cool to the touch. Seth examined the wall of the structure, his agile fingers running over the dark stone looking for hidden seams or indentations. After a few minutes, he gazed up and shrugged.

"If there is a doorway here, it is hidden by magic."

Glo thought back to his vision. The cultists had stood only a short distance from the structure and recited a phrase. Unfortunately, though Glo could see them through the crystal, he could not hear them. There was no way of knowing what those words were. The real question was, how did the cultists even know what to say? He turned to Elistra. "Any ideas?"

The seeress held a hand to her chin, her brow furrowed as she scrutinized the wall. After a few moments, she began to pace backwards. Glo and the others followed, watching her curiously. After a dozen or so steps, she stopped. "I believe they were standing back here."

Elistra squinted her eyes, as if searching for something in particular on the surface of the monolith. Glo stood next to her, following her gaze. The others lined up as well. After a few moments, Martan shouted, "I see something!"

The archer pointed at a spot about fifteen feet off the ground. Glo stared where Martan indicated, but didn't see anything at first. He squinted his eyes, then finally saw it. There appeared to be slight indentations in the dark stone, running a few feet across the outside wall. *Dragon's teeth! The archer does have keener eyes than an elf.*

Elistra leaned in closer to him and grabbed his arm. "I still don't see anything."

Glo stooped down so his head was next to hers, and pointed to the location of the markings. "Right up there."

Elistra leaned in even closer, placing her head against Glo's. Her hair brushed up against his face, and he breathed in its scent. He smelled the sweet odor of honeysuckle, as if walking through a glade in the middle of the summer. After a few moments, Elistra spoke, breaking him out of his reverie. "Yes, I see them now. They seem to form some kind of pattern."

"They're runes," Elladan said with certainty.

Glo stood up and scanned over the indentations once more. After a moment or two, he was able to trace out faint lettering. *Elladan is right! They are runes.*

"Can you read them?" Elistra asked, still holding onto him.

Whatever language it was, it appeared ancient, but Glo couldn't quite make it out from here. He strode closer, keeping his eyes fixed on the lettering. "Yes, I believe I can. They look to be in ancient Dwarven."

Elladan strode up next to Glo, and the two of them pored over the runes together. All at once, the duo burst out in laughter.

"You going to let us in on the joke?" Donnie's voice came from behind them.

Glo spun around and saw the others watching them curiously. "Well, if there was any doubt about who this place belonged to, we have our answer."

"Why? What does it say?" Lloyd asked.

"Larketh... is... master," Elladan recited the inscription. That elicited a mixture of snickers and groans from the others.

"Larketh always did have a high opinion of himself," Elistra noted dryly. Glo took a sidelong glance at her. The seeress was obviously well-versed in the history of the Thrall Masters, but that particular statement almost sounded like a personal assessment. "Or, so I've read," she quickly amended, returning his stare with an enigmatic smile.

Glo held her gaze for a moment or two, then shrugged. *Nah, it couldn't be.* He turned his attention back to the monolith. "Oh, well, here goes nothing." Glo raised his voice and repeated the words Elladan had translated, but this time in Dwarven.

"Larketh... bi... skilam!"

His voice reverberated across the clearing as if the monolith had picked up the sound and bounced it back at him. The echo continued for a few seconds then finally died down. The clearing went silent. Glo stared at the monolith expectantly, but nothing happened. *Did I translate it wrong? Perhaps the phrase was symbolic rather than literal?*

He opened his mouth to speak, but was stopped by a faint rumbling sound. It was coming from the monolith! Without warning, a section of wall directly in front of them began to recede. It recessed about a foot inward and then slid sideways, disappearing into the wall of the structure. When it was done, a rectangular opening the size of a large door was left in the side of the monolith.

Glo felt a slap on the back. "Nicely done!" Elladan exclaimed.

Glo nearly choked. "Th-thanks."

The rest of the company dismounted. While the companions gathered their gear, the Knights of the Rose began to set up camp. Sir Craven dispatched sentries to the four corners of the clearing, while the rest of his men unsaddled the horses, pitched tents and went to gather wood. Martan elected to stay outside and help them. He felt he would be far more useful in the forest. Glo left Raven outside as well, sending her winging up into the trees on the outskirts of the clearing. When they were done with their preparations, Seth, Lloyd, Alana, Glo, Elistra, Elladan, Aksel, Ruka, and Donnie all lined up in front of the monolith. Glo strained his eyes to see beyond the open door, but it looked pitch black inside. Sir Craven joined them as they filed toward the entrance.

"Good luck," he wished them solemnly.

Seth led the way, disappearing through the dark doorway. The inky blackness swallowed him whole, leaving no trace of the halfling. Lloyd went next, followed by Alana, both vanishing as completely as Seth. Finally, it was Glo's turn. He stepped reluctantly forward, casting a brief glance over his shoulder. Sir Craven had spun around, preoccupied with the business of assembling the camp. A strange shudder passed up Glo's spine as he watched those valiant men and women. It was as if he was seeing them for the last time. The eerie feeling was gone just as fast as it had come.

Must be nerves, Glo told himself. He then stepped through the doorway and all went black.

20

INSIDE THE MONOLITH

Only by obtaining the holiest heights
can one progress to the most glorious depths

Glolindir stood inside the monolith, the light from the entrance barely illuminating the area around him. He could just make out the darkened forms of Seth, Lloyd, and Alana a few steps away. Beyond the threesome there was nothing but blackness. It gave him an eerie feeling, almost as if they had stepped into a void. Glo reached into his pouch, pulled out a slightly phosphorescent material, and touched the end of his staff, a single word passing his lips.

"*Lux.*"

The end of his staff began to glow, its light fanning out as it grew steadily brighter. Seth, Lloyd, and Alana became visible, the latter two firmly gripping their swords. The radiance from his staff extended a few yards beyond them before fading into the blackness, yet Glo could still see nothing more than stone floor. There were no walls, doors, pillars, or steps of any kind in sight. Glo swiveled around and saw Elistra, Elladan, Aksel, Donnie and Ruka standing in the entranceway. All wore perplexed expressions except for the young teen, who appeared totally unphased by the encroaching darkness. Glo's eyes strayed to the top of the doorway and his heart skipped a beat—they had passed under an archway. *Just like in my dream.*

Glo took a deep breath and slowly exhaled, shifting his focus beyond the arch. The outside world was clearly visible. *Interesting trick, you can see out, but not in. It must be some kind of privacy spell placed permanently on the doorway.* Once his nerves settled, Glo returned his gaze to the top of the archway. There were more runes written across it. He briefly scanned them, filing their meaning away in his mind. Meanwhile, Aksel had walked past him and was speaking with Seth in a hushed tone.

"What's the matter?"

Seth's response was equally soft. "This is a wide open area—I'm not sure just how far it extends."

Once again, a shiver ran up Glo's spine. A vision of a huge chamber lined with glowing urns and a giant statue of a dwarf in the center passed before his eyes. *What are the odds?* True, there were no urns or statues in sight, but the light spell he used was supposed to extend up to forty feet in all directions. That was about the size of the common room back at the Charging Minotaur, or rather, the Golden Golem. That could only mean that this chamber was larger than that, perhaps even as large as in his dream. Glo felt his pulse quicken and took another deep breath. *Stick to the facts, Glo. This is no time to get caught up in visions and hallucinations.*

Someone strode up next to him. It was Elladan. The bard gave him a quick wink. "Then let's shed some more light on the subject."

Elladan made some hand motions, followed by two soft words. Above them, four globular-shaped lights winked into existence, twisting and turning as if dancing in place. With a wave of his hand, he sent the globes spiraling upward. They rose higher and higher, until they were far above their heads. The area was now bathed in a faint glow that radiated well beyond the light from Glo's staff. The outline of a huge pillar became visible straight ahead, but there was still no sign of the ceiling or the other walls.

Lloyd's voice was filled with awe. "Just how large is this place?"

"Let's find out," Aksel answered. The little cleric made the same hand motions as Elladan, and another set of globular lights appeared above them. Aksel waved his hand and the lights traveled up and away, floating past the pillar and onward, until the opposite wall finally came into view. Aksel waved his hand again and the lights stopped. Glo arched an eyebrow. Judging by the pattern of the dancing lights, that wall had to be about a hundred feet away. Aksel glanced at Elladan. The bard gave a short nod and then the duo created another set of globular lights. They sent them left and right simultaneously, until they found the other two walls. When they were done, the entire room was dimly lit.

Someone let out a soft whistle. This room was enormous, encompassing the entire length and width of the monolith, easily twice the size of the large main hall in Ravenford Keep. It was an amazing feat of architecture, the like Glo had not seen since leaving his home city of Cairthrellon. It was exactly like Glo's dream, except that in the center of the room stood a single huge pillar instead of a statue. A stone staircase wound up and around the outside of the wide column, disappearing into the ceiling far above. Directly across from them was another archway, though this one was completely black. Two more archways stood in the center of the left and right walls—they were dark as well.

"What an incredible feat of engineering," Aksel murmured softly.

Like everyone else, Glo continued to marvel at the chamber around them until a familiar voice broke them out of their revelry.

"If you're all done sightseeing, can we get on with this already?"

They all turned to see Seth standing there, his arms folded across his chest. Aksel wore a sheepish grin, probably none too different from the one on Glo's face. The little cleric ushered the halfling forward. "Very well, Seth, lead on."

"Thank you," Seth responded with mock gratitude. He cautiously led the party across the room, toward the large pillar. As they drew nearer, an opening appeared in the floor next to it. Steps could be seen spiraling downward, mirroring the staircase that climbed up its side.

Glo experienced another episode of mock déja vu. *This is starting to get freaky. Again, the spiral stairs lead downward, just like in my dream. Still, there were no stairs leading upward in that nightmare.*

When they reached the huge pillar, Seth raised a hand for them to halt. Glo lifted his head and gazed straight upward—the column towered over them, disappearing into the blackness far above. When he peered back down, Seth was kneeling over the opening in the floor. After a few moments, the halfling stood back up and turned to the others. "It's pitch black down there."

Donnie strode up next to him and briefly peered down the hole, then turned around to face the others. "So the obvious question is, do we go up, or do we go down?"

Glo glanced briefly up the pillar once more, then down the dark hole in the floor. The truth was they really did not have enough information to make an educated decision either way—unless there was a clue in those runes across the archway. Glo opened his mouth to voice his thoughts, but Elladan beat him to it.

"Maybe there's a clue in those runes over the entrance."

Glo eyed the bard, a thin smile spreading across his lips. "I've already deciphered those—they were a bit obscure, but if there are runes over the other three archways, maybe together they might give us a clue."

Elladan responded with a semi-smile. "Couldn't hurt. I'll take the arch to the north."

"Then I'll take the one to the south," Glo said with a nod.

Aksel held up a hand. "Hang on a minute. Although the room looks empty, let's not take any uncessary chances. Seth, Lloyd, you go with Glo. Donnie, Alana, you go with Elladan."

Seth brushed past Glo. "I'll take the lead," he said over his shoulder. Glo glanced at Lloyd who shrugged back at him. The two of them took off after the halfling. Sure enough, the southern archway had runes inscribed across the top. Glo examined them closely, forming a rough translation in his mind. When he was done, Glo peered across the wide room. Elladan still stood in front of the northern archway, Donnie and Alana by his side. Glo turned back to Seth and Lloyd. "Let's check out the west door."

The three of them crossed over to the western archway. Glo was halfway through the translation when Elladan, Donnie, and Alana joined them. When he was done, they compared notes, coming up with a full translation of all four doorways. The six of them then headed back to the pillar in the center of the room, and Elladan recited it to the others.

Lord Larketh is the Divine Master of all Constructs.
All hail he who is the sovereign ruler of all that has no rule.
He breathes life into that which never had.
He grants will to that which has none.
He binds the materials of stone, metal and earth to his command.
The Lord Larketh speaks the true name of the earth and calls it his own.
Only by obtaining the holiest heights can one progress to the most glorious depths.

Donnie wore a wry smile. "So, this monument is pretty much a dedication to the Golem Master's ego."

His comment elicited a few chuckles. Aksel, however, did not laugh, his brow furrowed in deep concentration. "All except that last line. *Only by obtaining the holiest heights...*"

"*...can one progress to the most glorious depths,*" Glo finished for him. He gave Donnie a wry smile. "It is the only line that doesn't speak to Larketh's ego."

"Then it's a clue," Donnie said with enthusiasm.

Seth's mouth warped to one side. "Obviously. The stairs leading down are just a sham, leading to a false basement."

Elladan gave a short, closemouthed laugh. "So the real basement can't be reached that way. Can't say Larketh wasn't clever."

"Yes." Glo nodded to the bard. "If we decide to take that statement at face value, then we need to ascend to the top of the tower to reach the sub-basement."

Aksel paced back and forth, drumming his fingers against his chin. "Sounds very plausible. Larketh was obviously a master builder, as evidenced around us." He gestured across the enormous room. "Anyone who could do this could easily build a secret chamber in the strata beneath this tower."

"It is in keeping with Larketh's nature," Elistra chimed in. "He was the most secretive of the Thrall Masters."

Glo gave Elistra a sidelong glance. Once again, that sounded like a personal assessment. It was certainly not common knowledge, at least, not in any of the books he had read on the Thrall Masters. Yet for all intents and purposes, Elistra appeared to be a human in her late twenties. If she was anything else, it would have been revealed during their fight with the succubus. The only reasonable explanation was that she had access to books that Glo had never seen before. He was about to ask her when Seth interrupted him.

"Then it's settled," the halfling said impatiently. "We go up."

Aksel nodded. "We go up."

Seth spun around and headed toward the stairwell leading upward. "Finally," he could be heard muttering under his breath.

The disc in Lloyd's hand had begun to glow, growing brighter and brighter until everyone had to shield their eyes

Glo felt a keen sense of relief as the company ascended the stairs. The journey upward had definitely broken the pattern of his dream, where he had descended into the basement to find his friends dead. The large party climbed upward in the same formation that they had taken when entering the monolith—Seth in the lead and Ruka bringing up the rear.

They wound their way up the staircase, around the huge pillar, toward the stone ceiling far above. Seth carefully scanned each step as he went—a few steps below the ceiling, he signaled a halt. The others waited in silence as the halfling scrutinized the stairwell ahead. Seth reached up and ran his hands along the ceiling above the stairwell until abruptly he stopped. A faint click could be heard followed by a barely audible, "Child's play."

A slim smile spread across Glo's lips. It was definitely one of the halfling's favorite phrases. Seth glanced over his shoulder and whispered, "Blades," indicating the kind of trap they had just avoided. Seth resumed his slow ascent, disappearing into the ceiling above. The others followed one by one. The staircase continued to wind upward through solid rock. After what seemed like forever, the stairwell opened up into another dark area, the light from Glo's staff illuminating a large circle around them.

The chamber appeared empty, nothing visible in the radius of the light except for stone floor and the stairway continuing its path around the pillar upward. Elladan and Aksel sent out more globes of light, brightening the room. It turned out to be another vast chamber, stretching the length and width of the monolith, except that this area had a number of pedestals spread around it at regular intervals. When viewed all together, the pedestals formed a large circle around tall central pillar.

Seth addressed the group in a soft voice. "You guys can check those daises out if you want. I'm going to examine the stairwell above—just don't touch anything until I get back."

Aksel gave him a grim nod. "Agreed."

Seth disappeared up the staircase, his small form reappearing farther above as he spiraled upward, then disappearing once more. Meanwhile, Aksel detailed his plan to investigate the room. "Let's split up into two groups. Lloyd, you go with Glo and Elistra. Alana, you come with me, Elladan and Donnie. Ruka, you keep watch on the stairs."

Ruka stood up as stiff as she possibly could, and gave Aksel a mock salute. "Got it, chief."

The little cleric paused in his tracks, raising an eyebrow. "Um, let me rephrase that. Ruka, can you please keep watch on the stairs?"

A wry smile crossed the young teen's lips. "Will do."

Glo, Lloyd and Elistra set out in one direction, while the others headed out in the exact opposite. Lloyd went first, cautiously leading the way across the dimly lit chamber. As they approached the pedestals, Glo observed that each one had a small disc upon it, and that each disc was emblazoned with a colored symbol. The disc directly in front of them was green, the one to the left yellow, and the one to their right blue. When they reached the middle dais, Glo examined the green symbol closely—the emblem on it looked strangely familiar.

"Where have I seen that before?" he murmured softly.

"It's a chakra symbol."

Lloyd and Glo turned to face Elistra.

"What's a chak—ra?" Lloyd repeated the word slowly.

"It's a spiritual energy point on the body. There are seven of them, running from the groin up to the top of the head." Elistra illustrated by running a hand up her torso, stopping at different points along the way.

Lloyd's eyes widened slightly and a small smile came to his lips. "Oh. you mean the seven gateways of power."

A small frown crossed Elistra's brow. "I guess you could call them that. You know of them?"

"Yeah," Lloyd said with a nod. "As a spiritblade, we learn to channel their energy—well, the first, third, and seventh that is."

A knowing smile spread across Elistra's face. "Ah, yes, body, mind and spirit."

"Uh huh. That's how a spiritblade can do the things we do, by combining body, mind and spirit." Lloyd stood there grinning brightly at both Glo and Elistra, obviously quite thrilled at being able to discuss this topic with someone else who would understand.

Lloyd was not wrong—Glo was also familiar with the seven chakras. He was perhaps not as well versed in them as Elistra, but he definitely knew about them. They were an integral part of psionics. One of his mother's books was devoted to chakras, meditation, and the focusing of spiritual energies. From what Glo could recall, each chakra was numbered and had a specific purpose, symbol, and color associated with it. "So the symbol on this disc in front of us, that's associated with the fourth chakra?"

Elistra smiled sweetly at him, her violet eyes lighting up at his understanding of her field. "That's correct. The first chakra is red, the second orange, the third yellow, the fourth green, the fifth blue, the sixth purple, and the seventh white."

"And each has a particular meaning then?" Lloyd asked, mirroring Glo's thoughts.

"Body, emotion, mind, heart, voice, sight, and spirit," Elistra recited, as if she had repeated that same list many, many times before.

Lloyd bent forward for a closer look at the disc. "So this is the heart disc?"

"Yes." Elistra nodded, a touch of amusement graced her lips as she watched the curious young man gaze intently at the little disc on the pedestal in front of them.

After a short while, Lloyd stood back up and spun around slowly to his right. "So if the fourth one is here, then the fifth one should probably be over there..."

Before they could say another word, Lloyd strode off toward the next pedestal in the circle. Glo gave Elistra a quick glance. She shrugged at him and the two of them took off after the impulsive young man. Sure enough, when they reached the next pedestal, there was a disc with a blue symbol upon it that was associated with the fifth chakra. Glo glanced at the next pedestal in the circle and observed that the disc on it had a purple colored symbol. "So each of the pedestals has a colored chakra disc on it." Glo scanned the room carefully, counting eight pedestals in all. "Hmm, eight pedestals and seven chakras. That's strange."

"What do you want to do?" Lloyd asked him.

Glo thought it over. The others were still on the far side the room. "Well, we've seen four pedestals so far, ranging from yellow to purple in color..."

"Chakras three through five," Elistra corrected him.

Glo gave her a brief smile. "Three through five. So let's see what the others have found."

They crossed the room, rejoining Aksel, Alana, Donnie and Elladan. They compared notes and found that seven of the pedestals contained a colored disc with the symbol for each chakra. The eighth pedestal was the oddball—that one contained a disc with all the other colors combined, fanning out from the center of the disc in small wedges.

Elistra stood over the multicolored disc, a single finger resting on her chin. "This is indeed odd. It appears to be a combination of all the chakras in one."

It appeared as if she was going to say more, but was interrupted by a familiar voice from behind them.

"Well, the way up is blocked."

They all spun around at once. Seth stood there with his arms folded across his chest.

Aksel eyed the halfling curiously. "Blocked?"

Seth's expression remained impassive. "As in solid stone. The stairs appear to just end at the ceiling."

Elladan stepped forward and peered up toward the top of the tall pillar, shaded in the darkness far above. "Well, there has to be a way up. We are no where near the top of the monolith."

"Hmm," Glo murmered softly, steepling his hands in front of his mouth. "A puzzle then." He spun back toward the pedestal behind them. "Perhaps these discs are the key. The question is how..."

Seth strode up next to Glo and eyed the rainbow disc on the pedestal. "Someone want to fill me in?"

Glo and Elistra repeated everything they had found, or surmised, so far concerning the pedestals and the discs. When they were finished, Seth squinted at the two of them.

"Whatever. I don't know much about all this chakra mumbo jumbo. I'll leave that to you. Meanwhile, I'll check this pedestal for traps." The halfling knelt down in front of the dais and began to search around.

"Elistra..." Lloyd said the seeress's name tentatively.

She turned to face the young man, a delicate eyebrow arched. "Yes?"

"Remember when I said spiritblades use three of their chakras?"

Elistra pursed her lips and nodded. "Uh huh."

Lloyd's expression grew sheepish as he continued. "Well, the truth is that most of my energy comes from the first one. The energy from the other two are not as strong, but they seem to help with flow and control, if that makes any sense."

A warm smile spread across Elistra's lips. "It more than makes sense. Your first chakra provides the physical power to do the things you do. The third and sixth help you to stabilize and direct that power. In truth, you resonate the most with your first chakra, though."

Resonate? For some reason that word sparked something in the back of Glo's mind. He turned to Elistra. "Did you say resonate?"

The seeress squinted at him curiously. "Yes, resonate. Certain individuals resonate more with specific chakras depending on their talents and interests."

The thought in the back of his mind suddenly came rushing to the forefront. "I've got it!" Glo exclaimed enthusiastically.

They all turned to stare at the wizard. Elladan raised an eyebrow and cocked his head to one side. "Got what?"

Seth let out a derisive snort. "I think he's finally snapped."

Glo put his hands on his hips and glared at the halfling darkly. "Perhaps I have, but I also think I have the answer to this puzzle."

"Well, don't just stand there. Spill it!" Elladan urged him.

Everyone gathered close around the elven wizard. "Okay then, based on what Elistra just said, someone might resonate with a specific chakra. So what if each of these discs are some kind of key?"

Aksel's hand went to his chin, his brow furrowing deeply as he considered Glo's theory. "If each disc is a key, then how exactly does it work?"

"It's actually quite ingenious. In order to unblock the staircase, a person has to resonate with the discs."

The little cleric stroked his chin as he deliberated over Glo's words. "You may be on to something there."

"Well, if anyone cares, the pedestal is clean."

They all turned to see Seth had finished examining the dais. Everyone stepped forward, crowding around the pedestal to get a better look.

Donnie bent down and eyed the multi-colored disc curiously. "So, how do we use these discs then?"

"Why don't you pick it up and find out?" Seth said to the slight elf, his tone dripping with sarcasm.

Donnie stood up and cast an acid look at the halfling.

"That is probably the idea," Glo said with a slight nod.

Seth folded his arms and stared at Donnie with a self-satisfied smile. "Told you so."

Donnie eyed the disc, but instead of reaching for it, he stepped back and proffered it to Seth. "After you."

Seth waved a hand at the slight elf. "Nah. I don't resonate with rainbow."

Donnie glowered at the halfling, but was interrupted before he could form a reply.

"So what happens if we pick up the wrong one?" Elladan asked the seeress. Elistra wrinkled her nose as she considered the possibilities. After a short pause, she answered his question. "Probably nothing. Either you resonate with the disc or you don't."

"Well, I'm game," Lloyd declared with enthusiasm. "I already know I resonate with my first chakra." The young warrior spun around and strode toward the next pedestal in the circle, the one with the red disc on it. The others followed close behind. When Lloyd reached the dais, he bent down to grab the disc. Before he could grab it though, a small voice interrupted him.

"Forgetting something?"

Lloyd spun around to face Seth, a sheepish grin on his face. "Um, sorry."

"You might have been," Seth chided him as he knelt down next to the pedestal. After a minute or so of searching around it, Seth stood up and announced, "All clear."

"Thanks." Lloyd gave the halfling a self-conscious smile, then bent down and grabbed the disc. Nothing happened. Lloyd stood there holding the disc in his hand then looked up at the others, a sigh escaping his lips. "I don't think it's working."

"Umm, you might want to check again," Seth told him with a nod toward the young man's hand. The disc that Lloyd held had begun to glow, growing brighter and brighter until everyone had to shield their eyes. Abruptly the light vanished. Lloyd was the first to speak, his voice filled with confusion.

"Where did it go?"

Glo unshielded his eyes. The disc was gone from Lloyd's hand, however, a bright red glow, the same shape and size of the small disc, now shone at his groin.

"Umm, Lloyd, you might want to look down," Seth said, staring unabashedly at the young man's torso.

Lloyd glanced downward, a single word escaping his lips. "Whoa."

The red glow slowly faded then finally disappeared. Elladan stepped forward and placed a hand on Lloyd's shoulder. "How do you feel?"

"I feel—great!" A smile slowly spread across Lloyd's lips until it broke out into a full-fledged grin. "I feel—stronger."

Elladan turned to Elistra with a questioning look. "Is that possible?"

Elistra pursed her lips, her expression growing reflective as she thought over this strange new development. "It might be, if the disc were some kind of chakra tattoo."

Glo eyed the seeress curiously, a single eyebrow raised, and repeated her last two words. "Chakra tattoo?"

Elistra peered back at him with a small smile. "It's a symbol that enhances the abilities associated with a specific chakra point."

Elladan let out a short, closedmouthed laugh. "So are you saying Lloyd has an actual tattoo down there?"

"More than likely." The seeress's eyes sparkled with amusement.

Lloyd's cheeks swiftly turned a bright shade of scarlet. "Well, I'm not going to check."

"Trust me, no one wants you to," Seth agreed fervently.

"So what did you say the second one is?"

Elistra turned to face Donnie, an amused smile on her lips. "Emotion. Although I've also heard it referred to as passion, creativity or sensuality."

Donnie gave Elladan a speculative glance. "That could be either of us."

"No, no, no." Elladan shooed him toward next platform. "I've got the voice one. You go for it."

Donnie shrugged, spreading his hands outward. "Okay, if you insist."

The slight elf led the way to the next platform in the circle, the others following close behind. When they got there, Seth knelt down to check the pedestal. A short while later, he stood up and backed away. "All clear."

Donnie gave him a brief nod, then slowly bent down to grab the disc. Before grasping, he turned toward Elladan one last time. "You sure?"

The bard nodded. "Positive."

"Okay then." Donnie turned back to the dais and grabbed the

orange disc. The same thing happened as with Lloyd. At first the disc lay quietly in his hand, then abruptly began to glow. A bright orange light filled the chamber then slowly faded and disappeared. When it was over, a bright orange symbol appeared on Donnie's torso, just below the navel. It soon vanished.

Elladan eyed the slight elf with thinly veiled amusement. "So how do you feel, Donnie?"

"I feel—"

"What are you feeling?" a voice interrupted him.

They all spun around and saw Ruka standing behind them.

"Ruka—" Donnie sputtered, "—what are you doing here?"

The young teen folder her arms across her chest, her eyes practically burning holes into the slight elf.

"I mean, aren't you supposed to be guarding the stairs?" Donnie swiftly amended.

Ruka nodded over her shoulder. Glo looked behind her and saw Lloyd now standing at the stairwell. When the young man realized they were looking his way, he waved to them.

"I asked Lloyd to swap with me," Ruka explained. Her eyes dropped to Donnie's lower torso, a wide grin crossing her lips. "So why were you glowing down there?"

Donnie's cheeks swiftly reddened. "Well... um..."

Elistra came to the embarrassed elf's rescue, going into a detailed explanation of what they had discovered. She told Ruka about chakras, their theory about the discs being keys, and finished with the chakra tattoos and their effects. When she was done, Ruka turned back to Donnie. The young teen wore a wicked grin. "So, Donnie, are you going to show us your tattoo?"

"Ruka!" Donnie cried, his entire face turning scarlet.

Elladan burst into outright laughter. Alana, Elistra, and Glo all chuckled. Aksel wore a faint smile on his lips, but Seth just shook his head. "Um, no. Just—no."

Ruka's eyes flickered around the group then back to Donnie, dancing with amusement as they fixed once more on the slight elf's lower torso. Aksel cleared his throat in an obvious attempt to stifle a laugh. "Ahem, back to the matter at hand. Ruka, would you like to try a disc?"

Ruka pointed to her chest, her eyes going wide. "Me? No, thank you—not really my thing." With that, the young teen spun around and strode away. "I'll send Lloyd back to you," she called over her shoulder.

"Well then, shall we move onto the next disc?" Glo tried hard to hold in his laughter.

The group moved over to the next pedestal in the circle, Lloyd rejoining them. This disc was yellow, the one Elistra referred to as "mind". Everyone agreed that Glo should try this disc. Once Seth cleared the platform, Glo stepped forward and bent down to grasp the disc. It felt cool to the touch. He stood up and held it in his hand.

After a few seconds, it began to glow. As the disc brightened, it also warmed to the touch. When it grew so bright that he could no longer look it at, it had become hot in his hand. Just when Glo felt he would have to drop it, the disc suddenly disappeared. The heat, however, did not. Instead, it traveled up his arm and into his body, shooting down his spine to a point between his heart and his navel. It stopped there, pulsing warmly in his abdomen.

Abruptly, the image of a yellow disc appeared over the spot. It glowed for about half a minute, then faded away. The warmth had disappeared as well. At that same moment, his mind began to race, images flooding through his head from the last few weeks. He re-lived everything that had happened since their first encounter with the orcs in the Bendenwoods. It all passed before his eyes in a matter of seconds, every color and every detail as vivid as if he was still there. It was as if his mind had somehow expanded and enhanced his memory.

"Glo, are you alright?" a gentle voice interrupted his thoughts. It was Elistra. His eyes refocused on a lovely pair of violet ones directly in front of him. Those eyes were filled with concern.

"I'm—fine," Glo answered slowly. "Just adjusting to the effects of the tattoo."

Elistra grabbed his arm and held onto him as the group moved on to the next dais. Upon that pedestal sat the green disc, the one associated with the heart chakra. While Seth checked the platform, the others debated who should try this disc. It came down to Aksel or Alana, but in the end it was decided that the spirit disc would fit Aksel the best. Therefore, Alana stepped forward to claim the heart disc.

The lady knight repeated the process Glo had just experienced, ultimately resulting in a green disc appearing over her heart. Once it disappeared, Alana's face softened, a wide smile spread across her lips. The lady warrior was rather lovely, a fact she usually kept hidden with her serious countenance. Alana's eyes swept fondly around the gathered group.

"I am so lucky to have comrades like you."

Donnie reached out and grasped her hand. "As are we in you, milady.

Alana peered back at him graciously, her eyes brimming with tears.

"Get a room, you two." Seth stood there gazing at the duo with a wicked grin.

The next disc down the circle was the blue one, the voice chakra. Elladan had already claimed that one for his own. When the blue glow disappeared over his throat, a tattoo appeared in its place. It appeared to be a blue flower with an inverted triangle in the center.

Glo arched an eyebrow at the sight. "So they do turn into tattoos."

The bard cleared his throat and softly sang a scale. His voice sounded as clear as ever, but there was a slight difference in timber, almost as if another person sang along with him. Elladan touched his throat, his eyes widening at the realization. "Now that's different."

The disc after that was the purple one, the one representing sight. Since Martan wasn't with them and Ruka had no interest, that left Seth as the most natural fit. After checking the platform, the halfling nonchalantly scooped that one up. When it was over, Seth lifted the locks of black hair off his brow, revealing a purple tattoo that appeared very much like a third eye.

Glo squinted at the halfling, but could detect no change in him. "Do you feel any different?"

"Nope. All I see is a bunch of idiots gaping at me when we should be moving on to the next disc."

Donnie let out a short laugh. "Well, he's obviously fine."

Seth snorted derisively. "Humph. Of course I am." With that, the halfling strode away, brushing by the slight elf as he headed toward the next dais. Once past Donnie, he called back over his shoulder. "Oh, and by the way—nice boxers, Donnie."

Donnie's jaw dropped open, his eyes going wide. "How'd you..." He stopped himself and gaped at Seth. "No..."

Seth continued to stride away, but Glo caught sight of a wicked grin on the side of his face. Meanwhile, Donnie turned toward Elistra, his expression incredulous. "He couldn't have," the elf declared rather firmly. "Could he?" he abruptly added, suddenly not sounding so certain of himself.

Elistra, however, did not respond, instead also brushing past him, wearing that all-too-familiar enigmatic smile. Donnie stared after her for a moment or two, then spun toward Glo.

Glo merely threw up his hands. "Don't look at me. I'm not the expert on this."

Donnie glared at the wizard, then spun around and chased after Elistra. As Glo watched the receding elf with amusement, he suddenly felt a hand on his shoulder. He turned to see Elladan standing there with a quasi-smile on his lips.

"Seth one, Donnie zero," the bard murmured. The two elves chuckled softly.

The next-to-last disc was the white one, the spirit disc. Seth checked the pedestal, then Aksel bent to pick it up. When it was over, the little cleric appeared momentarily dazed, much like Glo had been. Aksel recovered quickly, though, and addressed the group.

"Now that I think of it, this appears to be an extremely elaborate mechanism for opening the door to the next floor. I am sure there is a short cut."

Glo nodded. The spirit disc appeared to have a similar effect on Aksel as it did on Glo, expanding both his mind and awareness. "You make a good point. So you think the eighth disc is a universal key."

Aksel slowly stroked his chin. "Maybe. Then again, maybe not all the discs are required to open the door either."

Now that Aksel mentioned it, that made sense. Glo should have thought of that himself. "I see your point. However, we do have someone with us who may be able to use the universal key." He turned toward Elistra. "I've watched you meditate regularly. Correct me if I am wrong, but doesn't that practice attune all your chakras?"

Elistra's entire face lit up. "You really do know your psionics, don't you?"

Glo felt his face flush slightly. "I think the disc is helping quite a bit. Still, if you don't mind, I think you should try the last disc."

Elistra grew silent, pursing her lips as she thought it over. Finally, she gave him a short nod. "Very well then, I shall try it."

Elistra led the way back to the first pedestal, the one with the rainbow disc. Since Seth had already checked it out, there was no reason to wait, yet Elistra hesitated before bending down and grasping the disc. She gave Glo a brief glance, then scooped up the disc into her hand.

It began to glow like the others, but when this disc disappeared, seven images appeared along Elistra's torso, from the base all the way to the top of her head. Red, orange, yellow, green, blue, purple and white. When they finally disappeared, the seeress smiled, then abruptly wobbled in place.

Glo rushed forward with a cry. "Elistra!"

He grasped her around the waist and held her tight, supporting her against him. The seeress appeared quite dazed at first, but abruptly shook her head and steadied herself. Her eyes fixed on Glo, a slight smile spreading across her lips. "Whoa, what a rush."

Glo was relieved to see her recover, but still felt a measure of concern. "Are you alright?"

"I'm fine," she answered, placing a soft hand on his cheek. She mouthed the words, 'thank you,' then gently pushed away from him and turned toward Aksel.

"You were right. I can see it clearly now. The multi-colored disc is a universal key, but it is not the only one. Certain combinations of the other keys should open the door above as well. If I had to guess, I would say body, mind and spirit, or heart, voice and sight."

Glo was also impressed with her supposition. It made perfect sense in fact—so much so, that Glo was able to expand on her theory. "What you're saying is that someone like Lloyd could have picked up three of the discs and opened the door himself."

Elistra gave him a short nod. "I believe so."

"Well, on the bright side, at least we've all got these nice tattoos," Elladan said with a partial smile, pointing to the one on his throat.

"That is one way to look at it." Elistra winked mischievously at the bard.

"Or that we just wasted a whole bunch of time," Seth added with a derisive snort.

Elistra gave the halfling an ironic stare. "That as well."

Aksel spoke up at that point, refocusing everyone's attention to the matter at hand. "Well, what's done is done. We might as well head up the stairs and try to open the block."

Aksel was right as usual—there was no point in berating themselves for something they could not possibly have known ahead of time. The small company crossed over to the stairwell and filed one by one up the winding stairs, Ruka falling in behind them. When they reached the top, Elistra placed her hand on the solid stone directly above the stairwell. Just as had happened with the door from the outside, a section of ceiling receded then slipped sideways, disappearing into the stone above. It revealed a circular hole containing a set of stairs that spiraled upward through the solid stone ceiling.

Glo felt a keen sense of elation that their theory had proven true. "It worked!"

Elistra's eyes fell on him and she winked. "Indeed."

Aksel, a triumphant smile on his face, ushered everyone forward. "Well then, onward and upward."

22
BLADES

Never... ask... me... if... I'm... sure...

After opening the way up, Elistra moved to one side, allowing the others to pass. The marching order remained the same, with Seth in the lead, followed by Lloyd and Alana. Glo went next, Elistra falling in behind him as he passed. Once again, the staircase wound upward through solid rock.

Seth took his time, examining each step carefully for trip wires, pressure plates, and the like, thus their ascent was painstakingly slow. Abruptly, the halfling signaled a halt. Seth carefully scrutinized the stairwell ahead, checking both the steps and the walls. He finally stopped after a few stairs, closely examining a spot on the wall. Seth fiddled with something there for a minute or so, when they heard him swear softly, "Dragon dung."

Lloyd called to the halfling. "Is something wrong?"

Seth spun around, his face a mask of frustration. "It's just another stupid blade trap."

Aksel abruptly appeared on the stair right next to Glo. "Then what's the problem?"

Seth folded his arms across his chest and silently shook his head. "It's stupid, but the control mechanism is stuck—I can't get it to budge."

"Is it something I can help with?" Lloyd offered, though he didn't sound quite certain of himself.

Seth eyed the young man skeptically. "It would be tricky. You'd have to be careful not to touch anything else or you could set the whole thing off."

Before Lloyd could answer, a familiar voice drifted up from below. "Maybe I can help." Glo turned to see Donnie pushing past the others up the narrow staircase.

"And how do you intend to do that?" Seth asked, his tone filled with frustration and more than a hint of sarcasm.

"I've picked a lock or two in my time," Donnie said almost too casually. "How different could a trap mechanism be?"

Seth threw up his hands and rolled his eyes to the ceiling. As Donnie drew up next to him, he fixed the elf with a dubious stare. "You do realize the lock is already picked, right? All that needs to be done is to throw the switch..."

"...which is stuck," Donnie finished for him. "No offense to Lloyd, but I think I have a better chance of prying it free without setting off the trap."

Seth snorted contemptuously. "By all means then. Go ahead and get your head cut off."

"I doubt it will come to that," Donnie replied confidently, gazing up the staircase ahead of them. "So where is it then?"

Seth eyed the slight elf for a few moments more, then shrugged. "It's your funeral." He pointed up to a spot on the stairwell just above where they stood. "It's right there, three steps up on the left."

Donnie squinted his eyes, then nodded. "I see it."

Seth moved out of the way as the slight elf ascended the stairs. When Donnie reached the spot Seth had pointed out, he stopped and examined the area. There was a square-shaped box there that blended in perfectly with the color of the wall. Donnie slowly reached into the box and began fiddling with its insides. From the look on his face, it was obvious he was struggling with something. All of sudden, there was a sound like the popping of a spring, followed by the harsh grinding of gears. A moment later, the slight elf launched himself backwards, narrowly avoiding a huge blade that came swinging out of a previously-unseen slit in the wall.

"Donnie!" Alana cried.

She launched herself up the stairs, but then stopped short as Lloyd caught hold of the slight elf. Seth leaned casually against the opposite wall, his mouth curved sideways. "Told you so."

Donnie regained his balance and spun around, flashing Alana a brilliant smile. "Never even touched me." He then turned to Seth. "I almost had it," he said, holding two fingers about a half inch apart.

Above them, three huge blades now swung across the stairwell at regular intervals. They disappeared into the opposite wall, only to reappear again mere seconds later. The swinging blades effectively blocked their way upward. Seth glared at the slight elf. "So what now, genius?"

Donnie's hand went to his chin, his head tilted and his brow fur-rowing with deep creases. A few moments went by when, all of a sudden, his face lit up. He eyed Seth questioningly. "Do you hap-pened to have any spare knives?"

Seth let out a short laugh. "Heh. I always have spare knives. How many do you need?"

Donnie swiveled his head to the blades above. "Three should do it," he said, holding up that many fingers.

Seth produced three daggers and held them out hilt first. Alana eyes swept from the daggers to the blades above them then back to Donnie. "Are you sure you know what you're doing?"

Donnie grasped the knives without taking an eye off the blades, his response in rhythm with the lowest one. "Never... ask... me... if... I'm... sure..." As the last word died on his lips, the blade disappeared into the wall. Donnie suddenly leapt forward with one of Seth's knives in hand. The agile elf swiftly wedged the dagger into the opening, then quickly backpedaled down the steps. They all stood there, holding their breath, waiting to see what would happen next.

There was a loud clicking sound, and the knife handle moved slightly, but the dagger remained firmly stuck in the slit.

"It worked!" Donnie cried in triumph. He spun around and grasped Alana, hugging the lady warrior and rocking her back and forth.

Alana seemed uncertain how to respond, her arms askew as the slight elf held her tight. "I guess it did," she responded, sounding both surprised and amazed.

"Good thing too, or you'd be a head shorter."

Glo turned to see Ruka standing between him and Aksel. There was a strange yellow flash in her eyes as she stared at the embracing duo. Glo was not quite sure, but he thought he heard a faint roll of thunder off in the distance.

"Of course, if he had just disabled the trap in the first place..." Seth pointed out, his smirk even wider than before.

Donnie let Alana go, his eyes moving from Ruka to Seth. "I'm surrounded by doubters," he exclaimed perhaps just a bit too dramatically. The slight elf then spun around and began timing the next blade. "Anyway... it's... too... late... now..."

Donnie leapt forward just as the second blade disappeared into the wall and wedged another knife into the slot it came from. He quickly retreated and waited to see the result of his effort. The second dagger held as well. Donnie repeated his performance one more time, but on the last blade, the knife didn't quite wedge in all the way. He tried to correct his mistake, but instead was rewarded with a nasty cut across the side of his head. Had he been just a fraction slower, he wouldn't have had a head at all.

"Donnie!" Alana and Ruka screamed simultaneously. The pair rushed up the stairwell and dragged the elf back down.

"Let me see that," Aksel said, pushing through them all.

Donnie bled profusely from the scalp, but it turned out to be less severe than it looked. Aksel staunched the bleeding in no time and healed up the cut. When he was done, Aksel sat back and turned to Seth. "Do you want to give that a try?"

Seth threw up his hands in front of him. "Oh, no, no, no. I'm short enough already. This is Donnie's show. Let him finish what he started."

Donnie gave Seth a nod as got up and brushed himself off. "Much obliged."

Alana's eyes were filled with concern as she watched the elf prepare to try his crazy stunt once more. "Are you sure you're okay?"

Donnie flashed the lady knight a brilliant smile. "I'm fine now, thanks to Aksel." His gaze shifted upward to the last revolving blade. "I should have just left the last knife alone. I'll get it this time for sure."

Without warning, Ruka lashed out and punched him in the arm.

"Ow!" Donnie cried. He grabbed his arm and whirled around to face the teen. "What was that for?"

Ruka's expression was dark, her tone filled with more than a trace of anger. "You better not miss this time."

The young teen then spun on her heel and pushed past them as she charged back down the stairs. Donnie's jaw hung open as he gazed after her. Seth, grinning outrageously, held out another knife to the bewildered elf. Donnie absently grabbed it from the halfling, his eyes still focused on the retreating teen. Alana placed a hand on his shoulder and softly bade him, "Good luck."

Her words brought the elf back to his senses. He peered at Alana and replied with a soft, "Thank you."

Everyone stepped back as Donnie prepared himself for another attempt. The slight elf swayed back and forth, his body keeping rhythm with the huge blade. He was more cautious this time, waiting for a number of passes before finally launching himself up the staircase. As the last blade disappeared into the wall, Donnie reached the opposite side and quickly wedged the dagger into the slot. The wiry elf immediately leapt back down the steps, his eyes glued to the hilt that still protruded from the wall. The stairwell grew deathly quiet as the companions waited there, none daring to even breathe. Their silence was rewarded with a loud clicking sound as the last knife handle moved slightly, but nonetheless, stuck in the slit. All three blades were now effectively wedged into the wall.

"Phew." Donnie wiped his brow then spun around to face the others. "I suggest we move ahead quickly. This makeshift fix won't hold forever."

The companions resumed their ascent, the clicking sounds of the blocked blades garnering nervous stares from each of them as they passed. Seth, in particular, kept muttering to himself and shaking his head. Glo heard Aksel whisper to the halfling, "Don't say it."

"I can still think it," Seth murmured under his breath.

23
PHANTOM ARMOR

The second his foot touched the floor,
the suits of armor began to move

The small company continued up the stairwell as it wound through solid stone. Maybe two dozen steps above the blade trap, Seth stopped and raised his hand, signaling another halt.

"What is it now? Another trap?" Aksel whispered.

"There's light up ahead," Seth hissed over his shoulder.

Glo felt a sinking feeling in the pit of his stomach. Had they finally found the Serpent Cultists? If so, how did they get past the chakra puzzle and the blade trap in the stairwell?

"What kind of light?" he asked in a hushed tone.

"Daylight," came the soft reply.

Daylight? The queasiness in Glo's stomach disappated, but at the same time he felt confused. Glo tried to picture the exterior of the monolith in his mind, but could not remember seeing any windows. They began to climb again. Sure enough, when Glo reached the stair Seth had been on, he could see light at the top of the stairwell, and indeed, it looked like daylight.

The companions climbed a bit father until the stairwell opened up to yet another huge chamber—this one was not dark like the floors below. From where Glo stood, he could see three walls, each with a large archway embedded in its center. Through those arches, the treetops of the Darkwoods were visible, fanning out like a sea of fluttering greenery as far as the eye could see. Sunlight filtered into the room from all sides, completely illuminating the area around them. As in the lower rooms, the huge pillar rose up its center, the staircase winding around it all the way to the ceiling far above. Glo could only assume there was a fourth archway in the wall hidden behind the pillar.

"The magic on the archways must be the same used in the downstairs entrance," he murmured quietly. "Light can filter in but not out."

Elladan nodded and gave him a half-smile. "It is a nice trick."

The large chamber was barren, with one glaring exception—midway between the stairs and each archway stood a black suit of armor. Glo eyed the suits cautiously. They appeared to be full sets of armor, including a helm, breastplate, gauntlets, tassets, and greaves, all dull black in color. Furthermore, each suit held a large, jet black sword, point down with the tip resting on the floor, each pommel gripped firmly by two armored gauntlets.

The sight of the black-armored suits standing alone in the empty room was eerie. Yet despite their intrusion on this floor, the armor remained stationary, appearing for all intents and purposes to be just harmless decorations. Yet something nagged at the back of Glo's mind, something dark. He racked his brain, mentally scanning over the books in his father's library. Glo's mental eye abruptly stopped— he was looking at a large book with a dull black cover, the title written in swirling elvish runes along the thick binding. It read, *The Book of Undead.*

Glo's pulse began to race as he mentally leafed through the pages of that book. He sped through it, scanning for anything to do with armor. Suddenly he stopped—a dark visage stared back at him from the page, sending a chill up his spine. Glo frantically skimmed the text, his eyes growing wider as he realized what they were dealing with. Yet, before he could utter a single word, Donnie prempted him.

"I think I'll take a closer look," the slight elf declared as he casually took a step off the stairs.

"Donnie, wait!" Aksel cried, reaching for the elf just a split second too late. The second his foot touched the floor, the suits of armor began to move. Glo froze in horror as he watched three large jet black swords raise off the floor and spin around in those dull black gauntlets until they were held upright. Each suit then took a step forward, the clinking of metal armored plates echoing through the otherwise silent chamber. The motion broke Glo from his fear-driven paralysis, and he managed to utter two words.

"Phantom armor!"

The sound of those words seemed to draw a palpable darkness down around them. Phantom armors were undead creatures, raised from the corpses of slain knights, any shred of humanity ripped away from them, the empty metal shell filled with nothing but a cold spirit. Were they evil in life, the knight's soul remained bound to the armor, haunting the halls and battlefields where they were slain, forever seeking vengeance against the living. Yet even if they were good, the soul of the slain knight would be replaced with a violent spirit, one intent on death and destruction. Either way, phantom armors were terrible opponents, encased in steel and feeling no pain, battling until the bitter end.

While Glo quickly explained what they were up against, Donnie, Lloyd, Alana and Ruka fanned out in front of them. The sound of steel echoed through the chamber as the foursome drew their weapons. Donnie stood ready, rapier in one hand, short sword in the other. Lloyd, beside the slight elf, took a defensive stance, a large sword held in each hand, flames rising from their hilts and swiftly encircling the blades. Alana's holy sword gleamed with pure white light as she drew it from its sheath, as if the blade knew it was facing creatures of the dark. Ruka, next to Alana, drew her short sword and a dagger, the faint crackle of thunder adding to the mix as arcs of electricity played across her sword blade.

Glo finished his brief explanation, his eyes now fixed on the advancing armors. The entire scene seemed surreal, the black suits slowly and methodically marching forward, their huge blades pointed directly at the companions. They uttered no words or challenges of any kind, the only sounds coming from them being the clicking of their armored plates and the scraping of their steel boots on the stone floor. The eerie silence was shattered by a cry from the stairwell above.

"There's a fourth one!"

That was Seth's voice. Glo gazed up at the pillar, but could not see the halfling. He must have climbed the spiral staircase to see behind the pillar and was now on the opposite side. All at once, music filled the room. It was an invigorating tune, and Glo's nerves immediately calmed at the sound of it. He glanced over at Elladan, the bard responding with a semi-smile as his lively music dispelled the dark cloud that hung over them.

✳

Seth stood on the other side of the pillar, about two dozen stairs above his friends. Upon reaching the third floor, he had immediately spied the black armors and noted their positions in front of the archways. Seth was certain there was a fourth armor and archway behind the pillar, so he headed up the staircase to get a good look. Sure enough, as he rounded the curve in the pillar, another archway and armor came into view. That was when he heard Aksel's cry.

"Donnie, wait!"

A moment later, the armors within his view began to move. Seth planted his face in his palm. Leave it to Donatello—the elf was so impetuous he was giving Lloyd a run for his money. That's when he heard Glo yell, "Phantom armor!"

Seth wasn't exactly sure what phantom armor was, but whatever it was, he was certain it wasn't good. Some kind of spirit, or ghost, inside the armor perhaps? Either way, the armor appeared pretty solid—too solid, in fact. Two of the phantom armors had disappeared around the curve of the pillar, but the third was still advancing in his direction.

"There's a fourth one!" he cried loud enough for the others to hear. Unfortunately, there was no response. It appeared that Seth was on his own back here, but what was he going to do? His thoughts were interrupted by the strumming of a lute. Lively music filled the chamber, making Seth smile despite himself. *At least Elladan is making himself useful.*

The sudden clash of steel on steel rang throughout the chamber. The others had engaged the enemy. Seth returned his focus to the armor in front of him. The thing was huge, probably six feet tall and a good three hundred pounds. *There's no way I can take this thing alone.*

Seth's eyes swept the nearly-empty chamber, searching for anything that might give him an advantage. His eyes fell on the archway, and an idea popped into his head. It was crazy, but then again Seth never shied away from crazy. Making up his mind, the halfling grasped the railing and launched himself up and over, landing smoothly on the stone floor below. The phantom armor continued to advance straight for him. Seth reached into a bag on his belt, but this time did not withdraw a knife. Instead, he now held a small vial of oily liquid. Seth held out the vial and moved his hands in a slow, intricate pattern. As his hands came together, Seth spoke a single word, "*Arvina.*"

The oily vial disappeared from his hand. At the same moment, a film of blackish liquid appeared under the armor's feet. The puddle quickly spread until it reached about two yards in every direction. When the phantom armor took its next step, its foot started to slide. It shifted both feet in an attempt to stay upright, but then its back foot gave out as well. The entire suit of armor flipped up in the air and landed with a resounding crash in the middle of a pool of grease.

The corner of Seth's mouth lifted slightly. *Step one, check. Now for step two.*

While Seth was still busy with his phantom armor, Lloyd and Donnie engaged their own. The warrior and swordsman weaved in and out, slashing at the metal-encased creature and dodging its heavy blade. Neither of Donnie's weapons left a scratch, but Lloyd fared a bit better, especially with his black blade. Wherever that sword connected, it left a deep cut in the dull black armor. Meanwhile, Alana and Ruka fought another armor. The lady knight expertly parried its huge sword with her shield, and rang blow after blow on the armored creature. Her gleaming sword seemed equally as effective as Lloyd's black blade, slicing deep into the armored suit. Ruka hung back, slowly circling around the black-armored figure, looking for an opportune angle to strike.

Meanwhile, the enigmatic Elistra had revealed yet another psionic ability. She summoned an astral construct, a creature of pure ectoplasm, the material of the astral plane. The construct was roughly the size and shape of a large human, with a semi-transparent body and indistinct features. It bore no weapons or armor, its large, three fingered hands being its only method of attack. Elistra sent the creature to hold off the third phantom armor while the others dealt with the first two.

"It may not last long," she cautioned, her expression grim.

Glo watched with keen interest as the construct faced off against the phantom armor. As soon as it was within reach, the armor assaulted the creature, hacking and slashing away with its huge black sword. Pieces of ectoplasm flew everywhere but did little to deter the construct. The creature swung back with its large hands, hammering away mercilessly, leaving visibile dents in the dull black armor wherever it struck. A sudden cry drew his attention to the other combatants.

"Alana, move!"

Glo spun back in time to see the lady knight backpedal away from the black armor. A second later, Ruka let loose a bolt of lightning. The bolt passed through the armor and across the room, well away from the other combatants. It was a well-executed attack, but unfortunately had little effect on the phantom armor, resulting in only a momentary pause in the creature's movements. Once the bolt was gone, the black-armored fiend resumed its advance as if nothing had happened.

"Dragon dung!" Glo swore under his breath. "How are we going to stop these things?"

Around the other side of the pillar, Seth reached into his bag, this time pulling out a small parchment. He unrolled it and pulled out a sticky piece of white cobweb. Seth held the sticky material in his hand and began another set of intricate motions, ending with the words, "*Aranea Repere.*"

All at once, the soles of his boots adhered to the ground. He was able to lift them with some effort, but when he set them down again, they stuck fast.

"Nice," he whispered to himself. The phantom armor still thrashed about in the pool of grease as Seth advanced into the black puddle. His feet adhered solidly to the ground, as the effects of his spell negated the effects of the black liquid. When Seth reached the armor, he bent down and gave it a slight push. It moved easily. Seth chortled to himself. *This just might work.*

The halfling nimbly dodged out of the way as the armor lashed out at him, his mind still racing. It all came down to one thing—if these windows were like the door on the first floor, his plan would work. Seth hustled to the nearest archway and placed his hand into the opening. Sure enough, it passed right through. Seth could hardly contain himself. *It will work!*

The halfling spun on his heel and ran back to the other side of the pool. The armor still floundered in the middle, completely covered with grease. Seth grinned from ear-to-ear. *Even better.*

He crouched down and mentally crossed his fingers, then took off at a dead run. Seth slammed into the flailing suit and pushed against it with all his might. The armor was so heavily greased that it shot forward in front of him, sliding across the pool, not even slowing down when they hit the edge.

"Alana, move!"

Seth was still running full tilt when he heard Ruka's cry, but paid little heed. The archway was fast approaching when a flash went off behind him and a crash of thunder reverberated throughout the chamber. Seth ignored that too—the armored suit was flailing wildly, and if he slowed down he might not reach his goal. The arch was now dangerously close, but Seth continued to push until the very last second. He finally let go a couple of yards from the window, planting his feet and praying his boots would stop him in time. Unfortunately, they did not. Seth's forward motion continued, his speed and the grease from the armor counteracting his spell. He watched with grim satisfaction as the phantom armor reached the archway and slid through, immediately plummeting out of sight below, then Seth himself was over the edge.

As he fell, Seth made one last attempt to grab onto the edge. Miraculously, his hands caught hold, grasping a slight lip that was there. His body, however, continued to swing outward, dangling over thin air. Luckily, his grip held. In an amazing feat of agility, Seth pulled his knees up and managed to hit the side of the monolith with the soles of his boots. By the grace of the gods, his feet stuck. He hung there for a few moments on the side of the monolith, his breath coming in short, ragged bursts.

"Well, that was fun," he said to no one in particular.

Seth glanced behind him and saw the phantom armor broken into pieces on the ground far below. A brief smile crossed his lips, and then the halfling hauled himself back up into the chamber. As he pulled himself off the floor, Seth caught sight of something bright out of the corner of one eye. Above the archway, a Dwarven rune had lit up. Seth's eyes went wide. He suddenly understood. He spun around and screamed at the top of his lungs, "Elladan, grease them! Throw them out the windows!"

"Dragon dung!" Glo swore under his breath. "How are we going to stop these things?"

"You did say they feel no pain," Aksel reminded him.

"And that they won't stop until they're utterly destroyed," Elistra added.

Glo took in a deep breath and blew it out in an attempt to calm down. "Yes, yes, I know..."

He was interrupted by a shrill cry. "Elladan, grease them! Throw them out the windows!"

That was Seth, but this time his voice came from behind the pillar. The inspiring music abruptly stopped. Elladan peered at Glo, a single eyebrow arched. "Say what?"

Glo was just as perplexed as Elladan. *Grease them? And throw them out the window? Is he serious?*

Glo peered at Aksel, but the little cleric merely frowned and shook his head. Even the normally unflappable Elistra appeared surprised, her comely brow furrowed. Seth's voice rang out once more, nearer this time. "It's another puzzle! Throw them out the window they started from! A rune lights up!"

It was Glo's turn to raise an eyebrow. *Now that sounds just plain nuts.* He shouted back to the halfling, "Seth! If you are joking..."

Seth cut him off. "Always! But not this time!"

Glo didn't know what to think. The idea of greasing the phantom armors and throwing them out the windows seemed ludicrous. Elladan and Aksel appeared equally uncertain. Elistra, on the other hand, broke out into a wry smile. "If the chakra tattoos were any indication, Larketh did appear to have a strange sense of humor."

Aksel gazed at the seeress and shrugged. "I guess it can't hurt."

Elladan's eyes moved from Elistra to Aksel, then he shrugged as well. "Guess there's only one way to find out."

"Aim for the one battling Alana and Ruka," Aksel instructed him.

Elladan gave a brief nod, put away his lute, and started weaving his spell. Meanwhile, Aksel turned toward the armor between Lloyd and Donnie, and began a spell of his own. Glo was puzzled—as far as he knew, the spell to create grease was not a divine one.

"What are you going to do?" he asked the little cleric.

"I'm going to try to dispel the magic imbued in the armor," Aksel responded, not taking his eyes off his intended target.

Elladan's spell released first. A pool of black liquid appeared under the armor, causing it to wobble as it tried to maintain its balance. It teetered precariously for a moment or two, then hit the ground with a resounding crash, its large black sword clattering away across the stone floor. Unfortunately, Alana also lost her balance, landing unceremoniously on her steel-encased butt.

"Sorry, my lady!" Elladan called to her.

Alana spun her head toward him, a faint smile across her lips. "I'll forgive you this time—next time, perhaps a little warning might be in order!"

Ruka, in contrast, had no trouble with the grease pool. She slid over to Alana as if skating on ice, and helped the lady knight up to her feet, escorting her out of the pool while the black-armored phantom continued to splash around. While Ruka assisted Alana, Aksel cast his spell. *"Nullam Depelle."*

A circle of violet light appeared around Lloyd, Donnie, and the armor between them. Two things happened simultaneously—the phantom armor halted in its tracks, and the flames around Lloyd's blades winked out. Man and elf waited cautiously, but the black armor remained still. Suddenly, the armored suit began to shake, then all at once fell apart, crashing to the ground in a heap of steel.

"It worked!" Elladan cried, clasping Aksel firmly on the shoulder.

Glo, however, was not so certain. "For now maybe, but if the magic holding it together is stronger, it will just reassemble itself."

Aksel gave him a grim nod. "Good point." The little cleric cupped his hands around his mouth and shouted, "Lloyd, Donnie! Quick, throw the pieces out the window!"

The duo stood over the armored heap, cautiously inspecting it. They glanced up at Aksel's words, nodded briefly, then sheathed their weapons and scooped up as many pieces of the armor as they could carry. Lloyd grabbed the heavy breastplate, the tassets, and the helm while Donnie picked up the gauntlets and the greaves. As they hurried toward the nearest window, Ruka got Alana to solid ground. The young teen then turned toward the stairwell, a thumb pointed at the black armor still floundering in pool of grease behind her.

"What about this one?"

Glo immediately pointed at the archway behind her. "Out that window."

A half-twisted smile spread across Ruka's lips. "Got it."

Ruka strode back into the pool of grease, not slowing her pace in the slightest. Upon reaching the black armor, she bent down, knocked a flailing arm out of the way, and began pushing it in the direction of the archway. Glo watched appreciatively as the young teen sped faster and faster, but then noticed something strange. A faint golden glow appeared around Ruka's body, and her hair rose of its own accord.

Glo arched an eyebrow. *Just as Donnie had described during her battle with the troll.* He cast a quick glance at Elistra, but the seeress paid him no attention, her gaze fixed firmly on Ruka, that familiar enigmatic smile on her lips. When Ruka was about five feet from the archway, she gave the armor a tremendous shove. The motion stopped her in her tracks, and simultaneously launched the armor directly at the open archway. It quickly reached the window, then flew out into the open air, swiftly disappearing from view as it fell over the side of the monolith. Above the archway, a rune he hadn't noticed before suddenly lit up.

"It appears that Seth was right," Aksel said, with just a hint of surprise. Moments later, Lloyd and Donnie dropped their pieces out the window, a rune above them also lighting up.

"Looks like Seth already has the last one," Elladan said with a soft chuckle.

In all the excitement, Glo had forgotten about the third phantom armor. He spun around now and saw the last black armor flat on its back, flailing around in another pool of grease. Seth stood just outside the pool, his hands on his hips. There was no sign of Elistra's astral construct, other than pieces of what could only be ectoplasm scattered here and there. The four of them sprinted across the room toward Seth, Aksel calling out ahead of them. "What's the problem?"

Seth spun around to face them, his lips curved to one side. "I already pushed one of these things out the window. Someone else can take care of this one."

Glo, Aksel, Elladan and Elistra all exchanged glances, then burst into laughter. Leave it to Seth to make light of what could have been an otherwise disastrous situation.

"That's alright Seth, we'll get someone else to do your dirty work," Elladan said in between chortles.

Lloyd, Donnie, Alana, and Ruka all came running up at the same time. Ruka nodded toward the still-flailing suit of armor. "What's up with that?"

Elladan broke into a wide grin. "Seth's too cerebral to take care of this last one."

Seth's head tilted down, his eyes squinted as he glowered fiercely at the bard. "Yeah, yeah. I'm a fricken genius. Now can someone with a bit more mass than me push this thing out the window?"

24
RUNIC WHEEL OF FORTUNE

I think these rings are actually wheels

When the last suit of armor fell out the window, the final rune lit up. A few moments later, the grating noise of stone against stone drifted down from the ceiling far above. Seth climbed the stairwell and confirmed that the way up was clear, but the small company decided to rest a while before moving on.

Miraculously, other than a few bumps and bruises, no one had been harmed in the strange battle with the phantom armors. Still, everyone felt drained. Judging by the outside sun, it was now mid-afternoon. They had been inside the monolith perhaps a couple of hours now, but with all that had happened thus far, it felt like it had been a lot longer.

Elladan broke out some bread and hard cheese for everyone to share. They gathered around and ate the short meal, refueling their depleted bodies. At the same time, seeing the outside world again bolstered their spirits. A breathtaking view of lush treetops spread out like a dark green ocean before them. Off in the distance, to the north and west, tall black peaks rose up to meet the deep blue sky. Those were the Korlokesel Mountains, the range taller and more barren here than its greener counterparts that bordered the western edge of the Bendenwoods to the north.

After a short break, the companions gathered at the northern window. In the clearing far below, the Knights of the Rose were still setting up camp. Six smaller tents formed a circle around a large one. A number of small, silver-clad figures busily hammered long wooden stakes into the ground, creating a pike fence around the entire encampment. Directly below them, two tiny knights had gathered around a broken suit of black armor. Occasionally, they would look up at the monolith and shake their heads. Alana opened her mouth to cry down to them, but Aksel interrupted her.

"That may not be the best idea."

She turned her head and stared at him uncertainly.

Elladan placed a hand on her shoulder and explained in a gentle voice. "We still don't know what happened to the cultists, or where they might be now."

"Oh, right," Alana replied, her expression turning grave.

Glo understood her desire to communicate with her fellow knights. A lot had happened in the short time since they entered the monolith, and it would be best to keep them informed. He had an idea. "If you want, I can summon Raven. You can tie a note to her leg and she can carry it down for you."

Alana turned toward the wizard, her face lighting up. "That would be most kind of you."

Glo smiled back at her as he mentally called Raven. Their telepathic link unerringly led the bird through one of the darkened windows in the monolith's side. Alana quickly scribed a note, which Glo then tied to bird's tiny leg. Raven then flew back through the window and spiraled down to the clearing below. The companions watched on as she winged her way around the encampment, finally settling on the top of a pole bearing the pennant of the moon next to the center tent.

A silver-clad figure with short dark hair approached the bird, reached up, and took the note from it. The knight unfolded the parchment and read through it. Once done, he glanced up at the monolith and waved. From this height, they could barely make out the line of a dark beard across the figure's face. It was Sir Craven.

Sir Craven disappeared into the large tent, reappearing a few minutes later. He strode over to the waiting bird, attached something to its leg, then stood back as Raven spread her tiny wings and lifted up off the pole. She slowly spiraled upward above the camp, and winged her way back toward the monolith. Raven again unerringly navigated through the dark window and landed on Glo's outstretched arm. Glo retrieved the note from Sir Craven and handed it to Alana. The lady knight unrolled the parchment and read its contents out loud.

"All is well here. The fortifications will be done before dark. The woods are clear, and there is no sign of cultists. The black armors were crushed from the fall, but we will disperse the parts as you suggest. Good luck and godspeed. Sir Craven."

Alana breathed a sigh of relief, the tension fading from her armored shoulders. "Well then, gentlemen, whenever you are ready."

Aksel responded with a thin smile, then nodded. "I agree. We should get moving."

The small company gathered up once more and ascended the winding stairwell around the huge center pillar. Seth led the way with Donnie close behind, the latter wanting to learn more about spotting and handling traps. Seth begrudgingly agreed, with the caveat that Donnie was not to touch anything. Donnie appeared crestfallen, but agreed. The stairwell passed through another section of solid stone, but there were no blade traps this time. Other than Donnie, no one seemed disappointed.

Daylight filtered down from the top of the stairs here as well. When they reached the top of the stairwell, it opened up to another large chamber. Like the room below, this one had an archway in each wall, the mid-afternoon sun streaming in and brightening the entire area. Yet unlike the other rooms, the stairs ended here, the center pillar rising only a few feet above the floor, ending in a flat, round surface. Far above, all four walls rose to meet at a single point.

Glo let out a deep sigh—they had finally reached the top of the monolith. As he stepped into the room, his attention was drawn to the dais at the top of the pillar. The entire thing was covered with carvings. The others noticed it as well, the entire group gathering around to see what was engraved on it. The wide dais had three concentric rings around its perimeter. Inside the rings was a large circle, three yards in diameter, decorated with an intricate pattern of curved and crossed white lines on a purple background.

"That's the symbol of Larketh," Elistra explained to them. "It's supposed to depict how all life is interconnected and intertwined. Personally, I always found it a bit convoluted."

Glo gave the seeress a sidelong glance. He had seen the symbol before, but it was not widely known, only appearing in the most obscure of texts. His father, of course, had a copy, but yet again, he had to wonder where Elistra studied Larketh. Elladan mirrored his thoughts.

"You seem extremely well versed in history, milady, especially those things having to do with the Thrall Masters."

Elistra eyes moved from Elladan to Glo, her cheeks turning a light shade of scarlet. "Oh, it's just a hobby of mine," she said with a negligent wave of her hand.

Seth let out a derisive snort. "You have some weird hobbies, lady."

The rings around the dais were each divided into 36 sections, every section with a symbol carved on it. The symbols on the inner ring were immediately recognizable as a combination of letters and numbers from the Common tongue, starting with the letters 'A' through 'M.' The alphabet was interrupted at that point by the numbers '0' through '9.' Beyond that, the alphabet continued with 'N' and finished with 'Z' in the 36th slot.

Glo, Elladan, and Seth recognized the outer ring as depicting the ancient Dwarven language. That ring was laid out exactly the same as the inner ring, with numbers dividing the alphabet. The middle ring, however, proved to be a mystery—the symbols portrayed on it did not match any known language. Glo could state that for a fact since he was familiar with the basics of all written languages—in fact, he could speak sixteen of them, some better than others. While Glo fretted over the central ring, Aksel examined the entire platform.

"I think these rings are actually wheels," the little cleric mused softly. He reached a tentative hand toward the outside ring when Seth interrupted him.

"Um, are you sure you want to do that?"

Aksel glanced up, his face flushing. He immediately stepped back and shook his head. "Guess I got a bit carried away." Aksel ushered Seth forward. "Would you care to do the honors?"

"Thank you," Seth responded, in a mock polite tone. Yet, despite his obvious displeasure, he strode forward and carefully examined the platform. Donnie followed Seth around, hovering close over the halfling's shoulder. Every once in a while, Seth would look up and glare at the slight elf. Donnie would back off for a while, until Seth resumed his scrutiny of the platform, then Donnie would then return to his position over the halfling's shoulder.

After about a quarter of an hour of searching the dais, Seth finally pronounced it safe. The halfling puncuated his announcement by grasping the outer ring and giving it a good shove. The ring spun a few degrees clockwise, eventually coming to a stop. Unexpectedly, the middle and inner ring also moved, though each progressively less.

Aksel positively beamed with pride. "I was right; it is a wheel!"

For the first time in awhile, Glo smiled. "Indeed you are. So it's another puzzle, the key most likely being the lining up of all three wheels."

Seth gazed up at them and let out a short laugh. "Heh. Not going to be easy, especially with them all moving at the same time."

Glo grimaced, the intricacy of this puzzle causing his head to ache. He reached up and rubbed his temples with his fingers. "That and the fact that the middle circle is a language none of us has ever seen before."

"Look at this." Glo glanced up and saw Elistra bent low over the platform about a quarter way around the dais. Glo strode over to her side and followed her gaze. Elistra pointed to a few of the symbols along the center ring. "Notice how the markings around each symbol are lighter and flowing. It almost looks like they are surrounded by water, or wind perhaps..."

Glo took a closer look at the symbols. The designs around what had to be letters did indeed look like water and wind and...

"...even fire," Elistra finished his thought. "What's more is, the pattern repeats itself." She pointed to each letter as she went. "Water, wind, fire, and, assuming that last design represents earth, it starts all over again. Water, wind, fire, earth..."

Glo's eyes widened as he too now saw the pattern. "Every fourth letter. Brilliant!" he burst out in excitement. Before Glo realized what he was doing, he threw his arms around the seeress and kissed her on the cheek. Elistra turned toward him, and suddenly they were face to face, their noses no more than an inch apart. A small smile crossed the seeress's lips.

"You're welcome," she replied in a low tone that practically dripped senuality.

Glo felt the blood rushing to his cheeks. He quickly let go of her and took a step backwards. "S-sorry. I didn't mean to overstep myself."

Elistra's eyes twinkled with amusement. "Oh, I didn't mind at all."

Glo abruptly felt a hand clasp his shoulder. Elladan leaned in close and whispered, "Got yourself a live one there, Glo."

Glo spun around and saw everyone watching him. Seth and Ruka both wore bent grins. Elladan gave him his familiar half-smile. Donnie and Alana exchanged a knowing glance. Even Aksel wore a slight smile. Glo's cheeks grew even hotter, if that was possible. Now thoroughly embarrassed, the elven wizard spun back toward the dais and tried to focus on the puzzle of the middle wheel. Yet try as he might, his mind kept wandering back to a certain pair of violet eyes. The flustered wizard began to muse aloud in an effort to regain his focus.

"An elemental language. An elemental language. Who in the world would..."

All at once, it dawned on him. An unknown language, the four elements, all depicted in flowing script—there was only one race that would have developed such a language.

"The Titans!"

Glo and Aksel had called out the answer simultaneously. The elf and gnome turned toward each other, grinning from ear to ear. The Titans were purported to be masters of the four elemental forces.

Of course, there were none roaming the earth these days, but before the elves, during the Second Age of the world, the Titans ruled supreme. No known texts had survived that unnamed era, but it was always rumored that the Titans had a written language. Any books that may have existed were most likely destroyed during the Dragon-Titan War, the cataclysmic event that shook the world to its foundation and reformed the continents. Only the Dragons had any records of that age, and they jealously guarded that information. Now, though, in front of them, was clear evidence of a language that could only belong to the Titans. Glo was positively bursting with excitement.

"What a remarkable discovery!"

Seth, pragmatic as ever, interrupted his reverie. "Yeah, yeah, you can gush over it later. Right now we have a puzzle to solve, unless of course, you want to spend the rest of the day stuck up here?"

Glo took a deep breath and reigned in his enthusiasm. Seth was right. They needed to figure this out. A tap on his shoulder caused Glo to spin around. Donnie stood there, a paintbrush in his hand. "If you want, I can sketch out each of these symbols for you."

Glo smiled at his fellow elf, a bit of his former enthusiasm returning. "Thank you, Donnie." He cast a hard look at Seth. "At least some folks have an appreciation for the significance of this find."

"Oh, I understand it," Seth shot back. "I just don't care."

Before Glo could respond, Aksel held up a hand. "Not now, you two. Glo, come over here and help me figure this out."

Glo took another deep breath. Aksel was right. This was neither the time nor the place for a discussion on the significance of a long lost language. Glo cast a glance at Donnie, but the artist was already engrossed in sketching the newfound letters onto his pad. Glo decided to let him be, and joined Aksel in re-examining the platform. The little cleric was thinking aloud.

"We can assume this wheel has letters and numbers in the same order as the other two, so all we really need to do is decipher just one of these symbols."

"You all do that," Seth said with more than a just hint of cynicism in his tone, "while I try and figure out the movements of these rings and how to line them up."

It was rather obvious the halfling did not think much of their chances of finding a solution anytime soon. Askel chose to ignore the halfling's lack of faith in them.

"Good plan," was all Aksel said, not looking up from his study of the middle wheel. At the same time, Glo felt someone next to him. He turned and saw Elistra standing there, gazing up at him with those violet eyes.

"I have an eye for this sort of thing. Maybe I can help?"

"S-sure," Glo stammered, his concentration evaporating as she stood right next to him.

Since they had reached the top floor, Ruka had remained off to the side, silently watching their progress with the wheel puzzle. Perhaps not surprisingly, her patience had worn thin. "You all go ahead. I'm going to go and scout outside."

The young teen strode across the chamber toward one of the four windows in the top floor chamber. Alana gazed after her, a wistful sigh escaping her lips. "Wish I could come with you."

Donnie gazed up from his sketch pad at the lovely lady knight, his eyes glittering with obvious interest. "You can always keep me company..."

His expression remained hopeful as her gaze fell upon him. A small but satisfied smile spread across Alana's face, but then she shook her head. "That's alright, I'll just keep watch out the window."

With that, Alana spun around and trod after Ruka, the young teen having stopped in front of a window, preparing to shape shift. Lloyd, quite obviously just as bored as the rest of them, swiftly rushed to join her. "I'll go with you."

Donnie mooned after the lady knight as she crossed the chamber, continuing to watch her as Ruka shape-shifted into the now familiar visage of the white-tailed hawk and flew out of the monolith. Once the lady knight and young warrior took up positions at the window, Donnie let out a brief sigh and returned to his paintbrush and sketchpad. Glo lost track of the others after that. Elistra stuck close to his side, the warmth of her body, scent of her perfume, and the occasional brush of her hair a constant distraction. Of course, it didn't help that Seth kept turning the wheels at odd moments. Glo was not sure how much time had passed when the halfling called out, "Got it!"

Glo raised his eyes and saw Seth standing across the platform from them, his arms folded across his chest and a smug expression on his face. "The outer wheel turns twice for every turn of the middle wheel, and the same for the middle to inner wheel. So you have to turn the outer wheel four times to get one full turn of the inner wheel."

Aksel grinned at the self-satisfied halfling. "Nicely done, Seth."

Glo gave him a nod as well. "Yes, very nice piece of deductive reasoning there."

"Yeah, not bad for a little guy," Elladan chimed in.

Glo nearly choked—height was definitely one of Seth's buttons. Seth's smile abruptly faded, his eyes narrowing as he glared at the bard. Elladan stared back at the halfling with an innocent expression. "What? It was a compliment."

Aksel, trying to keep the peace, spoke up before Seth could respond. "Anyway—anyone having luck with this alphabet?"

Elladan, still trying to suppress a grin, turned to the little cleric. "Not so far. Other than the repeating pattern, there isn't much else to go on."

Elladan was right, neither Glo nor Elistra had gleaned much from the wheel either. What they needed was more information. Glo knit his brow as he stared down at the wheel and mused aloud. "If we only knew what element was primary, we could cut down the possibilities for the first letter..."

"Why didn't you just say so?" Elistra interrupted him. Glo gazed up at the seeress. She stood there with her hands on her hips and her head cocked to one side, wearing an expression of thinly veiled amusement. "Our present-day Zodiac signs were derived from ancient lore, dating to before the elves, all the way back to the age of the Titans. The first Zodiac sign is Ares, the sign of the Ram, and its associated element is—fire."

Glo's eyes went wide as her words sunk in. "Elistra, you're beautiful!" he cried, nearly throwing his arms around her again.

Elistra's eyes glittered. "Oh, Glo, you say the sweetest things..."

Glo, however, was too excited to respond, instead whirling back to the middle wheel. "That just cut the number of potential starting symbols down to nine..." Glo pored over the symbols with renewed vigor. If what Elistra had told them was correct, one of the fire symbols represented the letter 'A.' Of course, that meant that the symbol could also be 'E,' 'I,' 'M,' '3,' '7,' 'O,' 'S,' or 'W.'

After scrutinizing the wheel intently, Glo became convinced that one of the symbols was the letter 'I.' Abruptly he realized he was not alone. Glo looked up and saw Elladan on his one side, and Elistra on the other. The three of them hung over the same symbol. He exchanged a glance with Elladan, the two of the speaking simultaneously. "That has to be an 'I.'"

The duo exchanged grins. Glo turned to Elistra and saw her nod as well. Aksel came over to join them. "Which one?"

Glo pointed the symbol out to him. It was rather elaborate, with a curl over the top—it appeared to be a scripted letter I with flames shooting out from the bottom. Aksel bent over the letter, then stood up and nodded at the three of them. "Let's try it."

The little cleric strode over to Seth. Following Aksel's directions, the halfling spun the wheels. The outer wheel had to be spun three times to get the three rings lined up the way they wanted. Seth slowed the wheels down as the three letters approached each other. The inner and middle rings lined up first, the outside ring the last to fall into place.

Glo held his breath as the Dwarven letter for 'I' finally came even with the Common tongue 'I' and the Titan letter in question. They were rewarded with a loud click. A moment later, the symbol of Larketh in the center of the platform split in half, each side sliding away and disappearing under the wheels. A glowing circular disc, also with the symbol of Larketh emblazoned on it, appeared underneath. It was not attached to the platform, but merely hovered there in mid-air.

Elladan proffered his hands toward the floating disc, a bent smile on his face. "Ladies, gentlemen, it looks like our ride is here!"

Aksel and Seth slapped their hands together in triumph. Glo, equally elated, turned to hug Elistra. The seeress, however, had other ideas. As Glo wrapped his arms around her, she pulled close to him, stood up on her toes and firmly planted her lips on his. Glo was completely taken by surprise. He stood there wide-eyed at first, but then the softness of her lips, the smell of her hair, and the warmth of her body emptied his mind of all else. He closed his eyes and lost himself in that kiss, the world around him swiftly fading away.

From somewhere seemingly far away, he heard Donnie's voice. "Get a room, you two."

It was immediately followed by Elladan. "Shhh, don't spoil it. I've been waiting for this moment ever since they met."

Any other time, Glo would probably have been embarrassed, but at that moment he didn't have a care in the world. The lovely woman in his arms was all he wanted just now. She was smart, funny and beautiful, everything he could ever ask for. That amazing kiss went on for a while longer, until he heard Seth's voice.

"Okay, okay—I'm happy for you—I really am, but geez, guys, there's a time and a place."

Glo pulled back from Elistra, still holding her gently in his arms, and turned his head toward the halfling. Seth knelt on the platform, his mouth twisted sideways as he searched the floating disc for trip wires or the like. Donnie knelt beside him, grinning broadly at the duo. Aksel stood off to one side of the platform, wearing a bemused expression. Elladan stood next to him, grinning from ear to ear. Alana and Lloyd had returned from the window. The lady knight smiled and winked. Lloyd also wore a smile, but had a faraway look in his eyes.

Glo felt a sudden pang of sorrow for the young man. He could only imagine that he was thinking of a certain strawberry blonde young noblewoman. Ruka had returned as well, standing silently next to Alana with a twisted smile that mirrored Seth's.

"We really should get a move on," Aksel said in a gentle voice.

Elistra let out a brief sigh. "Yes, you are quite right, good cleric." She turned back to Glo and placed a slender finger on his nose. "We will continue this later," she told him, then gently pulled away.

Glo's cheeks burned hot. He imagined his face must be a bright shade of scarlet. Shortly thereafter, Seth declared the platform safe.

The floating disc was easily wide enough for the nine of them to comfortably fit on it. Despite that, Elistra snuggled close to Glo's side. The tall elf gladly draped an arm over her slender shoulders.

Seth was the last to join them. "All aboard!" he declared. "Next stop, the sub-basement."

"Is this thing ever going to move?" Donnie moaned impatiently. They had been standing on the floating disc for two full minutes, with no sign of it descending.

Seth eyed the elf darkly. "Did you see a control mechanism? Because I sure didn't."

"Maybe a vocal command?" Aksel suggested. He swiveled his head toward Glo. "How do you say 'down' in Dwarven?"

Glo had been half listening, his focus on the lovely woman by his side. Elistra nudged him with her elbow and whispered, "Glo, Aksel asked you a question."

Glo shook himself out of his reverie and looked at his gnomish friend. "Oh, right. The Dwarvish word for down. That would be 'Turzhr.'"

The disc they stood on started to descend, slowling sinking into the pillar. The movement was extremely smooth, as if they were floating on a cloud. The companions soon dropped below the top of the pillar and were surrounded by solid stone.

"Well, that was easy," Donnie said with a wry smile.

"Maybe a bit too easy," Aksel responded with just a hint of nervousness in his tone. "Who knows what's waiting for us at the bottom."

Lloyd's voice abruptly rang out from behind them all. "Should I get out my swords?"

"Not in these close quarters! Are you a moron?" Seth cried. Everyone spun around to look at the young man. Lloyd stood there with a huge grin on his face, his blades securely sheathed.

"Dragon dung, Elladan! You're rubbing off on him!" the halfling grumbled angrily.

Elladan responded with a closemouthed laugh. "Yes, I am, aren't I?"

As they descended, the light from above disappeared, but the shaft did not darken appreciably. The glow of the disc they stood on was rather bright, and every so often they would pass a row of glowing tiles. Glo gazed around in wonder—in all his studies, he had never heard of anything like this before. "Remarkable. The inside of the pillar is completely hollow and is traversed by this floating disc."

Aksel peered around as well, a look of wonder on his face. "It is quite a feat of engineering."

Glo was about to say more, but stopped as a calming tune suddenly filled the air. He glanced over his shoulder and saw Elladan strumming his lute. Glo eyed the bard quizzically—Elladan merely smiled and shrugged. "I don't know why, but I got the sudden urge to play. It somehow felt like we needed soothing music in here."

Glo spiked an eyebrow but said nothing. The bard continued to play tranquil tunes the rest of the way down. A few minutes passed until finally the top of an open doorway appeared at their feet. The disc slowed and came to a complete stop, even with the base of the door. Glo peered out the doorway and into a vast room. He estimated it was similar in size to the first floor of the monolith. Yet this chamber was not dark, lit by glowing tiles along the floor every few yards and on the ceiling far above.

Seth cautiously stepped out into the room, followed by Donnie, then Lloyd and Alana. After a short pause, Seth motioned for the others to follow. The rest of the companions piled out into the room—it was indeed identical to the first floor of the monolith, including archways on each of the four walls of the chamber. The exception was that there was a hall beyond each arch, there were no stairs spiraling up the pillar behind them, and there was a hip-high pedestal a few yards in front of them. Seth and Donnie approached it together, the others following close behind. As they drew closer, Glo noted a circular depression in the top of the dais. Donnie cautiously examined the pedestal all over. "I wonder what this is for."

"From the circular indentation, I'm guessing it used to hold some kind of sphere," Seth answered, as he knelt down and searched the base of the dais.

"Yeah, but where is it now?"

Seth's face bent into a half curved smile. "Do you really want me to answer that?"

"No. Probably not," Donnie responded almost immediately.

The duo concluded that the pedestal was not rigged with traps of any sort, and moved on to the rest of the room. The others waited patiently, but in the end they found nothing hidden, neither traps nor secret doors. They did, however, discover a plaque with a symbol on it above each archway. The hallways beyond the arches each led to a closed door. Every door was locked, but next to each was another plaque with the seven chakra symbols and circular indentations. Seth and Donnie returned to the others and described what they had found.

Aksel listened intently, his hand silently rubbing his chin. When they were done, he mused aloud over the archway plaques. "So we have four archways, each with a different symbol—a triple set of spirals, a circle with three consecutive spirals over three wavy lines, a flat-topped pyramid with a single spiral inside and lines across the base, and a single spiral with three flame-shaped objects extending upward from it."

"Air, water, earth and fire," Glo said with certainty. "The four elements once again."

Elistra pursed her lips and nodded slowly. "That does seem to be a recurring theme."

Seth spun around, gazing at all four archways that led from the chamber. "So each door represents a different element—probably another puzzle of some kind." He swiveled around one more time, then stopped, facing one of the arches. "I say we go to air first. I mean, if it is air, it's probably the least dangerous of the four. Right?"

"We'll see soon enough," Aksel responded, not sounding all that convinced.

25

AIR

The wind whipped harshly around the room,
its gale-like force making it hard to stand

The small company passed under the archway with the symbol of the three spirals above it, quickly reaching the door at the end of the short corridor. Just as Seth and Donnie had described, there was a plaque on the wall with the seven chakra symbols on it. Next to each symbol was a circular indentation Glo estimated to be the same size as the discs they had found on the second floor of the monolith. Seth turned to the others, his lips twisted to one side.

"Too bad we don't still have those discs."

"Maybe we do." Elistra stepped forward, knelt down in front of Seth, and stared at his forehead. "If you don't mind."

Seth eyed her curiously for a moment, then lifted up his black locks. The seeress took her index and middle finger and touched his tattoo. She hummed a deep tone, the same sound she sometimes made when she was meditating. A few moments later, the tattoo disappeared from Seth's forehead, reappearing in Elistra's hand in its original disc form. She held the purple disc out to him, a satisfied smile across her lips. "I believe this is what you were looking for."

"Nice trick," was all Seth said, but Glo knew him well enough by now to see that the halfling was impressed. Seth took the disc from Elistra's hand and inserted it into the plaque next to its matching symbol—the symbol immediately lit up.

Aksel stepped in for a closer look. "So the discs also function as some kind of key." He around to face Elistra. "Can you do that with the others?"

"I can," Elistra responded slowly, her tone dubious as she regarded Lloyd. The young man's face turned a bright shade of scarlet, nearly matching his armor. He leaned in close to Elistra, and asked in a soft voice, "Is there any way I can get my own?"

"Hmm," the seeress murmered, a slender hand going to her chin and her head tilting to the side as she mulled over his question. After a few moments, her face lit up. She peered at Lloyd speculatively. "Do you know how to meditate?"

"Yes..." Lloyd replied, his expression rather puzzled.

Elistra smiled warmly at the young man. "Well then, that's all you need to do. Place your two fingers over the tattoo, and then clear your mind."

Lloyd's face lit up. "Is that all?"

"That's all."

Lloyd let out a huge sigh, his coloring returning to normal. "Phew. No problem then."

The young warrior spun around and retreated down the corridor to meditate in private. In the meantime, Elistra knelt in front of Aksel and retrieved his disc. Seth took the disc and placed it in its associated slot, and once again the symbol next to it lit up. Lloyd returned at that point, holding a red disc in his hand. He handed it to Seth, and the halfling inserted that one as well. Elistra gazed approvingly at Lloyd. "See, that was easy."

Lloyd grinned back at her. "Yes, yes it was."

As Glo examined the partially-lit panel, he suddenly remembered Elistra's theory. "Elistra, do you think we need to retrieve all the discs, or do you want to test out your theory that certain combinations would work?"

Elistra pursed her lips, shifting her weight to one foot, and placing her hands on her hips. "Hmm—it might be worth a try." Her eyes fell on Aksel. "What do you think?"

Aksel gazed at the plaque, his brow furrowing as he thought it over. "It might be worth a try. How about this—let's retrieve all the discs just in case, but if your theory is correct, Elistra, we might just need to use Glo's."

"You mean body, mind and spirit," Lloyd said, ticking off the associated chakras with his fingers.

"Exactly," Aksel said with a nod.

Elistra gave Lloyd a sidelong glance. "You know—this would go a lot faster if you could help me."

"Sure!" came the immediate response, the young man practically beaming at the chance to help. The two of them split up, Elistra handling Alana and Glo, while Lloyd worked on Elladan and Donnie. When the seeress placed her hand on Glo's solar plexus, he was momentarily embarrassed, but that quickly passed. He noted with keen interest a tingling sensation in his abdomen as she chanted over him. It only lasted a few moments, then the chakra disc with the yellow symbol materialized in Elistra's hand.

Glo felt a bit strange once the disc was gone, empty somehow, but that feeling passed after a short while. Once all the discs were retrieved, they handed them over to Seth. With the red 'body' disc and white 'spirit' disc in place, the only thing needed to test out Elistra's theory was the yellow 'mind' disc. Seth picked that one out and placed it into its associated slot. The symbol lit up, and sure enough, the door in front of them slid open.

Glo tried to congratulate Elistra, but his words were drowned out by a loud whooshing noise. He peered through the doorway and observed a large, well-lit, circular room beyond. Abruptly, they heard a high pitched howl.

Donnie glanced around wide-eyed at the others. "What was that?"

Ruka's lips warped into a lopsided smile. "Sounds like the wind to me."

Everyone except Seth and Ruka gathered around the open doorway, trying to get a good look at the room beyond. Elladan motioned for the halfling to take the lead. "After you..."

Seth shook his head. "First things first."

One by one, he removed the four discs from the plaque. When he was done, he held all the discs in his hand once again, but the symbols remained lit and the doorway stayed open. "Well, that answers that."

Aksel gave him a nod of approval. "That was a good find, considering we will probably be needing those again."

Seth wore a satisfied grin as he redistributed the discs to their original owners. Once he was done, he led the way through the open door. The companions found themselves standing in the alcove of a large cylindrical chamber. It was quite bright in here, as if standing in the midday sun, but there was no evidence of those glowing tiles anywhere along the floor or walls. At the edge of the alcove stood a railing with an opening to a narrow walkway, leading to the center of the room. The walkway ended at a circular platform suspended in mid-air, which was no more than a few yards wide, and was barren except for a dais with a single lever on it.

As the companions approached the railing, they had to grasp it tight. The wind whipped harshly around the room, its gale-like force making it hard to stand. Glo peered downward, but could see nothing except swirling mists far below—a glance upward revealed a similar sight. The room appeared to have no real top or bottom.

Directly across the chamber stood a second alcove. In its center was another lever, similar to the one on the central platform. There were two more alcoves along the wall of the chamber, one to the left and one to the right. Glo leaned out over the railing and could just barely make out an additional lever in the back of each alcove. Floating discs, no more than a yard in diameter, traveled back and forth between the alcoves and the central platform. The discs would stop just outside each alcove, remain stationary for a few moments, and then float back toward the center.

More discs circled around the chamber. It appeared that to get to the alcoves, one would have to ride the floating discs, leaping their way across. To make matters worse, not all the discs were stable. The wind in the chamber gusted occasionally, attributing for the howling noise they heard, but also causing the discs to spin or flip over.

"Did you say something about this room being the easiest?" Aksel shouted over the sound of the wind.

"I never said that!" Seth yelled back.

"Actually, your exact words were, '*It's probably the least dangerous of the four.*'" Elistra repeated, staring at Seth with an impish smile when she was finished.

Seth tilted his head forward and glared at the seeress darkly. "Thanks, Elistra," he mouthed the words.

"Anyway—care to check out the center platform?" Aksel yelled to Seth.

"Sure!" Seth replied. "After all, how dangerous could it be?" he added with a glance back at the seeress. Once again, Elistra merely smiled mischievously at him.

Seth appeared cavalier about traversing the chamber, but Glo was worried. "Those winds are pretty fast! I'd say at least 70-80 miles an hour!"

"Try more like 90!" Ruka corrected him. All eyes turned to the teen. Ruka glanced around the group and shrugged. "Take it from someone who flies all the time!"

"Can't argue with that!" Donnie chimed in cheerfully.

"Can you stop with the shouting? Casting a spell here, people!"

Glo spun his head to see Seth making the motions of a spell. He watched the halfling's movements closely, barely catching the phrase at the end over the rush of the wind. "*Aranea Ascenditur.*"

Glo recognized the spell—it was called *spider crawl*. It was a rather clever idea, considering where Seth was going. The spell would make his hands and feet extra sticky, helping him to hold onto the walkway, even in those high winds. Nevertheless, Glo watched anxiously as Seth stepped out onto the narrow walkway. The wind buffeted him, his cloak and hair being whipped to the side, but the halfling's feet stayed firmly in place.

Glo felt a hand on his arm, and turned to see Elistra holding onto him. He gave her a brief smile, then turned his attention back to Seth. The halfling crouched down, keeping as low a profile as possible as he slowly working his way toward the central platform. Glo could feel the grip on his arm tighten as Seth moved along, mirroring his own nerves. Seth continued his slow advance, everything going surprisingly smoothly, until he reached the halfway point. Suddenly, a huge gust of wind blew across the chamber. Seth crouched down even further, but despite his best efforts, his feet began to slip. He slid to the very edge of the walkway, then his feet went out from under him all together.

"Seth!" Glo cried, his voice lost in the howling of the wind. He felt sharp nails dig into the skin of his arm but ignored them, intent on his friend's plight. Glo watched in horror, expecting to see the halfling whipped away, but by some miracle, Seth managed to hang on. His hands shot out and grasped the edge of the walkway, his body completely stretched out behind him, until the gust finally died down.

Once it did, Seth swung himself forward, and in an amazing feat of agility, planted his feet underneath the walkway. He was not done, though. Seth continued his forward motion, arching his body and grasping the other edge of the walkway. As he spun around, Glo could have sworn he heard the halfling cry out. Not taking his eyes off of his friend, Glo yelled, "Did anyone hear that?"

"You mean Seth yelling, 'Weeee! This is fun!'?" Elladan cried back, his ironic expression mirroring how Glo felt.

Glo wasn't sure whether to scream or applaud. Only Seth would make light of such a dangerous situation. Glo watched in awe as the halfling flipped himself up over the side of the walkway and back onto the top, once again solidly planting his feet. Glo let out a huge sigh, the grip on his arm finally relaxing.

"That was good. Really good!" Donnie cried over the rush of the wind. "I'd hate to have to pull that one off myself!"

"Don't be getting any ideas!" Alana retorted, elbowing him in the side.

Glo exchanged a brief, knowing smile with Elistra, then refocused his attention on Seth. The halfling was crouched down again, slowly inching his way forward. Thankfully, there were no more gusts of wind. After what seemed like an eternity, Seth finally made it to the center platform. Glo noted with keen interest that the moment Seth stepped onto the platform, his cloak and hair fell back into place.

It must be like the eye of a storm in there, Glo reasoned. He had studied natural phenomena including storms and earthquakes. All spinning storms had a calm area, the winds never quite reaching the center. As he understood it, this happened because of the spin—the winds wanted to move in a straight line, but got bent around. Either way, Seth was now safe.

"I think he's good in there!" Glo cried aloud.

"It appears so!" Aksel agreed.

The entire party seemed to breathe easier now that their friend was safely tucked away. Back on the central platform, Seth spent a few moments straightening out his hair and clothes, then proceeded to the center dais. He stood there for a minute or two, examining the pedestal, then reached up and pulled the switch. The platform began to lift on one side and lower on the other.

Glo did a double take. *The entire platform is turning over! So much for being safe.*

Elistra's nails bit into his skin once more as they watched Seth scramble up the rising end of the platform. He reached it moments before it went completely vertical and grasped the edge. As the platform continued to turn, Seth launched himself over onto what was now the top. Glo let out a sigh of relief, the nails in his arm releasing once more. The former underside of the platform now came into view. It turned out to be a mirror image of the top, with another pedestal, switch and all.

Seth waited until the platform stopped, then stood up and dusted himself off. He turned to the companions and gave them a brief thumbs-up before striding over to the new pedestal. Seth examined it closely for a short while, then reached up and pulled the switch. The entire platform began to turn over once more.

"You've got to be kidding me!" Elladan cried, the exasperation in his voice apparent even over the constant sound of the wind.

The companions watched on incredulously as Seth scrambled for the edge once again. As before, he waited until the platform began to flip over, then hoisted himself back on to the top.

"Well, it's official! Seth has a death wish!" Donnie cried over the continued whoosh of air around the chamber.

Seth dusted himself off, then turned toward his companions and shrugged. He then proceeded to the dais, sat down in front of it, took out his knife, and began to sharpen it.

Elladan turned to the others. "I guess he's done for now?"

"There's not really much more he can do!" Aksel cried over the perpetual noise of the rushing air. "We might need to pull those switches in the other alcoves!"

Donnie cupped his mouth and yelled, "I'll go and try one!"

Without warning, Ruka lashed out and punched him square in the arm.

"Ow!" Donnie cried, "What did I do this time?"

"Just be careful!" Ruka yelled, then stormed off to the back of the alcove.

Alana shook her head. "Be careful!" she reiterated, then went off to follow Ruka.

Donnie's expression was one of complete bewilderment. He eyed Elistra imploringly. "What'd I do?"

"If you don't know by now..." the seeress began, then fell silent.

Donnie flashed her one of his brightest smiles, then invoked his *Boots of the Spider*. Glo grabbed his friend by the arm and leaned in close. "Keep the wind at your back. Don't let it catch you from the side, or you'll go flying like Seth."

"Just like sailing." Donnie acknowledged.

Glo wished him luck, then let go of his friend's arm. The slight elf strode over to edge of the alcove, leapt onto the railing, and stretched his hand out to the wall. It stuck fast. Donnie reached out with his other hand and grasped the wall with it. Moments later, Donnie was crawling across the chamber like a spider.

Donatello slowly crept his way across the wall of the chamber, the wind steadily beating on him from behind. He looked down and saw nothing but grey mists. He looked up and saw the same. The slight elf gulped and refocused his attention on the alcove that was his destination, still quite far away. *Donnie, what have you gotten yourself into this time?*

The chance meeting with Elladan at the tailor's in Ravenford had led him down a breakneck path to his current perilous situation. True, it was not the first time his life had taken such an unexpected turn—in fact, it had been full of them. From his early days running with a gang of cutpurses, to his servitude to Lord Flynn, and then his time under Captain Mor'Findlas on the Pirate Coast, his life had been a series of near-disastrous events. If there was danger involved, somehow he always managed to be smack in the middle of it.

Still, this current little adventure had its share of moments. From their triumph over the Serpent Cult at Ravenford Keep, to the successful clearing of the monsters in Lake Strikken, this little group had made a name for itself. Heck, they were even close to finding the treasures of Larketh, the Golem Thrall Master. How many folks could say that?

There had been some surprises as well. Donnie had never placed much stock in psychics before, pegging most of them as con-artists and charlatans. Elistra, on the otherhand, had turned out to be the real deal.

"Stay the course and you may very well find what you seek," she had said back in Ravenford. Just how much did the beautiful seeress know about the past of which he never spoke?

It was a past that he was constantly reminded of whenever he saw the young teen, Ruka. It was more than just her physical appearance, though. It was the way she carried herself, her aloofness and cutting wit that was so hauntingly familiar. It would be so easy to let himself believe that she'd somehow come back to him, returned in the form of this young shape shifter. But the gods had never been that kind to him. *No Donnie, it's better to leave the past where it belongs.*

His thoughts then drifted to the Dame Alana. From the moment he first laid eyes on her, he had felt a strong attraction to the winsome lady knight. In fact, his heart skipped a beat whenever he was around the lovely red-head. Yet it was not just her appearance that drew him, for he had known many women and found beauty in them all.

What truly attracted him was the combination of strength and grace she displayed. It made her a force to be reckoned with on the battlefield, and yet none of that had hardened her. Fearsome as the lady knight was in combat, she was just as gentle-natured outside of it—well, most of the time. Still, her temper did not dissuade him, but rather fueled his interest even more.

Donnie roused himself from his musings—the alcove was now only a few yards away. When he reached the edge, he paused and scanned the niche carefully. Something didn't feel right. Nothing looked out of place, but still, he couldn't shake the feeling of impending danger. Donnie had learned to trust his instincts over the years, and it had saved his skin more than once. He wasn't quite sure what was amiss here, but he had an idea how to find out.

He pulled a coin out of his purse, stretched his arm out, and flipped it forward with two fingers. The coin flew through the air, end over end, landing on the floor of the alcove with a clink. As soon as it hit the ground, sparks began to fly everywhere. The entire floor of the alcove lit up, arcs of electricity dancing across its surface. It was so bright that Donnie had to shield his eyes. A few seconds later, it was over.

Donnie uncovered his eyes and searched for the coin. He quickly found it, or at least what was left of it. In place of the coin, a slag of melted copper sat on the floor. The discharge of electricity had been so intense that it melted the metal. Donnie let out a deep sigh. "Phew, guess I won't be stepping in there."

The slight elf climbed into the alcove, careful to stick to the wall. Donnie had always been a quick study, and his short time with Seth this day had paid off. He had not gone even a few feet when he spotted a set of cables running to the floor. They had been fairly well masked, inset and painted the same color as the wall, but Donnie found them nonetheless. He followed them up to a section of wall where they stopped.

Donnie saw nothing at first, but felt around there anyway. His fingers soon outlined a small, invisible box attached to the wall. He swiftly found the latch and popped it open. The entire box immediately became visible. Inside was a glowing bulb that connected to the two cables that ran from the box. Next to the bulb was a switch and a keyhole. Donnie tried the switch at first, but it was locked firmly in place. *No matter.*

Donnie reached into a pouch on his belt and pulled out his favorite lock pick. The little pick appeared quite well used, but it had seen him through many a tight spot through the years. Donnie inserted it into the lock and jiggled it around. The lock turned out to be a standard pin-tumbler. Donnie fiddled with the pins for a bit until he heard a loud click. The tumblers fell into place and the glowing bulb immediately went dark. Donnie felt rather pleased with himself. *Not bad, if I have to say so myself.*

Just to be safe, he reached into his purse and pulled out another coin. He then flipped it onto the floor and shielded his eyes. Nothing happened. Donnie smiled as he stepped down onto the floor, first one foot, then the other. Without warning, the floor shot out from underneath him! The force was so great that even his *Boots of the Spider* could not hold him in place. Donnie was launched backwards, out of the alcove where the wind swiftly grabbed hold of him. Before he knew it, he was being spun end over end, out into the center of the chamber.

26
ABOVE THE CLOUDS

When Ruka saw Donnie get launched out of the alcove, the young teen nearly jumped over the railing into the chamber. Alana had to grab her by arm and forcibly hold her back. "You can't get to him. The wind is too strong!"

Ruka jerked her arm free. "Oh, yeah? Just watch me!"

"Wait!" Elladan cried to the duo. "Look!"

Out in the chamber, Donnie flipped end over end, the wind whipping him through the air. As he drew near a floating disc, the slight elf pulled in his arms and legs, curling his body into a tight ball. Suddenly his hands shot out, barely catching the edge of the disc. Donnie yanked himself forward, flipping his legs under himself, and firmly planted his boots on the bottom of the disc. The disc wobbled precariously for a few seconds, then finally stopped. The onlookers breathed a collective sigh.

"Didn't I tell you?" Elladan yelled over the wind. "Nothing to worry about!"

The companions watched as the acrobatic elf carefully climbed over the top of the disc. He crouched there, both hands and feet planted on the surface. Donnie rode the disc until it neared another one, then deftly leapt to that one. He rode that disc to the center of the room, then jumped aboard the larger platform. Seth met with him, the pair having a brief conversation. When they were done, Seth headed to the right-most edge of the platform, while Donnie carefully crept his way down the narrow walkway toward them. A few seconds later, a disc reached the central platform and Seth leapt on board, beginning a journey toward the right side of the chamber.

"What's he doing?" Lloyd cried over the rushing wind.

"I think he's trying to make it to the right alcove!" Aksel yelled his answer.

The companions followed Seth's progress as he approached another disc. The halfling leapt to that one, bringing himself one step closer to the right side of the chamber. Donnie reached them while Seth was still in transit. The moment he entered the alcove, both Ruka and Alana rushed up to the elf. Donnie visibly flinched, but instead of scolding him, the duo threw their arms around his waist. His eyes went wide. "Whoa! What'd I do?"

Alana, not letting go, exclaimed, "You scared the heck out of us!"

Ruka, still holding him tight, yelled, "Don't you dare do that again!"

Donnie placed an arm around each of their shoulders. "Trust me, that is not a performance I want to repeat!"

Alana and Ruka slowly let him go and stepped back. Donnie gazed from one to the other with clear affection. "Unfortunately, I need to go back out there!" he yelled over the whooshing sound of the chamber.

Without warning, Ruka lashed out and punched him in the arm again. "Be more careful this time!"

Donnie grabbed his arm, but didn't complain, instead, gazing at the young teen fondly. Ruka spun around and stomped away, covertly wiping the moisture from her eyes. Alana stepped forward once more, this time embracing Donnie like a comrade. "Good luck!"

Donnie gave her a bright smile, then visibly steeling himself, strode to the edge of the alcove and climbed back out onto the wall.

A few moments later, Seth reached the alcove embedded into the right side of the chamber. After his discussion with Donnie, Seth knew the floor here was electrified, so instead of leaping directly to the alcove, he jumped toward the wall of the chamber. The wind buffeted him, but he had already accounted for that and landed neatly just outside the alcove. Seth carefully climbed into the recess, keeping to the wall. He swiftly found the trap mechanism just where Donnie said it would be. Seth had to admit he was impressed. *This elf learns pretty fast.*

Even so, Seth would never admit that to his face. Donnie also warned him about the spring trap underneath the floor. Seth could have searched for that box, too, but didn't feel like wasting more time. Instead, he climbed around the back of the alcove and stepped down on top of the lever, straddling it with either leg. He grasped the lever with both hands and gave it a hard yank. It easily pulled back, clicking into place. Outside the alcove, the wind began to slow down. Seth's lips twisted with satisfaction. *So these levers do serve a purpose after all.*

The halfling quickly climbed back onto the wall and out of the alcove, beginning the long crawl across the chamber toward the recess opposite the entrance.

Just as Donnie reached the alcove on the left side of the chamber, the winds began to die down. Although he couldn't see from this angle, Donnie assumed that Seth had pulled the switch across the way. Donnie carefully climbed along the wall until he reached the back of the alcove. It took a bit of balancing, but he reached for the lever while still standing on the wall. Donnie grasped it with both hands, giving it a good tug. The switch moved toward him, clicking into the opposite position. Out in the chamber, the winds died down even more. Donnie grinned in triumph. *So it is the levers!*

Donnie swiftly climbed out of the alcove and made his way along the wall to the one opposite the entrance. When he got there, Seth had already arrived and disabled the electrical trap. Donnie watched as the halfling straddled the last switch and pulled it. Once it clicked into place, the wind in the chamber died down and stopped. Across the way, Donnie heard cheering. He spun around and saw the others waving and crying out in triumph. With a brief wave, he turned back to Seth.

"And just when I had gotten used to the ringing in my ears," Donnie quipped.

Seth, however, paid little attention to him. Instead, the halfling seemed fascinated with the back wall of the recess. Donnie squinted his eyes and followed Seth's gaze, but saw nothing. "Find something?"

"False wall," Seth answered, reaching for a spot on the back wall of the alcove. He moved his fingers up and down, then abruptly stopped and pushed against a section of the wall. A door slid open in the wall next to him. Donnie could see a small room beyond the doorway, with another lever. He eyed the floor suspiciously. "How much you want to bet it's electrified?"

Seth's face remained impassive. "Probably. I'll check for traps if you get the switch."

"Sure."

Halfling and elf climbed their way along the walls into the backoom. Sure enough, Seth found another trap mechanism. He quickly disabled it, then Donnie, already in position, climbed down and pulled the last switch. Out in the main chamber, the middle platform disconnected from the walkway and floated upward about a foot.

"Interesting," was Seth's only comment.

Donnie cocked his head to one side and stared at the platform curiously. "I wonder what it does now?"

"Won't know until we try it."

Donnie peered at Seth and shrugged. "Let's go, then."

The duo climbed along the wall, back into the alcove, when Donnie got a sudden idea. He stopped halfway across the wall and turned his body around so he was facing toward the inside of the alcove. Seth stopped and glanced at him over his shoulder. "What are you doing?"

"You'll see," Donnie replied mysteriously.

Before Seth could say another word, Donnie jumped into the alcove. The floor immediately shot up, sending him flying out into the main chamber. Donnie heard cries of dismay from across the room, but he was too busy concentrating to pay them much attention. He flew through the air across the chamber, toward the central platform. When he started to lose momentum, Donnie pulled in his arms and legs and flipped through the air twice. The circular motion increased his speed just enough, allowing him to land on the central platform.

Donnie landed in a crouch, then immediately stood up, and bowed to the folks at the entrance. He then turned around and bowed to Seth, feeling rather pleased with himself. Seth, however, was not to be outdone. The halfling repeated Donnie's performance, launching himself into the chamber just as he had.

Donnie stepped back and watched with keen appreciation as the halfling flew through the air and executed three perfect flips before landing on the platform in front of him. Donnie strode up to Seth, clapping slow and loud. "Nicely done—had to get in that third flip, I see."

"Yep," Seth responded with a self-satisfied smile.

"You two are crazy!" Alana yelled from across the walkway.

Donnie spun around and grinned at the lady knight. "You just figuring that out now?"

After a short chuckle, the pair went over to the switch on the dais. Donnie stood back, proffering it to Seth. "Care to do the honors?"

Seth nodded graciously. "Don't mind if I do."

The halfling reached up and pulled the switch. The central platform rose slowly upward. After a few moments, Seth pulled the switch a second time. The platform stopped and descended back to its original position, hovering about a foot above the walkway.

"Anyone want a ride?" Donnie called out from across the chamber.

"I do!" Lloyd cried back, obviously eager to do something other than just standing and watching.

"I'm coming, too," Ruka shouted, though the teen sounded more annoyed than excited.

Glo cast a quick glance around the group and shrugged. "Guess I should go. Someone has to keep them out of trouble."

Aksel gazed back at him and grimaced. "Unfortunately, you're right." He let out a brief sigh. "I'll come along as well."

"I think I'll be staying here," Alana said, peering over the railing and cautiously eyeing the bottomless chamber below.

"Me, too," Elistra said, standing herself next to the lady knight.

Elladan cast a quasi-smile at the others. "I guess I'll stay and keep them company."

Aksel's eyes flickered briefly around the alcove, and then he gave a brief nod. "Probably a good idea."

After a short goodbye, Lloyd, Glo, Aksel and Ruka crossed the narrow walkway to the central platform. When everyone was aboard, Seth pulled the switch.

"Next stop, who knows where!" the halfling cried as they rose up toward the mists above.

"Be safe," Elistra called after them. Glo glanced down at seeress, noting the concern on her face. She stood at the railing of the alcove, not moving until the platform blocked her from view.

"Wonder what we're going to find up there?" Lloyd speculated aloud.

Glo turned his gaze upward as the mists enveloped them, then everything went gray.

The platform continued to rise through the mists, or at least that is what it felt like—it was hard to tell, with nothing but fog surrounding them. Glo held his breath, straining his ears to pick up any sound, but all he heard was the shallow breathing of his companions around him. Not even the rising platform made any noise. Finally, after what seemed like an eternity, they rose out of the clouds. A long stone bridge stretched out before them, its piers rising out of the mists below. Glo searched the mists, but could not tell what those piers were resting on.

"Nice little trick there," Seth said, with a nod toward the free-standing bridge.

"Indeed," Glo agreed.

There was a circular hole in the bridge directly above them. The platform continued to rise until it passed through the hole, stopping when it was level with the bridge. Glo glanced toward both ends—the one side of the bridge ended in a blank wall, but the other side led to two large doors, inset into a tall archway.

"Guess that's our destination," Glo observed dryly, with a nod toward the arched doorway.

"From the size of those doors, I hope the giant isn't home," Donnie quipped.

"If he is, we'll be sure to feed you to him first," Seth said as he carefully stepped off the platform. He planted one foot, then the other, but the bridge didn't move. Seth jumped up and down in place, but the bridge appeared soild. He turned to the others and said, "Seems sturdy enough."

While the others disembarked, Seth strolled over to the side of the bridge. "I wonder," he mused aloud.

Aksel eyed him curiously. "Wonder what?"

Without anwering, Seth pulled a copper coin out of his purse. He held it in his open palm and stuck his arm out over the side of the bridge. Seth then turned his palm over, letting the coin slide off of it. Glo pulled up next to Seth just in time to see the coin disappear into the mists below.

✳

Down in the air chamber, Elladan, Alana and Elistra waited for the others to return. Alana was clearly the most impatient of the three.

"I should have gone with them," she declared with a fierce scowl.

Elistra eyed the lady knight with keen curiousity. "Why didn't you, then?"

Alana didn't answer at first, her face flushing slightly. "It's—personal."

"Oh, I see," Elistra responded with a soft chuckle. Alana glared at the seeress, her cheeks reddening even further.

"See what?" Elladan asked, curious as to what the seeress had divined.

Elistra turned to him, placed a hand to the side of her mouth, and said in a confidential tone, "She's afraid of heights."

"Am not!" Alana huffed, turning her back on them and storming away from the railing.

Elladan and Elistra could not contain themselves, both laughing aloud. Alana spun around, an accusing expression on her face. She opened her mouth to retort, but suddenly halted.

"What's that?" she said, her eyes focusing beyond them.

Elladan spun around, following the lady knight's gaze. His keen eyes caught sight of a small, shiny object falling from above. It quickly fell past them and out of sight into the mists below. Elladan spun back around and exchanged a bewildered look with the seeress and the lady knight. "I think it was—a coin."

Aksel eyed Seth as if he were crazy. "What was that for?"

"Just testing out a theory," the halfling responded mysteriously.

Everyone but Ruka leaned over the edge of the bridge, searching the mists below for the coin Seth had dropped.

Glo cocked his head to one side and squinted at the halfling. "And that theory is what, exactly?"

Seth's lips curved into a lopsided smile. "Wait for it..."

About two seconds later, Donnie yelped, "Ouch!"

The slight elf jumped back from the edge of the bridge, rubbing the back of his head. Lloyd placed a hand on his friend's shoulder. "What happened?"

"Something hit me!" Donnie said, spinning around in search of his invisible assailant. At the same moment, Seth knelt down and picked a small, shiny object off the bridge. He held it up for everyone to see, a wicked smile across his lips. "There you are!"

Donnie's gaze fixed on the object in Seths hand, his eyes going wide. "Noooo!"

"But how?" Lloyd asked, his expression incredulous. The young man peered over the railing, glancing up, then down.

Glo was equally perplexed. He turned to Aksel. "Maybe some kind of portal?"

Aksel appeared as mystified as Glo. He threw up his hands and shrugged. "Maybe."

Lloyd shook his head, his face a mask of confusion. "This place gives me a headache."

"Tell me about it," Donnie agreed, still rubbing the back of his head.

The companions moved out across the bridge. When they reached the large doors, they found another chakra lock. "Good thing we don't need all the discs," he said dryly, holding out his hand to the others.

Glo, Lloyd, and Aksel all reached into their belts and pulled out one of the chakra discs necessary to open the lock. All three deposited their disc into the halfling's waiting hand, and then stood back while he inserted them into the lock mechanism. While they waited, Aksel brought up an interesting point. "I wonder if Elistra's disc could be used on these locks somehow."

Glo arched an eyebrow—it was something he hadn't thought of before. "That's a good question. Her disc did clear the way to the third floor all by itself."

"Maybe we could try it on the next lock?" Donnie said with a shrug.

Aksel pursed his lips and nodded. "That's a good idea."

At that moment, Seth finished inserting the discs and the large doors swung open. Beyond them lay a long, sparsely decorated room, with a plain stone floor. At the far end stood a podium with a gold-colored object hovering above it. As they drew closer, Glo saw that it was an eighth of a sphere. Seth let Donnie check the pedestal for traps then gave it the once over himself. It was all clear. Glo reached out and removed the piece of sphere from the podium, turning it over on all sides. It was completely smooth. "Well, seven more of these and we'll have a sphere."

Donnie leaned in for a closer view of the piece. "Bet you when we're done, it fits into that podium in the center room."

Seth let out a derisive snort. "Ya think?"

Aksel's eyes moved back and forth between the duo, then he let out a deep sigh. "Are you two ever going to learn to get along?"

A wicked grin spread across the halfling's features. "Probably not."

Donnie placed his hand on his hips and feigned being insulted. "But I'm such a nice guy. "Everybody likes me!"

"Except for certain husbands," Glo answered before anyone else could speak. "Oh, and boyfriends... and brothers..."

Donnie put both hands up in front of him. "Okay, okay. I give. I give."

Ruka folded her arms across her chest and regarded the slight elf with a suspicious stare. "Quite the reputation there, slugger."

Donnie spun toward her, a hurt expression crossing his face. "Me? I'm just a misunderstood artist."

"How so?" Ruka asked, still appearing rather skeptical.

"I see beauty in all things, especially the fairer sex. It would be a crime against art not to grace my canvas with them," he told her with clear passion.

Ruka's cheeks turned bright red. She glanced down at her boots, trying to hide her embarrassment. Seth, of all people, came to her rescue. "If you two are done—does it seem weird to anyone else that there are four element rooms and only one eighth of a sphere here?"

Glo exchanged a curious glance with Aksel. "Now that you mention it, yes, that is weird."

Aksel's eyes slowly swept the room. "So you think there might be a second piece around here somewhere?"

"There's one way to find out." Seth turned to Donnie. "You take one side and I'll take the other."

The pair thoroughly searched the room. Before long, Donnie found a secret compartment in the very back, just behind the podium. There was another electrical trap attached to it, but Seth easily disarmed it. Inside the compartment was another eighth of a golden sphere.

Donnie shook his head in wonderment. "Wow, this Larketh guy really didn't trust anyone."

Seth handed the second piece to Glo. The wizard held up both pieces, and slowly brought them together. The moment they touched, they instantly merged into a quarter sphere with no seams of any kind.

Donnie leaned in close and whistled. "Neat trick there."
Glo silently agreed.

27
WATER

Water began pouring out of the large holes at the top of the room

A short while later, Aksel, Donnie, Glo, Lloyd, Seth, and Ruka rejoined the others down below. Donnie gave the others a vivid description of the mists, the bridge, the giant doors, the room they found, and finished with the golden sphere pieces.

Elladan let out a soft whistle. "Ya gotta love this Larketh guy."

"Actually, you don't. You really don't," Seth practically spat the words, then spun around and stomped out the exit.

Elladan turned to Glo, his face a mask of confusion. "What's with him?"

Glo raised a single eyebrow as he watched after the retreating halfling. "I'm not sure."

"Let's find out," Aksel said, walking out the door after Seth.

They followed the halfling back into the main room, catching up with him in front of the dais. Aksel strode up next to Seth and quietly said, "You want to tell us what's going on?"

Seth spun around, mixed emotions playing across his face. "You really want to know?" His eyes flickered around the group. "Well, I'll tell you. Wizard or sorcerer or psioricist or whatever this Larketh was, I mean, who does this?"

He waved his hands around the vast chamber. "Who sets up a whole building with elaborate rooms and weird traps and hides these strange keys all over the place where almost no one can get to them?"

Seth paused for a moment to catch his breath. "I mean, don't get me wrong. I've known people who hide away their treasures. They keep them in nice, secure places, with plenty of traps around to protect them. But this place—" Seth's eyes swept around the room once more "—this place takes it to a whole new level."

When Seth was finished, silence pervaded the chamber. Glo stared at the halfling with a raised eyebrow, not quite sure how to respond. In truth, he had discussed this very phenomenon with his father. The older mage had warned him that wielding arcane magic did not come without a price. The more power a wizard achieved, the more distrustful they became, seeing enemies and rivals at every turn. Those mages tended to surround themselves with warning spells and elaborate traps.

Living in the relative safety of Cairthrellon, Glo had dismissed his father's warning outright, thinking it merely another attempt to scare Glo and slow down his studies. Now he realized that Amrod was right. Maltar's house was a prime example of a paranoid mage's sanctum. Larketh, on the other hand, had indeed taken it to a whole new level. Glo opened his mouth to speak, but Elistra beat him to it.

"Larketh was a very paranoid individual..."

Seth snorted contemptuously. "Ya think?"

Elistra let out a short, tight-lipped laugh, then continued. "...but not completely without reason. Remember, although he was a Thrall Master with unparalleled control over his constructs, there were three other Thrall Masters equally as powerful as he, if not more. I suspect that this monolith, with all its puzzles and traps, was meant to keep someone like them out, rather than anyone else."

"From what I've read, they weren't exactly one big happy family," Elladan said in support of her premise. Elistra gave the bard a brief smile, then turned back to Seth. The halfling listened quietly as Elistra continued, his arms folded across his chest.

"As Elladan intimated, although the Thrall Masters worked together in their bid to conquer Thac, it was not of their own free will. The Thrall Lord was the one who forced them to band together, and he was more terrible than all of them. So in the end, they bent to his will, although not in all things."

When Elistra finished, Seth remained silent, but he did not appear quite as aggravated. Glo took the opportunity to add to her words, telling the others what his father had shared with him about the pitfalls of being an arcane magic user. When he was done, Elladan clasped him on the shoulder. "Well, then, you have a head start."

Glo stared at the bard uncomprehendingly. "How so?"

Elladan ushered a hand around the chamber. "When we're done here, all this can be your lair."

Glo cast a glance at the bard and saw that he was grinning from ear to ear. The wizard burst out laughing, as did nearly everyone else.

Seth's entire demeanor had softened—he now wore his usual half-twisted smile. "Yeah, Glo, I think you'd make the perfect crazy wizard, holed up underneath this black stone monstronsity."

Before Glo could retort, Elistra swooped in and grabbed him by the arm. "As long as you give me a key so I can come and visit."

Glo blushed in spite of himself, but attempted to cover his embarrassment with humor. "Oh, I will, to be sure. In fact, you can all have keys. Heck, this place is big enough that you can have whole rooms." He turned to Seth. "You can have the air chamber."

Seth fixed him with a scathing stare. "Gee, thanks."

Aksel cleared his throat, holding up a single hand. "Ahem, let's not get ahead of ourselves just yet. We still have at least three element rooms to go. Seth might find a 'more dangerous' room he likes better."

The halfling turned his dagger-like gaze on Aksel. "Very funny."

"The room above the clouds was nice and quiet," Donnie pointed out with a shameless grin.

Before Seth could retort, he was interrupted by Elladan. "Oh, that reminds me, when you were up there, did one of you happen to lose a coin?"

Glo, Lloyd, Seth and Ruka all stared at Donnie and burst into laughter.

"It's not that funny," the slight elf declared, absently rubbing the back of his head.

A short while later, Glo stood over the dais and placed the quarter sphere into the indentation. It was a perfect fit. He removed it and handed the partial sphere to Elladan, asking the him to place it in his portal bag. Elladan gladly complied. When he was done, Aksel addressed the group.

"Well, now that that's confirmed, what element do we want to tackle next?"

Donnie reached into his vest pocket and pulled out a shiny silver ring. "How about we try water? I just happen to have this nice ring of underwater breathing, and Ruka here takes to water like a fish." He reached over and put an arm around the teen's shoulder. Ruka gazed up at him, her face turning slightly red. She immediately recovered, elbowing the him in the side.

"Flatterer," she said, the corner of her mouth rising.

Donnie grimaced and bit back a yelp.

Elladan was hard pressed to hold back his laughter. His eyes danced as he addressed his elven friend. "You've been holding out on us there, Donnie. Where'd you pick up that little trinket?"

Donnie waved a hand nonchalantly at the bard. "Oh, I came across it quite awhile ago. Just never had any reason to take it out until now."

"You mean 'lifted' or was given to you by one of your admirers," Elladan gently corrected him.

A sly grin broke out across Donnie's face. "Maybe..."

Seth squinted suspiciously at the slight elf. "Anything else you've got hidden away you'd like to tell us about?"

"Nope!" came the immediate response.

"Water it is, then," Aksel declared, before anyone else could speak.

The water corridor stood directly across the main chamber from the air room. Aksel led the companions in that direction, passing under the archway with the circle containing three consecutive spirals over three wavy lines. At the end of the corridor stood a locked door with another chakra key mechanism on the wall next to it. Glo, remembering their conversation on the bridge above the mists, turned to Elistra. "Do you think your disc can open one of these locks by itself?"

Elistra wrinkled her nose and tilted her head to one side as she mulled over his words. "Hmm. I don't really know. Well, I guess there's only one way to find out. Give me some room, please."

As Elistra closed her eyes, the others stepped back from the seeress. She began to hum, just as she had when retrieving the others' discs, then reached up and placed her index and middle finger on her forehead. A few seconds later, the multi-colored disc formed in her hand. Elistra handed the single disc to Seth. The halfling stared at it for a few moments, then glanced up at her skeptically. "So, which indentation do you expect me to put this in?"

"Do you really want an answer to that, Seth?" Glo asked with a dry smile.

The halfling tilted his head forward and glared at the wizard.

"Whichever one you feel like," Elistra responded before Seth could fire off a response.

Seth glanced at the seeress, his dark demeanor disappearing as quickly as it came. "Okay then." He turned toward the plaque and ran the disc over a few indentations, reciting the words, "Eenie, meenie, miney, mo…"

"For the gods sakes, Seth, just pick one already!" Aksel cried impatiently.

"Spoilsport," Seth retorted. His hand was currently over the green indentation, so he shoved the disc in there. Nothing happened at first, then, abruptly, there was a flash where the disc lay. A moment later, there was a pair of flashes in the indentations above and below the green one, and another multi-colored disc appeared in each of those. That was immediately followed by two more flashes above and below those with two more discs appearing. There were two more final flashes, and the last two indentations were filled. All the lights went on, and the door opened.

Elladan stared in awe at the panel. "That was cool."

Glo exchanged a glance with his fellow elf and grinned. "Very."

Through the open doorway stood another alcove. Beyond that, Glo could see a large pool of water. Seth pulled out the original disc, and all the copies disappeared. He handed it back to Elistra and then led the way inside. Before them was another chamber similar in size to the air room, but this one was shaped like a hemisphere. Once again, this room was very well lit, but the source of illumination was obvious this time—those glowing tiles they had seen before were spaced at regular intervals across the curved ceiling.

A large, round pool of water completely encompassed the floor of the room, except for another platform in the center, and a narrow walkway leading out to it. Similar to the air room, the central platform had a dais with a lever. Embedded in the apex of the ceiling was a large circular door. It appeared wide enough for the central platform to fit through. The door was surrounded by numerous holes, each covered with a grate.

"I wonder what all that is for?" Glo mused aloud.

"I have a sneaking suspicion we're about to find out," Elladan answered, with just a hint of trepidation.

"Look down there," Seth called to the others. He pointed down into the crystal clear water of the pool. The lower half of the room was another hemisphere, this one filled with water. At the very bottom of the water were what appeared to be two more levers. Next to those underwater levers stood two large grey figures. One marched back and forth, while the other one stood perfectly still.

Donnie squinted at the figures at the bottom of the pool. "Are those..."

"...stone golems," Seth finished for him.

"Well, this should make things interesting," Donnie said with a slightly nervous laugh. The problem was, this was no laughing matter.

Glo's mind flashed back to the first time they crossed paths with the Boulder, at the keep on Stone Hill. The nine-foot-tall golem had battered down the door to the pantry and nearly killed their warrior friend, Titan. Luckily, they were able to escape down the chute to the basement, or they would have all perished.

These two golems looked exactly like the Boulder, their great heads decorated with eerie glowing eyes that sat atop a massive pair of shoulders. Their thick arms hung down to their knees on either side of wide torsos, supported by thick legs ending in large flat feet. Glo had no doubt that these creatures were equally as deadly as the Boulder, nearly impervious to damage, and able to kill any one of them with a single punch.

Aksel was equally aware of the dangers involved. "Donnie, why don't you and Ruka see if you can get close to those two levers? But be careful—whatever you do, stay out of reach of those golems."

"Will do," Donnie said with a nod.

While Donnie and Ruka prepared to go diving, Aksel turned to Seth. "Feel like checking out that center platform?"

Seth responded with a nonchalant shrug. "Why do I feel like I've done this before—but sure, why not."

The halfling stepped out onto the walkway that led to the central platform, carefully scanning his path as he went. Meanwhile, Donnie had put on his ring and taken off his boots. As he removed his shirt, Ruka started to blush furiously. The young teen immediately dove into the water, resurfacing moments later and calling out to Donnie, "You going to be all day?"

"Coming," Donnie answered, throwing his shirt to the ground.

"Be careful, you two," Alana said to the pair.

Donnie flashed her a pearly white smile and winked. "I'm always careful." He then executed a perfect swan dive into the water.

In the meantime, Seth reached the center platform. The halfling scanned the dais for a minute or so then finally pulled the switch. A transparent purple bubble momentarily appeared over the platform, then winked out.

Elladan peered curiously at Glo. "Was that…"

"…a force bubble," Glo finished for him.

Lloyd appeared perplexed, his brow furrowing into deep creases. "To keep the water out?"

Glo shook his head and shrugged. "As good a guess as any."

Seth tried the lever once more, but the same thing happened. The halfling cast a glance at the others, threw up his hands, and then sat down and waited.

Donnie met up with Ruka underwater. She signaled for him to follow, then took off toward the bottom. Donnie was hard-pressed to keep up with her, but she finally stopped just above the floor of the pool. Donnie caught up to Ruka and signaled for her to stay put. She folded her arms across her chest and gave him a withering stare, then motioned him forward with a nod.

Donnie flashed her a bright smile, then spun around and swam toward the levers. He stayed just far enough above the marching golem so that it could not grab him, then quickly darted down to the unguarded lever. Donnie grasped the switch and pulled, half expecting it not to budge, but it gave easily. The second he switched it, the marching golem stopped, turned around, and came right for him.

Up top, Glo saw Donnie pull the lever and called over to Seth. "Donnie got the first one. Try the switch."

Seth got up and pulled the lever. This time the force bubble appeared over the platform and stayed on. It lasted for about thirty seconds, then went out again.

"What happened?" Seth called over to them.

"The golem flipped the switch off again," Glo cried back.

"And nearly got Donnie, too!" Elladan added.

A few seconds earlier, Donnie saw the large golem heading for him. He swam away as fast as he could, but the golem's long arm shot out after him, nearly latching onto his leg. At the last second, he was grabbed from behind and whisked away, out of its reach. Donnie turned his head to see Ruka hanging on to him. He flashed her an appreciative smile. She grinned back, then let him go and nodded toward the lever. Donnie followed her gaze and saw that the golem had reset the switch.

Dragon dung. Now what do we do?

Ruka tapped him on the shoulder. Donnie spun around again and saw her pointing downward toward the stationary golem. He raised his eyes and saw her point to herself. Donnie shook his head vigorously.

Too dangerous, he tried to mouth the words.

A wide smile spread across Ruka's lips. She swam up to him and patted him on the cheek. Without warning, she shot forward, passing him so fast that he couldn't stop her. Donnie spun around and took off after the teen, but it was no use. He would never be able to catch her. He watched on in horror as she came within reach of the golem. It grabbed for her, but she neatly dodged its grasp and swam away, the large stone creature lumbering after her. Donnie had no choice—he swam down to the second switch and threw it.

The moment the second switch was thrown, Glo heard the door to the main chamber shut behind him. At the same time, water began pouring out of the large holes at the top of the room. Everyone exchanged alarmed glances.

"Check it out," Aksel said, pointing down into the water.

At the bottom of the pool, Donnie and Ruka swam away from the second lever. The golem Ruka had drawn off now lumbered back toward the switch. The companions watched as it reached the lever and flipped it back into place. Just as suddenly as it started, the water stopped pouring in from the ceiling and the door to the main chamber opened up behind them.

Elladan let out a short sigh. "Phew, well that's a relief. I don't know about the rest of you, but I'm not exactly dressed for a pool party."

Donnie and Ruka abruptly resurfaced, and Aksel waved Seth over to rejoin them. When they were all back together, Donnie explained what had happened underwater, ending with why they had given up. "I don't think we can do this with just two people. I think we need a third person."

Aksel listened thoughtfully to Donnie's account of the situation down below. When he was done, the little cleric absently rubbed his chin. "Well, I can cast spells of underwater breathing, but I would need to rest overnight and then pray for that spell in the morning."

"It has been a long day," Glo acknowledged, feeling rather fatigued himself after all they had faced since entering the monolith. Just then, they heard a loud grumbling noise. Everyone turned and saw Lloyd standing there with a sheepish grin, holding his hands over his abdomen.

Elladan let out a short chuckle. "I think Lloyd's stomach agrees, too."

28
A WALK IN THE PARK

As she drew close, a huge stone arm shot out toward her

The companions left the water room and headed back to the main chamber. They set up camp in the center of the room around the huge pillar. Elladan brought out some slices of cold, dried fish, a few loaves of bread, cheeses, fruits, and nuts for everyone to share. They all gathered in a circle and began to eat.

"What time do you think it is?" Lloyd asked in between mouthfuls.

Glo thought it over as he gobbled down a piece of cheese. "Let's see. It was late afternoon when we finally solved the runic wheel puzzle. The ride down wasn't that long, but we spent a lot of time in the air chamber. If I had to guess, I would say between eight and nine at night."

Donnie took a swig of water from a canteen, then yawned and stretched. "Why does it feel so much later?"

Glo, watching Donnie, had to stifle a yawn himself. "It does, doesn't it?"

Seth reached over and tore off another hunk from a loaf of bread. "I've got a better question." He paused a moment as he took a bite. "Why haven't we seen any sign of the Serpent Cult?"

Everyone but Seth stopped eating. Glo felt his face redden—he had completely forgotten about the cultists. His eyes swept around the circle of companions—they all appeared as embarrassed as he felt. There were a few moments of silence, then Aksel finally spoke up.

"That is a very good question."

Lloyd sat cross-legged on the floor, a half loaf of bread in one hand, his brow deeply furrowed. "Could they have left the monolith?"

Donnie grimaced and shook his head. "No, the only tracks went into the monolith."

Alana sat next to the slight elf, pieces of her armor removed so that she could sit comfortably. The lady knight put down her plate of half-eaten dried fish, her eyes flickering around the group, her expression perplexed. "Could they have gotten past these puzzles somehow?"

This time Seth shook his head. "All the traps were untouched. There is no way they got past them."

Alana threw up her hands in frustration. "Well they have to be in here somewhere!"

Elladan, directly across from the lady knight, snapped his fingers. "I think I've got it!" All eyes turned toward the bard.

"So, what is it?" Lloyd asked impatiently.

Elladan waved them all closer, then spoke in a soft voice, as if he were afraid the very walls might hear what he was about to say. "What if they couldn't get past the first puzzle? I mean, without Elistra we might not have figured it out."

Elistra gave the bard an appreciative smile. "Thank you, Elladan."

Elladan responded with a partial smile and continued with his train of thought. "So instead, they hid out in the monolith, knowing we would eventually show up..."

"...hoping we would solve the puzzles for them," Donnie finished for him.

Glo arched an eyebrow. If Elladan's theory was correct, then even though the Serpent Cultists had reached the monolith days before them, they had not gotten very far on their own. Yet, they couldn't just leave empty-handed. Glo had gotten a glimpse of their dark mistress, and she did not appear to be the type who would accept failure gracefully. If that were the case, it would make sense that the cultists would bide their time, skulking around inside the monolith somewhere. *Perhaps in the basement...*

A vision suddenly flashed before Glo's eyes, of a room filled with treasure, four large serpents in its center, and his companions' dead bodies scattered all around. Glo felt a shiver run up his spine, but immediately pushed the thought out of his head. *It was just a dream.*

"The cultists will have to surface again eventually," Aksel was saying. "If I had to guess, probably once they think we're done with all the puzzles."

Elladan gave the little cleric a short nod. "Exactly. They're making us do all the dirty work for them."

"What do you mean us?"

All eyes turned to Seth—the halfling sat with his arms folded across his chest, a smug smile on his face. Elladan responded with a closemouthed laugh. "If you're fishing for compliments, then thank you for risking yourself with all these weird traps and puzzles."

Seth responded with an overemphasized, "Thank you."

"Anyway—if they are waiting for us, there's not much we can do about it," Aksel said, glancing around the circle at each companion in turn. "The best we can do is be on our guard."

"Leave that to me," Lloyd said solemnly, rising up from the gathered group and placing his hand on his sword hilts. "I'll take first watch. If they do show their faces, they'll find my blades stuck in them."

Glo couldn't help but smile at the young man's fierce determination, but he was positive the cultists would not show just yet. "I think you can take the time to finish your meal, Lloyd. We still have a few more puzzles to solve."

Elladan stood and placed a hand on Lloyd's broad shoulder. "Still, we appreciate the sentiment."

Alana also stood, placing her hand on Lloyd's other shoulder. "Agreed."

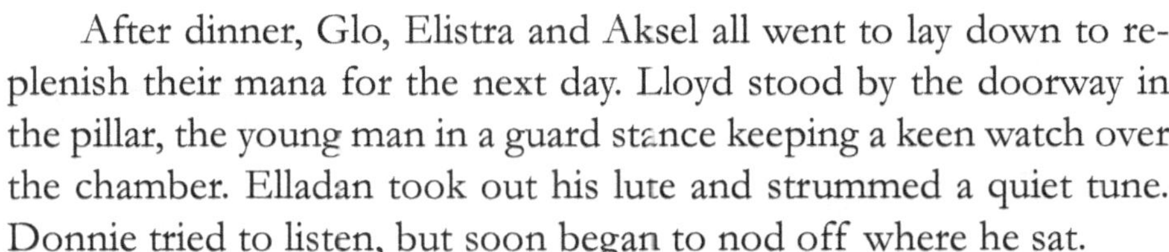

After dinner, Glo, Elistra and Aksel all went to lay down to replenish their mana for the next day. Lloyd stood by the doorway in the pillar, the young man in a guard stance keeping a keen watch over the chamber. Elladan took out his lute and strummed a quiet tune. Donnie tried to listen, but soon began to nod off where he sat.

"Go to bed, Donnie," Elladan admonished him.

"Guess I will," the slight elf agreed. He got up with a yawn, then stretched and went to find his blankets.

A minute later, Ruka also rose from her seat. "I'm going to go sharpen my sword," she announced to no one in particular. "It got a little nicked up fighting that stupid suit of armor."

Ruka walked off a short distance and sat down on the stone floor of the chamber, her back up against the huge pillar. She then took out her sword and a stone and began slowly and methodically sharpening her blade.

Seth stood up next. "That's it for me, too. I should take over for Lloyd in a few hours." He strode over to his blankets, dove in, and disappeared underneath them.

Elladan kept playing his lute, softly strumming a peaceful tune. It was just him and Alana now. The lady knight had removed her plate armor for the night and now sat in a tunic and light chain, silently listening to the music. She should have been comfortable, but Elladan detected an air of tension about her, as if something played on her mind.

He had become quite good at reading people's expressions and body language, mostly from his years playing in taverns to small crowds. The patrons there often came in to soothe their souls with music and drink, to forget their daily troubles, even if for a short while. As an entertainer, it was Elladan's job to read the mood of the crowd. He had learned to recognize when they needed to dance, to laugh, or just be lulled. Alana appeared to require the latter. He was also not surprised when, after a while, she began to speak softly over the music, almost as if to herself.

"I just don't understand him. Sometimes he can be so charming, and other times, he just seems so careless. Is he trying to get himself killed?"

Elladan watched the lady knight closely as he continued to softly strum his lute. She was, of course, talking about Donnie. It seemed that his charms had finally gotten under her skin. Elladan had not known Donnie long, but he was a fairly good judge of character. The slight elf was a carefree spirit, one that was not easily tied down. He also fancied himself a bit of a swashbuckler, always rushing in to the rescue, with little regard for his own safety. Elladan had to admit, it was an enticing lifestyle, especially for a young elf. He measured his words carefully as he decided how to explain all this to Alana. When he spoke, he kept his voice low.

"You have to understand us elves. We live very long lives by human standards. That kind of gives you a different perspective on things. Some of the things you humans take very seriously, we elves don't exactly see the same way."

The lady knight glanced up, her eyes mirroring her inner anguish. She tilted her head and eyed him questioningly. "Like what, for instance?"

Elladan let out a soft chuckle. "Oh, a great many things. It is why someone like Donnie might seem so careless at times. When your life is as long as ours, it can sometimes feel—empty. That is why folks like Donnie, Glo and myself crave adventure. It makes life seem that much more worth living."

Alana eyed him intently, an ironic smile crossing her lips. "You know, the elves don't have a monopoly on that."

Elladan grinned back at the winsome lady knight. "No, I suppose we don't, but I'll ask you this—would you like him any more if he were not the adventurous type?"

Alana blinked at him, surprise registering on her face at his question. She pursed her lips, her gentle brow furrowing for a few moments as she thought it over. Finally, she let out a deep sigh. "No, I suppose not."

"Well then, you have you answer." Elladan flashed her a quasi-smile.

They fell silent once more, Elladan continuing to strum relaxing music, the lady knight still his sole audience. After a while, he spoke up once more. "So when are you going to tell him?"

Alana tilted her head and squinted at him. "Tell him what?"

"How you feel about him?"

"Oh, that," she responded, a playful smile crossing her lips. "Let's just say, he'll know it when it happens."

A roguish grin spread across Elladan's face. "He's one lucky elf."

"Isn't that the truth?" Alana winked.

The night passed uneventfully. Seth switched with Lloyd after a few hours, then Alana took over after that. Early the next morning, they had a quick breakfast, then Aksel went to pray, Glo to study his spellbook, and Elistra to meditate. Meanwhile, the others packed up camp. When they were all ready, everyone gathered in front of the pillar, Aksel next to Donnie and Ruka. The little cleric's eyes swept across the remaining companions. "Okay, so who's going swimming with these two?"

Lloyd's hand immediately shot up. "I will!"

One side of Ruka's mouth lifted, her eyes twinkling with amusement. "Not the worst choice. You weren't too bad back at the cape."

Aksel peered around once more. "I assume there are no objections."

Seth leaned against the pillar, his arms folded across his chest. "Nah. Lloyd's got this."

Alana gazed down at her steel-encased torso and shook her head. "Don't look at me. Do you know how long it takes to get in and out of this thing?"

Glo respectfully declined, as did Elladan and Elistra.

"Very well." Aksel faced Lloyd, his arms slowly weaving the pattern of the spell that would allow the young man to breathe underwater. Once it was cast, they all headed back to the water room. Ruka dove in immediately while Lloyd and Donnie stripped off their shirts and boots. When they were ready, the two of them dove in after the teen. Glo glanced upward, his eyes fixing on the holes that spouted water into the room the day before. "I think it might be best if we head to the center. Once the water comes pouring down, we're going to want to be under that dome."

Seth let out a short laugh. "Heh. Ya think?"

Below the waterline, Donnie, Ruka and Lloyd swam to the bottom. Both golems were at their regular routines, one marching back and forth in front of the first switch, while the other remained stationary next to the second switch. The trio had worked out the plan on the way over to the water room. Ruka would once again distract the stationary golem, drawing it off when the marching golem was farthest away from its lever. Donnie and Lloyd would then quickly swim in and pull both levers simultaneously. Hopefully, that would end the puzzle, and the golems would not reset the levers.

Ruka swam off and positioned herself a short way from the immobile golem. Lloyd and Donnie waited just far enough away for the golems to ignore them. When the marching golem neared its farthest point, Ruka swam for the standing one. As she drew close, a huge stone arm shot out toward her, yet once again, Ruka proved too fast for the creature, nimbly swimming around the long stone arm and dodging its grasp. As she shot off across the pool, the golem took off in pursuit. Donnie motioned to Lloyd and the duo simultaneously launched themselves toward the levers.

A moment later, the other golem reached its farthest point and turned around. It immediately spotted them and stomped back toward its lever, doubling its usually slow pace. At the same moment, the golem chasing Ruka halted and spun about. It also saw the two swimmers and charged across the bottom of the pool. It was a race now. Lloyd and Donnie redoubled their efforts, swimming as fast as they could. Twenty feet, fifteen feet, ten feet, five feet. The two golems continued to bear down on them and would be in grabbing distance any moment. At the last possible second, both man and elf reached their levers and yanked them hard, slamming them into place.

Above the waterline, the door to the main chamber slid closed and water began pouring in from the ceiling. Seth pulled the lever on the central platform, and a clear purple force bubble appeared around them. Elladan's eyes swept around the group, his face breaking out into that all too familiar half-smile. "Alright! I love it when a plan comes together."

A few minutes went by with still no sign of Lloyd, Donnie or Ruka. With the force bubble surrounding them, there was no way to get a clear view down into the water. Glo grew increasingly concerned as the minutes went by. "Where could they be?"

The chamber was beginning to fill, the central platform rising with the water level. Abruptly, two figures broke the surface—it was Lloyd and Donnie. A second later, Ruka surfaced. Glo let out a hugh sigh. Seth flipped the switch, turning off the bubble, allowing Lloyd to climb aboard. Donnie and Ruka, however, remained in the water. Alana knelt down at the edge of the platform. "You two coming aboard?"

Donnie and Ruka exchanged a quick glance before he answered. "No, I think Ruka and I will stay out here—just in case."

"Suit yourself," Seth said, pushing the lever back the other way.

The purple force bubble immediately reappeared, surrounding them once again. The platform continued to rise with the water level. About a half an hour later, they had nearly reached the ceiling. The chamber was almost completely filled with water. The companions watched with keen anticipation as the top of the force bubble hit against the closed door in the ceiling above them. Nothing happened.

"Why isn't it opening?" Elladan asked, with more than just a trace of concern in his voice.

It was indeed a good question. Glo had thought that the door would open as soon as the field pressed up against it. Around them, the chamber continued to fill with water. It began to rise past the bottom of the platform. Luckily, the force bubble remained intact.

Seth called out to Donnie. "Check around for a hidden switch around the door."

"Will do!" Donnie cried back.

The slight elf spoke two soft words then climbed out of the water and up the side of the force bubble, sticking to it like he had to the walls of the air chamber. He reached the ceiling and then crawled up onto it, searching around the perimeter of the closed door. Around them, the water continued to rise—it was now waist level outside the bubble. Ruka tread water just outside the bubble, watching Donnie climb around the ceiling.

Seth cupped his hands and called up to the elf. "What's taking you so long?"

"This is not as easy as you make it look!" Donnie yelled back, continuing to crawl around and run his hands around the ceiling as he spoke.

Elladan glanced nervously at Glo. "What happens if the bubble shuts off?"

Glo arched an eyebrow. He hadn't thought of that. Up till now, Glo assumed the bubble would stay on and the water would just stop once the chamber was filled. He suddenly felt queasy in the pit of his stomach. He glanced over at Aksel. From his expression, he was having the same thoughts as Glo.

"That would be a problem," the little cleric answered apprehensively.

Glo placed an arm around Elistra. The seeress smiled back at him, but he could see the worry in her eyes.

Alana tried to bolster their confidence. "Don't worry. I'm sure Donnie will find something.

Seth said nothing, instead carefully scanning the ceiling from where he stood. Suddenly he called up to Donnie. "Try over to your right!"

Seth pointed to a spot about three yards away from the sight elf. Donnie swiveled around and headed toward where Seth was pointing. "Found it!" he suddenly cried, and began fiddling with something on the ceiling. The water was now even with their necks.

"Hurry!" Elladan shouted up to him. "If the bubble turns off, we're all gonna need gills!"

"I'm working on it!" Donnie yelled, not taking his eyes off whatever he was tampering with. "Almost there..." he added a few moments later.

The water was now over their heads—it had nearly reached the top of the bubble. Glo tightened his grip on Elistra. Seth climbed up on the pedestal to get a better look at what Donnie was doing. Aksel began to pray. Elladan glanced nervously at Glo. He opened his mouth to speak when they heard a loud click. Everything happened at once. The door above them opened, the bubble disappeared and the platform began to rise. As water rushed in to soak them, Donnie and Ruka dove onto the platform. The platform then shot up through the opening, leaving the water-filled room behind.

Glo turned to Elistra and hugged her tight. Aksel made a sign across his chest in thanks to his goddess. Elladan wiped his hand across his brow. "Phew, that was close! I thought I had sung my last song there for a minute."

Lloyd clasped Donnie on a sopping wet shoulder. "Nicely done!"

"Even if you cut it way too close," Seth added, his lips bent sideways.

Donnie got up and winked at the others while ringing out his trousers. "I just wanted to see you all sweat."

"Gods, now he sounds like Seth!" Elladan declared, a semi-smile spreading across his lips.

"No." Seth shook his head. "Just no."

✳

The companions were now in another place entirely. This area above the water room was park-like, a carpet of lush green grass spreading out underneath their feet with what appeared to be blue skies overhead. Around them stood groves of well-groomed trees and neatly trimmed bushes. Two stone pathways cut through the grass, leading off in different directions. The companions decided to split up. Seth, Lloyd, Glo and Elistra went one way, while Donnie, Alana, Aksel and Elladan went the other. Ruka shape-shifted and took off upwards to investigate.

The park turned out to be far larger than anyone anticipated. The stone pathway led through a garden area with a large stone fountain, behind which was a tall hedge maze. Seth led the way through the maze, his instincts unerringly guiding them through to the other end.

As they exited the tall hedges, Lloyd cried out in excitement. "We found it!"

Ahead of them in a small courtyard stood an old fashioned gazebo. It was rather elegant with ornate sage green columns, decorative white latticework, and a majestic concave sage green roof that rose up to a white octagonal cupola at the very top. In the very center of the gazebo stood a pedestal. Floating above the pedestal was another golden eighth of a sphere.

"Well, that doesn't look too conspicuous," Seth noted wryly. The halfling searched carefully around the gazebo. He quickly discovered a pressure plate on the steps leading up to the structure. Seth traced it back to a box hidden in the grass just at the base of the gazebo. He disarmed it in less than a minute.

"What was that?" Lloyd asked when Seth rejoined them.

The halfling responded with a nonchalant shrug. "Nasty little trap. Looked like it set off another force field around the gazebo and filled it with water."

Glo raised a single eyebrow. "A drowning trap?"

"Apparently."

Glo shook his head and sighed. Where Larketh was concerned, paranoid was an understatement. The companions entered the gazebo and approached the pedestal. Seth made a sweep of that as well, but then pronounced it all clear. Lloyd reached forward and grabbed the piece of sphere, spun around, and handed it over to Glo. Glo carefully scrutinized it, swiftly determining it was just like the others. He then put it in his robes and glanced around the interior of the gazebo. "Based on the last room, there should be another one around here."

"Here it is," a familiar voice called out from behind them.

They all spun around and saw Ruka saunter up the steps of the gazebo. In her hand she held another piece of globe. Lloyd eyed the young teen incredulously. "Where did you find that?"

Ruka halted in front of them, balancing the piece of sphere in one hand. "Oh, just floating around," she answered in an almost too-casual manner.

Seth eyed her suspiciously. "Sure ya did."

Elistra strode up next to Ruka and stared at the others, her hands on her hips. "Does it really matter?"

Seth stared at her a moment, then broke out into a wicked grin. "No, not really. It's just a natural reflex."

Ruka snickered softly as she handed Glo the other sphere. He held a piece in each hand and slowly brought them together just like before. Once again, when they touched there was no sound, but they instantly merged and became a quarter sphere. Elistra leaned in close, staring at the golden object in wonder. "Now all we need is the other quarter sphere and we'll have an entire half."

Ruka flew off to tell the others they had found the pieces, while Seth, Lloyd, Glo and Elistra retraced their steps. They all met back at the platform from the water room. Glo held up the quarter sphere for the others to see.

Aksel appeared quite pleased with the find. "Nicely done."

Glo turned to Elladan. "Shall we join the two pieces together?"

"Certainly," the bard responded, reaching into his portal bag, and pulling out the other quarter sphere. He handing it to Glo, the wizard holding the two quarter spheres apart, one in each hand. Glo slowly brought them together, and once again, when they touched, they noiselessly merged into a hemisphere.

Elladan leaned in close, examining the sphere from all sides. "I don't think I'll ever get over how cool that is."

Glo handed the half sphere back to him for safekeeping. "Okay, where to next?" Elladan asked, as he put the hemisphere into the portal bag.

There were a few moments of silence, everyone either glancing around uncertainly at each other, or lost in thought. Glo was one of the latter, mulling the choice over carefully. The two elements they hadn't tackled yet were earth and fire, but no matter how he looked at it, there was not enough evidence in support of one element over the other. Seth finally broke the stalemate.

"I say we save fire for last."

Aksel gazed at the halfling and nodded. "That may be wise."

"Then onward to earth," Donnie declared, raising a finger above his head exuberantly.

Everyone seemed enthused, except for Lloyd. The young man's brow was deeply furrowed. Glo glanced at him curiously and asked, "What's the matter?"

Lloyd's hand went to the back of his neck, a sheepish grin spreading across his face. "I just have one question—how do we get out of here?"

29
EARTH

Steam began to rise as the greenish acid quickly ate the edges away

It turned out that pulling the switch on the circular platform emptied the water out of the chamber below. It took about an hour, but the water finally receded to its original level. The platform lined back up with the walkway, and then the door to the main chamber slid open.

The companions disembarked the circular platform and left the water room, crossing through the main area over toward the earth chamber. They passed under the archway with the flat topped pyramid and walked to the end of another short corridor. The door here had the same chakra disc lock mechanism as the others. For expediency's sake, they used Elistra's multi-colored disc once again.

The door slid open, and the companions got their first view of the chamber beyond. Unlike the air and water rooms, this chamber appeared to be a large, rocky cavern. It was not as well lit as the others, the source of light being a strange greenish glow emanating from the ground ahead. A rocky bluff was visible on the other side of the chamber, but the roof of the cavern was hidden from view, lost somewhere in the darkness above.

The companions filed into the chamber one at a time, Seth and Donnie leading the way. They found themselves at the top of a cliff, a wide pit stretching out below them, filled with a bright green glowing liquid that bubbled and popped in spots. Thin streams of smoke rose out of the pool here and there, an acrid smell reaching their nostrils as they approached the edge of the cliff.

"Acid," Seth hissed.

Glo's eyes went wide with surprise. Seth was right—the entire pit was filled with acid! This was perhaps the most dangerous room yet. The elven wizard slowly exhaled, his eyes scanning the length of the cavern. There was a faint purple shimmering in the air in front of the opposite cliff. *Another force screen.*

The rocky bluff was further separated from them by the pool of acid which stretched all the way from one side of the cavern to the other. Near the cliff edge closest to them, a lever jutted out of the ground. Atop the opposite bluff was another lever, behind which stood a pedestal. Over the pedestal floated yet another golden piece of sphere.

Donnie turned to Seth. "Were you saying something about elaborate traps and strange keys?"

Seth tilted his head downward and glared at the slight elf. Any retort he may have had, however, was abruptly cut off.

"What is that?"

Lloyd stood at the edge of the cliff, pointing at the pit below. Glo followed his gaze—a reddish-brown mound rose out of the pool of green liquid and shambled about. Glo's breath caught in his throat. "Clay golem," he managed to croak out after a moment's pause.

Clay golems were large, ponderous, vaguely humanoid creatures made entirely of clay. Their muddy bodies, while soft to the touch, were extremely resilient, actually reforming over any wound. There were even recorded cases of combatants' weapons being stuck and engulfed in the amorphous body of these creatures. Lloyd appeared awestruck, his mouth hanging open as he gaped at the large creature. "I didn't think anything could live in a pool of acid."

Elladan drew up next to the young warrior and placed a hand on his shoulder. "They're immune," he said softly.

"There's another one!" Donnie yelled. Glo looked at where the slight elf pointed. Sure enough, another creature had risen out of the green liquid. The form was similar to the first golem, but this one was gray in color.

"The pool is full of them," Ruka called out. The companions watched in awe as four more golems rose up out of the acid. The creatures were of various shades of red, brown, and gray. They roamed around the glowing green pool, submerging and resurfacing here and there. Thankfully, the cliff they stood on was high enough that the clay creatures disregarded their presence.

"Guess swimming across is out of the question," Donnie quipped. No one laughed. The sight of the acid pool filled with clay golems was perhaps too sobering a sight.

After a few moments of silence, Seth rubbed his hands together. "Okay then, let's pull the switch and see what it does."

He strode over to the lever, knelt down, and carefully examined around the base. After about half a minute, he stood up, grasped the lever, and gave it a hefty yank. The lever moved easily, clicking into the opposite position. As soon as the switch was thrown, a set of large stone tiles appeared out of thin air directly in front of them. There were dozens of them, hovering at about the same level as the cliff they stood on.

The tiles, about a yard square each, were evenly spaced about two yards apart. and stretched all the way across the pool of acid. Each tile had a lightly scripted, flowing symbol inscribed on top of it. Donnie stepped nearer to the edge, bent forward, and squinted at the hovering tiles. After a few moments, he turned to Glo. "Aren't those the elemental runes of the Titans?"

Glo had been thinking the same thing. He nodded to Donnie. "I believe so."

Seth stood next to the lever with his arms folded, wearing a smug expression. "Well, we've found our way to the other side. Can one of you geniuses detect a pattern? Glo? Elladan?"

Elladan glanced at the halfling and laughed aloud. "You hear that?

He wants us to translate Titan for him. No one has spoken Titan in ages." Elladan paused a moment and gave Elistra a sidelong glance. "Unless..."

Elistra fixed the bard with a withering stare. "No, Elladan, I do not speak Titan. If I did, then why wouldn't I have translated those runes on the wheel upstairs?"

The wheel upstairs? Of course. Glo's eyes moved from the bard to the seeress, his lips spreading into a slim smile. "But we do have a translation—Titan to Dwarvish, and Dwarvish to the Common tongue."

Elladan tilted his head to one side and eyed Glo curiously. His face suddenly lit up as the realization hit him. "The two other wheels—Glo, you're a genius!"

The three of them stood there grinning at each other, but their relvelry was cut short by a derisive snort. Seth stared at the trio, his arms still folded and his lips curved into an ironic smile. "Yeah, yeah, you can start a fan club later. So, do any of you masterminds remember how those wheels lined up?"

Glo opened his mouth to speak, but Donnie beat him to it. "I think I can help with that."

All eyes turned to the slight elf as he doffed his backpack. He reached inside and pulled out a large piece of parchment as the others all gathered around him. Donnie slowly unrolled it, revealing a clear representation of the three wheels from the top floor of the monolith. Even better, all the symbols were lined up.

Elistra gazed fondly at the slight elf. "Donatello, I could kiss you right now!"

"No!" Glo, Alana and Ruka cried almost simultaneously.

The others turned to stare at the threesome. Glo felt his cheeks burning, while both Ruka and Alana turned a bright shade of scarlet. There was an awkward silence, until the wizard finally stammered, "What I meant to say is, 'Seth is right.' This is no time to be congratulating each other."

Seth fixed the elf with a bent grin. "Sure, that's what you meant."

Glo glared at the halfling for a moment or two, then turned his attention back to the portrait of the wheels. His eyes moved from it to the tiles and back again.

"Can I have this?" Glo asked the elven artist.

Donnie gave him a brief nod and cautiously handed the parchment over. "Just be careful with it."

Glo responded with a quick smile, then moved closer to the edge of the cliff, motioning for the others to follow. Elladan and Glo held either side of the wide parchment, while Elistra and Aksel stood behind them. The four of them pored over the portrait, comparing it to the lettering scripted on the tiles just a few feet away.

Aksel stepped back and gazed out at the hovering tiles. "So this is obviously another puzzle. There's probably some phrase that spells a path across the pit." He paused a moment, absently stroked his chin. "Since Larketh was a Dwarf, it's most likely something in his native tongue."

"You mean something like 'I'll have a pint of that'?" Donnie quipped.

Seth fixed the slight elf with a scathing stare. "Yeah, I'm sure that's the phrase Larketh used."

Aksel cleared his throat, drawing their attention back to him. "Ahem. I was thinking more in lines of those inscriptions across the entryways upstairs."

Glo raised a single eyebrow. *Now that was genius. Why didn't I think of that?* Glo's eyes flickered between the portrait and the tiles, examining them up, down, and even diagonally, but nothing appeared to spell out any of the Dwarvish inscriptions they had found. He did catch bits and pieces of words here and there, some even in the Common tongue, but nothing that spelled out the inscriptions they were looking for. After a while, his eyesight began to blur. Glo reached up and rubbed his eyes, then turned to Elladan. "Do you see anything?"

Elladan glanced back at him and slowly shook his head. "Nothing that makes any sense."

By now, Seth had lost all patience. He stood with his hands on his hips, his eyes sweeping from Glo to Elladan to Aksel. "Well, we can't just stand here all day. I guess we'll have to do this by trial and error." Before anyone could stop him, the halfling spun around and strode to the edge of the cliff.

"Are you sure about this?" Aksel called after him.

"Piece of cake," Seth responded, as he peered out at the nearest tiles. "Kind of reminds me of a game I used to play as a wee lad…"

"You're still a wee lad," Donnie responded immediately.

Seth tilted his head forward and eyed the elf with a wicked stare. "Shut it, Donnie."

Donnie let out a short, closemouthed laugh. "Sorry. Reflex response."

The sudden sound of a musical chord drew everyone's attention to Elladan. The bard's eyes were fixed on Seth, a bent smile on his lips. "How about a rousing tune before you leap head-long into this?"

Seth's mouth warped into a half-curved smile. "Well, I was going to use my feet…"

Elladan let out a short laugh, then played the song of inspiration. It did indeed lift everyone's spirits, but despite that, Glo still found himself worried for his halfling friend. He cleared his throat as he anxiously eyed the glowing green pool of acid below. "How about we give you a bit more protection on top of that. Just in case…"

Seth's eyes fell on the wizard. "Works for me," he said rather nonchalantly, but Glo noticed the slightest hint of moisture in the halfling's eyes.

Glo nearly welled up himself—though it remained unsaid between them, he had grown rather fond of Seth over these last few months. Glo fought back his emotions, and began the hand motions of the spell he was going to cast. A few seconds later, he released it with the words, *"Donec A Diam."*

A column of sparse green energy rose from the ground around Seth and rushed up to the top of the halfling's head. It quickly disappeared, but left a momentary greenish glow around Seth's body. That, too, abruptly faded. Glo eyed the halfling with a slim smile. "At least now if you fall, you have a chance of escaping the pool unscathed…"

"Thanks," Seth said simply. There was no mock gratitude in his tone, nor did he follow it with a smart remark. Glo started to wonder if the halfling was alright.

"Be careful, then," Aksel admonished him.

"When am I not?" Seth responded, the telltale smirk returing to his lips.

Glo breathed a sigh of relief. Now there was the Seth they all had come to know and love. The halfling swiftly spun around, and without hesitating, leapt across the two yards to the first stone tile. He deftly landed in a crouch, prepared to jump again if necessary. The onlookers held their breath, but nothing happened. The tile did not waver in the slightest, hovering firmly in place over the bubbling acid.

The only response was in the pool below—a clay golem surfaced nearby and shambled through the glowing green liquid toward the stone tile Seth knelt on, its long arms reaching far above its amorphous head. Luckily, the tiles were just out of the golem's reach.

Elladan called Seth's attention to the spectacle below. "Looks like you've got an admirer down there."

The halfling carefully shifted his body around and peered down into the pit. The clay creature was now directly below him, its long arms still reaching up in vain for the stone tile above. Seth's lips rose to one side. He cried down to the creature, "Sorry, no autographs today."

The golem merely groaned in response, blindly grasping at the tile Seth sat on. Seth slowly got up and stepped to the center of the small slab of stone, gingerly scanning the surrounding tiles.

"That's an 'L' you're standing on," Glo called out to him.

"What do I have next?" Seth responded, his head still spinning between the tiles.

This time Elladan answered, his eyes continually shifting between the small stone tiles and the portrait of the wheels. "A 'D' to your left, an 'O' behind you, and an 'A' to your right."

Seth rubbed his hands together again. "Alright then, let's try 'O.'" He carefully stepped to the edge of the tile then launched himself over the pit again. The onlookers held their breath, but the halfling easily landed on the next tile. Once again, the small stone slab did not waver, hovering in place over the green bubbling pit below. The clay golem followed the halfling and parked itself underneath the next tile, now reaching for this stone slab instead. Seth stood back up and scanned the new set of tiles around him.

"What next?" he called over his shoulder.

Glo translated for him this time. "'R' to your left, 'G' in front of you, and 'S' to your right."

Seth's eyes swept across those three tiles a few times, before turning around and facing the others. He shrugged his shoulders, an ironic smile on his lips. "Ideas anyone?"

Glo exchanged glances with Elladan, Aksel and Elistra. No one seemed to have an immediate answer. The little cleric absently stroked his chin, his brows knit together in concentration. "'R' and 'S' are the most common letters..."

"I vote 'S,'" Donnie interjected cheerfully. "Maybe it spells out *Lost in the caverns.*"

There were a few snorts and snickers in response, but Glo merely spiked an eyebrow at the slight elf. The combinations 'Lor' or 'Los' made far more sense than 'Log,' but Glo had no idea which of the two was correct. He turned his gaze toward Elistra. "Any feelings on this?"

The seeress tilted her head upward, her eyes momentarily glazing over as she tried to divine the answer. After a few moments, her eyes shifted back down to him. "It definitely spells out a specific phrase— but as to what that phrase is, I cannot tell."

Her insight was met with a derisive snort. "Well, that was help-ful," Seth called from his precarious position over the pit.

Elistra gave the halfling a feeble smile. "Sorry, psionics is not an exact art."

No one seemed to have a good answer one way or the other. Seth spun his head from his left to his right a few times, then finally reached a decision. "Guess I'll try 'S' then."

The companions watched on anxiously as the halfling stepped to the edge of the small stone slab, and abruptly launched himself across the empty space toward the adjacent one. Seth landed deftly on the tile with the 'S' on it, but as soon as his feet touched it, the entire thing began to shake. Glo's breathe caught in his throat, a nervous gasp escaping his lips. He was not alone, the entire party ac-companying him. Meanwhile, Seth performed a nervous "dance" on the shifting slab, doing his best to maintain his balance. The tile con-tinued to wobble, its motions increasing, making it more and more difficult for the halfling to stand. If it didn't stop soon, even the agile Seth was sure to fall. As the left side of the stone slab dipped down again, Seth suddenly crouched and launched himself backwards off of it.

"Seth!" Aksel cried in fright.

Glo felt his heart skip a beat as he watched the halfling flip through the air. Time seemed to slow as Seth spun backward, end over end, sailing over the bubbling acid. He arced through the air, landing back on the 'O' tile with his hands and knees simultaneously, barely skidding to a halt before reaching the other edge.

"Phew." Glo expelled a lungful of air from his mouth. He hadn't realized he had been holding his breath the entire time.

In the meantime, the shaking tile finally stopped moving. A moment later, it fell straight down into the acid below. Greenish liquid sprayed up in all directions, splashing on the clay golem that had just moved out of its way. Steam rose all around it as the greenish liquid quickly ate away the edges of the little stone slab. Finally, the small amount that was left sank into the pool, disappearing from sight.

"That was *close!*" Donnie exhaled sharply.

Seth fixed the elf with a withering glare. "Ya think? Next time you pick a letter, I'm going the opposite way."

"Sorry." Donnie responded, his shoulders slumping and his head sinking down as he turned away. "I was just trying to help," he murmured under his breath.

Alana reached over and placed a steel-encased hand on the slight elf's shoulder in an attempt to console him. Meanwhile, Seth got up, dusted himself off, and then spun around to face the tile to the left.

"Guess it was 'R' then," he said with a wry smile.

The companions watched on anxiously as Seth leapt across the chasm between tiles again. He landed squarely on the 'R' slab in a crouch, his body tensed as if ready to leap again immediately. Luckily, this tile remained motionless like the first two. The only movement was below him, where the clay golem continued to shadow his movements. After a few moments, Seth stood up, his eyes sweeping the area. He was at the leftmost edge of the tiles now, his only options jumping either forward or backward.

"And now what's next to me?" he called out to the others.

It was Elladan's turn to respond. The bard scrutinized the two tiles, his eyes swiftly shifting between them and the portrait of the wheels. "There's a 'B' in front of you and a 'D' behind you."

The halfling's lips bent to one side. "Well, '*Lorb*' just makes so much sense."

"'L-O-R-D,'" Glo murmured to himself.

"Didn't one of those inscriptions begin with Lord?" Aksel eyed Glo curiously, mirroring his thoughts.

"*Lord Larketh is the Divine Master of all Constructs*," Elistra said, her eyes glazed over as she recalled the exact phrase that Elladan had recited to the group when they first entered the monolith.

Seth tilted his head and stared at Glo incredulously. "I thought you said you couldn't find any translations?"

Glo threw up his hands and shrugged. "Well, there weren't any in Dwarven. Nor are there any in a straight line. How as I supposed to know it twisted around in a circle?"

Glo felt a small hand on his shoulder. He spun his head and saw Elistra gazing up at him, her eyes filled with sympathy. "Lord is obviously in Common. So what if the phrase is in Dwarven, translated into Common, and phonetically spelled out with Titan runes."

Glo spiked an eyebrow as he mulled over her theory. "Isn't that just a bit convoluted?"

"Have you looked around recently?" came Seth's reply. He turned to see the halfling waving his hands around the chamber, indicating the crazy monolith they stood in.

Glo bowed his head, a sheepish grin spreading across his face. "Point taken."

Elistra leaned in close and wrapped her arms around his waist. He shifted his eyes and saw the understanding expression on her face. "There's no use in berating yourself. Perhaps it would be better to solve the phrase now that we know what we are dealing with?"

A thin smile spread across Glo's lips. Elistra was right—this was no time to pout over his previous oversight. He bent over and gently kissed her on the forehead, then carefully unwrapped her arms from around his waist.

Glo motioned to Elladan to join him, then pored over Donnie's diagram with renewed vigor. The two elves feverishly scanned the tiles fanning out from where Seth currently stood, painstakingly discovering the next ones in an ever-growing chain. The trail they uncovered wound circuitously around the little stone slabs, but when they were done, the duo had mapped out a clear path across the tiles using the Dwarven inscription, translated into Common, and then into Titan, as Elistra had theorized.

Elladan wiped the sweat from his brow and cried out in triumph, "Phew. We got it!"

Glo, equally excited, spun around, grabbed Elistra around the waist and hoisted her up into the air. "You're beautiful!" he shouted exultantly, spinning her around him. He then drew her back down, and kissed her passionately on the lips.

Seth waited impatiently for the two elves to figure out the rest of the puzzle. It was not exactly pleasant out here, the acrid smell of the pit below wafting up to makes his eyes water. Over on the ledge, Glo and Elladan conferred excitedly. While he waited, Seth snickered to himself. *Lord Larketh is the Divine Master of all Constructs.* Larketh definitely did not have self-confidence issues. Finally, after what seemed like ages, Elladan cried out, "We got it!"

Seth watched on with amusement as Glo picked up Elistra and spun her around in the air. Then, much to his surprise, Glo brought her down and kissed her.

Well, that was something, Seth thought wryly.

Ever since he met him, Glo had prided himself on his keen intellect, and his ability to think logically. Yet Seth immediately noticed the effect the merchant's granddaughter, Xelda, had on him—even if Glo didn't notice it himself. Even more recently, Seth observed the way both Ves, and later Kailay, made the elf blush and get all flustered. But then Elistra came along, and it was more than obvious that the two were attracted to one another.

Seth still didn't completely trust the seeress, but he appreciated the effect she was having on Glo. The wizard had definitely mellowed, and was far less stiff than when Seth had first met him. Glo finally put Elista down, and turned to face him. Seth noted with amusement the seeress standing behind the elf, her fingers going to her lips, a satisfied smile spreading across them.

Glo and Elladan then began shouting directions his way. Seth let the two elves guide him across the chasm, and it wasn't too long before he landed on the final tile. As soon as his feet touched it, the force screen in front of him shimmered and winked out of existence. Seth leapt from the last tile to the rocky bluff only a few feet away. Cheers erupted from behind him—Seth turned and executed a short bow. He grinned briefly, then strode over to the second switch.

After a brief examination, he found two nozzles hidden in the base of the lever. Considering the room they were in, Seth could only guess that it was some kind of acid spray trap. He traced a well-hidden wire around the base to an invisible control box. Seth swiftly cracked it open, and disabled the pin-and-tumbler mechanism inside.

"Child's play," he muttered to himself absently.

Seth then stood up and threw the switch. Over the chasm, all of the tiles began to grow. They melded together and solidified into a bridge across the acid pit.

"Nice trick," Seth said to himself. He had to admit, he was impressed with Larketh's level of magic.

As soon as the bridge finished forming, the ground beneath his feet began to rumble, and he heard a grinding sound over his shoulder. Seth spun around and saw a section of the cavern wall slide away, a rock tunnel appearing beyond the doorway. He spun back toward the others and waved them across, his attention then returning back to the pedestal. Much to his surprise, it was not rigged with any sort of traps. Seth gingerly reached up and retrieved the golden piece of sphere. The others soon joined him and he handed the piece to Glo.

Donnie motioned toward the tunnel behind them. "Guess the other piece is somewhere in there."

"You want to go first?" Seth said with a wicked smile.

Donnie took a quick glance around the acid room, then ushered Seth forward. "Um, after you."

Seth and Donnie approached the tunnel entrance. It was a long, dim, rocky corridor, another chamber visible at the far end. That room was well-lit, clearly displaying a second pedestal with another golden piece of sphere hovering over it.

Donnie eyed the tunnel cautiously. "That has to be trapped."

Seth quickly described the acid jets he had found on the lever. "Cute," Donnie said.

"You two might want to be careful in there," Aksel said with clear trepidation.

Seth let out a short, ironic laugh. "Heh. Ya think?"

Elladan drew up next to them and said, "Maybe this will help."

The bard cast a quick spell and four globes of light appeared in front of him. With a wave of his hand, he sent them floating through the rocky entrance and down the tunnel. He stopped them halfway, effectively lighting the entire corridor. Seth gave the bard a grateful nod. He still didn't completely trust him, but Elladan had proved himself useful more than once now. With a quick glance at Donnie, Seth crept forward into the narrow tunnel. He did not turn his head, but felt the slight elf close behind him.

Seth took one step at a time, slowly moving down the corridor, careful to scan the floor, the walls, and even the ceiling. He was prepared to jump back at any second, but things went smoothly for the first dozen yards or so. At that point, Seth spotted a pressure plate on the floor. He quickly found the control box and disabled the mechanism. Meanwhile, Donnie discovered more jet nozzles hidden in the walls.

The slight elf stared cautiously at the site. "Did you say an acid spray trap?"

Seth shook his head. "I don't ever want to find out for sure."

A few more yards down the tunnel, they found a second trap. Donnie actually spotted this one first. It was an extremely thin wire running across the tunnel, three inches off the ground.

Seth gave the slight elf a grudging nod. "Not bad."

Donnie was actually getting rather good at this. The duo swiftly found the trap mechanism and disarmed it. They moved on down the tunnel in tandem, finding more pressure plates and trip wires along the way. In one particularly nasty spot, they found a pressure plate on the other side of the trip wire. If someone had stepped over that wire instead of handling the trap, they would have gotten sprayed with acid anyway.

Finally, after what seemed like an eternity, the duo reached the end of the tunnel. They entered a small, circular chamber, no more than ten yards in diameter, the podium standing in its very center. Seth and Donnie cautiously crossed the room together. When they reached the pedestal, they examined it carefully, but there were no more pressure plates, trip wires, or anything of the like.

Seth ushered Donnie toward the piece of sphere. "Be my guest."

Donnie responded with a short bow. "You did most of the work."

Seth could not help himself—he actually grinned. "I know. I'm just in a good mood."

Donnie grinned back at him. "If you insist."

The slight elf reached up and grasped the golden piece of sphere. The duo then strode back down the tunnel and rejoined the others. Donnie gingerly held out the sphere piece to Glo, and the wizard took it, joining the two pieces together. Elladan then brought out the hemisphere, and they attached the pieces together. When it was done, they had a three-quarter sphere.

Everyone seemed elated by their success, though Seth still had his reservations. Aksel and Lloyd slapped hands together enthusiastically. Glo and Elistra hugged each other, joyfully rocking back and forth. Donnie clasped Alana and Ruka on the shoulders, and ardently shouted, "One last room to go!"

Only Elladan appeared as cynical as Seth. He gazed at the halfling and winked. "Yeah, the fire room. That should be a real blast."

30
FIRE

One more time, the companions crossed the main chamber. This time they were headed toward the fire room, the archway with the single spiral at the bottom and the three leaf-shaped objects extending upward from it. The small company strode purposefully to the end of the corridor, their excitement noticeably building as they reached the door to the last of the elemental chambers.

Once again, they used Elistra's multicolored disc to open the chakra lock. The panel lit up, the door slid aside, and the companions were immediately hit with a wave of sweltering heat. Through the doorway, they spied another dim, rocky cavern, which on first glance appeared quite similar to the earth room. However, the major difference between the two became quickly apparent. The pit in this chamber was filled with a thick, bubbling, yellow-gold liquid.

Molten lava! Glo had never been near a volcano, nor seen the searing liquid rock before, but it was impossible to mistake for anything else. Scattered amidst the bubbling lava were a number of large, rocky outcroppings, but none that came near the opposite bluff. There was no force screen in front of that cliff, either, and the door in the rock-faced wall at the back was clearly visible. Despite that, the entrance appeared just as unreachable as the one in the earth chamber.

Donnie mirrored Glo's thoughts. "Wonder how we're supposed to get over there?"

On top of their seemingly unattainable goal, the environment in this room was extremely inhospitable. It was easily twenty degrees warmer in here than in the main chamber. Many of the companions loosened their clothing as soon as they entered the room. Glo felt especially bad for Alana, the lady knight having no recourse, being encased in steel armor. Alana removed her helmet and wiped beads of sweat from her brow.

"Phew," she exclaimed, flinging the sweat away with the back of her hand. "Now I know how a roast feels in the oven."

The only ones seemingly unaffected by the change in temperature were Lloyd and Ruka. There was not a drop of sweat on either of them, nor did they seem the least bit uncomfortable. Glo found the phenomenom quite curious. "Lloyd, pardon me for asking, but—why aren't you sweating like the rest of us?"

The young man spun around, his eyes fixing on Glo. "Oh, it's nothing, really. As a spiritblade, we are taught that the body's reactions are mostly in the mind. Part of my spiritblade training was learning to control bodily functions that most people are unaware of."

Seth let out a cynical snort. "Does that include blushing?"

Lloyd's face immediately reddened and he grinned sheepishly. "Guess I never got the hang of that one."

Donnie eyed Ruka curiously. "I don't suppose you've had spiritblade training?"

The young teen's expression remained impassive. "Never even heard of it till I met a Stealle."

Donnie hesitated a moment, his suspicion filled eyes flickered around the group before returning to Ruka. "Then I don't suppose you want to tell us why you're not sweating?"

"No, not really."

The young teen spun away from the slight elf, and strode off along the edge of the cliff, effectively ending their conversation. Donnie gazed after her dubiously, but Glo merely shrugged. At this point, nothing Ruka said or did surprised him. It didn't seem to shock Aksel, Seth, or Elistra either. Any further discussion was cut short by a shout from somewhere over the side of the cliff.

"There's a ladder here!"

That's Lloyd! Everyone rushed to the edge of the cliff. The young warrior waved up to them from a rocky ledge perhaps twenty feet below, just at the edge of the bubbling, molten pool of lava. A ladder with a strange metallic sheen ran along the side of the cliff directly below them, down to where Lloyd now stood. Glo reached down and cautiously touched the top of the ladder, but was surprised to find it did not feel warm at all. He briefly wondered what kind of material it was made of, but then his attention was diverted elsewhere.

"Would you look at that?" Elladan cried out in amazement.

Glo shifted his gaze to where the bard was pointing. Inbetween the two cliffs, down near the cavern wall, a large figure emerged from the molten lava, and waded up near a small isle of rock. It lumbered around the little isle, seemingly unaffected by its bath in the searing yellow liquid. From its metallic sheen, the figure was made from the same material as the ladder they just found. What was more interesting though, was the object it circled around—yet another lever.

"That's an iron golem," Aksel said in a hushed voice.

Glo felt a chill run up his spine, despite the fact they were in the hottest room in the monolith. *An Iron golem? This is serious.* Iron golems were massive creatures, much like stone golems, but as their name implied, they were made exclusively of iron. Appearing for all intents and purposes to be a giant suit of armor, their metallic bodies were not only harder than their rocky cousins, but also stronger, their powerful fists able to punch through even solid metal. In a one on one between a stone golem and an iron golem, the iron golem was sure to be the victor.

"This is not going to be easy." Aksel stared intently at the golem, a hand on his chin, and his brows knit together.

Lloyd abruptly reappeared at the top of the ladder, his expression one of confusion as his gaze moved from Aksel to the large iron creature. "Why's that?"

Aksel spun to face the young warrior. "You've obviously never faced an iron golem. Fire heals them."

Lloyd's mouth fell open. "Oh."

The young man's expression grew deadly serious as he mentally reassessed their huge, iron-clad opponent.

"It gets better."

All eyes turned to Seth. The halfling gazed at the other side of the room, straight across the lava pit from the marching golem. Glo spiked an eyebrow—another iron golem had appeared, patrolling around a second lever on a similar islet.

"Let me guess—both levers need to be pulled at once," Donnie noted wryly.

"Just like the water room." Ruka nodded, an ironic smile on her lips as she strode back to join them.

Donnie eyes narrowed as he gazed back and forth between the two iron creatures. "Unfortunately, unlike the water room, both golems are right next to their levers."

"A distraction might still work, though."

All eyes turned to Lloyd. The young warrior's brow was furrowed with concentration. "They don't appear to be very fast. If one of us can draw them away from the lever, the other can pull the lever."

Seth let out a loud snort. "Sure—as long as you don't get yourself killed doing it."

Elladan leaned in close to Lloyd, the back of his hand going to the side of his mouth. "Iron golems hit hard," he said in a confidential tone.

"Even harder than stone golems," Seth added, his expression completely serious for once.

Lloyd's eyes widened, the color draining from his face, most likely envisioning Titan after her battle with the Boulder back at Stone Hill. He just as swiftly recovered, firmly setting his jaw.

"I don't think we have a choice," the young warrior declared, his voice unwavering.

Alana stepped up to stand beside him, placing a steel gauntlet on his shoulder. "I agree. Lloyd and I will distract the golems. Donnie, perhaps you and Seth can work your way around and pull the switches then?"

Donnie and Seth exchanged a brief glance and a nod. The halfling's eyes then shifted back to Lloyd and Alana. He gazed intently at the pair for a few moments, then shrugged. "Your funerals."

"Not if I can help it." Ruka stepped in front of Alana, folded her arms, and glared at the lady knight. "I'm coming with you."

Alana eyed the young teen carefully. Ruka's expression was defiant, as if daring the lady knight to argue with her. Alana remained silent for a few moments, then a slight smile spread across her lips. When she spoke, her tone was formal, but there was a trace of moisture in her eyes. "Your assistance would be most welcome."

"I might also be able to help." Elistra stepped forward, her expression grim as her gaze shifted from Ruka to Alana, finally coming to rest on Lloyd. "I can summon another astral construct. The fire won't hurt it, and it should be able to help keep the other iron golem busy for a while."

Glo had been listening quietly to their proposed battle plans, his stomach in knots as he thought about what his friends might be facing. Yet, based on what he heard just now, Glo began to think they might stand a chance. His eyes swept around the group, a slim smile sprouting on his lips. "This might just work. I can cast fire protection spells on the lot of you—that will help with the lava, and as for the golems, they are immune to all magic, except—electricity."

Glo's eyes came to rest on Ruka as he uttered that last word. The young teen's mouth curved sideways as he finished his speech. "Really now? You don't say."

Aksel snapped his fingers together, his eyes coming alight. "Of course! Electricity slows down iron golems."

Lloyd eyed the little cleric curiously. "How's that work?"

Aksel shifted his gaze to the young warrior. "Since they're metal, the electrical charge messes with their insides. It won't damage them, but it will slow them down until the charge dissipates."

"How long?" Lloyd asked, his brows knit close together as he tried to plan out his strategy.

"Not very," Glo answered this time. "Not more than half a minute."

Lloyd nodded solemnly. "Got it."

"I can also help," Elladan offered, holding up his lute. "An inspiring tune to increase your battle prowess."

Lloyd's expression softened and he smiled at the bard. "Thanks, Elladan."

"Yes, that would be most appreciated, good bard," Alana concurred.

Aksel's eyes swept over the small group, mixed emotions playing across his face. After a moment or two, he set his jaw and nodded. "Very well then, let's do this."

Lloyd carefully picked his way across the pit of molten lava, hopping between rocky outcroppings, toward the isle that held one of the golems. Out of the corner of his eye, close to the cliff face, he spied Seth mirroring his steps, the halfling hoping to dash across to the lever once Lloyd got the golem's attention.

Across the pit, far behind him, Alana, Ruka, and Donnie closed in on the other golem. Their approach was similar—Alana and Ruka would distract the golem, while Donnie crept around to the other lever. Once Seth and Donnie were in position, they would pull their levers simultaneously. The plan sounded simple, but in reality these things never were.

Lloyd stood on a rocky islet halfway between the entrance and the iron golem. It was extremely hot, the yellow-gold liquid rock bubbling and steaming around him. Even the rocks at his feet were scorched, glowing a dull shade of angry red from the heat. Luckily, he did not feel it. Aside from his spiritblade training, Glo had cast a protection spell on Lloyd and the others. It would not last indefinitely, but it should be long enough for them to get the job done.

Lloyd scanned the way ahead, looking for a good place to leap across to the next islet. In truth, with Glo's spell, he could have just waded through boiling lava. However, that would sap the spell's energy, and it wouldn't do for it to run out in the midst of battle. At best, the heat would quickly fatigue him—at worst, he could misstep and fall into the lava. That would be certain death.

The young warrior found a good place to cross, and leapt to the next outcropping, bringing him one step closer to his confrontation with the iron golem. He continued this process until he was nearly within reach of his metallic foe. The closer he drew, the more aware Lloyd became of its true size. It was more of a small giant, easily twice Lloyd's height, and even taller than the Boulder.

The golem's helmet-like head sat low on its broad shoulders, a strange, reddish glow emanating from the V-shaped split in its visor-less metallic skull. The golem's massive, armor-clad arms hung down to its knees, ending in fists the size of cannonballs. Its thick legs, each the width of a tree, disappeared into the lava below, its feet hidden as it plodded through the thick, molten rock.

Up until now, the golem had ignored him, continuing its circular path around the islet it guarded. Lloyd stopped one isle over and turned toward Seth. The halfling had positioned himself on an out-cropping near the wall of the chamber, awaiting Lloyd's signal. Di-rectly across the chamber, Alana and Ruka were also in position, within a few strides of the other golem. Donnie mirrored Seth, stick-ing as close to the wall of the pit as possible. Ruka peered over at Lloyd and gave him a single nod, signifying they were ready.

Lloyd nodded back, then shifted his gaze to the cliff top, locking eyes with Elistra. The seeress gave him a nod as well, then closed her eyes, her brow furrowing with concentration. A couple of yards from where Lloyd stood, a shimmering appeared in the air. It grew bright-er and brighter, then abruptly coalesced into a humanoid form. The creature was roughly Lloyd's size, although a bit bulkier, the vague outlines of a face sitting atop its semi-transparent body. As soon as the creature finished forming, it marched forward toward the golem.

"Go!" Lloyd cried across the pit. He caught a brief glimpse of Ruka and Alana wading forward as he drew his own blades. The young warrior then spun around and rushed after his strange com-panion as they began their assault on the iron giant.

Donatello watched with trepidation as Alana and Ruka lined up for battle. The two women warriors stood on a wide patch of rock, one islet over from where the golem plodded through the lava. Donnie's eyes shifted from the duo to the golem itself, his jaw dropping as he got a true perspective of the creature's size.

That thing is huge! Donnie had to bite his tongue to stop from crying out. The iron creature towered over the duo, even being knee deep as it was in the molten lava. Luckily, the golem continued to ignore them. Donnie crouched a short distance away, near the base of the cliff, surveying the surrounding area. He was supposed to wait until the two women warriors distracted the creature, then get to the switch behind it without being seen.

Thankfully, this side of the pit was dotted with numerous rocky outcroppings and islets. Still, he wanted to find the quickest path to the isle with the lever on it. As soon as both he and Seth were in position, they could pull the levers and be done with it. The plan was not at all to Donnie's liking—he was too afraid that someone would get hurt.

It should be me out there. Donnie might not be able to hurt the golem, but it would have little chance of hitting him either. He had no choice, though—he and Seth were the only ones who could reach the switches undetected.

Donnie chided himself. *Alana is a seasoned warrior, and Ruka has proven time and again that she can handle herself.*

Still, he could not get the knot out of his stomach. If anything were to happen to either of them, he would never forgive himself. *Well then, you just need to reach that switch as fast as possible.*

Donnie peered across the pit and saw Lloyd and Seth were in position. There was a sudden shimmering in the air next to the red-clad warrior, and then Elistra's construct appeared. The creature immediately charged the golem in front of them.

"Go!" Lloyd shouted from across the pit.

Donnie shifted his focus back to Alana and Ruka. The duo separated, Alana's shield up, her sword springing to life with a brilliant white glow. Ruka had her short sword out and pointed it at the golem.

Kraaaaacccckkkkk! Thunder rolled as a bolt of lightning jumped from her sword and caught the iron creature square in the chest. The golem immediately slowed down, arcs of electricity skirting across its torso.

Alana charged into the lava, the molten liquid nearly up to her waist. She came within striking distance of the golem, then slashed at its knee viciously with her glowing sword—once, twice, three times in quick succession. The golem slowly turned to face its attacker, but the lady knight had already backpedaled out of the lava and onto the islet where Ruka still stood.

Donnie nodded approvingly. *Very clever.* They were attempting to draw the golem out of the lava and onto dry ground. That way it couldn't heal itself with the hot liquid.

Kraaaaacccckkkkk! Thunder rolled once more across the cavern, this time from the other side of the pit. Donnie chanced a quick glance in that direction and saw a purple robed figure hovering high in the air, while the red-clad form of Lloyd rushed forward into battle.

"C'mon, big guy!" Ruka voice drew his attention back to the clash in front of him.

Alana waved the golem on. "Yes… this way."

The creature ponderously marched through the lava and out onto the rocky outcropping. The two female warriors backed away, drawing the iron giant toward the center of the isle. The creature's back was almost to him now.

This is my chance, Donnie realized. He spurred himself forward, moving across the rocky ledge as far as he could go without stepping into lava, all the while without taking his eye off the battle in front of him. The golem had swung at Alana, but the skilled warrior ducked under the creature's blow. Meanwhile, Ruka had run in and slashed across the golem's legs, another charge leaping from her blade.

Kraaaaacccckkkkk! Thunder rolled yet again. Arcs of electricity danced across the golem's torso, causing it to slow down once more. Alana took advantage of the moment and rushed in, landing three more blows in quick succession on the creature's knee. She was so skilled with her weapon, that every blow landed in precisely the same spot.

Even from here, Donnie could see the gash opening in the golem's thick leg. A few more blows and she just might sever it completely. Donnie looked away for a moment as he leapt across the lava to another outcropping. He deftly landed on solid ground, then turned his attention back to the battle.

The electric arcs around the golem had dissipated, the huge creature already turning after its foe. Suddenly, a large limb lashed out, and a cannonball-sized fist hurtled directly toward Alana, giving her little time to react. At the very last second, the lady knight sidestepped, and raised her shield arm defensively.

Bam!

The sound of metal on metal resounded across the lava pit. The force of the glancing blow was so great that it backlashed on Alana.

"Ooofff!"

The air was forced out of the lady knight as her entire body rebounded from the collision, pushing her back a few steps. Donnie froze in his tracks and nearly called out her name. He had to clamp both hands over his mouth to stop from screaming as he watched Alana struggle to maintain her balance. She finally managed to regain her footing, but the golem had followed her. As the creature recoiled for another blow, a cry rang out from the cliff above. "Alana! Watch out!"

The switch be damned! Donnie swore silently. As he launched himself toward the lady knight, something flew through the air toward the golem's back. It was Ruka!

"Oh, no, you don't!" the girl warrior screamed. She hefted her short sword high above her head, its blade crackling with electricity. Before the golem could unleash its blow, Ruka slammed into it, her weapon digging deep into the creature's back. Sparks flew as an aura of electricity encircled the golem's large frame. The creature stopped in its tracks, seemingly frozen in place, as the loud hum of electrical current filled the pit around them.

Donnie had pulled up short, and watched in awe as Ruka continued her electrical assault. Her feet planted firmly on the golem's broad back, she held onto the embedded blade and fired bolt after bolt of electricity into its innards. Once, twice, three times, and more.

So many times that Donnie lost count. Steam rose from the space in the golem's visor, and then from its joints. Still Ruka continued her unrelenting assault.

Finally, the young warrior stopped, heaving heavily on her short blade, and wrenching it from the golem's back. Ruka crouched, then pushed off the golem's back, flying backwards in a long arc, then summersaulting in mid-air and landing on her feet a few yards away. In the meantime, Alana was not idle. She launched herself at the still frozen golem with a loud cry over her shoulder.

"Move, Donnie!"

Donnie, still astonished, forced his feet into motion once more. He changed directions back toward the lever, but refused to take his eye off the incredible battle. Alana rushed the golem, once again hacking away at its wounded knee. She expertly slashed at it over and over, cutting deeper and deeper with every blow. The golem did not react, still frozen in place, steam continuing to rise from its innards.

Alana hit the knee with one last heavy blow, nearly slicing through the entire leg, then quickly backpedalled as the golem teetered precariously on the nearly severed limb. The large form finally tipped over and crashed to the ground with a loud boom, the pit around them trembling from the shock.

Donnie shook his head in amazement as cheers broke out from the cliff above them. *What a team those two make!* He was still grinning from ear-to-ear as he made the last leap to the isle with the lever on it.

31
STEALLE

He was flung across the islet, crashing hard into the rocky surface

While Ruka and Alana waged war with their foe, the assault began on Lloyd's target. He had worked out a strategy with Elistra, Glo and Alana, the seeress' construct already wading in, and drawing the creature out of the lava. Meanwhile, Lloyd turned his focus inward to bring his mind, body, and spirit together.

Kraaaaaccccckkkkk!

A roll of thunder momentarily broke Lloyd's concentration. He allowed himself a brief smile—Ruka certainly wasn't wasting any time.

The young warrior turned his focus inward once more, this time his body, mind and spirit converging. He was rewarded with a patch of metallic grey appearing near his abdomen, quickly spreading from there, and covering his entire body.

Stealle Skin his father called it, a thin layer of tensile steel, flexible and lightweight, that would protect him without slowing him down.

The golem was nearly at the center of the rocky islet, trailing after Elistra's construct, the astral creature already missing large chunks from its torso. As the golem reached the center of the small isle, a flash of light crashed down on it from above.

Kraaaaacccckkkkk! Thunder rolled once more across the chamber, marking Lloyd's entrance into battle. The young warrior rushed forward, his black blade readied, not looking up to see Glo still hovering there. The golem had been slowed down, arcs of electricity skirting across its torso. As the astral contruct lumbered forward, Lloyd raced under the golem's arm and slashed fiercely at the exposed knee joint. His black blade bit deep into the giant hinge, opening a gash in the creature's leg. Lloyd pulled the blade back, swiftly spun around and sliced into its knee from the other side, the black sword once again cutting deep into the exposed joint.

Kraaaaacccckkkkk! Another roll of thunder rumbled from across the cavern, but Lloyd had no time for even a quick glance. The huge leg suddenly pulled away as the golem swiveled around to face him. Lloyd swiftly spun around and retreated, instinctively ducking as something large passed overhead. He turned about and saw the iron giant following him, the construct all but forgotten.

A sudden cry came from across the pit—"Alana! Watch out!"—but Lloyd couldn't manage even the briefest of glances as the golem marched up and swung at him once more. The young warrior tumbled out of the way and came up at a dead run toward the golem's legs. As the creature recoiled, Lloyd lashed out once more, his blade biting nearly halfway through the joint this time. Not daring another blow, Lloyd continued on past the golem. He had only taken a few steps when he heard a frantic cry from above.

"Lloyd, look out!"

Lloyd tried to duck down, but something smashed into his back, sending him flying haphazardly across the islet. He tried to pull in his arms and legs, but the ground rushed up at him and he slammed into the rocky surface. The entire world around him went hazy, everything spinning out of control.

He heard a voice cry out his name. "Lloyd, get up! Get up, Lloyd!"

Lloyd fought down the urge to puke and rolled himself over. A huge metallic figure filled his view, growing larger and larger by the second. The young warrior forced himself up onto one knee, but the world around him started to spin again. Lloyd tried to focus on the metallic creature, but something abruptly blocked his view. He steadied his head with his free hand and the world suddenly came back into focus. The iron golem towered over him, but was being held at bay by Elistra's construct.

Lloyd took advantage of the brief respite, calming his mind and effectively shutting off the pain. The young warrior then forced himself to stand, grasping his black blade firmly in both hands. At the same time, the iron golem reached down and grabbed the astral creature by the arms. Lloyd watched in horror as the golem pulled the helpless creature from two directions. There was a sick, tearing sound, and the poor construct split right down the middle. The iron golem callously dropped the two halves to the ground, the remnants of the contruct quickly dissolved with a faint hiss into nothingness.

Lloyd was momentarily aghast, but then felt a deep, unabiding anger well up from inside him. *That construct saved my life! It didn't deserve to be ripped apart like that.*

Cries of victory suddenly rang across the chamber. It could only mean that Alana and Ruka had won. *Well if they can do it, so can I!*

The young warrior set himself for another assault, the combination of those triumphant cries and his own anger fueling his determination. The iron golem took a step toward him, when suddenly, the air around them lit up with a brilliant flash.

Kraaaaacccckkkkk! Thunder rolled again across the chamber. Lloyd had nearly forgotten about Glo, but the wizard had given him his chance. The golem slowed down again, arcs of electricity skirting across its torso, yet instead of rushing forward, Lloyd reached down inside himself once more. The world appeared to slow to a crawl as Lloyd touched that spark of spirit, his surroundings blurred, and he found himself directly behind the golem.

Lloyd did not hold anything back, letting his anger and frustration out in one vicious swing. His black blade connected with the creature's wounded knee, cleaving straight through what was left of the metal joint. Lloyd swiftly backpedaled away as the golem teetered precariously on its one good leg. Finally, the creature toppled over onto the ground with a resounding crash.

Cheers went up again across the cavern. The golem was down. They had won!

Seth and Donnie signaled each other from across the chamber, and then pulled the two levers simultaneously. The result was nothing short of spectacular—all the molten lava flowed toward the center of the chamber, welled up and slowly formed into the shape of a long bridge, connecting the two cliffs on either side of the pit. The thick, yellow-gold liquid then cooled, hardening into solid rock. During the solidifying process, Glo, Seth, Ruka and Donnie helped Lloyd and Alana rejoin the others—the young warrior and the lady knight had each taken a major beating in their battles with the golems. Aksel immediately began healing the lady knight, while Seth tended to Lloyd.

"You guys go ahead," Seth told the others as he knelt down beside the young warrior and ran his hands over his torso.

Donnie peered speculatively across the room at the door on the other side of the cavern, then shifted his gaze back to Seth. The expression on his face was tentative at best. "You sure about this?"

"Sure," Seth drawled, "what's the worst that could happen?"

Elladan placed an arm around the slight elf's shoulder, and let out a short laugh. "Donnie here could get himself fried."

Seth did not look up, but the side of his mouth lifted slightly. "Like I said, what's the worst that could happen?"

Donnie's hands went to his hips, his eyes shifting between the amused duo. "Thanks, guys."

Meanwhile, Glo had gone to examine the newly formed bridge. It appeared completely solid, but the young wizard had learned as of late not to take anything for granted. He stopped at the edge, bent down and held a hand out over the solidified rock. Though it had only cooled a short while ago, there was no sense of heat coming off the stone. Glo tentatively reached down and placed a finger on the bridge, but it was cool to the touch.

"Larketh's work with golems required a level of control over the elements that few have matched, even to this day."

Glo spun about and saw Elistra kneeling next to him. He had been so entranced with the bridge, that he had not even heard her there. Glo responded with a weak smile. "It is rather amazing."

The seeress' eyes danced with amusement. She reached out and placed a gentle hand on his shoulder. "You are not the first to marvel over the Golem Master's works."

Abruptly, Glo felt a hand on his other shoulder. He whirled around and saw Elladan standing above him. The bard nodded toward the bridge, his expression one of awe. "Larketh definitely had a flair for the dramatic."

"You can say that again," Glo agreed fervently.

So, while Aksel and Seth continued to tend to the injured, the rest of the companions proceeded across the newly-formed bridge. Donnie led the way across, halting at the door on the other side. There was another chakra lock here, but Elistra once again provided the key. The door slid open, revealing a cave beyond that split off into two separate tunnels.

Since Seth was preoccupied, the others decided to stick together and explore the passageways one at time. That turned out to be an excellent decision since, like the earth room, there were jet traps embedded into the walls. Donnie nearly got burnt by the first one, leaping out of the way just as a spray of flames burst out of the tunnel wall.

"Yow!" the slight elf cried, gingerly brushing the hot embers from his clothes. Unfortunately, he was not quick enough—the edge of his vest caught on fire. Donnie danced around, trying to pull it off, until Ruka rushed forward. In one swift motion, she yanked the burning cloth from his body, threw it to the ground, and stamped up and down on the vest until the flames went out. When she was done, Ruka picked up the still smoking cloth and held it out to Donnie, her mouth twisted sideways. "Next time you might want to watch where you step."

Donnie ignored the dig, his attention fixed on the smoldering, tattered vest before him. He took it from Ruka, and turned it end over end, a strained smile on his face as he stuck his fingers through the newly-formed holes in the material. "So much for my lucky vest…"

Glo was uncertain how to react. The sight of Donnie dancing around had indeed been comical, but he felt it rude to laugh at his friend's loss. Glo cast a sidelong glance at Elistra—the seeress' expression was impassive, but her eyes danced with amusement. Elladan, on the other hand, had a hard time containing himself, coughing vigorously into his hand in a vain attempt to hide his laughter. The sound drew Donnie's attention away from his vest, his eyes flickering around the group.

"Not a word," the slight elf cautioned, his gaze lingering a moment longer on Elladan. He paused a moment to stuff the tattered cloth into his backpack, then dropped down to his hands and knees, searching the ground ahead. Donnie soon discovered the pressure plate that had set off the stream of flames that nearly fried him. He traced it along the ground and up the wall to its control box. After disarming the mechanism, Donnie turned to face the others, his hands on his hips and his eyes narrowed as they swept across the group. "Well… any more comments?"

Elladan peered at the slight elf with a partial smile. "No, not really… although if you keep it up, you are going to be naked in no time."

Donnie fixed the bard with an acid stare. "I'm sure I can manage without losing any more clothes."

"I wouldn't mind," Ruka chimed in.

"Ruka!" Donnie gaped at the young teen, his face turning a bright shade of scarlet.

"Just don't singe any of the important parts," she added, her smile widening as she spun around and walked away.

Donnie stared after her, his mouth still agape. His eyes abruptly shifted to Elladan. "Why do I feel like I've suddenly lost my edge?"

The bard chuckled for a moment or two, then reached out and placed a hand on his bewildered friend's shoulder. "Ah, Donnie… she's a teen… there's no winning with them."

Donnie let out a long sigh, then finally shrugged, a wry smile returning to his lips. "I guess you are right. Some things will always be beyond our control." As he spoke those last words, his eyes shifted between Elistra and Glo. Donnie gave his fellow elf a sly wink, then spun around and rubbed his hands together. "Might as well be moving on."

The small group continued down the tunnel, Donnie finding two more pressure plates and a trip wire. He disarmed all of them without further incident. Finally, the companions made it to the end of the tunnel. There was a pedestal there with another piece of globe floating above it. After finding and disarming yet another fire trap, Donnie retrieved the sphere piece and handed it over to Glo, who swiftly merged it with the larger piece. When he was done, Elladan grinned at the elven wizard. "Just one more to go…"

The small group backtracked their way to the beginning of the tunnel and found Alana waiting there. Donnie strode up to the lady knight, gazing at her with a mixture of fondness and concern. "How are you feeling?"

Alana dismissed his question with a wave of her hand. "Just fine."

Donnie's face fell at her abrupt treatment of his affections. Alana must have noticed, because her entire demeanor changed. A tender smile spread across her lips, her eyes filling with warmth for the slight elf. "After all, Aksel is a rather expert healer."

Donnie's face lit up. "That's what I've heard."

The pair stood silently staring into each other's eyes, until Ruka interrupted them. "So where's everyone else?"

Alana's eyes shifted toward the young teen, her skin momentarily flushing. She covered her discomfort with a quick nod toward the cave entrance. "Aksel finished healing me, then went to help Seth with Lloyd. Last I saw, they were still working on him."

Donnie's eyes narrowed as he peered at the lady knight. "So… do they know you came looking for us?"

Alana briefly met his gaze, then averted her eyes. "Well… not exactly. He did say I was fully healed, though."

Donnie folded his arms across his chest, and stared at her accusingly. "Still, I'm sure he wanted you to rest."

Alana nudged a pebble across the ground with a steel-clad toe. "Now that you mention it, I believe he said something about that."

At that moment, Ruka strode up and punched Donnie solidly in the arm. The slight elf yelped, and grabbed his shoulder. "What was that for?"

"For the gods sakes, you are not her mother!" the young teen declared vehemently. She grabbed the lady knight by the arm, and steered her toward the second tunnel. "Come on, Alana, before he decides to tuck you in for the night."

Donnie stared after the two women, his expression dumbfounded. Elladan, chuckling softly, sidled up next to him, and placed a hand on his friend's shoulder. "You were getting a bit carried away there, Donnie."

The slight elf arched an eyebrow at the bard. "Was I that bad?"

Elladan nodded and grinned. "Smothering."

Donnie hung his head. "I *am* losing my edge."

Glo felt a momentary pang of sorrow for his elven comrade. He was obviously quite smitten with the lady knight, and was just as much out of his element with the young teen. Glo thanked the gods he was not in Donnie's position… heck, it was hard enough having a relationship with one woman, let alone two. He was about to say something to that effect, when he noticed the pair had reached the entrance to the other tunnel. "Um, Donnie… you might want to go after them."

The slight elf roused himself, and peered across the cave. On seeing the fair duo, he immediately took off with the cry, "Wait! Let me go first!"

Glo exchanged a brief glance with Elladan, the two elves chuckling softly as they strode after the others.

A short while later, the small group reached the other end of the tunnel. Strangely, there had been no traps of any kind along its entire length—they soon found out why. The passageway abruptly opened into a small cavern, the pedestal containing the last piece of sphere situated in a small alcove on the other side. Between the companions and their objective sat a steaming pool of bubbling lava. The molten liquid stretched a good ten yards in front of them, and from one wall of the cave across to the other. The group stopped at the edge of the bubbling lava, deliberating what to do next.

Donnie's eyes swept across the length of the cavern, his lips pursed. "I could try climbing across the walls… although they do look kind of hot."

Donnie was right—on closer inspection, Glo noticed that the walls had a reddish glow to them. Donnie's hands would be burnt beyond recognition were he to try climbing his way across. Glo cocked his head to one side. "I could cast the fly spell on you…"

Before he could finish his sentence, something rushed past their heads. Glo ducked down instinctively, then looked up, his eyes focusing on a white-tailed hawk as it glided over the steaming pit of yellow-gold liquid.

"Ruka! Stop!" Donnie cried, but it was far too late. The hawk flew into the alcove, hovered over the pedestal, and grasped the golden piece of orb with its sharp talons. The moment the piece lifted off the platform, the entire alcove was flooded with flames. Jets of hot fire streamed into the nook from every direction.

"Ruka!" Donnie shouted in horror.

Glo felt a sinking feeling in the pit of his stomach. There was little chance the young teen could survive such an onslaught. He reached out to place a hand on Donnie's shoulder when, without warning, something shot out of the flames. It was the white-tailed hawk—by some miracle, she had survived the fiery death trap. The bird now flew over the pool toward them, still grasping the piece of orb firmly within her talons.

As one, the companions stepped back from the edge of the pool, making room for the hawk to land. Ruka shape-shifted in mid-air, and landed neatly in a crouch on the ground in front of them. Her leathers looked a bit scorched, and there were traces of soot upon her skin, but otherwise she appeared unharmed. Donnie rushed forward to meet her. "You scared the heck out of us, young lady!"

Ruka's mouth twisted as she stood up. "Aww, Donnie, you do care."

Donnie stood there for a moment with his mouth agape, then

let out a huge sigh. "Of course I do." he said finally, reaching forward and wrapping his arms around the young teen. Ruka's eyes went wide, most likely startled by the slight elf's sudden affection, but her surprise just as quickly faded, the teen closing her eyes and sinking into Donnie's warm embrace.

"We all do," Alana added, stepping forward and hugging the girl from behind. Ruka stood there between the two, her head on Donnie's chest, practically purring with delight. At the same time, Glo felt an arm wrap around his—he glanced down and saw Elistra snuggling into his side, wearing a serene smile on her lips. Glo felt his insides practically melt, a warm smile spreading across his face in response.

After a moment or two, the elven wizard swung his gaze back to the enfolded trio. Suddenly, Ruka's eyes snapped open, her face flushing and her eyes going wide. She disengaged herself, pushing away from Donnie and Alana, her eyes sweeping around the group, finally coming to rest on Elladan. "Don't you have anything better to do than stand there and gawk?"

Elladan let out a short laugh, seemingly unphased by her accusation. "Oh, I wasn't gawking...I was just trying to figure out how you survived that fire trap."

Ruka folded her arms across her chest, and glared at the bard. "Does it really matter?"

Glo had been wondering the same thing, but the answer suddenly dawned on him. He cleared his throat, a wry smile on his face. "I think I can answer that." All eyes turned questioningly toward the elven wizard. "I had cast a fire protection spell on her, Alana, and Lloyd just before the battle with the golems. That was less than an hour ago, so it was still in effect."

"Yeah, yeah, whatever," Ruka responded, her tone a tad more sarcastic than usual. "How about focusing on what we came for instead," she added, striding deliberately toward Elladan, and dropping the last piece of orb into his hands. The young teen then brushed past him and strode away toward the tunnel entrance. "Let me know how it turns out," she called over her shoulder.

As Glo watched Ruka's small form recede down the passageway, he heard Alana's strained voice behind him. "I think I might have embarrassed her. Perhaps I should go apologize." The lady knight abruptly pushed her way past them in pursuit of the angst-filled teen.

Elistra was the next to speak. "I think I should probably go too, and help smooth things over."

Before Glo knew it, the seeress brushed by him as well, striding swiftly down the tunnel after both Alana and Ruka. Glo's eyes remained fixed on the lovely retreating form, until he felt a hand on his shoulder. He turned and saw Donnie standing between him and Elladan, an arm around each. "Life would be far less interesting without them."

All three of them exchanged a grin. "Truer words were never spoken," Elladan added with a nod.

After a few moments, Donnie let go of his fellow Elves and said, "How about we finish what we started?"

"Good idea," Elladan responded, holding out the last piece of orb for Glo to take. The elven wizard took the piece, and brought it together with the rest of the sphere. It silently merged into place, and Glo now held a perfectly round, golden orb in his hands.

Donnie's eyes shifted between his two friends, a satisfied grin on his face. "Well, we got what we came for."

Elladan fixed them both with a partial smile. "Now to see what it does."

32
GOLDEN SPHERE

A set of stone stairs descended into the depths below

The elven trio retraced their steps, crossing the bridge to the cliff on the other side of the now empty pit. Aksel and Seth sat with Lloyd, the young man sitting on the ground, looking healthy but tired. Alana, Ruka and Elistra stood off by themselves, the two women talking quietly with the teen. As the elves approached, Seth stood up and strode over to them. "So I hear you got the final piece."

"As a matter of fact, we did," Donnie responded, his chest puffing up with pride as he motioned to Elladan. "Show him."

The bard reached into his portal bag and pulled out the completely round, golden orb, holding it up for the halfling to see. Seth moved in closer and examined the artifact critically. When he was done, his eyes swept across the threesome, finally coming to rest on Donnie, the half-twisted smile they had come to know so well upon his lips. "Nice… and Donnie's even in one piece."

Elladan responded with his own half-smile. "That's because Ruka did his dirty work for him."

Donnie spun to face the bard, a hurt expression on his face. "Hey! How about all those traps I disarmed in the first tunnel."

Elladan let out a short laugh. "You mean after nearly getting fried by the first one?"

Donnie glared at his elven friend. "One time… one time and everyone's a critic. Geez, what's an elf got to do around here to get some respect?" Donnie hung his head in a comical manner, feigning a "poor me" expression. His acting elicited a round of chuckles from his companions, his own expression changing quickly to a grin. The moment of amusement died down as swiftly as it had started. Glo peered over toward Aksel and Lloyd, the former still fussing over the young man, while the latter argued with him. Glo's sensitive ears caught some of the quiet conversation.

"…but I'm fine now," Lloyd was saying.

Aksel folded his arms, staring intently at the young warrior. "I'm your healer, and I'll determine when you are fine…"

Glo shifted his eyes back to Seth. "Is Lloyd alright?"

Seth's mouth rose to one side as he watched the duo argue. "Yeah, he's fine. Aksel is just mother-henning him is all."

Glo arched an eyebrow. "Over a couple of bumps and bruises?"

Seth responded with a derisive snort. "Hmph. That, and a broken bone or two…"

"Broken bones?" Elladan exclaimed, his voice rising an octave.

Seth, not turning around, merely shrugged. "Mostly ribs—although there was a hairline fracture in the one arm…"

Donnie's mouth dropped open, his eyes shifting from Seth to Lloyd, and then back again. "I had no idea. Lloyd seemed battered when we left him, but not much more than that."

The halfling turned to face the slight elf, the smirk on his face widening. "It must be one of the drawbacks of spiritblade training. That steel skin coating thing Lloyd did just before the battle probably saved his life. However, that shutting off pain thing he also does, masked just how serious his injuries were."

Elladan's eyes narrowed, his face filled with concern as he gazed over at the still-arguing Lloyd and Aksel. "But he's okay now, right?"

"Oh, yeah, he'll be fine," Seth replied with a nonchalant wave of his hand. He spun around again to watch the scene still going on between the young man and the gnome "Aksel wants him to rest, but Lloyd, of course, is raring to go." The halfling then turned his gaze to Alana, Ruka, and Elistra. "What's up with those three?"

Elladan laughed rather loudly, then reached out and placing a hand on Donnie's shoulder. "Let's just say that Donnie managed to get himself into even more hot water."

Seth let out a short, wicked laugh. "Heh. What else is new?"

Donnie glared at the duo, but never got the chance to reply as Aksel's voice rang out across the chamber. "…that's all well and fine, but when I say rest, you better rest… unless of course you don't want to be healed next time!" The little cleric folded his arms across his chest and glared at Lloyd as if daring him to challenge his authority.

Lloyd hung his head, a chagrinned expression on his face, as he responded with a sullen, "Okay."

Aksel gave him a firm nod, then spun around to face Alana. "And the same goes for you, young lady!"

Alana looked up from her own argument, and blushed at the little cleric's admonishment. Yet, before she could reply, Ruka answered for her.

"Yes, Dad," the young teen drawled. Her response elicited a round of laughter from everyone in the chamber. Glo had to admit, she hit the nail on the head with that one.

✳

After a short rest, mostly for Lloyd's and Alana's sake, the companions left the fire room. They headed back into the main chamber, Elladan gingerly leading the way, all the while cradling the now-complete golden orb in his hands. When they reached the pedestal, the bard spun around to face the others. "All things considered, I think it only fitting that those who put their lives on the line for this thing should have the honors."

All eyes turned toward Lloyd and Alana. The duo appeared surprised at first, then turned to eye each other. After a few moments, the young warrior stepped back and bowed to the lady knight. "The honor is all yours, good Dame."

Alana smiled at the young man's chivalry, but then shook her head. "We were not the only one's to risk our lives." Her eyes swept across the others, stopping first on Ruka.

"You can count me out," the teen responded immediately, folding her arms squarely across her chest.

Alana let out a short sigh, and then turned her gaze to Seth. The halfling shook his head. "Thanks... but no thanks. Let Donnie have the honors." Donnie's eyes fixed on Seth, his expression a mixture of wonder and gratitude. "After all, he nearly killed himself in both the air and water rooms," Seth added with a wicked grin.

"Gee, thanks," Donnie drawled, with a wry smile on his lips. The slight elf shifted his eyes back to Alana. "I still think it should be either you or Lloyd... especially after facing those iron golems."

Alana winced briefly at the painful memory, then gave the slight elf a brief smile. The lady knight turned her attention back to Lloyd, her expression tentative. "Together?"

Lloyd peered back at her, his own expression uncertain, then a broad smile broke out across his youthful features, and he nodded to the lady knight. "Together it is, then."

"Finally," Elladan drawled. "My arms are getting tired of holding this thing!"

Alana and Lloyd smiled warmly at the bard as they trod forward and took the sphere from his hands. Elladan stepped back to join the others, and watched as the duo strode up to the pedestal. They stood on either side, holding the orb aloft above the circular indentation. The lady knight and young warrior exchanged a brief glance, then gently lowered the sphere into the depression on the dais. It was a perfect fit. Everyone held their breath, all eyes focused on the golden orb as it sat unchanged on the top of the pedestal. Glo felt a hand on his arm, and glanced briefly down to see Elistra holding on to him. In fact, everyone was huddled close together, all eyes firmly fixed on the dais before them. As Glo shifted his gaze back to the pedestal, he noticed something strange. The golden sphere had begun to sink, slowly disappearing into the platform. Donnie's voice rang out in a semi-hushed tone. "Would you look at that?"

Elistra responded in a soft voice. "Yet another case of Larketh's dramatics."

Elladan chuckled softly at her comment. "I said it before—the dwarf had flair."

The golden sphere continued to sink into the pedestal, the top edge finally vanishing below the surface. At that point, an audible click sounded from somewhere underneath the dais, and the entire pedestal slid backwards noiselessly across the floor. There was a square hole in the floor where the platform had stood, revealing a set of stone stairs descending into the depths below. Donnie stared wide-eyed at the stairwell. "There's a sub-sub-basement?"

"It would appear so," Aksel responded, his mouth slightly agape.

"It figures," Seth added, his tone unmistakably laced with sarcasm.

The companions gathered around the newly discovered entrance, peering down as far as they could see. The staircase was illuminated by glowing tiles in the wall, similar to the floor and ceiling tiles in the large chamber where they currently stood. It spiraled downward, disappearing from sight around a bend a dozen or so steps below.

"Well, shall we?" Donnie asked with mock enthusiasm.

"Not just yet," Aksel said slowly, his eyes sweeping across the gathered group. "If I'm right, it's only about midday, and we've all been through a lot already. I don't think it would hurt to stop and replenish ourselves before moving on."

Donnie motioned toward Lloyd and Alana. "Too bad we can't have a hot meal. Somehow, I don't think cold rations are going to do our warriors here much good."

As if on cue, a loud growling noise erupted from Lloyd's midriff. The young man placed a hand over his stomach, and grinned sheepishly. Seth's mouth twisted sideways. "I think Lloyd's stomach agrees."

His comment elicted a few minor chuckles. Alana stepped over to the young warrior and placed a gauntleted hand on his shoulder, a hopeful smile gracing her lips. "We may be in luck. If it is indeed lunch time, they'll have a pot stewing in the camp outside." Her eyes swept around the rest of the circle. "It's fairly standard procedure, especially with large groups. That way, anyone in the camp can grab a quick meal and get back to their post."

Glo was impressed. He was not familiar with the procedures of regimented groups out in the field, but what Alana said made a lot of sense. Aksel seemed to think so as well. "That would be excellent if we could take advantage of it." His hand went to his chin, as he thought it through aloud. "We'd have to take the floating disc back up the shaft, probably fly down to the camp to save time, pick up the hot meals, and fly them back." After a moment's pause, he gave the lady knight a nod. "That seems feasible."

Glo agreed, but there was one thing that nagged at him. He voiced his concern to the others. "The only problem I forsee is that the windows in this place are covered with some kind of 'privacy' spell. We might be able to fly out, but you wouldn't be able to see them on the way back."

"Not a problem. I can find them."

All eyes turned to Ruka. The young teen stood there with her arms folded, wearing a self-satisfied smile. Glo raised an eyebrow at her confident attitude. "How's that possible? From what I can tell, the spell on those windows block all sight and sound from the outside."

Ruka cocked her head to one side, her smile widening even further. "You've obviously never spent any time as a hawk. Their senses are extremely sharp compared to a human's. Trust me when I say that in that form, I will know exactly where the window is, even if I can't see it."

Ruka seemed so sure of herself that Glo was not going to argue with her. Aksel also appeared convinced. "Okay then. Glo, you fly down with Ruka." He paused, his gaze shifting to Lloyd. The young man's face had lit up at the mention of flying, but Aksel immediately dashed his hopes. "I still want you to rest, so if you could lend your cloak to someone, they could follow along to lend a hand."

"I'll take it!" Donnie said, raising his hand excitedly. He immediately regretted his outburst when he saw the disappointed look on Lloyd's face. The slight elf curbed his enthusiasm, and swiftly added, "That is, if you don't mind."

Lloyd gazed back at Donnie with a wan smile. "No... that's fine." He doffed his cloak and held it out to the excited elf, his expression turning wistful. "It is a lot of fun."

Donnie gingerly took the cloak and held it up in front of him, staring at it with obvious intrigue. He then gazed back at Lloyd, his expression turning solemn. "I promise to take good care of it."

Aksel cleared his throat. "Alright then. While you're there, meet with Sir Craven and bring him up to date. Then gather up as much stew as the two of you can carry, and follow Ruka back."

Seth, standing silently through all of this, finally spoke up. "I'm coming with you—at least to the top floor." Aksel gazed at the halfling curiously, but before he could ask, Seth answered his question. "We have no idea where those Serpent Cultists went. So while they go get 'take out,' I'll keep a watch on the shaft."

"Ah," Aksel said, nodding with understanding, "sounds like a good idea."

Lloyd's stomach chose that moment to growl again. Everyone chuckled. "Sorry," Lloyd apologized, grinning sheepishly once more as he placed a hand over his wayward stomach.

Donnie grinned at the young warrior. "That's okay, Lloyd. We'll have that taken care of in no time!"

33

THE WOMAN IN THE WOODS

They described her as strangely alluring

There had been no sign of the Serpent Cult when they reached the top floor of the monolith. Seth remained stationed near the shaft as planned, using his cloak to make himself invisible. Outside the monolith, the knight's camp bustled with activity. The entire campsite was now surrounded by a barrier of pitched wooden spikes, and in its center, a large black cauldron sat suspended over a roaring campfire.

A number of armored warriors gathered around the huge pot, spooning from bowls what could only be stew. Donnie's stomach grumbled at the sight. Glo and Ruka exchanged grins at the expense of the slight elf. Donnie grinned sheepishly back at them. "I guess it's catching."

Ruka's lips bent sideways, and then, without a word, shifted into the now-familiar shape of the white-tailed hawk. Glo followed suit, casting the fly spell upon himself, while Donnie invoked Lloyd's flying cloak. The hawk lifted off the floor, and with a great beat of her wings, shot out through the window and into the open air.

Donnie and Glo exchanged a quick glance, then launched themselves after the magnificent winged creature. The hawk sped away from the monolith, and then began to bank. She slowly arced into a graceful circle, and spiraled downward toward the camp far below. Glo and Donnie glided straight down as the hawk flew circles around them.

Abruptly, a small dark form zipped out of the trees, and winged its way toward them. It was Raven! Glo felt a warmth inside at the sight of his childhood companion. He hadn't realized just how much he missed her. Raven soon joined Ruka, spiraling around the two elves as they descended toward the camp below.

The Knights of the Rose had already spotted them, the dark-haired form of Sir Craven appearing out of a large pavillion in the center of the camp. The head knight waved upward to them, bidding them to land next to him. The two elves adjusted their flight pattern, angling themselves toward the waiting knight. When they were within a few yards of the ground, Sir Craven called up to them.

"Well met, Glolindir and Donatello! Where are the others?"

"Well met, Sir Craven," Donnie responded in kind. "They are all well—merely waiting inside."

As the two elves touched down, Sir Craven strode to meet them, extending a gauntleted hand. The knight smiled grimly as he shook with each of them in turn. "We were beginning to get worried."

Glo opened his mouth to answer, but was momentarily distracted by the feeling of tiny feet latching onto his shoulder. He swiveled his head, reached up, and stroked Raven's feathers gently. He had indeed missed her. Meanwhile, Donnie spoke for the two of them. "There's no need for that. Everyone's"—Donnie suddenly grimaced as the large, white-tailed hawk landed on him, its sharp talons latching onto his shoulder—"fine."

Glo did his best to suppress a laugh. Ruka never seemed to miss an opportunity to get under Donnie's skin—figuratively or literally. Sir Craven covered his mouth with his hand, pretending to cough into it. "Ahem, yes. So have you found what we came for?"

"Not just yet," Glo answered for them, as Donnie tried to shoo the hawk off his shoulder.

"And no sign of the cultists?"

Glo shook his head. "None."

Sir Craven's expression grew troubled. "That is indeed strange."

As the conversation continued, Glo spied a familiar figure striding across the camp toward them. It was a man dressed in brown leathers, a bow slung over his shoulders, and a quiver of arrows sticking out behind his head.

"Martan!" Glo hailed the tracker.

"Glo, Donnie." Martan nodded to each of them in turn.

Sir Craven gave Martan a nod as well. "Glolindir and Donatello were just telling us of their progress inside the monolith."

Martan gazed from Donnie to Glo, his expression rife with curiousity. "Oh. Find anything?"

"Not really…" Glo began.

"…other than a whole bunch of traps and puzzles," Donnie finished for him, still trying to shoo the white-tailed hawk off his shoulder.

Martan appeared quite surprised. "No sign of the Serpent Cult?"

"None," Glo answered, still finding it hard to believe himself.

Donnie finally gave up trying to get Ruka off his shoulder. He turned to Sir Craven and Martan, still grimacing. "What about… out here?"

Sir Craven pointed around the campsite with his open hand. "The fortifications are done as you can see, and it's been relatively quiet—with the exception of one strange occurrence."

Glo's eyes shifted between the tracker and the knight. The duo exchanged a brief glance, their expressions somewhat strained. Glo raised an eyebrow at their odd behavior. "What happened that was so strange?"

Martan's complexion reddened slightly. When he spoke, his tone was rather tentative. "I believe it was that succubus, again."

Glo felt a sudden sinking feeling in the pit of his stomach. "Are you sure?"

Martan raised his hands and shrugged, his faced reddening a bit more. "I didn't see her myself, but listen to Sir Craven's story, and you'll see what I mean."

Glo peered at the knight, who seemed most uncomfortable with the topic. After a few moments of silence, Sir Craven began to tell the tale. "Well... it was the middle of the night. Most of us were asleep... but the sentries were on duty..." The head knight paused, his face flushing further. Glo and Donnie exchanged a brief glance, but waited silently for him to continue. "This strange woman appeared out of nowhere at the edge of the woods... she was absolutely stunning from the way the sentries described her... and... she was completely naked."

When Sir Craven finished, his face was quite flushed. Donnie, completely unabashed, questioned the embarrassed knight further. "Was she full figured, with fair skin, pouty lips, and long flowing red hair..." The slight elf abruptly halted, grimacing as Ruka dug her talons deeper into his shoulder. "What?" the hapless elf yelped, wincing from the hawk's strong grip. "I was only trying to be accurate!"

Sir Craven's face was filled with mixed emotions—embarrasment from the story he had just related, and amusement at Donnie's current predicament. "As a matter-of-fact, that is exactly how the sentries described her."

Glo glanced at Martan, his head slighty cocked, his expression apologetic. "It appears you were right."

Martan responded with a weak smile. "I wasn't sure at first either, but you have to listen to the rest of it."

Glo arched an eyebrow, his eyes shifted back to Sir Craven. "There's more?"

The knight nodded, the redness draining from his face as his expression turned grim. "The sentries reported that she tried to lead them away into the woods. They described her as strangely alluring, and almost followed her. Now knowing what she is, I am sure they would have, if they had not been devout followers of Cormar."

Glo nodded slowly in understanding. "So their holy vows protected them from her charms."

Sir Craven responded with a curt nod. "Yes. Without our god's favor, we would be little more than ordinary warriors—but enough talk of this evil creature," he declared, with a dismissive wave of his hand. "It is midday, and you must be starving. Let's adjourn inside, and you can tell me all about your adventures inside the monolith, over a bowl of stew of course."

Donnie bowed graciously to the thoughtful knight. "Thank you, that would be wonderful, but it will have to be quick, I'm afraid. Our comrades still wait inside, and we were hoping we could trouble you for hot meals for them as well?"

Sir Craven peered at the slight elf, his eyes filled with understanding. "And so it shall be! I will have the squires fetch it for you." He looked past them and called across the camp. "Lamorn, can you and Syndir gather some empty casks, and fill them with stew?"

The young squire stood by the cauldron, ladle in hand, dishing out meals to the gathered men in armor. He put the ladle down, and responded with a crisp salute. "At once, Sir Craven."

"But first, bring three bowls into my tent," Sir Craven added.

A thoughtful expression crossed Donnie's features. "Umm, ifI might ask—what kind of stew is that exactly?"

Martan was the one to answer him. "It's fish stew."

Donnie and Glo peered curiously at the tracker. Martan shrugged, a self-conscious expression crossing his face as he explained further. "On our way here, I noticed the streams were teaming with trout. So a few of us went back this morning, and did a bit of fishing." He finished with a motion mimicking the casting of a fishing rod.

Donnie grinned at the tracker, then glanced up at the hawk sitting on his shoulder. The bird peered back at him, its head spinning back and forth, then responded with a single, "caw." Donnie shifted his gaze back to Sir Craven, holding up all his fingers sans the thumb. "Four bowls then," he corrected the knight.

Sir Craven gave the elf an odd look, but repeated his words without question. "Make that four bowls!"

"Yes, Sir Craven!" came Lamorn's response.

The knight spun around to face the pavilion and motioned the others to follow. As they stode toward the large tent, he glanced over his shoulder at Donnie and Glo. "So then, tell me what I've missed."

A little more than half an hour later, Glo, Donnie, Ruka and Seth returned with enough hot stew for everyone. Good to her word, Ruka unerringly led the elves back into the monolith. The top chamber remained empty except for Seth, who reported no sightings of the Serpent Cultists. During lunch, Donnie reported the succubus sighting to the others.

"So the witch followed us here, then," Elladan said in between spoonfuls.

"I had a slightly different word in mind for her," Elistra added, an impish smile upon her lips.

There were a few chuckles around the group, but Aksel managed to remain impassive. "Well, either way, if she's lurking around outside, she might have seen you three come in and out of the upper floor."

Glo let out a soft groan. "Which means, we more or less showed her a way past the sentries into the monolith."

Elistra reached over and patted him gently on the shoulder. "There's no way you could have known."

Aksel's eyes shifted from Elistra to Glo. "Elistra's right. I wasn't trying to blame anyone. I was just pointing out that she will most likely find her way inside."

Elladan's eyes swept across the entire group. "So when the cultists finally rear their ugly heads, the succubus will most assuredly be with them."

Aksel gave the bard a brief nod. "Exactly."

"Good!" Alana declared firmly, unsheathing her sword and running a finger across the glowing blade. "I wanted another crack at that... witch, anyway."

Elistra grinned at the lady knight. "You and me both."

Glo glanced from Alana to Elistra, noting the fire in their eyes. *Woe be that succubus if she shows herself in front of these two*, he thought wryly.

A few hours later, after a much-needed nap, Lloyd and Alana were raring to go once again. The companions swiftly gathered up their belongings, and prepared for the descent into the "sub-sub-basement," as Donnie called it. The party took up the same marching order they had used on the ascent up the monolith—Seth led the way, followed by Lloyd, Alana, Glo, Elistra, Elladan and Aksel, with Donnie and Ruka bringing up the rear.

The companions entered the stairwell single file, Seth a few steps ahead of the others. The staircase spiraled downward, lit every few yards by glowing tiles on the outside wall. The walls themselves were extremely smooth, just like those between the floors of the monolith above. Seth cautiously examined the stairwell as they descended, but there were no traps on these stairs, nor in the walls around them. Despite that, the climb down was rather lengthy. After about ten minutes, Glo heard Elladan whisper, "Just how long are these stairs?"

Glo had been mentally counting them as they wound their way down. He responded to the bard, "Two hundred, so far."

Elladan's pursed his lips and nodded. "That's a lot of steps."

Glo maintained his mental count as they continued their descent. He was nearing three hundred, when Seth held up his hand for them to halt. "We're nearly at the bottom," the halfling whispered. "Wait here while I check it out."

While the others waited, Seth carefully climbed down the spiral staircase, soon disappearing around the bend of the stairs. About thirty seconds later, Glo heard a low whistle filter up from below. Shortly thereafter, Seth reappeared.

"What's going on?" Aksel called down to him anxiously.

Seth's eyes were uncharacteristically wide. "You're not going to believe this," he responded rather dramatically.

Seth was not easily impressed. Glo couldn't begin to imagine what had elicited such a response from him. The companions picked up their pace as they followed Seth the rest of the way down. The stairs abruptly ended at a tall archway, beyond which appeared to be a rocky cavern. Lloyd and Alana stepped out of the stairwell after Seth and turned, each going wide-eyed just as the halfling had. When Glo finally trod out behind them, his eyes shifted in the direction they were peering.

The companions stood in a wide alcove that opened up to a huge underground cavern beyond. The alcove was rather well lit, the walls once again sporting those embedded, glowing tiles. Glo paid little attention however, his eyes riveted on the cavern beyond. A long walkway led out into the dimly lit cave—at the other end stood what appeared to be a huge stone head! It lay partially in the shadows, but Glo could just make out two darkened eye sockets, a large nose, and a wide mouth underneath.

The elven wizard arched an eyebrow. It was hard to tell from this distance, but if that head was connected to a body, that entire thing had to be at least fifty feet tall. Once again, a shiver ran up Glo's spine—this time, the vision of a tall stone statue flashing before his eyes, the image of a dwarf holding a large tome.

Glo immediately berated himself, silently proclaiming it was just a dream, yet this was uncanny. First his view of the clearing, then the huge ground floor chamber, and now this giant stone statue. It was just too much to be a mere coincidence.

Glo felt a gentle hand on his arm. He turned to see Elistra standing there, her eyes gleaming with sympathy. She leaned in close and whispered, "Perhaps more than just a dream, but still not prophecy."

Glo peered at her a moment, then glanced around, letting out a huge sigh. *Elistra is right.* There were no large serpents, or black mages, anywhere in sight. Glo's shoulders sagged, the tension leaving his body, but he silently vowed to himself that if they did run into the cultists, he'd be the first to step forward. None of his friends were going to die on his account. Another low whistle broke him out of his anxious musings. "Look at the size of that thing!"

He spun to see Elladan, the bard's mouth uncharactistically hanging open, his eyes wide as he stared at the huge stone statue. The corner's of Glo's mouth upturned at the sight of the normally un-flappable bard's astonishment.

"It's nice to see you smiling again," Elistra whispered to him. Glo eyed the seeress, his heart warming and a genuine smile spreading across his lips. She grasped his arm with both hands, her eyes sparkling with delight. "Now that's more like it."

Glo gazed at her affectionately, then returned his attention to the cavern before them. The walkway leading from the alcove was rather wide—there was easily enough room across it for two people to stand side-by-side. Seth and Lloyd went first, followed closely by Alana and Glo. The elven wizard had lit his staff, but found it immediately unnecessary—the moment Seth and Lloyd stepped out onto the walkway, the cavern lit up, large tiles in the rough hewn walls illuminating the natural chamber.

The companions strode a short distance foward, then, as one, halted and glanced out over the railing. The giant head indeed sat upon an immense stone body, its huge rock feet clearly visible on the cavern floor far below. Glo mentally adjusted his initial estimate—the stone statue was more like sixty, or even seventy feet tall. Donnie and Ruka brought up the rear, the slight elf gaping as he leaned over the railing. "Whoa… that thing is huge!"

An enigmatic smile spread across Elistra's features. "As Elladan so aptly stated, 'Larketh definitely had a flair for the dramatic.'"

Her comment elicted a few short laughs. Glo cocked his head to one side and peered at the seeress, making a mental note to be careful what he said from now on. That was the second time she had quoted someone verbatim. Elistra seemed to have an uncanny memory, rivaling, if not surpassing, his own. She gazed back at him, her eyes dancing with amusement as if she had read his thoughts. Glo gave her a brief smile, the turned his attention back to the colossus below. The body definitely did not look like a dwarf's. Still, it appeared quite familiar—in fact, it looked like a larger version of...

"It looks just like the Boulder," Lloyd said, mirroring Glo's thoughts.

Alana eyed the young man curiously. "You mean, your stone golem?"

Lloyd nodded to the lady knight. "Yes… but much, much larger."

Aksel's mouth abruptly fell open. "It couldn't be..."

Glo's own mouth hung open, his mind numbing at the realization of what was in front of them. "I think… it is…"

"I'm afraid you're right," Elistra said softly. "That, ladies and gentlemen, is a giant stone golem."

"No way..." Donnie said with clear astonishment.

Glo squinted his eyes and peered intently at the giant for a few moments, then looked up, his eyes sweeping across the group. "I know Larketh was the Golem Master, but I would never have imagined something like this."

The corner of Seth's mouth twisted upward. "Overcompensating much, you think?"

The halfling's comment broke everyone out of their reverie, genuine laughter echoing out from the walkway, and bouncing off the walls of the immense cavern. Glo, still half-chuckling, peered at his smirking friend, and slowly shook his head. "Only you, Seth. Only you."

The halfling stared back at the wizard and shrugged, his mouth widening into a wicked grin. "What can I say? I have a unique perspective on these things."

34
SHADOW OF THE COLOSSUS

The skeleton sat there unmoving on its throne,

its empty eye sockets staring forward, unseeing

Once the laughter died down, the companions returned to examining the colossus. Glo noticed that farther down, the walkway split in two, encircling the head of the giant golem. He also observed a large stone chair that looked like a throne atop the head—in it was seated a skeleton.

"Think that's Larketh?" Lloyd asked, his voice hushed.

Elladan placed a hand on the young warrior's shoulder. "Not according to bardic lore. Based on what I was taught, the Golem Master died along with his fellow Thrall Masters northwest of here, in the mountains around the Silver Lakes"—he paused and eyed Elistra curiously—"unless other folks have heard differently."

"No, no, good bard, that is what I had heard as well," the seeress agreed.

Lloyd squinted his eyes, as if to get a better look at the skeletal figure that sat above the colossus. "So then, who could that have been?"

"We may never know," Aksel answered this time. "If those bones have been here since the Thrall Wars, then not even a *Speak to the Dead* spell would work on it."

Lloyd shifted his gaze to the little cleric, then shrugged. As one, the companions pushed away from the railing, and continued down the walkway toward the huge head. Elladan still wore an expression of awe. "This is amazing—to think this thing has been hidden here underneath the monolith for the last hundred years."

"At least that long," Aksel corrected him. "Larketh must have been working on this golem for a long time before his demise."

"Either way, it'll make one heck of a story," the bard said with a wink.

The companions reached a point about halfway across the cavern to the colossal head, when the light on Glo's staff suddenly winked out. Everyone froze in their tracks. Donnie had dropped down into a crouch, glancing anxiously around them. "What was that?"

Silence pervaded the cavern for a few moments, until Aksel finally answered him. "I suspect we've just entered an anti-magic field."

An anti-magic field was an invisible barrier that suppressed the use of mana within its borders. Neither spells nor supernatural abilities would work inside the field. Glo silently agreed with Aksel's hypothesis, but there was an easy way to confirm the cleric's suspicions. He turned to Lloyd and said, "Try to light up your blades."

The young warrior eyed Glo uncertainly for a moment, but then drew his weapons. His brow furrowed with concentration, but nothing happened, his blades remaining cold and dark. Lloyd shook his head and tried again, a fierce look crossing his face, but the result was the same. Lloyd gazed at Glo, his frustration quite clear. "I... I can't."

Glo smiled with keen sympathy at the young man. "It's okay, Lloyd—step around behind me and try it again."

Lloyd eyed him uncertainly, but then wove through the others until he was behind Glo. The young warrior then tried once more to light his blades; this time the flame ignited when he called it, the red glow starting at the base of his weapons, and quickly flowing outward toward the tips. Lloyd let out a deep sigh. "Phew. I thought I had lost it there for a minute."

An understanding smile crossed Glo's lips. "No, my friend… Aksel was right, and you just proved it. There is an anti-magic field in this cavern… perhaps to keep anyone from magically finding this stone colossus."

Aksel nodded in agreement, his hand slowly rubbing his chin as he thoughtfully surveyed the surrounding area. "My guess is it extends in a circle all around the golem. We're about fifty feet away, so that would make it a one-hundred-foot wide field."

Elladan scrunched his nose, staring skeptically at the little cleric. "That's a mighty big area." His eyes shifted to Glo. "How wide is a typical spell cast field?"

Glo did not know the spell as of yet, but had a basic knowledge of its workings. "About… ten feet in all directions."

Elladan let out a short laugh as he glanced around the cavern. "Heh. So this one is five times the size of what any wizard can do."

Glo threw up his hands and shrugged. "Pretty much."

Elladan winked at the elven wizard. "Like I said before, this will make one heck of a story."

The companions resumed their forward progress, Lloyd's blades winking out as he re-entered the field. Glo fell in behind Lloyd, but abruptly halted when he heard Donnie's voice.

"Is something wrong?" the slight elf asked.

Glo spun around and saw Donnie facing Ruka. The young teen stood with her arms folded across her chest, staring at Donnie defiantly. "I'm not getting any closer to that… thing."

Glo raised an eyebrow. Incredulous as it seemed, was it possible that the normally acerbic Ruka was actually afraid of the colossus? He peered closely at the young teen, but could detect no hint of fear about her. *What is her problem then… unless, I've been right all along?*

If this girl they saw before them was not the real Ruka, then the anti-magic field would dispel any magic and reveal her true form. As Glo came to this realization, Alana pushed past the others, and stood next to the young teen, draping an armor-clad arm over the teen's shoulders. "You all go ahead. We women warriors will wait back here."

"Thanks," Ruka responded under her breath, so softly that Glo almost didn't catch it.

Donnie gazed from Alana to Ruka, then back again, and finally threw up his hands and shrugged. "Suit yourself."

The slight elf spun around and shooed the others forward. Glo gave the two women a faint smile, then also turned and followed the others toward the giant stone head. Elistra fell in beside him and whispered so softly he could barely hear her. "It's just as well. I'm not quite sure how Donnie would take it if he saw her true form."

Glo gave the seeress a sidelong glance. He knew Elistra mirrored his own suspicions about Ruka, but now she not only sounded certain, but also implied that she knew the girl's true form. Glo wanted to question her further, but now was not the time. He pushed any thoughts about Ruka from his mind, turning his attention back to the colossus. The closer they drew to the stone giant, the more details about it became evident. One thing in particular seemed to catch Askel's attention—there was a crown atop the skeleton on the throne.

"I want a closer look at that," the little cleric stated definitively, not taking his eyes off the strange artifact. The companions reached the walkway that encircled the huge head, and swiftly discovered a set of stairs in back that led up to the top. Aksel headed straight for those stairs, and began to ascend them, his eyes fixated on the throne above.

"Umm, Aksel?" Seth called out after the little cleric.

"What?" the gnome replied, not turning his head, his voice sounding empty and hollow.

"Maybe I should go first?"

"Oh, right. Sure," Aksel responded, his eyes still fixated on the throne above.

Seth gave Glo a brief sidelong glance, his eyes filled with concern, then climbed up the stairs, taking a position in front of Aksel. Glo squinted his eyes, watching the little cleric carefully. He was acting rather strangely, almost possessed, in fact. Glo wasn't sure what had come over Aksel, but he, too, was now concerned. He turned to Lloyd and whispered, "Maybe you should follow them?"

Lloyd's eyes swept from Glo to the ascending gnome and halfling. He gave Glo a quick nod, then took off up the stairs after them. Meanwhile, Elladan sidled up next to Glo.

"What's with Aksel?" the bard whispered.

Glo shook his head. "I'm not exactly sure." He peered over at Elistra. "Any ideas?"

The seeress watched the trio ascend the stairs, a single finger resting on her lips. After a few moments, she shook her head. "It can't be a compulsion. That wouldn't work inside an anti-magic field."

"He's from Caprizon, right?" Donnie asked from the other side of the seeress.

"Yes," Glo said with a nod.

"That city is built into stone cliffs. Perhaps he's just fascinated with the enormity of Larketh's creation," Donnie reasoned.

Glo peered back at the trio on the stairs. They had nearly reached the top. "Perhaps," Glo answered softly. At least he hoped that's all it was.

Aksel slowly followed Seth up the stairs that led to the peak of the colossus. Just below the top, Seth halted and held up his hand. Aksel and Lloyd came to a sudden stop, and waited silently as the halfling crept up the last few steps. When he reached the peak, Seth carefully peered around, then waved the duo upward. Aksel rushed up those last steps, Lloyd right beside him, both pulling up short next to Seth.

The top of the stone giant's head was barren, except for the throne he had seen from the walkway below. The solid stone chair sat abreast a small circular platform, that was in turn attached to the enormous golem's head. Seth silently motioned for the others to follow, then cautiously circled around the platform, till the front of the stone chair came into view. The skeleton sat there, unmoving on its throne, its empty eye sockets staring forward, unseeing.

Aksel found himself strangely drawn to the crown the skeleton wore. He had felt a strange pull the moment he had first laid eyes on it, almost as if it was calling out to him. Yet he knew that was crazy. Magic couldn't work here, nor could telepathy, or any other form of psionic ability. Still, there was no denying the weird attraction he felt. While Aksel mused over the strange lure of the crown, Seth knelt in front of the throne and searched all around. After a minute or so, he stood up and nodded to Aksel. "All clear."

"Thanks..." Without realizing it, Aksel had stepped up onto the platform and reached for the crown. Suddenly, he felt something grab his arm. Aksel nearly jumped, his eyes going wide as they fixed on a skeletal hand firmly wrapped around his wrist.

"Yahhh!" Aksel screamed in terror. He tried to jerk his arm away, but found that the bony appendage held him fast. Furthermore, the creature's other arm was now reaching for his throat! Aksel nearly screamed again, when a huge black blade swept down from nowhere, neatly severing the arm that had been reaching for him.

Aksel spun his head and saw Lloyd standing beside him, the warrior's star metal sword held firmly in both hands. Lloyd lifted the black blade high up into the air, and brought it down in a sweeping motion, cutting through the arm that still held him in place. Aksel, suddenly free, stepped swiftly backward, almost falling off the platform. He teetered there on the edge for a moment, but finally regained his balance.

"Th—Thanks, Lloyd," Aksel stammered.

Lloyd gave him a grim nod, but any reply he may have had, was abruptly drowned out by a cry from Seth.

"Watch out!"

Aksel whirled around to a terrifying sight—the skeleton had risen out of its chair, its empty eye sockets fixed directly on him. Aksel shrank back in terror, but Lloyd's tall form was suddenly there, interposing itself between him and the murderous creature. The tall warrior's black blade sailed over Aksel's head as he swung it in a sweeping arc, the blade not stopping until it had wrapped all the way around Lloyd's other side.

Aksel watched with fascination as a skeletal head flew out from behind the tall warrior, landing on the golem's scalp a short distance away. The head bounced twice and came to a stop, but unfortunately, the crown popped off and kept rolling. Aksel took off after the crown, frantically trying to catch it before it rolled off the edge, but was too late. The little cleric watched in dismay as the crown sailed over the edge, barely stopping before he too would have fallen.

Aksel held his breath as the object of his desire bounced away, apparently headed toward its inevitable demise some seventy feet below. Just when it appeared that all was lost, the crown took a large hop off the golem's head and hit the curved walkway, rolling swiftly along the circular path, till it finally came to stop, right in front of Elladan's feet.

Elladan watched with fascination as the crown bounced down the side of the colossal stone head, landed on the walkway, and rolled to a stop right in front of him. Donnie, Glo, and Elistra stood beside the bard, all staring in wonder at this odd turn of events.

"I always thought of you as a prince among elves, but that's just ridiculous," Donnie quipped.

Elladan gave Donnie a sour look, while Elistra and Glo audibly groaned. The bard shifted his attention back to the crown at his feet. He knelt down and picked it up, scrutinizing the crown intently. It appeared to be a rather plain circlet, with eight peaks protruding at regular intervals around the ring. There were no fancy carvings, or jewels inlaid around its circumference, but it did appear to be made of solid gold. He was interrupted from any further examination, as Aksel's voice rang out from above.

"Can you bring that back up here?"

Elladan stood and peered upward—Aksel stared down from atop the colossal head, his eyes fixated on Elladan. Lloyd and Seth stood to either side of the little cleric, their expressions filled with clear concern.

"Sure!" Elladan called back up to Aksel in a placating tone. He gave Glo and Elistra a sidelong glance. "Do you think it's safe to give to him?" he asked underneath his breath.

Glo gazed back at him and shrugged. Elistra, however, closed her eyes, her brow knitted with concentration. After a few moments, her eyes snapped open and she responded in a soft voice. "I can detect nothing from it. I do not believe it is inherently evil."

"I still think it's a gnome thing," Donnie whispered. "Stone is kind of in their blood."

"Hey! Are you going to stand there all day, or are you going to bring me my crown!" Aksel cried down once more.

"His crown, he says," Elladan muttered. "I'm telling you, something is definitely wrong here."

"Better to just humor him for now," Elistra whispered. "Perhaps Donnie is right, or maybe it is something else entirely. But we won't know for certain unless we see this through."

Elladan shook his head as he ascended the stairs. "I just hope you're right."

Seth watched Aksel with growing concern. The little gnome had been acting strangely since he first caught sight of the crown atop the colossus. Aksel rarely showed any kind of emotion—the only time Seth had ever seen him lose control was when dealing with the bigots from Dunwynn. Yet now, Aksel seemed obsessed with that crown.

The little gnome fidgeted nervously as Elladan climbed the stairs, practically ripping the crown from the bard's hands when he finally reached the top. Without a word, Aksel spun around and headed straight for the throne. Elladan stared after him wide-eyed, his gaze shifting to Lloyd and Seth. Seth responded with a quick shrug, then took off after Aksel.

Aksel now sat on the throne, the crown still in his hands. Seth, Lloyd and Elladan stood before him as he slowly lifted it and placed it on his head. The little gnome let out a deep sigh. "Phew. That's better."

Seth eyed Aksel intently, wondering what effect the crown would have on his friend now that he wore it. Aksel, finally realizing that they were there, swept his eyes around, his gaze coming to rest on Seth. He paused a moment, then lifted a hand, waving them off. "You may go now."

The little gnome then turned his gaze forward, and appeared to go into a trance. Seth exchanged a worried glance with Elladan and Lloyd. The bard backed away a few paces, motioning for the two of them to follow. They huddled together there, and Elladan whispered, "We can't just leave him here like this."

Seth wasn't about to leave Aksel alone with that crown. The little cleric was the closest thing he had to a brother in this world, and Seth wasn't about to let some stupid artifact take over his mind. Still, if they all continued to hover over him, it might just agitate Aksel further. Seth gazed from Lloyd to Elladan, and spoke in a hushed voice. "You two go. I'll keep an eye on him."

Lloyd peered behind them at Aksel, then looked back at Seth and gave him a nod. Elladan cocked his head to one side, eyeing Seth carefully. "You sure about this?"

Seth responded with a curt nod. Elladan glanced at Lloyd, then shrugged. "Okay. I just hope you know what you're doing."

Lloyd gave him a hopeful look, then the duo headed to the stairs, soon disappearing out of sight. Once they were gone, Seth spun around and headed back to Aksel's side, silently wondering if he had done the right thing.

Elladan and Lloyd descended the stairs, leaving Seth to look after Aksel. Donnie, Glo, and Elistra met them at the bottom, the trio practically bursting with curiousity. Elladan briefly explained what had happened with the crown, finishing with, "…he's definitely not himself."

Before anyone else could utter a word, the walkway suddenly lurched. Everyone scrambled to stay on their feet, Elladan grasping the nearby rail. Donnie ended up next to him, the slight elf pointing over the railing. "Look!"

Elladan peered over the side, his eyes going wide as a giant stone arm rose up from the depths below.

Seth stood a short distance from Aksel, keeping an intense watch on his silent friend. Suddenly, Aksel's eyes snapped open. The little cleric sat straight up and slowly lifted his right arm. At the same moment, Seth felt the colossus lurch. He ran over to the edge of the huge scalp and peered over the side, his eyes locking on a giant stone arm that rose up from the depths. Seth spun his head and stared at Aksel—it was the same arm!

The halfling did a double take, but there was no doubt about it. The colossal golem was mimicking Aksel's movements. A silent smile spread across Seth's lips. His friend wasn't going crazy after all. The crown was obviously the control mechanism for the colossus, and Aksel seemed to instinctively know it. Somehow he had recognized the crown for what it was—something neither magical or psionic, but that allowed the Golem Master to control even magically immune constructs. Maybe Aksel's experience with the Boulder, another of Larketh's creations, had given him the foresight to spot the crown for what it was. Either way, Seth was impressed. A sudden shout interrupted his thoughts.

"Incoming!"

Seth peered down and saw Alana, still halfway across the walkway, with sword and shield in hand. Ruka stood beside her, with her blades drawn as well, both women facing the other end of the cavern. Seth followed their gaze to the alcove at the other end of the walkway. There, in the entranceway, stood four giant serpents, one larger than the rest, accompanied by four robed figures in black. Hovering above them all, her bat-like wings keeping her aloft, was the demonic succubus. Giggling manically, the creature's voice echoed across the cavern, "I told you you hadn't seen the last of me!"

"It's that witch and the Serpent Cult!" Elladan's voice drifted up from below. Seth peered down and saw Lloyd and Donnie already on the move, weapons drawn as they raced across the walkway to join their comrades. Glo, Elladan, and Elistra were not far behind.

Seth cast a quick glance at Aksel. The little cleric's brow was creased with concentration as he returned Seth's gaze. "Go! I've got this."

Seth gave his friend a quick nod, then turned invisible, and launched himself over the side of the colossus.

Glo sped across the walkway behind Lloyd and Donnie, his mind racing, his body tense with apprehension. *Four serpents and four casters, just like my dream.* The black-robed figures had begun spells that were surely aimed their way. Unbeknownst to them, Glo and the others were safe inside the antimagic field, yet Alana and Ruka were not. Worse, they were still too far away to be reached in time. Glo yelled ahead to the duo, "Back up and you'll be safe!"

Ruka cast a quick glance back over her shoulder. "I can't!" she cried in protest.

"Why not?" Donnie shouted as they barreled down the walkway.

"Because... I can't!" Ruka practically screamed. Without warning, the teen spun around and shoved Alana. Caught off-guard, the lady knight went flying backward, clattering onto the walkway nearly three feet away. "Sorry!" Ruka yelled, as her form swiftly shimmered into the white-tailed hawk. A moment later, the winged creature hovered where the teen had been.

A split-second later, two red-hot glowing orbs left the hands of the dark mages. Ruka responded with a huge flap of her wings, launching herself off the walkway, and swiftly spiraling down underneath. Just as she vanished from sight, the flaming balls reached their destination, expanding out and exploding into huge fiery spheres. The eruptions swept across the walkway, but died out not a yard from where Alana lay prone. A moment later, two arcs of electricity flashed past the erupting fire balls, but thankfully winked out as they hit the invisible field. Glo exhaled with relief. "Phew, that was way too close."

Lloyd and Donnie arrived at Alana's side, and helped the lady knight to her feet. Donnie shook his head, gazing at Alana with concern. "I don't know what's come over her." He spun his head and screamed with frustration, "Ruka!"

Alana grasped his cheek with a gauntleted hand, turning his face back toward her. "It's alright, Donnie, she saved my life."

Glo had drawn up next to the others. Across the way, the black mages were regrouping. It wouldn't be long before they attacked again. "We can't worry about her now," Glo said stepping around the others. "Stay back in the field. I'll handle these mages." Before anyone could stop him, the elven wizard reached into his pouch and stepped out of the anti-magic field.

35

THE TRUTH ABOUT RUKA

The giant serpent that had fallen from the walkway now hovered in mid-air far above them!

Glolindir stepped out of the anti-magic field, his eyes locked on the black-robed figures, his hand already weaving an intricate pattern through the air. Too much of his dream had already come true, and he was not going to take any further chances with his friends' lives. Before the dark mages could react, he brought his hands together and uttered a single word.

"Augue."

A ball of fire shot away from Glo's outstretched arms, rocketing across the cavern toward the unprepared mages. It flew over the four serpents who had slithered onto the walkway and hurtled into the alcove beyond. The black-robed figures cringed as the angry red ball exploded in their midst. The ensuing storm of flame swept across the alcove, engulfing all four mages inside. Screams of pain echoed across the cavern then abruptly stopped. A few short seconds later, the flames winked out. Glo swiftly surveyed the aftermath of his spell. Two charred bodies lay on the ground where the mages had been moments before. However, two black-robed figures still stood, smoke rising from their otherwise untouched robes.

"Kill him, you fools!" came a shrill cry from above.

A determined smile crossed Glo's lips, as he smoothly grabbed another pinch of sulfur. The demoness, hovering far above, stayed out of reach while the serpents slithered closer—yet neither were important at that moment. He needed to take out these last two casters. Only when they were gone would he feel safe letting Lloyd and the others jump in. Glo was already weaving the intricate pattern in the air, but now so were the two remaining mages. The race was on! He wove his spell with practiced experience, ending the pattern a split second before the others. A bright red ball of light came to life between his palms, and he uttered the word once more.

"*Augue.*"

The ball rocketed away from him just as the other mages finished their patterns. Without warning, two strong arms wrapped themselves around his waist, yanking him backwards just as the mages released their spells.

"Whaaaa..." The cry exploded from Glo's mouth at the same moment a bolt of lightning shot across the cavern. It came so fast that he didn't even have time to blink. The blinding bolt nearly seared his eyes, winking out of existence not a foot from his face. Nothing was left but a shadowy trail across his field of vision. Glo barely had time to gasp for air when his own spell exploded across the way. He only caught a glimpse—a second red ball came streaking at him and erupted less than a yard away. Hot flames leapt forward, threatening to engulf him, but thankfully stopped, instead arcing around himself and his savior. Not even the heat penetrated the bubble they were in. A few seconds later, the flames abruptly winked out.

"Phew, that was close," Lloyd's voice sounded behind him.

"Thanks," Glo said simply, pushing the young man's arms away. Lloyd had just saved his life, but he would thank him properly later. Right now, his sole concern was those mages. Across the cavern, three charred figures now lay on the ground. One black-robed figure still stood, its robes smoking more than before, hot embers showing at the edges here and there. The serpents were only a few yards away, but Glo was determined to take one last shot at the mage.

"Glo, don't!" Elistra cried as he started forward.

Across the way, the last mage glared at him. Suddenly, the figure spun around and bolted for the stairwell, quickly disappearing from sight.

"Get back here, you coward!" came a shrill shriek from above.

"Ha! You better run!" Elladan cried out from behind him.

Glo's mouth fell open in sheer astonishment. He had never expected the mage to cut and run. Peering upward he saw the succubus still hovering there. Abruptly, she pivoted in mid-air, and with a great flap of her wings, launched herself toward the alcove. As Glo stared after her, he felt a strong arm push him to the side.

"Nice job, Glo, but now it's our turn," Lloyd said with a grin, stepping past the wizard. The young warrior's countenance turned grim as he exited the field, his swords swiftly igniting, red hot flames racing up the blades. Alana and Donnie followed close behind him, the lady knight's sword glowing brilliantly. Glo let out a deep sigh as he watched the threesome march forward to meet the giant serpents. He nearly started as a pair of gentle arms slid around his waist.

"I'm glad to see you are still in one piece," Elistra cooed in his ear. "You do realize just how stupid that was?" she added in an admonishing tone.

Glo let out a soft chuckle and gave her a short nod. "Perhaps, but necessary nonetheless."

Further conversation was cut short, as their three comrades engaged the serpents.

Donatello, rapier in one hand, short sword in the other, followed Lloyd and Alana toward the impending battle. Thankfully, the walkway was only wide enough for two serpents at a time. Two of the "smaller" serpents had lined up in front, leaving no room for the third, nor the largest one, to get past. Unfortunately, that also left no room for him either. Ever the gentleman, Donnie had tried to move up in front of Alana. The lady knight, however, had barred his way.

"Back me up," she told him firmly.

It was against his nature to stay behind when others fought. He had nearly railed against her comment, but then thought better of it.

"As you wish," was all he replied.

The tall warrior and lady knight now engaged the frontmost serpents. The large creatures were near twins of the ones they had fought back at Ravenford Keep a mere week ago. Huge, yellow, glowing eyes were inset into massive reptilian heads, covered with mottled, green-scaled skin. Long snouts with huge gaping jaws protruded outward, their open maws exposing long dripping fangs with forked tongues that darted in and out. The massive, snake-like bodies, easily as thick as Lloyd, were also green-scaled, except for the undersides, which were a pale yellow in color.

It was a daunting sight that should have worried him, but his mind was not wholeheartedly on the battle. He was still trying to fathom Ruka's disappearance. Her apparent "fear" of the colossus was totally out of character. She had indeed saved Alana, and shifting and dodging the mages' spells was smart, but where was she now? The Ruka he had come to know would never miss a fight like this. His stray thoughts were abruptly cut short, as a frantic cry rang out behind him.

"Fall back!"

Donnie glanced over his shoulder, and saw Elladan, the bard's head turned upwards. Donnie adjusted his gaze, just as a huge shadow fell over them. His eyes went wide as they fixed on a giant stone hand passing overhead. The slight elf instinctively ducked, the huge hand no more than a few feet above their heads. Donnie quickly backpedaled out of the way, Elladan before him, as they made room for their comrades' retreat. A glance behind showed Lloyd and Alana disengaging as well. The duo ducked down and backed away as the serpents' attention shifted toward the colossal hand.

Donnie watched in awe as the large serpents writhed back and forth, trying to avoid the grasp of the colossus. The front two abruptly flattened themselves on the walkway, the giant hand barely passing over them, yet the rearmost serpents did not fare as well. The colossal hand closed on them, the smaller serpent getting caught in its grip. Donnie thought the huge serpent would be caught as well, but at the last second, the large creature twisted its torso, avoiding the grasp of the enormous stone hand. Still, that proved to be its undoing, as the serpent's heavy torso tipped it way too far over the edge. The serpent hung there for a moment, trying to maintain its balance, then abruptly fell off the walkway, disappearing out of sight below. Meanwhile, the colossal hand continued to close on the serpent it had caught. The stone hand lifted off the walkway, the large creature disappearing inside its enormous grasp.

"Alana, Donnie, go!"

Donnie ripped his eyes away from the sight of the huge stone fist, and saw Lloyd rushing the two remaining serpents. He immediately spurred himself into action, trailing close behind the warrior and lady knight.

"Donnie, get ready!" Lloyd cried over his shoulder.

Donnie wasn't quite certain what Lloyd was planning, but he kept his eyes glued on the young warrior. Lloyd closed on the serpent, the creature lunging for him. Just when it appeared it was going to catch him in its wide jaws, Lloyd suddenly vanished! The serpent couldn't stop itself, continuing its forward motion, and chomping down on thin air. Donnie watched in amazement as Lloyd flashed into existence directly behind the large creature. The serpent, thrown off-balance, tried desperately to recoil, but Lloyd's jet-black blade was already whistling through the air. It passed right through the serpent's torso, the creature's body going rigid. It stayed that way a moment or two, then the upper half of its torso went limp.

Abruptly, it dawned on Donnie what Lloyd wanted him to do. Alana appeared to have things well in hand, the second serpent unable to break past her guard. Satisfied, Donnie sheathed his sword, and took off at a run toward the dead serpent. He reached it just as it slammed into the walkway, and with a quick leap, vaulted onto its back. Donnie ran straight across the scaly torso toward Lloyd, the warrior waiting there with cupped hands.

The second serpent cast a brief glance his way, but paid for it dearly as Alana slashed its snout. Completely forgotten, Donnie traversed the last few feet, and leapt into Lloyd's waiting hands. With a great heave, the young man sent Donnie airborne, the slight elf flipping high up above the other serpent. Drawing his rapier, he twisted around in mid-air, and plummeted toward the unsuspecting creature, point first.

Donnie slammed into the large serpent, driving his rapier straight through its skull. His sword sank deep into its head, the beast shuddering violently as Donnie held on for dear life. The creature continued to writhed back and forth, then Alana was there, stabbing deep into the serpent's torso with her gleaming sword. The beast suddenly stopped thrashing, its body going momentarily rigid, then it sank to the ground, unmoving. Donnie slowly withdrew his rapier from the serpent's skull, then gazed up and saw Alana standing there.

"Well, that was a nice little warm up," she said with a wide grin.

Donnie grinned back at the winsome knight, but his answer was cut short as a roar sounded from above. His head snapped back, his eyes taking in a strange sight—the giant serpent that had fallen from the walkway now hovered high in the air above them!

"What in all of Thac?" he heard Elladan cry.

Donnie silently agreed. Serpents didn't fly, and they most certainly didn't roar, yet this was one was wrapped around something—something nearly as large as the serpent itself. From this angle, he couldn't see much of the serpent's prey, other than a long, spiney tail whipping around frantically beneath the hovering duo. The tail was yellow-brown with light green stripes, and had an almost metallic sheen to it. Donnie's eyes suddenly widened as he realized what the serpent was wrapped around.

Elladan must have figured it out too, the bard's voice filled with wonder. "Is that a bronze…"

"…dragon!" Donnie finished for him, equally astonished. *What in Arinthar is a bronze dragon doing all the way down here?*

"Quick! Somebody do something!" Elistra cried, her voice cracking with emotion.

"Don't worry, I'll fly up and…" Lloyd began, but abruptly halted. The young warrior let out a huge sigh. "Sorry, I forgot. Stupid anti-magic field."

Donnie felt a brief pang of sympathy, but another roar drew

his attention skyward. The combatants must have lost altitude—he could see them clearly now. The dragon could not have been fully grown. A full adult dragon would have dwarfed the serpent, and dispatched it with ease. As it stood, they were locked in a death grip, the serpent trying to squeeze the life out of the young dragon, the dragon in turn clawing and biting the giant snake. The dragon, however, appeared to be losing, the serpent's deadly hold restricting its movements. It was a foolish tactic—the dragon's wings were the only thing keeping the two aloft. Pinned as they were, the wings slowed their descent, but if the serpent didn't let go soon, they would both die when they hit the ground.

"We have to help her!" Elistra shouted, sounding completely distraught.

Donnie shook his head in dismay. He had no idea how to help the young dragon. He dropped his gaze toward Elistra and saw Glo holding her, the seeress' eyes brimming with tears. Donnie didn't understand why she was so distraught, but he spoke sympathetically nonetheless. "Much as I'd love to help the dragon, I have no idea how. Maybe its best we just look for Ruka instead."

Elistra glanced up, her violet eyes glaring with such intensity that it nearly made him wince. "That *is* Ruka, you dolt!"

Donnie's jaw went slack, his entire world suddenly turning upside down. *The dragon... Ruka?*

Glo gave him a brief nod. "She's right, Donnie. It all makes sense. She's a shapeshifter, she's young, so is the dragon..."

Donnie half listened as Glo ticked off point after point, softly muttering to himself, "Ruka's a dragon?"

Alana abruptly pushed between them, the lady knight's face flushed with anger. "We can sort this out later. Ruka or dragon, that noble creature needs our help!"

Alana's chiding brought Donnie back to his senses. At some level he had accepted that the young dragon was indeed Ruka, and he was not about to let her die.

"I'm not sure what we can do," Glo answered the lady knight somberly. "We have no magic inside this field."

"Magic be damned!" Donnie cried, rushing forward to the railing.

The young dragon and the giant serpent had spiraled below them, but they were still too far away to reach.

"Look down there!" Elladan shouted.

Donnie followed the bard's finger—the colossus' other arm rose from the depths, its hand opening to catch the duo. From what Donnie could tell, they would just miss it, but if he timed it right… A crazy plan suddenly formed in the slight elf's head, but Donnie never shied away from crazy. He spun around to Lloyd and yelled, "One more time!"

Recognition sparked in the young warrior's eyes as Donnie back-pedaled away from the railing. Lloyd rushed over to the rail, and cupped his hands just like before. Donnie backed up as far as he could, then took off at a dead run for the young warrior. He caught a brief glimpse of Alana's face, her features frought with fear, then he leapt up into Lloyd's waiting hands, and was flipped out far over the side.

Donnie dove through the air, straight for the colossal arm, Lloyd's extra push giving him the distance he needed. The arm came up on him fast, the slight elf tucking into a ball just before he hit. Donnie slammed into the stone arm, his body wracked with pain, but he ignored it and rolled forward, leaping swiftly to his feet. The slight elf half-ran, half-slid, down the giant stone arm, reaching the out-stretched hand just as the combatants spiraled past it. Donnie did not hesitate, swan-diving off of a giant finger after the falling dragon and serpent.

They were falling faster now, the young dragon's wings tiring from the extra weight. Donnie flattened his arms against his side and sped his descent, quickly gaining on the spiraling pair. The ground was coming up fast—he would only have one chance at this. Donnie closed the gap until he was within arms' distance of the large serpent, then reached forward, barely managing to grasp onto its huge head. So intent was the serpent on its prey, that it totally ignored the slight elf. Donnie yanked himself closer, and wrapped his legs around the creature's neck. His grip was too precarious for either of his swords, so he leaned down and yanked a hidden dagger from his high boot. Lifting the dagger up, he plunged it into the back of the creature's neck. The huge serpent ignored him at first, but Donnie pulled out the small blade and plunged it in once more.

"Stupid… thing! Why… won't… you… let… go!" he cried, frantically plunging the small dagger over and over into the serpent's thick neck.

Blood spurted everywhere, the huge snake just now realizing its peril. It swung its head back and forth, trying to dislodge the slight elf. Donnie had to drop his dagger and grab on with both hands to keep from falling. Yet, in its efforts to throw him off, the serpent had loosened its grip on the dragon.

Now the dragon came to Donnie's aid, the bronze head lunging forward and sinking its teeth deep into the serpent's neck. The huge serpent shuddered as the dragon tore into its throat. It made one last effort to pull away, then the serpent's body went slack, slowly unwinding from around the dragon. Donnie held on for dear life as the serpent suddenly let go and fell away from the young dragon. It plummeted downward, the ground below coming up far too fast.

Donnie braced himself as the ground rushed up to meet them, resigned to the fact that he had made the supreme sacrifice. He only had a few small regrets, and death might reunite him with his greatest regret of all. About fifteen feet from the ground, something sharp jabbed into his shoulders, and he was suddenly plucked from the serpent's back. He hovered there in mid-air, watching wide-eyed as the large serpent slammed into the ground with a huge *thud!*

Donnie cast a glance upward, and saw a large reptilian head staring down at him, its emerald green eyes hauntingly familiar.

"Ruka?" he said in a tentative voice.

The young dragon suddenly swooned and lost its grip on him. Donnie plummeted down the last fifteen feet, tucking and rolling as he hit the ground. He finally came to a stop, sore and aching all over.

"Well, that was a wild ride," he quipped to himself, as he slowly rose to his knees. The flap of large wings drew his attention behind him. He whirled around in time to see the bronze dragon land a few yards away. Their airborne struggle must have carried outside the antimagic field—Donnie now watched in awe as the creature began to glow and the large form shrank down in size. When the glow finally faded, Ruka stood there in place of the dragon, smiling at him awkwardly.

"Thanks for the assist," she said, looking as if she could barely stand. His body aching all over, Donnie nonetheless forced himself onto his feet and slowly limped over to her. Tears welled in his eyes as he observed her arms and legs. They were covered with wounds, puncture marks from the serpent's fangs. Perhaps more frightening, her skin had turned a pale green.

"Do me a favor," she asked breathless as he reached her.

"Anything," he replied softly, his heart in his throat.

"Hold me a minute." She smiled up at him, then the young teen swooned into his arms. Donnie caught her, gently lowering her to the ground. He knelt down beside her and placed her head onto his lap, gently stroking her short, sandy-blonde hair.

"You'll be... fine..." His throat caught. "Aksel will have you healed in no time," he told her, though he immediately knew it was a lie. From the looks of those wounds, and the coloration of her skin, she had been seriously poisoned. Donnie wasn't sure whether Aksel could counter that.

Ruka smiled up at him. "Cursed snake... *cough*... had enough venom... *cough*... to kill a dragon..." She began to laugh, but it quickly turned into a coughing fit.

"Foolish child, you have only sped the poison by taking human form," said an unfamiliar voice. It sounded like that of an old man, yet as Donnie's eyes swept the area, he saw no one.

"Totally worth it," he heard Ruka whisper as she buried herself further into his arms.

Donnie heard a noise that sounded like an exasperated sigh. "You would trade your continued existence for a chance embrace with this... elfling!"

It's the sword, Donnie realized. Seth had said the blade could talk, but Donnie had thought the halfling was pulling his leg. He glanced at the blade, and tried speaking to it. "Can you do anything for her?"

His question was met with silence at first, then the old voice answered him in a tone clearly filled with sorrow. "I'm afraid her wounds are beyond my power."

"Hang on, Ruka!"

That was Alana! Donnie glanced overhead, and saw a giant stone hand descending from above, carrying his companions in its palm. They all jumped off as it neared the ground, Alana leading the charge. She quickly reached their side and knelt down next to the duo. Alana placed one hand on Ruka's head, and the other on her heart, glancing at Donnie as she whispered softly, "I may not be a healer, but Cormar has granted me some divine power."

Ruka barely opened one eye. She fixed it on Alana and whispered, "Take good... care of him... *cough...*"

"Hold still," Alana admonished her. "You're not going anywhere just yet." With that, the lady knight's hands began to glow. They gleamed bright white, then healing light poured from them across Ruka's still form. Alana held her hands there for a number of minutes, bathing Ruka in healing light. Donnie glanced up and saw the others gathered around, watching the spectacle with sad eyes. Finally, Alana's light faded and disappeared. Many of the wounds had closed, but those that remained still festered, and Ruka's coloring had not changed. The lady knight sat back and let out a weary breath. "That is all I can do. The rest is up to Aksel."

Alana stood up and stepped away, making room for the little cleric. Aksel stepped forward and knelt down across from Donnie. He quickly ran his hands over Ruka's body, then gazed up, his expression grim.

"How bad is it?" Donnie asked, his heart in his throat.

Aksel responded in a soft voice. "I can heal the rest of the wounds, but the poison is rampant throughout her system."

"Is... is she going to die?"

Donnie glanced up to see Lloyd's eyes filled with moisture. Glo and Elistra stood nearby, holding each other gently, their faces heavy with sadness. Elladan held the weary Alana, the lady knight's arms wrapped tight around her own midriff.

"Don't worry," the bard tried to assure them, "Aksel will think of something."

Aksel stood up, his eyes sweeping across the group. "I do have an idea, but she will need regular healing and a comfortable place to rest for the next few hours."

"I'll carry her all the way up the monolith and down again if necessary," Donnie declared, meaning every word of it despite his aching bones.

Aksel peered at him, a warm smile gracing the cleric's lips. "That may not be necessary. On the way down I spotted another stairwell behind the colossus' foot. It must have been underneath, but the foot moved when I extended the arm."

"Seth! Can you check it out?" Donnie glanced all around, but the halfling was nowhere to be seen.

Aksel's face fell. "That's another problem. Seth's disappeared."

Donnie felt his anger rise, frustration spilling out of his lips as his eyes swept across the others. "Disappeared? He picked a fine time. And just where did he go? Doesn't he know we need him?"

Elistra gazed upon the slight elf with keen sympathy. "I don't think he has any idea of our current predicament. The last I saw him, he was chasing after the dark mage, the one who ran away."

"I should go after him," Lloyd declared, grasping the end of his cloak.

"No!" sounded a chorus of voices, all at once.

Lloyd halted in mid leap and spun around, gazing wide-eyed at his companions. A semi-smile spread across Elladan's face as he tried to explain to the young warrior. "That succubus is still up there, and you know what happened the last time you ran into her."

"Plus Seth was invisible. The mage may not even know he is being followed," Elistra added.

Lloyd began to waver, but still did not appear entirely convinced. Glo stepped forward and placed on hand on the tall man's shoulder, a wry smile on his lips. "Seth can take care of himself. Aside from being almost impossible to find, he's fairly adept with those knives of his."

"Just ask Telvar and Voltark," Aksel added, with a faint smile.

Lloyd let out a long sigh. "You're right. I guess I just got carried away."

Elladan gazed fondly at the young man. "It's okay, Lloyd. Your heart was in the right place."

Lloyd grinned sheepishly back at the bard, his embarrassment slowly subsiding.

Aksel cleared his throat, and turned toward Donnie. "Ahem. Meanwhile, we still need to check out those stairs. In lieu of Seth, you're our next best choice."

Donnie thought it over for a moment, then nodded. "Very well."

Alana, unhooking her sword belt, came around and placed a hand on his shoulder. She spoke to him in a soft voice. "I'll keep watch over her."

Donnie gently got up, holding Ruka's head still until Alana knelt down in his place. The lady knight folded the tails of her surcoat over her armored legs, making a comfortable cushion, then Donnie placed Ruka's small head on her lap.

"I won't be long," Donnie promised, glancing down at the still form of the fragile young teen. Without another word, he spun around and headed off toward the colossus' feet.

36
ABOVE THE COLOSSUS

*Everything on the floor of the cavern will be crushed—including
your precious little friends*

Glolindir held Elistra gently in his arms as they watched the desperate scene before them. The seeress was right, the young dragon entangled with the giant serpent had indeed been Ruka. Just as Glo had suspected, the human girl they were all used to was not Ruka's natural form. Still, dragon or human, Ruka was Ruka. She was their friend, she was in trouble, and she needed their help.

Donnie had just left to investigate the stairwell behind the colossus' foot. With any luck, he would find something down there that could help with their current predicament. Meanwhile, Aksel worked on healing the rest of Ruka's wounds. He knelt over the young teen, white healing light pouring down from his hands over her poison-wracked body.

Even so, Ruka would still need some kind of cure for the toxins. The poison would continue to damage her until it was completely out of her system. Aksel appeared to have some kind of plan in mind—Glo was certain he would tell them once he was done heal-ing the young teen. The sudden sound of flapping wings roused Glo from his musings, but before he could pinpoint the source, Elladan cried out in warning.

"Duck!"

Glo pulled Elistra down, covering her with his body, just as some-thing strafed overhead. As soon as it passed, Glo swung around, his eyes locking on their attacker. It was the succubus—she had returned to plague them once more. The demoness swung back around, but this time did not attack, instead hovering just out of reach. "Awww, it looks like your little friend there isn't going to make it."

Lloyd growled at the creature, drawing his black blade and falling into a fighting stance. Aksel paused in healing Ruka, and switched places with Alana as the lady knight stood. She drew her gleam-ing sword and glared at the demoness, her voice like steel. "How… dare… you…"

The sucubbus placed a hand on her chest, and continued to taunt them in an innocent tone. "Was it something I said?"

Elistra pushed away from Glo and stomped forward, motioning the evil creature away. "There is nothing more here for you. Go back to your master and tell her you failed."

The sucubbus regarded the seeress for a moment, then stuck out her blood red lips and began to pout. "Ohhh… but there are still plenty of toys to play with."

Her eyes swept around the group, finally coming to rest on Lloyd. Glo was sure Lloyd could handle himself, but the succubus was fast on those wings. If he fell under her spell right now, it would prove disastrous for them all. Glo knew it wouldn't really hurt her much, but he pointed his arm anyway. "Play with this—*Radius Ardens.*"

A red hot beam of light leapt from his fingertips and struck the demoness square in the chest. She seemed shocked at first, touch-ing the burnt spot with her fingertips, but then she bared her fangs, and hissed at him. "How could you!" The demoness spun around in mid-air and with a great beat of her wings rocketed away, her voice trailing behind her. "I'll be back..."

Once she was gone, Elladan turned to face the others, his brow deeply furrowed. "You know, we have to do something about her. If she keeps coming back, sooner or later she's going to get to Lloyd or Donnie again."

Elistra placed her hands on her hips and cocked her head to one side, eyeing the bard curiously. "What do you have in mind?"

Elladan hesitated, a pained expression crossing his face before he replied. "I know it isn't going to be easy, especially in the air, but we're going to have to go after her."

Elistra narrowed her eyes as she considered the bard's words. "Who's we?"

"I'll go," Glo responded immediately. He wasn't their best flyer, but he still had a few spells he hadn't used yet.

Elistra shifted her gaze toward him, and regarded him for a moment or two, mixed emotions playing across her face. Finally, she nodded and said, "As will I."

Lloyd let out a short sigh, his shoulders slumping. "I wish I could go, but we all know how that turned out the last time."

Alana strode over and placed a hand on the young man's shoulder, smiling at him warmly. "We understand. I'll go in your stead— that is, if you'll lend me your cloak."

Lloyd glanced up and gave the lady knight an appreciative smile. "Certainly." He stepped back and unclasped his cloak, and held it out to her.

Alana smiled at him once more, but held up a hand in front of her. "Thank you, but can you hold onto that for a few more moments? There's no way I can fly effectively in this."

The lady knight pointed out the heavy armor she still wore. Lloyd grinned for the first time since Ruka had been hurt. "Probably not."

As Alana divested herself of her armor, Glo peered skyward, his eyes soon finding the succubus. She was flitting around up by the colossus' head. Abruptly, she disappeared from sight. Glo shifted his eyes back toward the others. "I think we should go on ahead, or we run the risk of losing her."

Elistra eyed Glo once more, but then gave him a short nod. "Perhaps you are right."

"Go on ahead," Alana told them, as she peeled off her armored greaves, "I'll be right behind you."

Glo gave her a nod and cast the fly spell upon himself. Elistra summoned an astral construct that looked vaguely like a horse-sized hummingbird. She swiftly mounted it and glanced at Glo. "Ready."

The wizard gave her a brief smile, then nodded to the others. "Here we go!"

A number of things ran through Alana's head as she swiftly doffed her armor. She had never had many friends growing up, life revolving around her family and training to be a knight. Alana never thought she needed more, knighthood being her life's ambition, yet something had changed in the last few days. These "Heroes of Ravenford" were an unregimented, and sometimes unruly bunch, but their camaraderie was infectious, and their teamwork exceptional. Still, there was something more to them—they were true friends, beyond what she had found amongst her fellow knights.

Alana had grown closer to them as the days passed, especially Elistra. She had shared things with the seeress she would never have told a fellow knight, not even the lady knights. Then there was Donatello—a warm smile came to her lips as she thought about the slight elf—his attempts to "woo" her had been corny at first, but they started to grow on her. Donnie had a roguish charm about him, and he had slowly, but surely, won her over. And most recently, she discovered a protective side to herself, in particular when it came to Ruka.

Ruka. Alana's eyes drifted over to the young teen, lying still in Aksel's arms, the little cleric trying to heal her without moving around too much. Alana was not close to the little gnome, but he was a jewel among beings, his caring for the misfortune of others going far beyond the norm. Alana didn't know much about the Soldenar, the goddess of the gnomes, but if she was anything like Cormar, she must be proud to have Aksel as one of her followers. Lloyd's voice interrupted her thoughts.

"Can I help you with that?"

Alana had gotten to her heavy breastplate. She could lift it on her own, but time was of the essense. She nodded to the young man with a genuine smile—he was an excellent sparring partner and a human being of the highest caliber. Lloyd would make a fine lord one day, his primary concern being the welfare of others. All Alana had left now was the fauld and tassets. As she doffed the last of it, she heard Elladan speaking to Aksel.

"Can I lend a hand?"

The little cleric gave the bard a grateful nod, then carefully switched places with him, thus freeing Aksel to heal Ruka more effectively. Alana caught Elladan's eye and gave him a grateful nod. His good looks had thrown her at first—she'd thought him a preening peacock, but the bard had proven her wrong. He was actually rather humble, with a boyish charm about him that was nearly as appealing as his handsome features. He had truly surprised her, though, with his attempt to allay her concerns about Donnie the other night. The bard had far more depth than most would give him credit for.

Alana let out a huge sigh as the last of her armor came off. She now stood in linen underclothes, her feet covered with woollen stockings. She re-donned her surcoat for a modicum of protection, then spun around for her backpack. Alana pulled up short, Lloyd standing there holding her spare pair of leather boots.

"Is this what you're looking for?"

Alana gave him another smile and gratefully accepted them, quickly pulling them on. She stood and belted her sword around her waist, then took Lloyd's cloak and fastened it around her shoulders. Alana grasped the edge in her hand, spoke the word Lloyd had taught her, and steeled herself as she lifted off the ground.

Far above, Glo was having a hard time with the succubus. The winged demoness was quite at home in the air, banking, weaving and diving around him as if he were standing still. Glo had already missed her with one ray of fire, a miscalculation he had paid for with blood. The succubus had caught him with her sharp claws, raking his chest as she dove past. Yet it might have been worse, if Elistra hadn't been right on her tail. The "hummingbird" she rode was nearly as fast as the succubus, and its long pointed beak looked deadly. The winged demoness had made it a point to steer clear of that lethal beak.

The succubus had drawn Elistra off, then quickly turned for another pass at Glo. She banked and rose upward, taunting him as she closed. "You can't hit me, little elf. The air is my domain!"

The demoness was right—she was way too fast for his ray of fire. Still, fast or not, Glo knew something that wouldn't miss. He aimed his fingers in her general direction and spoke two words, *"Nullam Telum."*

Three purple projectiles erupted from his fingertips, one after the other. They spiraled down toward the succubus, following her every move. The demoness tried to bank away, but all three missiles veered after her. They finally caught up with her, exploding with concussive force as they connected with her midriff. The succubus reeled at each explosion, causing her to momentarily flinch. After the last one, she righted herself, a wicked smile crossing her red lips.

"Do you really think that would stop me?" she said in a mocking tone.

"That may not, but this will!" a familiar voice cried.

Glo looked down and saw Alana just below them, her holy sword gleaming as she rose through the air. The demoness' eyes went wide, her wings beating wildly as she scrambled to get away, but Alana was too close. The lady knight's sword sliced through the air, its tip catching the succubus along her torso. The succubus flitted away and screamed in pain, a wide gash across her upper abdomen.

Alana stopped and spun around, her sword readied as she hovered a few yards away. Elistra pulled up at the same time, reigning in her mount on the other side of the succubus. Dark blood seeped from the open wound across the demoness' stomach. Her mouth agape, she reached down and touched it with her fingers. She pulled her hand away, her eyes wide as she stared at her fingertips covered in blood. A snarl escaped the demoness' lips, and she bared her fangs, her dark eyes shifting toward Alana.

"You fool! Now you've done it. I'll kill you. I'll kill you all." The demoness hissed at Alana, then launched herself upwards, her wings beating furiously as she rose.

"Follow her! Don't let her escape!" Elistra cried.

The three of them took off after the succubus, trying to keep up as she rose higher and higher. They followed her past the catwalk, over the head of the colossus, and beyond. The cavern ceiling grew steadily closer, a giant stalactite coming into view. The huge stalactite hung from the cavern roof, directly over the head of the colossus. The succubus continued her ascent, flying up the side of the giant formation.

"Where's she going?" Alana cried, as the three of them continued to give chase.

Glo silently wondered the same thing. He peered ahead at the fast approaching ceiling, his eyes focusing on a dark circular patch near the base of the giant stalactite. It was too round to be a natural formation—it had to be a door. Elistra must have seen it at the same time, the seeress crying out, "She's headed for that hole in the roof!"

The three of them were only a short way behind as the succubus reached the door in the ceiling. She paused there a moment, as the door slid opened, then disappeared inside. Glo, Elistra, and Alana reached the door a few moments later. Light filtered down on the three of them through the open doorway. Glo started for the door, but Alana placed herself in his way. "Let me go first."

Glo glanced at Elistra, the seeress responding with a short nod. Glo shrugged, then turned back to Alana, motioning her forward. "Very well. Lead the way."

The lady knight flew up through the doorway, Glo right after her, and Elistra behind him. The trio came up on the side of a wide circular chamber, numerous crates spread around the room in a large circle. Long cables extended from each crate like the spokes on a wheel. At the very center of the "wheel" stood a single switch, similar to the ones in the element rooms above. The succubus stood next to the lever, a saccharine smile on her lips.

"You see this little switch?" she practically purred. "One little pull and all these nice crates around the room will explode."

Glolindir glanced around the chamber once more, his eyes going wide. There were sixteen crates that made up the circle, each large enough for a person to sit on. *That's a lot of explosive power.* He exchanged a nervous glance with Elistra and Alana. *If she pulled that switch, none of them would get out of here alive.*

The succubus knew she had them at her mercy, yet she continued to gloat. "Oh, and that's not the worst of it. That giant stalactite is just below us. So when this room blows, the stalactite will fall."

Glo's breath caught in his throat, the blood draining from his face. *If that huge stalactite falls...*

The succubus finished his thought for him. "It will shatter the colossus, causing a huge avalanche of stone. Everything on the floor of the cavern will be crushed—including your precious little friends."

Glo found himself speechless, there was nothing he could do. Alana, however, tried to reason with the creature. "If you do that, you'll destroy yourself along with us."

The demoness threw back her head, and let out a wicked laugh. She fixed her eyes back on Alana, a hand on her scorched and bleeding chest. "Oh, this body will be, for sure. I'll be banished to my home plane for a while, but no, little girl knight, I will not die. I will return to rule this world when you are nothing but a sad memory."

Alana's face went pale as she realized the truth of the demoness' words. The creature stared at her with obvious satisfaction, still reveling in the upper hand that she had finally gained on them. She gloated for a few moments more, then placed a hand upon the switch. An evil smile graced her lips—she licked them and said, "Might as well get this over with."

Glo had watched the entire exchange, feeling utterly powerless to stop the inevitable. Now, in these final moments, he wanted nothing more than to hold Elistra. He went to grasp the lovely seeress, but abruptly halted. Elistra's brow was furrowed with concentration. Glo had seen that look before, just as she was about to unleash a psionic power. Beyond hope, he spun around to see three crystalline coils appeared out of nowhere, and constrict around the unsuspecting succubus. She was bound into place, unable to pull the switch. The demoness screamed in frustration. "No! You cannot stop me now! Not when I'm this close!"

The succubus struggled fiercely against the bonds, straining to break free from their hold. Elistra gasped, sweat forming on her brow as her concentration began to waver. "I can't hold this for long! You have to finish her now!"

"I'm on it!" Alana cried, launching herself across the room.

Glolindir took a deep breath and set his jaw—he would do his part to save his friends. He cleared his mind, lifted an arm, pointed straight at the succubus, and spoke the words, *"Radius Ardens."*

A red hot beam leapt from his fingers and shot across the room, catching the succubus square in the chest. She screamed and writhed in pain, but the crystalline coils still held her fast. A moment later, Alana reached her, holy sword poised to strike. With a great cry, she brought it down, and with all her might, cleaved the demoness nearly in two. A shrill scream erupted from the creature's lips, but was suddenly silenced as she disappeared in a brilliant flash of light. The light expanded out in all directions, shining so bright that Glo had to shield his eyes. A few seconds later, it faded away—there was not a trace of the foul demoness left to be seen.

Alana, still hovering in mid-air, spun around to face them. She wiped the sweat from her forehead with the back of her hand. "Phew, that was a little too close."

Glo grinned at the lady knight, then turned to smile at Elistra. The seeress returned his warm smile, then suddenly wavered, nearly falling off her mount. Glo rushed forward and grabbed her around the waist, steadying her in her seat. The moment of dizziness quickly faded, and Elistra smiled up at him, snuggling into his arms.

Glo stared at her a moment, a mixture of relief and desire flooding through him, then he reached down and lifted her chin, kissing the seeress passionately on the lips. She returned his kiss with equal ardor, the world around them seemingly fading away. Glo lost track of time—he had no idea how long they stayed like that, but eventually Elistra pulled away. Their foreheads still touching, she gazed up into his eyes and whispered, "Much as I'd love to stay like this, I'm afraid Ruka might still need our help."

A wry smile crossed Glo's lips, yet he held her close just a bit longer. "Yes, you are right. We should go."

A tiny, bell-like laugh came from the seeress. "I don't see you letting me go."

Glo laughed in response. "Okay, okay. Give an elf a break."

He reluctantly let Elistra go, and stepped back from her mount.

Alana floated there next to them, a knowing smile on the lady knight's face. "When all this is over, we need to get away to someplace nice and private."

Elistra grinned at the lady knight and winked. "The more private, the better."

Glo shifted his gaze from Elistra to Alana, blushing furiously, the two women bursting into laughter at his embarrasment. Elistra placed a soft hand on his cheek, a warm smile across her lips. "Oh Glo, promise me you'll never change."

Glo, Elistra, and Alana flew back down to join the others. Below them, Ruka still lay on the ground, her head resting on Elladan's lap. Donnie had returned and now knelt beside her, gently holding Ruka's hand. Lloyd stood watching over them, a melancholy expression on the young man's face. Aksel knelt a short distance away from the others, the little cleric deep in prayer.

Lloyd glanced up as they approached the ground, his expression turning grim. "What happened with the succubus?"

Glo responded with a thin smile. "She won't be bothering us again."

The trio landed, all eyes turning once again to their fallen comrade. Ruka's wounds had disappeared, and her coloring was definitely better, but the young teen lay uncharacteristically still on Elladan's lap.

Alana's face was drawn, as she softly asked, "How is she?"

Elladan gazed up, his normally carefree expression gaunt, more than a hint of sadness in his voice. "Aksel finished healing her. Her wounds are closed, but the poison is still in her system."

Donnie gazed up at them, the slight elf's face ashen. Glo had never seen him this serious before. He looked as if he had aged a thousand years.

"What is Aksel doing now?" Glo asked quietly.

Donnie remained silent, so Elladan explained for them. "He's praying for divine knowledge. He's beseeching his goddess for a spell that will help with the poison."

"Ah," Glo responded, not wanting to say anymore. What Aksel was attempting could have severe consequences. Glo was not that familiar with the Soldenar, but the gods had a tendency to be fickle when it came to that sort of thing. Often times, they only provided their clerics with the knowledge they deemed fit. If Aksel were to anger his goddess, he might jeopardize his connection with her—the little cleric would never be able to cast divine spells again.

Alana shifted her gaze to Donnie, her voice just barely above a whisper. "Did you find anything below that might help?"

Donnie glanced up again with a long, drawn out sigh. "I found what appears to be living quarters below. Once she's better"—the slight elf's voice caught for a moment—"once she's better, there's a nice couch we can lay her on."

Glo wiped a hand across his eyes, drying the excess moisture that had built up there. Unless Aksel could pull off a miracle, then dragon or not, Ruka was probably not going to make it. Elistra had been holding on to Glo's arm. She gave him a brief squeeze, then slowly stepped forward and placed a hand on Donnie's shoulder. She spoke softly into the elf's ear. "There may be something I can do, but it won't be without consequences."

Donnie's head immediately spun around, a ray of hope returning to his features. "Whatever it is, I'll do it!"

Elistra knelt down next to him, a slim smile across her lips. Her voice was measured as she explained to him further. "You must first understand, this is not something to be entered into lightly. It will prove dangerous for you."

Donnie gave his head an emphatic shake. "I don't care. I promised her she would be fine, and I always keep my word. Just tell me what I have to do."

The slight elf's expression was one of desperation. Elistra took a deep breath, and then explained in detail. "I can link your fates... sort of a karmic channel, where you can temporarily share life-forces. You would bolster her life with your own, but it will also distribute the pain and any damage she continues to suffer."

Alana interrupted them, her voice filled with more than a touch of concern. "So he would be poisoned, too?"

Elistra shifted her gaze to the lady knight and slowly shook her head. "No, he would not… but any further damage she takes from the poison… would affect the both of them."

Donnie had already made up his mind, the color returning to his face and his jaw set determinedly. "I can live with that. Let's do this already."

Elistra placed a hand on Donnie's arm, her expression deathly serious. When she spoke, her voice was very firm. "There's just one more thing you need to know. You would be so closely linked, that if she were to die, you might die as well. At the very least, it would cut your life short."

Glo's eyes went wide. If Donnie were to do this, he might pay the ultimate price. Glo practically wanted to scream, *don't do it*, but caught himself. If the tables were turned, and it was Elistra laying there, Glo wouldn't hesitate for a moment.

Donnie's resolve hardened even further, his face taking on a grim cast. He stared Elistra right in the eye, and responded, emphasizing each word. "I… don't… care…" The slight elf then waved his hand and added, "Link us together already, or whatever you need to do."

"Wait!"

The cry came from Alana. All eyes turned to the lady knight. Alana glanced around self-conciously, but then her face hardened, her gaze returning to Elistra. "I'll do it." She folded her arms across her chest, her eyes sweeping around the group. "I care about her just as much as the rest of you"—her eyes finally settled on Donnie—"and no offense, Donnie, but I am a lot tougher than you."

Donnie stared open-mouthed at the lady knight, then his features softened, a gentle smile crossing his face. He let go of Ruka's hand, stood up and crossed over to Alana, his hand gently caressing the side of her face. "What's a few hundred years to an elf like me? And what would be the alternative? Let you do it, and rob this world of your beauty? I have painted a million faces, across many lands, and never seen one as lovely. Robbing the realms of a face such as yours, would be the true crime."

Alana blushed furiously at his heartfelt response. She grasped his hand, and gazed deep into his eyes for a few moments, then finally whispered, "Donatello… I still stand the better chance…"

Elistra shook her head as she spoke, putting an end to the passionate debate. "Perhaps, but in order for this to work, I have to overcome Ruka's will—and the will of a dragon, even poisoned and dying, is a tremendous thing."

All eyes spun toward the seeress. Elistra wore a wan smile. Her head fell, her voice turning to a whisper as she added, "I only bring this up because I thought... perhaps... if it was Donatello, she wouldn't resist..."

Alana opened her mouth to speak, then stopped herself. She hung her head in defeat and sighed, "Very well."

Donnie leaned forward and gave her a brief kiss on the cheek, then spun around and strode back to Elistra, kneeling down next to the seeress. "Alright, let's do this."

Elistra responded with a curt nod. "Very well."

The seeress placed a hand over both Donnie's and Ruka's hearts, her brow deeply furrowing as she began to concentrate. Glo watched on with renewed admiration for the slight elf. Not many would do what Donnie was about to do for Ruka. Despite his sometimes devil-may-care attitude, the slight elf had a heart of pure gold.

A wry smile suddenly crossed Donnie's lips. "Plus anyway, this will give me the chance to answer an age-old question that has plagued my gender since the beginning of time."

Elistra hesitated, her expression turning curious as she gazed at the elf. "And what question would that be?"

"What *does* go on inside a woman's head?"

37
HOPES AND PRAYERS

Greater than the gods? What is greater than the gods?

Seth stood quietly in the darkness, listening to the sharp, ragged breaths that came from just a few feet ahead of him. They were on the ground floor of the monolith, a short distance from the archway that led outside. Night had fallen, the clearing surrounding the monolith dimly lit by the campfires of the Knights of the Rose. The darkness of the forest lay just beyond, the nearest trees flickering with a dull yellow glow that radiated from their fires.

When the Serpent Cult finally showed its face, Seth had turned invisible, and launched himself off the colossus. He had skidded down to the walkway below, intent on sneaking down the path and surpising the black mages. What he hadn't counted on was Glo rushing in and starting a fire fight.

Seth wracked his brains for a way around the conflagration, until he noticed the colossus' arm rising over the top of the walkway. It appeared that Aksel was going to use the golem against the serpents that had slithered forth. He had also inadvertently provided Seth with a clear path across the chamber.

Seth had leapt onto the Colossus' broad shoulder, and raced down the giant's arm. He reached the hand just as the fire fight ended, the last black mage shaking his fist defiantly, then turning coat and running for the stairwell. Seth rushed across the stone hand, and leapt through the air just over the tops of the serpents, landing in a ball on the walkway behind them. He leapt back up, and sped the rest of the way to the staircase, reaching it just moments before the succubus. Seth narrowly avoided her, and raced up the stairs after the receding mage.

The succubus, unable to fly in such close quarters, quickly fell behind. Seth had chased the mage all the way up the monolith, and back down again, until they stood where they were now, waiting quietly just outside the monolith entrance. The succubus was nowhere to be seen, most likely having given up the chase, and returned to the battle below.

Seth was not worried in the slightest—he knew his friends could handle the demoness. His primary concern was putting an end to the Serpent Cult once and for all, and that would not be possible unless they routed them out at the source. They needed to find the cult's home base, and destroy it along with the cult's leader. That was the only way to end their mad plans to rule Thac.

The black mage in the darkness just ahead of him was the ticket to that goal. Seth was certain that if the mage got away, he would make a beeline for the cult's base, leading Seth straight to it. The only problem with that plan was that the mage appeared afraid to move. The armored guards outside kept a tight watch on the clearing, and the black mage didn't seem prepared to sneak past them.

Seth sighed inwardly. *Do I have to do everything myself?*

He was going to have to sneak past the mage, and get the company to relax their guard. It was the only way his plan was going to work. Shaking his head, the halfling crept forward on silent feet. He slowly crept past the heavily breathing mage, and slipped through the archway to the clearing beyond.

The night around him was clear, the stars twinkling brightly in the black sky overhead. The moon was just barely visible below the tree tops, its pale silvery face nearly full at this time of month. Seth would have to make this quick—once the moon peaked out overhead, the mage might completely lose his nerve.

He scanned the clearing, focusing his gaze on the large tent in the center of the camp. Seth headed directly for it, passing unnoticed through the campground, and swiftly reaching the tent's entrance. He peered inside—a dark-haired knight knelt before a makeshift altar, reciting his evening devotions—he had found Sir Craven. Seth slipped silently into the tent, and crept up next to preoccupied knight. He dispelled his invisibility and said, "Hey, Sir Craven. What's up?"

To the knight's credit, he barely flinched, turning toward the halfling with the hint of a smile on his lips. "It is good to see you, Master Seth. To what do we owe the honor of this impromptu visit?"

The duo sat down at the knight's table, and Seth quickly explained what had happened below. Sir Craven listened carefully as Seth outlined his plan, remaining silent until he had finished. The knight sat there stroking his bearded chin for a few moments, then nodded.

"A sound plan, Master Seth. He'll probably head for straight for the horses. I'll have one saddled as if for patrol, and relax the guard on this side of the clearing. I trust you will want your riding dog?"

A lopsided smile crossed Seth's lips. "Better than trying to keep up with him on foot."

"Agreed." Sir Craven gave him a wry smile, but his expression swiftly turned serious again. "What about Dame Alana and the others? Do you think they will require any assistance?"

Seth shook his head. "No, Glo already took out the other mages. Between Lloyd, Alana, and the colossus, those serpents don't stand a chance."

Sir Craven gave him a curt nod, then stood. "Very good. Prepare yourself then—I will have the horse and dog saddled, and then draw back the guards."

The tall knight strode from the tent, leaving Seth all alone. A half-eaten bowl of stew still sat on the table. Seth quickly wolfed it down, not sure of the next time he would get a hot meal. The halfling then stood and wiped his mouth on his sleeve, the corner of his lips rising. *Well then, here goes nothing.*

Aksel Alabaster knelt at the foot of the colossus, far below the Darkwoods monolith. He was beseeching his goddess, the Soldenar, for the power to counteract the poison that coursed through the veins of his friend, Ruka. Communion with his deity was a very personal experience for Aksel. It was not an easy connection to achieve, requiring a still mind, a pure heart, and an utter devotion to the sanctity of life. Further, it also demanded a keen wit, for the Soldenar was unlike any of the other gods.

The goddess of the gnomes extolled the virtues of faith, but also of cleverness, emphasizing brains over brawn. Her doctrine taught that outthinking one's enemy was more important than overpowering them. Thus, a direct prayer to the deity never received a direct answer. It was usually met with a riddle, the success of the prayer solely based on answering it correctly.

Luckily, not all prayers were direct questions. For instance, as Aksel had grown both in mind and spirit, the Soldenar had rewarded him with the knowledge to cast more complex spells. Once provided with that knowledge, Aksel merely had to renew his vows to the Soldenar in prayer each day. Yet now he had a direct request, and to make matters worse, it was for a spell whose complexity may very well be beyond him. Still, he had to try, for Ruka's sake. As Aksel reached the deepest level of prayer-state, the question formed in his mind.

Soldenar, Goddess of all Gnomes, I beseech you. Please grant me the power to cleanse the poison from the blood of one who is pure, honorable, and just.

Aksel's request was met with utter silence. That had never happened to him before—his goddess had never ignored a direct query from him. The longer the silence lasted, the more perplexed he became. Perhaps he had worded it incorrectly? Aksel repeated the question with a slight variation.

Soldenar, my Lady and Master, I beseech you. Please grant me the power to cleanse the poison from the blood of one who is pure, honorable, and just.

Aksel was met with silence once again. He began to grow anxious.

Did his goddess already know what he was going to ask for? Was she upset about it? Aksel considered repeating the question one more time, when the lilting voice of his goddess reverberated through his mind.

'Tis a tall order ya ask for, lad. Are ya certain of the nobility and purity of the lassie for whom ya ask this boon?

I am, Aksel responded with certainty.

There was a long pause before the Soldenar replied. *Very well. Then first ya must answer me this simple query:*

What be greater than the gods,
more evil than demons,
the poor have it,
the rich need it,
and if ya eat it,
ya will die?

Aksel mentally winced. He knew a riddle was coming, but this one was a doozy. *Greater than the gods? What is greater than the gods?* There were the greater powers—Illitar, the Essence of Life, being chief amongst them. That might even fit the second line, for the greater power Dirbane, also known as the Dark Flame, was the very essence of evil. Still, that did not answer the rest of the riddle. Aksel continued to rack his brains.

What was greater than the gods? Love? Perhaps, but could it be considered more evil than demons? If one considered the pain love could cause, then maybe. In fact, it almost fit the rest of the riddle. Love might be the only thing the poor have, and the rich tended to sacrifice love for wealth and power. As for eating it, that might be a reference to the statement, "One cannot survive on love alone."

Well, lad, do ya have an answer?

Love? Aksel responded, the thought tentative at best. He was met with another long pause. Finally, he heard his goddess' reply in his mind.

Ah, I'm sorry, lad. A good answer to be sure, but not the right one.

Aksel mentally hung his head. He had failed, and poor Ruka would pay the price. Yet, just when he thought all was lost, the Soldenar's voice reverberated through his mind once more.

Still, ya obviously put a lot of thought into that one, and yer cause is just. So, I will grant ya a boon. Not the one ya asked for, but a boon nonetheless.

Aksel's hopes rose—at least he had not completely failed. He waited in silence for his goddess to tell him what this boon might be.

While I cannot grant ya the power to cure the poison, that is still well beyond ya, lad, I will grant ya the spell to halt its progress now, instead of on the morrow.

Aksel felt both disappointed and relieved. It may not be what he originally asked for, but it would certainly help. Otherwise, Ruka might not survive until the morning. He had already lost too many people from his life—his parents, his grandparents, all his aunts and uncles—he was not about to lose another person. At least with this spell, Ruka would be immune to the poison. It would remain in her system, but she would take no further damage from it. Still, they would need an actual cure to restore her to full health.

Aksel took a deep breath, and thanked his deity for the boon she had granted him. *Thank you, Soldenar, Goddess of all Gnomes. Your wisdom is only surpassed by your kindness.*

Yar welcome, lad. Now go heal the wee dragon lassie.

Aksel's eyes snapped open. He rose to his feet, and rushed across the chamber with new hope for his ailing friend.

Elistra knelt between Donnie and Ruka, a hand over each of their hearts. Her breathing slowed as if she were deep in meditation, her brow knitted with concentration. A purple glow formed around her heart, then spread out across her torso, through her arms, all the way down to her hands. The light flowed out of her palms and into Donnie's and Ruka's chests.

Glo, Lloyd, Elladan, and Alana all watched in silence as the seeress linked together the fates of the dragon girl and the slight elf. As time went on, Ruka's breathing became more regular, the color returning to her face. At the same time, Donnie's complexion grew more and more pale. The exchange of life force went on for a little while longer, then finally the purple glow faded. Elistra opened her eyes and sat back, her voice quite soft. "It is done."

Ruka now appeared to be resting comfortably in Elladan's lap, looking far better than she had before. Donnie, on the other hand, looked more than a bit haggard. Yet, he completely ignored his own plight, his main concern still being Ruka. His eyes shifted to Elistra, his voice sounding rather weary. "How... how is she?"

Elistra returned the slight elf's gaze with a fondness in her eyes that had not been there before. "Much better... your life force has strengthened hers immensely..."

She trailed off, leaving the rest unsaid. Glo thought perhaps it better that way, but Donnie apparently wanted it spelled out. He continued to stare at the seeress, his eyes narrowing. "Where's the 'but'?"

Elistra's face fell, a deep sadness in her voice as she answered. "But, as I warned you before, it won't stop the poison from still hurting her... and now you."

Silence pervaded the little group. Glo strode up behind Elistra, placing a hand on each of her shoulders. She tilted her head up toward him, and responded with a weak smile. He could feel the tension in her shoulders—this had been a difficult thing for her to do. She had bought the young teen a bit more time, but at what cost to their elven friend?

Donnie broke the silence once more. "How much time?"

Elistra shifted her eyes to the slight elf, her expression pained as she slowly shook her head. "It is not clear to me right now..."

"I think I can help with that."

Glo looked up to see Aksel rushing toward them. The little cleric hurried over and knelt down at Ruka's side.

"Did it work?" Alana asked, sudden hope in the lady knight's voice.

Aksel stretched his hands over the young teen as he answered. "Somewhat. I cannot cure the poison, but I can make her immune to its effects..."

Donnie tilted his head and eyed the little cleric curiously. "Which means what exactly?"

Aksel had begun to move his hands in a pattern, but paused, not taking his eyes off Ruka. "It means, she will not get any sicker, but she will not get any better either—at least not until we find a cure for the poison in her system."

Donnie's face brightened significantly, his voice thick with emotion. "Thank you, Aksel."

Aksel merely nodded, and once again started to weave an intricate pattern over their ailing friend. It only took a few moments, the little cleric finally finishing with two soft words, *"Mora Detegere."*

The magic released from Aksel's hands and a pale green light enveloped Ruka's body. The glow lasted for a few scant seconds, then appeared to dissolve into her skin, finally disappearing altogether. When it was done, Aksel sat back and took a deep breath.

Donnie sat there, still holding Ruka's hand, staring at the little cleric impatiently. "Well?"

Aksel's eyes shifted to the slight elf, a thin smile spreading across his mouth. "It worked. She's now immune to the poison in her system."

As if on cue, Ruka's eyes fluttered open.

"Ruka!" Donnie cried in excitement, his haggard face lighting up once more.

The young teen lifted herself up onto her elbows, her eyes sweeping around the hovering companions. A familiar smirk spread across her lips. "What's everybody staring at?"

Elladan's quasi-smile returned to his lips for the first time in quite awhile. "Oh, she's definitely better."

There were a few subdued chuckles around the group. Donnie, however, did not laugh, instead leaning forward and grasping the young teen in a tight embrace. "You had us worried sick!"

Ruka flushed furiously. She pushed Donnie away and stammered, "I'm... fine. Really."

Aksel folded his arms across his chest, and stared at her with a stern expression. "No, you're not."

Ruka turned to face him, her head tilted quizzically to one side. Aksel explained to her about the poison and how it was still in her system. When he was done, Ruka sat up and stretched out her arms. "But I don't feel any different."

Aksel tilted his head to once side, his expression dour as he eyed the young teen. "You'll find your strength is not quite what it was before."

Ruka stared back at him, her own expression rather skeptical. "If you say so."

Elistra placed a hand on Ruka's shoulder. "There's one more thing you should know."

Ruka spun toward the seeress, her brows knitting together as she saw the serious expression on Elistra's face. "And what's that?"

Ruka's eyes went wide as Elistra described the fate link she had imposed between her and Donatello, and the consequences it further entailed. When she finished, Ruka bowed her head, her face paling as she sat there quietly.

"Donnie..." she choked out his name, her voice thick with emotion.

The slight elf sat forward and placed a hand under her chin, lifting up her face, and flashing her a pearly smile. "I promised you that you would be alright, and I *always* keep my promises. Or at least I try to," he added softly.

"Well then, are you done talking the poor girl's ear off?" Elladan interrupted. All eyes turned toward the bard. Elladan stared at Donnie with that all-too-familiar half-smile. "I thought you wanted to bring her downstairs once she was feeling better?"

Ruka shifted her eyes from Elladan back to Donnie. "Downstairs?"

Donnie looked at her with a sheepish grin. "I almost forgot. There was another stairwell hidden under the colossus's foot. It leads to what appears to be living quarters. There's a couch down there and everything."

Ruka yawned at the mention of the couch. "That sounds... very comfortable..."

The young teen yawned once more. Alana bent down and grabbed Ruka behind the back and under her legs. She lifted her up, and nodded to Donnie. "I'll carry her. You lead the way."

"I'm not... a baby..." Ruka started to protest, but her complaints swiftly subsided as her head came to rest on the lady knight's shoulder. She struggled to keep her eyes open, but after a few moments, she gave up and kept them closed.

Donnie gave Aksel an anxious glance. "Is she alright?"

"She'll be fine," Aksel assured him. "She's been through a lot. She just needs to rest now."

"I'm... fine..." Ruka said sleepily, still nestled comfortably in Alana's arms. "Couch..." she added before drifting off once again.

Alana gazed fondly down at the young teen, a serene expression on the lady knight's face, and Donnie practically beamed as his eyes swept over the duo. The slight elf gazed at them for a few more moments, then strode out ahead of everyone, motioning for them to fall in behind. "Okay everyone, follow me."

38
THE GOLEM MASTER'S SECRET

The translucent crystal-blue statue began to move

Donnie led the way down the spiral staircase, Glo and Elistra right behind. Alana came next, carrying Ruka, immediately followed by Elladan and Aksel. Lloyd came last, bringing up the rear. The stairwell, well-lit by those strange glowing tiles, ended another fifty steps down, opening up to a wide circular room. More glowing tiles stretched across the ceiling, every ten feet or so, illuminating the rounded chamber.

A fine rug lay on the floor before them, and a number of high-quality chairs were spread about. A very comfortable-looking couch sat in front of a small fireplace, which just happened to be lit. There was no wood in the fireplace—the fire must have been a permanent magical effect. Next to the hearth stood a translucent crystal-blue statue of an elven woman, holding a silver tray in her hands. At the other end of the room were three closed doors.

Elladan gazed around the room with an approving nod and smile. "Larketh sure knew how to live in style."

Donnie gave the bard a knowing grin. "You think?"

As the companions spread out into the room, the translucent crystal-blue statue began to move. Lloyd stepped forward, his hands on his blade hilts, but Donnie put an arm out in front of him. "It's okay Lloyd—watch this."

Donnie strode up to the statue, and said, "I'm hungry."

The statue responded to him in the Common tongue. "Would you like something to eat, Master?"

The tray in the statue's hand began to glow. The light swiftly faded, slices of bread, cheese, and a silver goblet appearing on the platter. The food smelled fresh and the goblet held a clear liquid. Donnie picked up a piece of cheese and popped it in his mouth. "Mmm… good." He spun around to face the others, and ushered them toward the tray. "You should really try some."

Lloyd's stomach grumbled loudly as he stared at the tray full of food. Ruka popped her head up for a moment, the young teen mumbling a single word. "Food…"

Donnie immediately responded by grabbing some bread and cheese off the plate, and rushing it over to the half-asleep teen. Ruka's eyes popped open and she grabbed the bread from him, laying back and munching on the piece of loaf, as she lay comfortably in Alana's arms. Donnie stepped back and smiled at the young teen until Elladan smacked him in the arm. Donnie spun around and gave the bard a questioning stare. "What was that for?"

"You've been holding out on us," Elladan said in a mock serious tone.

Donnie placed his hands on his hips and glared at the bard with fake defiance. "I had more important things on my mind than feeding you."

Their pretend face-off was interrupted by Lloyd. The young man stood in front of the elven "maid" statue, stuffing his mouth with as many delectables as he could at once. "Yu tu shud rally stop arg-u-ing, n' try al' dis' de-lic-tus fud."

Donnie and Elladan shifted their gaze toward Lloyd, and suddenly burst into laughter. The two elves threw an arm around each other's shoulders, and strode over to join the starving young man.

Alana watched them with a raised eyebrow, then shifted her gaze to Elistra. "What is it with men and food?"

Elistra, standing back and watching with Glo and Aksel, wore an amused expression. "They have always been that way… as far back as I can remember."

Glo gave the seeress a sidelong glance. He silently wondered just how far back the seeress really could remember. Alana shook her head, then went to lay Ruka on the couch next to the warm fire. Donnie managed to tear himself away from the food tray, and found a blanket to cover the young teen with. Meanwhile, Elladan took a sip from the silver goblet and made a face.

Aksel eyed the bard with concern. "Is there something wrong with your drink?"

Elladan turned to little cleric and shook his head. "Oh, sorry. No its fine. It's just water is all. I was just hoping for something a bit stronger—after all, Larketh was a dwarf."

Elladan finished his assertion with a wink, causing the group in general to laugh. It was a great tension breaker after all they'd been through this day. Everyone grabbed some food, and took a seat, Alana and Donnie taking turns bringing more to Ruka. The amount of food available was never ending—whenever the tray or goblet emptied, either would automatically refill with bread, cheese and water. Soon, everyone had eaten their fill.

Once their appetites were sated, Aksel reminded them it was not time to rest just yet. He nodded toward the three doorways at the other end of the room. "We should probably check out where those lead."

Alana sat down on the couch next to Ruka. "You all go. I'll stay and keep an eye on Ruka."

Aksel gave her a brief smile, then turned to Donnie and ushered him forward. "Donnie, if you please."

Donatello carefully examined the three doorways and the floor around them for trip wires, pressure plates and the like, but there were none to be found. Neither were the doors locked. One door led to a bed chamber, one to a library area, and the last to a study—this was indeed Larketh's living quarters, or at least one of them. The companions explored the rooms in depth, starting first with the bedroom.

This was another circular room, though smaller than the main living area. The highlight of this room was an elaborate, cherry wood poster bed, draped on three sides with sheer material that reached from its canvas covered top, down to the floor. A matching nightstand stood next to the bed, and along the walls were two cherry wood dressers, one with a large mirror, the other a tall wardrobe.

Elladan eyed the bed with clear interest. "Now that looks inviting." The bard strode over to it, pushed the sheer curtains aside and plopped himself down. A look of sheer delight crossed his face. "This is cushy!" Elladan threw out his arms and fell back onto the bed, sinking deep into the plush mattress. "Ahhhh... call me in the morning."

While Elladan enjoyed himself, Donnie began a thorough sweep of the room. At the base of the wardrobe, the slight elf found a secret panel. Inside that panel lay a locked chest. Donnie deftly picked the lock, and threw open the lid.

Glo half expected to hear the words, "child's play." The elven wizard let out a small sigh, sorely missing their cynical friend. He briefly wondered where Seth was, and sincerely hoped the halfling was alright.

His concern for their missing friend was cut short as Aksel waved him over to the chest. Glo peered inside and saw that the interior was lined with gold pieces. On top of those rested a silver crown with an opal inlay, a large silver brooch, and three ivory scroll cases. Glo examined each item thoroughly. The crown turned out to be non-magical, but the brooch definitely had magical properties, and the cases each contained scrolls with high-level spells in them.

"What's this for?" Elladan's voice came from behind the bed curtains.

Without warning, a section of wall beside the bed slid open. Lloyd and Donnie moved in front of the others, and drew their weapons. Elladan leapt through the curtains, and rushed to stand with Aksel,

Glo, and Elistra. Behind this new door was a small, dark closet. As the companions peered anxiously inside, a familiar figure abruptly emerged. It was another translucent crystal-blue elven woman, similar to the serving statue in the "living room." This construct, however, wore a very skimpy outfit. She sauntered up to the astonished companions and said, "How can I serve you today, Master?"

Lloyd took a step back, blushing furiously at the sight of the scantily-clad blue woman. Glo spiked an eyebrow—Larketh was indeed a master of all forms of golems, but he was also obviously quite... decadent. Donnie and Elladan exchanged a glance, the former lowering his sword. The duo slowly approached the blue woman, eying her carefully up and down. The blue elf eyed both of them back, a flirtatious look upon her face.

"This Larketh did seem to have interesting tastes," Donnie noted wryly.

Elladan nodded, his brow furrowed. "Indeed."

Before anyone else could comment, Elistra strode up to the blue elven woman, a finger on her chin as she circled all around her. Donnie and Elladan politely moved out of the seeress' way. Elistra made a full circle, the blue elf watching her as well. "She's got curves in all the right places, but I don't imagine that she is as soft or warm as a real woman."

A seductive smile crossed the blue woman's face as she gazed alluringly back at Elistra. "I am built for the comfort of my master... or mistress."

Elistra shifted her gaze toward Glo, a single eyebrow raised. She folded her arms across her chest, and slowly backed away from the blue woman. "Thanks... but no thanks."

The blue elf then spun her head toward both Donnie and Elladan. "May I please either of you masters, then?"

Donnie raised both hands in front of him and backed away as well. "Maybe another time—things are a bit too complicated at the moment."

Elladan shook his head as well. "Sorry, darling, but I think our dragon girl friend needs the bed more than me right now."

The blue elven woman raised an eyebrow. "Oh, good. May I please her, then?"

"No!" came simultaneous shouts from almost everyone in the room.

The blue elf began to pout, but then stopped, a smile returning to her face almost immediately. "Very well then. Ring me if you need me."

With that, the elven woman spun on her heel, and strode seductively back into the closet, the door sliding closed behind her.

Aksel, silent this entire time, finally spoke. "Okay then, how about we move on to the next room."

The companions slowly filed out the door. Elladan gave one last look over his shoulder. "I still can't believe she isn't real."

Donnie gave his friend a wry smile. "That didn't seem to stop Larketh."

"What didn't stop Larketh?" Alana asked from her seat on the couch, the lady knight's head tilted curiously to one side.

Elistra slowly shook her head, a look of revulsion on her face. "You don't want to know."

The lady knight arched an eyebrow. "That bad?"

The seeress nodded. "That bad."

✳

The companions explored the library next. This circular room had a long table down the middle, and two huge curved bookshelves on either side, each reaching from the floor to the ceiling. Those shelves were packed from end to end with bound texts of all sizes and shapes. Lloyd, Glo, Elistra, Aksel, Elladan and Donnie split up, examining each shelf thoroughly. There were nearly a thousand texts here, many of them quite ancient, yet very well preserved, as if untouched by time.

Glo had explored a few shelves, when a particularly ornate binding caught his eye. He gingerly pulled that volume off the shelf and cracked it open, his eyes going wide.

Elistra, another book in her hand, must have seen the look on his face. The seeress strode over and gazed questioningly at the volume he was holding. "What is it?"

Glo responded in a hushed tone. "It's a history of the Titans."

Lloyd, Aksel, Elladan, and Donnie came over as well. Donnie let out a soft whistle. "That text must be priceless."

Aksel shifted his gaze from the volume to the others, and nodded his head, his lips tight together. "This is an impressive find. Still, it's not what we came for."

Aksel was correct, of course. They had come in search of the golem master's secrets, not a history book on the Titans. Glo flushed with embarrassment, swiftly closing the book and holding it out to Elladan.

"Can you hang onto this for safekeeping?"

"Certainly," Elladan said with a sympathetic smile, taking the book and placing it gingerly in his portal bag.

The six of them explored the rest of the shelves, but found no works that contained the golem master's secrets. Mentally exhausted, they moved onto the last room. This last chamber was most definitely Larketh's study. A large ornate cherry wood desk sat in the very center of the room, with a single plush chair behind it. There was yet another bookshelf behind the desk, and a large painting of a dwarf off to one side.

The dwarf in that portrait was a rather imposing figure, with long red hair, a well-groomed mustache, and a long, neatly braided red beard. He wore black robes, and held a large tome in his left hand with the same symbol on it they had found on that dais at the top of the monolith. In his other hand, the figure held a golden staff. Glo's heart nearly skipped a beat. He immediately envisioned the huge Dwarven statue he had seen in his nightmare—this portrait was frighteningly similar.

"So I'm guessing that's Larketh?" Lloyd said, scratching the back of his head as he gazed at the portrait.

Aksel responded with a short nod. "More than likely."

"Well, if he's still alive, at least we know what he looks like," Elladan said with a semi-smile.

"Unless he was reincarnated," Donnie added with a wry smile of his own.

Elladan peered at the slight elf, and let out a short laugh. "Yeah. He could be a kobald."

Glo snorted. He didn't know if he was just tired, but somehow the idea of someone reincarnating into a sprite-like creature such as a kobald struck him as funny at that moment.

Aksel tore his eyes away from the imposing portrait and gazed at Elistra questioningly. "You wouldn't happen to have any insight on Larketh's state of being, would you?"

The seeress responded with a slow shake of her head. "I have no idea whether Larketh actually died, or is still alive somewhere." She shifted her gaze to Elladan, an impish smile on her lips. "...let alone if he has been reincarnated into a kobald."

"I thought you knew everything about the Thrall Masters," Elladan replied with a mischevious grin of his own.

Elistra pretended to be insulted, arching a delicate eyebrow and glaring at the bard with mock anger. She responded in a lofty tone. "Compared to most."

"Ahem," Aksel cleared his throat, drawing all eyes back to him. "Fun as this is, can we get back to searching this room?"

Elistra and Elladan both laughed. "Of course," they responded in unision.

Donnie made a thorough sweep of the room, in the end finding a section of the bookshelf that swung open with a hidden panel behind it. That panel slid open to reveal two large, ornate chests, both locked. Donnie picked lock on the first chest and lifted the heavy lid. This chest was lined with gold pieces just like the one they had found in the bedroom.

Laid carefully on top of that pile of gold, was a pair of jet black armbands with filigree carvings, made of similar material to Lloyd's sword. Next to the armbands lay a silver-plated scabbard, decorated with polished black gemstones, a pair of red leather gloves with black striations, and a small flask of white liquid. The only items that turned out to be magical were the gloves, and the potion in the flask. The gloves carried the ability to disrupt spells. The flask, unfortunately, was not a potion which would cure poison.

Donnie eyed the gloves with keen interest. His eyes swept across the group as he asked, "May I have those? You never know when something like that might come in handy."

Aksel pursed his lips and nodded. No one else seemed to have any objections, so Glo handed the gloves over to the slight elf. Donnie immediately removed his brown leather gloves, and put these on instead. He held up his arm and twisted his hand around in a circle, grinning at the others. "Stylish, don't you think?"

"Red's not exactly my color," Elladan replied, running a hand over his own nearly all-white outfit.

Glo could not help smiling at the duo's cavalier attitude. Neither elf seemed to have a problem with being flamboyant. Donnie gave Elladan a grin, then returned his attention to the second chest. The others held their breath as the slight elf picked the lock and pushed it open. This chest was also lined with gold, a number of precious items sitting on top of the pile of coins. There was a carnelian gemstone, a glowing fire opal, a life-sized darkwood cat sculpture with yellow topaz eyes, a carved darkwood harp with ivory inlay and zircon gems, and a ten-inch wand of rotted wood.

Though a very expensive find, the chest did not contain what the companions were looking for. Glolinder was crestfallen—the elven wizard hung his head, a deep sigh escaping his lips. "No tome."

Glo felt a soft hand on his arm. He turned and saw Elistra standing by his side, both disappointment and sympathy playing across her features.

"No tome," the seeress repeated, her tone subdued as well. Glo wrapped his arm around her slender shoulders, and pulled her to his side, the two of them silently consoling each other.

Aksel, true to form, managed to find the silver lining in this disappointing turn of events. "Well... at least we know no one else will find it in here."

Elladan tried to lighten the mood as well. "Of course, there's still that colossus upstairs." He pointed a thumb upwards. "Just imagine if the Serpent Cult got their hands on that thing."

Glo peered at the bard, Elladan flashing him a pearly smile. Glo felt a smile slowly crease his face—Elladan was right, of course, they had found the colossus. Keeping that out of the hands of the cultists was paramount. Feeling a bit more positive, Glo shifted his eyes from Elladan to Aksel. "You're both right. We accomplished what we set out to do—keep Larketh's works out of the hands of the Serpent Cult. Who knew that work would be so *large*?"

Everyone shared a good laugh, his comment releasing the tension they all had been feeling. Afterwards, Elladan placed all that they had found in his portal bag. The six of them left the study behind, rejoining Alana and Ruka in the living room. The young teen, now wide awake, sat on the couch rubbing her hands together.

"So what did you find?"

Donnie plopped down on the couch between the two women, and detailed to them all they had discovered. Ruka's eyes widened with each treasure he described, but Alana appeared as disappointed as the rest of them had been. The lady knight turned her eyes from Donnie to Aksel.

"No tomes?"

Aksel shook his head, returning her gaze with sympathy. "No tomes, but as Elladan pointed out, we do have a rather large golem on our side."

Alana's face brightened markedly at the thought.

Aksel swept his gaze across the group, his eyes finally coming to rest on Ruka. "Well then, that's that. Let's all rest up. It has been a long day, and some of us should still be sleeping."

Ruka gave him a dark stare as she snuggled on the couch between Donnie and Alana. "Not tired at all," she declared, an unexpected yawn escaping her mouth. Her head sank down onto Donnie's shoulder, her eyes getting quite heavy. "And you're not my mother…" she added, her voice fading as she drifted off to sleep.

Glo grasped Elistra around the waist and shared a smile with the seeress, the two of them gazing fondly at the young teen. She seemed remarkably content for a poisoned young dragon.

Outside the monolith, it was close to midnight. The moon had risen over the treetops, the forest bathed in the soft glow of moonlight. The fire had died down in the Knights of the Rose camp, the night still as Martan stood watch at the edge of the forest. Most of the encampment had bedded down for the night, only Martan and a few other sentries standing guard over the clearing. The archer spun around and glanced up at the tall monolith in the center of the glade, its dark frame glistening in the moonlight, framed against the backdrop of the black, starlit sky.

Most of the companions were still inside that structure—there had been no sign of them since Glo, Donnie and Ruka had shown up around midday, with the exception of Seth. Martan had not seen the halfling, only hearing about his visit afterward from Sir Craven. Martan sincerely hoped that Seth could track the black mage to the Serpent Cult's headquarters. If anyone could, he was sure it would be Seth.

Martan sighed as he shifted his gaze back to the camp. The fortifications had been finished, ringing in the area with a spike-pitched wooden fence. Inside the fence, smaller tents formed a ring around a single large tent, the one which housed Sir Craven.

The tent nearest to Martan belonged to the squires, Syndir and Lamorn, who the archer had befriended over these last two days. The lads were bright and full of zeal, but they were young and less aloof than the Knights of the Rose. Martan found them far more down to earth and easy to talk to. The boys seemed to like the archer as well. They appeared impressed with his wood tracking skills and his expertise with a bow.

Martan smiled to himself as he turned back toward the forest. The woods around him remained quiet, the only sound coming from the company's horses tied to a makeshift hitching post only a few yards away. The scene would have been idyllic if the surrounding woods weren't so dark and oppressive.

Hence the name Darkwoods, Martan thought wryly.

The wind kicked up, a sharp breeze flowing in from the east. Martan shivered slightly at the sudden chill. It felt like a storm was rolling in. He peered up into the sky, but there was not a cloud to be seen.

Strange.

Martan looked away just a moment too soon, barely missing the dark shadow that passed over the nearly-full moon in the night sky above.

Here ends Book Three of
the Heroes of Ravenford
the story continues in Book Four
Princess of Lanfor

ABOUT THE AUTHOR

F.P. Spirit writes high fantasy fiction inspired by the likes of Tolkien, Eddings, Brooks, and Piers Anthony. An avid science fiction fan, he became hooked on fantasy the moment he cracked open the Lord of the Rings in high school. When he is not writing, F.P. is either spending time with his wife and sons, gaming, doing yoga, Tai Chi, or walking their dog.

A long-time lover of fantasy and the surreal, he hopes you enjoy his fun contributions to the world of fantasy and magic.

You can learn more about F.P. Spirit by visiting his website at:
Fpspirit.com

www.ingramcontent.com/pod-product-compliance
Lightning Source LLC
Chambersburg PA
CBHW031928110726
47902CB00001B/83